Lovers and Enemies

Ashley Gordon Hollister. The beautiful, talented daughter of Napa Valley vineyard workers, she found the glamour and success with her art that she had always desired, along with the love of one of the wealthiest young men in the world. But could she rise above the tragedy that suddenly swept it all away?

Collin Deverell. The gorgeous, globe-trotting heir to half of a vast fortune, he turned to crime in hopes of reclaiming his legacy. But would the trail of stolen pride, stolen wealth, and stolen hearts lead him to his ultimate goal?

Justin Deverell. Collin's weak-willed twin brother, he manipulated the family empire to the verge of financial disaster. Would his sordid involvement with the criminal underground save the dwindling fortune? Or bury it forever—along with Justin himself?

Bradley Hollister. Ashley's unaccepting father-in-law, he was a powerful industrialist who alone held the key to both Ashley's and Collin's happiness. How many souls would his driving obsession eventually destroy?

Berkley Books by Norma Beishir

DANCE OF THE GODS
ANGELS AT MIDNIGHT

ANGELS AT MIDNIGHT

NORMA BEISHIR

B

BERKLEY BOOKS, NEW YORK

ANGELS AT MIDNIGHT

A Berkley Book/published by arrangement with
the author

PRINTING HISTORY
Berkley edition/April 1989

ISBN: 0-425-11406-6

A BERKLEY BOOK ® TM 757,375
Berkley Books are published by The Berkley Publishing Group,
200 Madison Avenue, New York, N.Y. 10016.
The name ''BERKLEY'' and the ''B'' logo
are trademarks belonging to Berkley Publishing Corporation

PRINTED IN THE UNITED STATES OF AMERICA.

10 9 8 7 6 5 4 3 2 1

With love, for my son Collin . . .
the ultimate con artist

Thieves for their robbery have authority
When judges steal themselves.

Shakespeare, *Measure for Measure*, II, ii

AUTHOR'S NOTE

Though I am deeply indebted to those who contributed to the background of this novel through their special skills, expertise, and memories, they have invariably chosen to remain anonymous—for reasons that will be obvious. I respect their wishes. Each of them knows who he or she is, and I thank them again for sharing their knowledge with me. I would also like to thank those who contributed in other ways, for they are equally important and deserving of credit:

Maria Carvainis, agent, friend, and confidante, who stood by me through the best and worst of times and gave me the benefit of her friendship as well as her professional capabilities. I couldn't have done it without you. (I hope you become a millionaire on your 15 percent.)

Damaris Rowland, my unfailingly supportive editor, who did all of the things a good editor should do, and yet has always been more than an editor to me. You told me once that you were going to be beneficial to me—and you certainly lived up to that prediction. (We never did go off to the rest home as we agreed.)

Sabra Elliott, Berkley's publicity director, whose

continued support has meant more to me than I can ever express. I can never put a dollar amount on that. (How would you like to create a *real* monster?)

Karyn Witmer-Gow, fellow author and good buddy, she's shown me, through her concern and compassion, what the best alliances are all about. (Still got those sweat socks you threatened to stuff down my throat?)

Tony Relling, my husband, the only man I ever loved. He gave me the one thing I could never get from my long hours of research—the ability to write about love, and the courage to follow my dreams. (You're no longer with me in body, but you'll always live in my heart.)

Norma Beishir
St. Louis, Missouri
February 14, 1988

New York City, July 1987

The penthouse was in darkness. Out on the terrace, a man and a woman, dressed in loose-fitting black overalls, prepared to make an unauthorized entrance. The woman, holding a large canvas rucksack, looked on as her partner ran a gloved hand expertly along the frame of the large glass door until he found what he was looking for: the wire connected to the burglar alarm. He reached into the rucksack and took out a pair of pliers and a long section of wire with an alligator clip on each end. Turning his attention to the alarm once again, he traced the wire to its source, moving slowly, deliberately. He stripped the wire and attached one of the alligator clips to the alarm. As he used the pliers to cut the wire, the woman tensed, an involuntary reaction, as if she expected the alarm to go off. When it didn't, her entire body sagged with relief. Why did it still bother her? she wondered. After all the times they had been through this in the past few months, shouldn't she be used to it? Shouldn't she be convinced that he knew what he was doing, that nothing would go wrong? She kept thinking of something he had told her when she first entered into this devil's bargain with him: one wrong move could be their last. He had said it himself. She looked at him, still amazed by how cool he was, how confident. Now he was taking a small glass cutter from the sack. Carefully, he cut a small hole in the glass, just large enough to allow him to reach inside and release the lock.

"Thank God that's over," she breathed as he slid the door open and stepped inside.

He turned to look at her, the strong, angular planes of his face shadowed in the moonlight, a lock of his thick, dark brown hair falling across his forehead. "Unfortunately," he said in a low, deep voice, "this is only the beginning."

He took two pairs of infrared goggles from the pocket of his overalls and gave her a pair. He slipped his on and gestured for her to do the same. As she pulled them down over her face and adjusted them on the bridge of her nose, she looked around. The room was suddenly bathed in an eerie red glow, but now it was possible for them to see the infrared beams of light crisscrossing throughout the room, deadly beams that would have been invisible without the goggles, beams that would instantly set off the electronic security system the minute they sensed the change in temperature that would occur when they passed through the invisible light. She stood in the doorway, looking at her partner questioningly as he appraised the situation.

"It's impossible, isn't it," she muttered.

He shook his head. "Not impossible—just difficult." He turned to face her. "Shall we?"

"You must be crazy!" she gasped. "There's no way—"

"You're wrong," he said quietly. "There's always a way. You should know that by now."

She hesitated for only a moment. "You really think we can pull it off?"

He grinned. "There's only one way we're going to find out, isn't there?"

She took a deep breath, then nodded reluctantly.

They moved cautiously yet swiftly through the room, dodging the beams by crawling under some, jumping over others, finally making their way to the wall safe that was concealed behind a priceless Matisse in an alcove at the opposite end of the room. She watched as he let the beam of bright light from his large flashlight play on the painting for a few moments. Then he passed the flashlight to her and took the painting down from the wall, turned it over, and placed it facedown on the floor. He cut it from its frame, rolled up the vellum, and handed it to her. She put it in the rucksack. He looked up at her and nodded toward the safe. "Let's get to it."

As she held the flashlight, focusing the light on the safe, they saw that a series of buttons replaced the traditional round combination dial. He went to the rucksack again, producing a small, rectangular device resembling a pocket calculator with a long wire attached to it. He connected the free end of the wire to the safe just beneath the panel of buttons with a soft, pliable substance he jokingly referred to as Silly Putty. He switched it on, and the digital display began to flash wildly as the device methodically sought out the combination. Swiftly, he opened the safe and swept its contents into the sack his accomplice held open for him. Then he closed the safe again, disconnected his equipment, and hastily stuffed it into the large rucksack, slipping his arms through the heavy straps that secured it to his back.

"Let's get the hell out of here," he told her as he pulled the goggles down over his eyes again.

Dodging the beams again, they made their way back to the terrace. As they prepared to make their escape, she looked apprehensively at the heavy cable strung from the terrace to the roof of another skyscraper several hundred feet away, the same cable on which they had entered. Though she had done this countless times in the past few months, and knew this particular cable to be safe, she doubted she would ever really get used to doing this sort of thing. She could not imagine ever being comfortable with the idea of her life literally hanging by a thread, five hundred feet above the ground. She leaned over the railing and stared down at the glittering lights of midtown Manhattan below. Normally, she would have found the view spectacular, but now all she could think of was the danger. *One wrong move could be your last.* His words echoed through her mind. One wrong move could be fatal.

"Come on!" he urged, perching himself on the railing. He swung his long legs over the side as casually as if he were getting out of bed, and grasped a heavy metal loop attached to the cable. Using his body weight to propel him, he swung forward forcefully, a motion that sent him sailing through the night, speeding toward the other building.

She studied the cable for a moment, thinking about something he'd told her the first time she used the cable: *My life happens to mean a great deal to me . . . when I string a cable, it's so safe you could sail a baby on it.* She took a deep breath and climbed onto the rail, moving with the natural grace of a dancer. The wind whipped her long, dark hair about her face as she gripped the loop and launched herself forward. Now, as she sailed through the darkness like some night bird in flight, those old familiar doubts and questions flashed through her mind: *When did it all begin to go wrong?* she asked herself. When did the world as she knew it begin to fall apart?

And how had she ended up here—doing this?

St. Helena, California, September 1975

The brilliant sunlight seemed to bathe the Napa Valley in a white-hot glow. The bronzed bodies of the shirtless men working in the vineyards glistened with perspiration as they toiled at the long, exhausting task of harvesting the grapes that would be used to make some of northern California's finest wines. Already, the process of pressing some of those grapes had begun, filling the air with their intoxicating aroma. It was a scene as common to that region as the crowds and the bumper-to-bumper traffic have always been to New York City, but perhaps not quite as well known.

This was wine country, and the many vineyards and wineries dominated the landscape as far as the eye could see in any direction.

On a grassy knoll overlooking one of those vineyards, Abby Giannini sat under a large oak tree, a sketchbook and several well-used pencils lying at her side as she pondered the scene. Dressed in faded jeans and a loose-fitting handwoven shirt, ivory with brightly colored flowers embroidered about the neckline and down the front, her long, heavy dark hair hung in soft waves about her shoulders, framing her delicate oval face perfectly. Abby's dark coloring, her wide, dark brown eyes, olive complexion, and fine, almost perfect features were unmistakable evidence of her Italian heritage, of the ancestors who had come to this country from Tuscany in the nineteenth century, bringing with them generations of experience in the making of fine wines— and the hope that here, they would be able to start over, to found their own vineyards and carry on traditions that had been in their families for centuries. It had always seemed unfair to Abby that the Gianninis had been masters of the wine industry in Tuscany, yet had been reduced to nothing more than "hired help" here in California. Ever since the first of them, her great-great-grandfather, Roberto Giannini, had arrived here over a century ago, they had always worked for someone else. Their expertise had made others rich, while their own incomes remained marginal.

Abby looked up at the cloudless sky, marveling at how clear and blue and infinite it seemed. It made her think of a song she'd heard somewhere, "On a Clear Day You Can See Forever." It was almost true, she thought as she reached for her sketchbook. As she opened it and stared with displeasure at the unfinished drawing on the first page, the old familiar frustration surged up within her. How many times had she attempted to sketch this particular scene—the men working in the vineyards, the intensity of the sunlight, the depth of that sky—yet failed to capture it as her eye and her heart saw it? She stared at the drawing with a critical eye. She knew it was good. There was no vanity in that appraisal, only a simple assessment of facts. She understood the strengths and weaknesses of her own artistic talents far better than anyone else ever could. She knew what she was capable of. This realization was what frustrated Abby Giannini most. She knew she had the ability to effectively recreate the richness and depth of this particular scene, yet when she tried to put it down on paper, the results always seemed somehow inadequate.

Unlike her ancestors, unlike her own parents, Abby had no intention of following tradition. Her future, she knew with certainty, was not in the wine business. She had discovered her artistic talents at an early age, and knew immediately that hers would not be the quiet, uneventful, working-class lifestyle of her parents, the way of life in which she had grown up. Abby was going to become a painter. She was sure of it. She was going to have a rich, exciting life in San Francisco. For starters. Perhaps she would go on, later, after she had achieved recognition in San Francisco, to New York or London or even Paris. Maybe she would travel, exhibit her works all over the world. Whatever happened, she promised herself she would *not* remain here, in the Napa Valley.

Abby scrambled to her feet and dusted blades of grass from the seat and legs of her jeans. She collected her things and made her way down the steep hill, headed for the small cottage on the winery grounds where she lived with her parents. Tony and Lucia Giannini had lived and worked here most of their married life. Their two children, Roberto and Abigail, had been born here. It was here that Roberto died at the age of five, a victim of acute lymphatic leukemia. Abby herself had taken her first hesitant steps in these same vineyards, spoken her first words in this vine-covered cottage, hewn of stone. She had gone to school in nearby St. Helena, two miles away. Her first serious drawings had been sketches of the impressive German Gothic-style winery, of the men working out in the vineyards, of the owners' wives and daughters, elegantly turned out in their stylish sun hats and designer fashions. For most of the children born to the laborers—particularly those like herself, whose families had been in the business for generations—it was an accepted fact of life that they would follow in their parents' footsteps, that they would either become laborers themselves or the wives of laborers. For Abby, however, it had been different. She'd known when she was very young that she was not going to spend the rest of her life here, that she was not going to marry one of the boys with whom she had grown up. Though a part of her would always love the valley, would always think of it as the closest thing to heaven on earth, she knew that the quiet, leisurely pace at which the people here lived when they were not working was not for her. There was something deep within the soul of Abby Giannini that demanded more.

And somehow, she was going to go after it.

"I'm going to San Francisco after graduation," Abby announced over dinner one night.

Her mother, a short, heavyset woman in her mid-fifties, a woman whose heavily lined face betrayed years of hard work and whose rounded, overweight form was the result of her love of the rich Italian dishes she prepared every day for herself and her family, looked up from her plate. "Whatever for?" she asked, genuinely surprised.

"To work, Mama," Abby answered simply. "I've told you before . . . I want to be an artist. A painter."

"But can't you be an artist here?" Lucia Giannini wanted to know. "Maybe you could sell your paintings in one of the shops in town—"

"It wouldn't be the same, Mama," Abby insisted. "I could paint, yes—maybe even sell some of my work in town—but I could never really learn what I need to here." There was an urgency, a passion in her voice. "I could never have any real success here."

"Success!" Tony Giannini spat the word out as though it had left a bitter taste in his mouth. He leaned back in his chair, a large, portly man with gray, thinning hair, a thick mustache, and a reddened, weatherbeaten face. "You're settin' yourself up for a big disappointment, girl,'' he growled. ''This world you want so much—it's not what you expect. That's for the rich people, the kind of people who *own* these wineries, not those like us who work for them. You wouldn't fit in. You'd just end up gettin' hurt.''

''I can make it as an artist, Papa,'' Abby argued, fighting to control her temper. ''I do have talent—I know I do!''

''You dream big, *figlia mia*,'' he said in a somewhat harsh voice. ''And dreaming is okay as long as you know that's all it is. Our kind doesn't go to San Francisco to become rich and famous. We don't mingle with society people. We're simple people, and we're better off when we mingle with our own kind, marry our own kind. Girls like you are happier, believe me, when they marry the boys who'll work out there in the vineyards like their fathers. They're happier when they settle down right here in the valley and have babies and—''

''I am *not* going to marry one of the 'boys' and have babies and spend the rest of my life here!'' Abby exploded, leaping to her feet with such force that she knocked over a pitcher of milk. Lucia scurried to clean it up, but Abby made no move to assist her—or to apologize for her actions. She turned on her father in anger. ''I am going to San Francisco, Papa. I am going to make it as an artist—you'll see!'' She turned abruptly and stalked out the back door.

Trembling with rage, Abby leaned on the heavy wooden rail surrounding the small porch at the rear of the cottage, trying as hard as she could to rein in her emotions. She loved her father dearly, but he could be so terribly narrow-minded sometimes. Couldn't he see that no one had to be locked into a way of life simply because it was the way of his or her parents or grandparents? Their ancestors had not been laborers, for God's sake! Back in Tuscany, they had been the *masters* of the wine market—the standard by which all others were measured. Had her father so conveniently forgotten that fact? Didn't he see that it was possible to rise above one's given station in life? Didn't he know that it wasn't necessary for one to have to spend one's life poor because he or she had been born poor? Why couldn't he understand that she wanted more from life than their world had to offer? Why couldn't he be more supportive of her, of her ambitions?

"Abby, your dinner is getting cold, *diletta mia.*"

She turned to see her mother standing in the doorway, a look of concern on her face. "I'm not very hungry, Mama," she said in a tired voice, shaking her head.

Her mother came closer. "Your papa worries about you, as I do," Lucia Giannini said gently, placing a hand on her daughter's shoulder. "His heart is in the right place, if his methods are not. He does not want to see you get hurt."

"Does he expect me to be hurt, Mama?" Abby's eyes met her mother's. "Doesn't he think I'm good enough to make it as an artist?"

"Of course he does," Lucia insisted. "But he is afraid that others may not see your gift as clearly as we do. He does not want you to be disappointed."

"And?" Abby had the distinct feeling that there was more, that her mother wanted to say something else but was fumbling for the right words.

Lucia drew in her breath. "Tony is very old-fashioned in many ways, Abby," she said finally. "He believes in families staying together, following the old traditions. He does not think much of their world."

" 'Their world'?" Abby looked at her questioningly.

"The rich people who go to the galleries and patronize certain favored artists can just as quickly turn their back on you. He does not trust the rich." Lucia Giannini paused. "Your papa looks upon our world as a safe one, and a good one, and thinks we would be wise never to forget it."

"But I can become one of them, Mama!" Abby cried passionately. "I have what it takes—I know I do!"

"I am sure that you do, *figlia mia,*" her mother responded. "But try to understand, Abby, that it is very hard for your papa and I to let you go, to think of you being so far away, in a strange city, alone, where we cannot protect

you. You are all we have now. After your brother died—"
She shrugged helplessly.

Abby embraced her gently, blinking back tears. "I'm so
sorry, Mama," she said softly. "I didn't realize . . ." She
had been so preoccupied with her own needs and wants that
she had not stopped to think about how painful it would be
for her parents to lose another child. To them, allowing her
to go off to San Francisco alone would be painful, even
though it could not be as painful or as final as Roberto's
death had been. Still, she could not bear to give up her
dream. *How do I make them understand?* she asked herself. *How
do I make them see that this is something I have to do for myself?*

"I am worried about Abby," Tony Giannini told his wife.

Lucia smiled patiently as she scraped the remnants of
their dinner from the chipped white plates into a large iron
pot. "Why, Tony?" she asked. "Because you think she
might be hurt if her dreams don't come true—or because
you think *you* might be hurt if she leaves the valley for
good?"

He looked at her for a moment. "You know me too well,
cara," he said, shaking his head sadly. "I suppose you think
I am a selfish father because I do not want to see our Abby
leave us, because I would like to see her married to a nice
young man and settled down right here in town—where I
can watch our grandchildren grow up."

"No, I don't think you are selfish," Lucia said gently,
looking at her husband with love in her eyes. "I think perhaps you love our little girl a bit too much, but that is hardly
a crime." She took the tablecloth, now stained with tomato
sauce from the veal dish she had served for dinner, and
tossed it into a large basket near the door. "I don't want to
see her leave any more than you do—but Abby's a woman
now. She's twenty years old. She's got a right to make a
life of her own—away from us, if that's what she wants."

"She's got too many big ideas, Lucia," Tony said, ex-
asperated. "She dreams too much. She *wants* too much.
She's settin' herself up for a big fall."

Lucia stopped what she was doing and sat down at the table, facing her husband. "I know how you feel, Tony—I *do*. I don't want to see her hurt any more than you do," she said quietly. "But we can't always protect her from what life brings. This is something she has to do for herself."

"But she's trying to be part of a world that's very different from ours," Tony said, his concern growing. "She's trying to become a part of a world that can chew her up and spit her out again."

"If that's true, then Abby will have to deal with it," Lucia said with simple wisdom. "She's strong, Tony. Rejection won't make her fall apart."

Tony Giannini's smile was tired. "Perhaps you are right," he said finally. "Perhaps she is, after all, her mother's daughter." He paused, reaching for a cigar and lighting it. "If only she would learn to curb that fierce temper of hers."

Lucia reached out and gave his left shoulder an affectionate squeeze. "That she will not find easy, *caro*—because she is also her father's daughter," she said with a sigh.

Abby prowled through a small art supply store in St. Helena, enthralled. She recalled how, as a little girl, she had watched the artists who came to the Napa Valley, watched them attempt to capture the true, natural beauty of the land on their canvases. It had amazed her then, the way they would squeeze paint from the tubes onto their palettes, mixing a dab of this and a dab of that with a large glob of a third color to create a totally new color. Even now, she was still amazed by her own ability to create a dozen different shades of green with which she would create a landscape as varied in shade as nature's own. It would always be magical to her how the sun might reflect differently from one patch of grass to another in the same meadow . . . the way the green of the vines differed from the green of the grapes themselves and the green of the tall grass in a nearby field. Looking now at a still life on display in the store, she was intrigued by the artist's ability to capture the reflection of light off one unevenly rounded side of an apple that was brilliant red in some places, pale yellow in others.

Dimitri Sarnoff, her art instructor at Napa College, had been the first to encourage her ambitions, fueling her desire to paint with stories of his own dreams of becoming a celebrated painter while growing up in postwar Europe, describing the magnificent paintings his own parents had smuggled out of Austria during World War II. He talked of the works of art that had sparked his imagination and filled him with the desire to create, to paint his own unique vision of the world. He told her of the years he'd spent at the Ecole des Beaux-Arts in Paris, of the painful discovery made there that he did indeed have talent, but not enough to enable him to make a name for himself in the international art world. "But you, Abby . . . you have the vision and you have the talent. Your ability will take you to the heights," he had promised her. "You will find the success you seek." He had been her mentor, her source of support and encouragement. He had given her the strength she needed to persevere. He had instilled in her the belief in herself she would need to keep her going, to pursue her goal.

Hastily, Abby selected her supplies, buying as many tubes of paint as she could afford, selecting colors she knew could be used with others to create even more colors. Since she did not have much money, she had learned early on to make the best of the resources available to her. She passed over the stretched canvases available in the store, planning to use her own homemade canvases—old white sheets treated with a kind of sizing made by covering them with a gluelike substance she made at home by boiling rabbit bones, a technique she'd come across in one of her art history books. Necessity truly was the mother of invention, she thought wryly as she drove back to the winery in her 1970 Ford Fairlane. She still used the easel her father had made for her when she was twelve years old and just beginning to take a serious interest in art. She painted whenever she could, wherever she could find a spot to set up her old easel. It was inconvenient, yes, and often frustrating, but no one would ever hear her complain. She promised herself it would not always be like this. She could put up with anything as long as she knew it was only temporary. One day, she thought with confidence, she would have a studio, a real studio, with the correct lighting and all the finest supplies—and perhaps a few luxuries as well. One day, those rich, influential people who looked down at the Gianninis would clamor for her paintings. One day, she thought, filled with determination, she would be recognized by all of them. Their money would make her reputation!

Abby had never been to San Francisco, but she knew almost as much about it as the people who had lived there all of their lives. She had been fascinated with that magnificent, magical city since she was a little girl, and had read everything she could lay her hands on that had ever been written about it. As she grew older, she'd focused her attentions on the art world in particular. She'd also read the society columns in the San Francisco newspapers avidly. She studied the photographs of the elegantly dressed, bejeweled women, knowing deep within her soul that one day many of them would buy her art. She was fascinated by who wore what, the way they wore their hair, what jewelry was good for daytime and what was best left for those "special" evenings. She took note of which restaurants they preferred, knowing the importance of being seen in the "right" places, and what cars they drove to get there. Knowing this knowledge was essential if Abby Giannini were going to prove herself to be a part of their world.

Abby Giannini. The name her parents had given her seemed somehow inappropriate for the new life she'd mapped out for herself. Her father would have her head for even thinking such a thing, she mused; she'd been named for his mother, her grandmother, whom he quite literally worshipped. Neither of her parents would understand why she felt it was necessary to change her name.

They would think she was ashamed of them, of her heritage, but that wasn't true at all. How could she make them understand that whatever she did, she did to fit in, to become a part of that new world she'd dreamed about?

Abby knew why her father was concerned about her ambitions. She knew he didn't approve of the people she'd meet or the lifestyle she craved. He felt they looked down on decent, hardworking people like the Gianninis, who weren't "their kind." But even knowing that, Abby longed to be a part of that different and exciting world. There were times she felt a little guilty for wanting it so much, but that did not change her dreams. She wanted the glamour and the excitement. She wanted the beautiful clothes and the nightlife and all the parties. She wanted to dine in the best restaurants. She wanted to be accepted into that world, and she was convinced that Abby Giannini, the daughter of a grape picker from the Napa Valley, wouldn't be greeted with open arms. But if she arrived in San Francisco as one of their own. . . .

She would need a new name, a more glamorous name, to go with that glamorous life. She'd decided to change Giannini to Gordon. It had an upper-class sound to it and was easy to pronounce. Abby Gordon? No, somehow that didn't sound right. What would go with Gordon? Anne was a nice name, a well-bred name. But Anne Gordon *sounded* as though someone had made it up. Angela? No, she'd never cared for that name. Alicia? It conjured up images of a little girl with pigtails and ruffled dresses. Of all the names she could think of, nothing seemed right. Nothing seemed to fit.

Abby seldom dated. Though she was pursued by some of the most attractive young men in the valley, she had no interest in any of them. They were laborers and the sons of laborers, and they were part of a life she was preparing to leave behind. To allow herself to become involved with any of them would only complicate her life, and that was exactly what she didn't need right now. Besides, she saw no reason to encourage any of them, to offer hope where there was none. Soon she would be leaving this life behind her. On those rare occasions when she did accept an invitation, it was always for an informal evening, one that included dinner and a movie in St. Helena or Napa. Abby loved movies. She adored the magical worlds created up there on the silver screen, worlds that had once seemed impossible for her to ever experience firsthand. She was fascinated with the glamour and excitement of those distant lives. They were her escape from the quiet, peaceful world of the Napa Valley. Sometimes she would try to picture herself living the lives of the characters portrayed in those films. *It is going to happen*, she promised herself again and again.

One evening during the harvest, in early October, she went to see a re-release of *Gone With the Wind* at the movie theater in Napa with Sam Cavelli, who worked in the winery. She and Sam had grown up together. Sam was every inch the so-called "macho man," both in looks and in attitude, but Abby had never been bothered by his caveman tactics; on the contrary, she'd always found them amusing. Of all the young men who had pursued her, Sam was by far the most attractive—and the most persistent. He never gave up, no matter how hard Abby tried to discourage him. No matter how many times she rebuffed his advances, he always came back. Sometimes she wondered why she bothered with him at all, but a part of her was genuinely fond of him, much as a sister was of her brother. It was unfortunate that Sam didn't see it that way.

As they sat in Sam's Chevy Malibu convertible under a clear, star-filled sky, parked high on a hill overlooking the winery, he attempted to impress her with talk of his recent raise and promotion. "I'll be foreman here before I'm thirty, babe," he bragged. "Then we can go out in style— if you play your cards right." He was trying not to be too obvious about it when he slipped one arm around her shoulders and moved a little closer.

"If I play my cards right," Abby repeated, amused. How many times did she have to tell him that he didn't fit into her plans for the future, that she had no intention of staying there, of playing his games?

His face moved closer to hers. "That's right, baby," he muttered as his lips met hers, his mouth coming down on hers with an unmistakable urgency. Abby tried to pull away, but Sam pressed her back against the white vinyl seat, forcing his tongue between her lips, making it difficult for her to breathe. He held her tightly with one arm while his free hand snaked up under her top, squeezing her breasts, pinching her nipples. She squirmed furiously but was unable to free herself from his grasp.

"Let go of me, you bastard!" she hissed when she was finally able to turn her face away from his. She struggled to break his hold, but her efforts were in vain.

"You don't have to keep playing the ice princess with me, Abby," he growled, pulling her top up as far as it would go under her arms, exposing her. "I'm not gonna talk. Nobody'll ever know . . . but you and me . . ." He bent his head to her breast, seizing one of her nipples in his mouth. She fought him, tearing at his hair, trying to push him away, but he was too strong. Finally, galvanized by her swiftly mounting anger, she lashed out, driving one elbow into his eye socket. He gave a sharp cry of pain as he rocked backward, one hand clasped over the injured eye. Quickly, Abby adjusted her tank top and reached for the door handle, but Sam grabbed her again. "You're nothin' but a lousy little cock tease," he growled in a menacing tone. "You flaunt yourself all over the vineyards, but when us guys start respondin' you shut us down cold." He pushed her down on the seat and pulled up her linen skirt. With one of his large, powerful hands, he ripped away her panties and forced her legs apart. She tried to scream when he plunged two fingers up inside her, but he stopped her mouth with his own. "How long did you think you could get away with it?" he muttered in her ear as he fondled her roughly. "Didn't you know that eventually I'd get tired of these games and just take what I wanted?"

"Is this what makes you feel like a man?" she gasped breathlessly. "Taking a woman who doesn't want you?"

"Taking a woman every other guy in the valley is hot for

sure as hell feels good,'' he muttered as he pressed himself into her. She could feel the tip of his penis, like a large, evil serpent, pressing against her, trying to force its way inside. As her fear merged with rage, she summoned up one final burst of strength, thrusting her knee into his groin. He fell off her, doubled over in agony. Abby pushed the door open and flew out of the car, determined to get as far from him as she could as quickly as she could.

She didn't stop running until she reached her cottage. *Thank God they're asleep*, she thought as she let herself into the darkened house and took off her shoes, tiptoeing down the hall to her bedroom. If her father ever found out about this, he would kill Sam with his bare hands. Not that she would have cared—she would have enjoyed doing so herself—but she did not think Sam Cavelli was worth going to prison for, dead or alive. Of all the nerve—he actually thought a movie and a five-dollar dinner entitled him to have sex with her! She had always liked him in spite of his womanizing attitude, but after tonight, he no longer existed for her.

As much as she would have liked to see him pay for his actions, she knew she was never going to tell anyone what had happened. Never. She told herself it didn't matter as she took off her clothes and stood naked in front of the full-length mirror, surveying the damage. There were bruises on her thighs and scratches on her breasts and groin. In spite of the anger and humiliation she felt, she told herself it didn't matter because she was not going to be here much longer. The day she left the valley was the day she would put her past behind her. Including Sam Cavelli.

She went into the bathroom and ran a steaming hot bath, impatient to scrub away every last vestige of Sam and what had happened. As she stepped into the hot water, she looked down at her naked body and thought of the way Sam had touched her, the things he had done to her with his hands and his mouth. She thought of the alien sensations that had swept through her body when he put his mouth to her breast, his hands between her legs. No one had ever touched her there before. No one had ever done such things to her before. Her responses to his actions disturbed her even more than Sam's attempt to force himself on her. He had aroused her against her will—but it changed nothing, she thought stubbornly. If anything, it had served to reinforce her belief that she did not belong here, that she needed desperately to put some distance between herself and the valley.

Abby could not admit, except to herself, that she wanted a lover. Sometimes, when she was alone in the darkness of her bedroom late at night, she would fantasize about a handsome, dashing man who would come and make love to her . . . a gentle yet passionate man with whom she would become one, not at all like Sam Cavelli or his kind. A man she knew instinctively she would not find here. Abby Giannini would never find such a man. But perhaps that other woman—the artist, the woman who had dwelled within the depths of her soul for so long, fighting to finally emerge— would find him in San Francisco. Maybe the woman she was trying to become would have everything she'd ever dreamed of, everything that now eluded her grasp. *But first,* she thought, *that woman must have a name, an identity.*

She'd been thinking about that same thing earlier, while she was watching the movie. She had been intrigued by one of the characters' names, a name she found entirely suitable for a man or a woman. It was glamorous and it was different. A name that suited that other woman, that other life, perfectly. Now, as she stepped out of the tub and dried herself thoroughly, her anger and her humiliation seemingly disappearing down the drain, she realized that she'd found exactly what she was looking for. When the time did come, when Abby Giannini finally ceased to exist, she knew who was going to take her place.

Ashley Gordon.

Boston,
February 1976

"En garde!" Two men in traditional white fencing attire moved around on the floor of the gymnasium with lightning speed, the blades of their French foils flashing in the harsh glare cast by the fluorescent lighting high above them. One of the men, his foil raised menacingly, took full advantage of a miscalculation on the part of his opponent, lunging forward in an aggressive move that caught the second fencer completely off guard. He backed off hastily, attempting to regroup his forces while using his own weapon to block the attack. The aggressor moved swiftly, and it seemed to his opponent that he was suddenly everywhere—parrying, lunging, feinting, counterparrying, and thrusting with the skill and assurance of the experienced swordsman he was. He scored one touch and then another and another, until he had made the required five touches on his opponent's target area to take the match in the allotted six minutes.

Once won, however, the aggressiveness of his manner vanished as quickly as he removed his wire mesh face mask, revealing a lean, angular face flushed with triumph, the velvety brown eyes crackling with fire. His thick, wavy dark hair was touseled and damp with perspiration as he faced his defeated opponent and bowed gallantly from the waist, displaying the natural grace of a superbly conditioned athlete. As he straightened up again, he grinned. "We really should do this more often, Farnsworth," he commented with a twinge of amusement in his voice.

The other man laughed wearily. "I don't think my heart could take it, Deverell," he responded breathlessly. "You weren't playing a game out there—you were waging war!"

Collin Deverell laughed heartily as he pulled the leather glove and gauntlet from his right hand and ran his fingers through his hair, pushing it into place. "Didn't anyone ever tell you that there's no crime in playing to win?" he asked in a mocking tone.

"Playing to win?" Derek Farnsworth said with a laugh. "Come on, Collin—for a minute there, I was beginning to wonder if you'd forgotten that there was a friend behind this mask! I felt as though we were actually engaging in combat!"

Collin grinned. "You're slowing down, pal," he warned. "Not equal to the challenge anymore?"

"I'm hardly a match for a former world champion," Farnsworth reminded him. "Look, I think I'll hit the showers and get back to my law books, okay?"

Collin nodded. "Tomorrow, then?"

Farnsworth gave an exaggerated groan of despair. "*Please*—it's going to take me a week to recover from to-day's match! Give me a break, will you?"

"I keep forgetting I have to go easy on you softies," Collin teased. "All right—I'll just have to find someone else to take me on."

"Keep this up and you're going to run out of friends," Derek Farnsworth joked as they walked back to the locker rooms together. "They'll all be mounted on your wall with your swords and other trophies!"

At that moment, the doors at the far end of the gym opened and a third man entered, a tall, slim blond man Collin recognized immediately from one of his classes at Harvard. "Hey, Deverell! I've been looking all over for you!" he called out loudly with an unmistakable New England accent.

Collin waved him off. "Whatever it is, I didn't do it!" he yelled back.

The other man ignored his quip. "Your father's in town—he's been looking for you. He called here twice. Your brother also called."

"My brother," Collin said ruefully, so low that only Derek Farnsworth, who stood next to him, could hear him. "Baron Stormcloud himself." He turned back to the other man who stood poised in the doorway. ''My father knows where I live,'' he said loudly.

''Sure he does, and he also knows that you spend most of your time here,'' the blond man responded. ''Better give him a call. He said he'll be staying at the Ritz-Carlton.''

''As if I wouldn't know where to find him,'' Collin said in a casual tone. ''I guess I'd better make this fast. When he flies up from New York instead of calling, it's usually urgent.''

In spite of the bitter cold, the Boston Common was crowded. A group of demonstrators marched in formation, brandishing large, crudely lettered signs while a soapbox orator delivered his impassioned—and very loud—speech from the center of the group. Several children bundled in warm winter attire ran off in the direction of the playground while two bag ladies rummaged through a trash can. Three young girls sat on a bench, lacing up their skates as they prepared to go ice skating on Frog Pond. Collin walked through the Common, oblivious of everything around him except the cold. Turning up the collar of his heavy winter coat, he pulled his gray cashmere muffler up over the lower half of his face. His cheeks stung from the icy wind and his eyes felt uncomfortably dry. The wind whipped through his hair, still damp from the shower, as he walked along the pond, headed for the underground parking garage just beyond the Public Garden at the west end of the Common. Breaking into a run, he dashed through the park and into the garage, not slowing down until he reached his silver Ferrari. Pulling off his gray leather gloves, he dug into his coat pocket for his keys and unlocked the door hastily, his breath visible in the bitterly cold air. He slid behind the wheel and closed the door. As he put the key in the ignition and turned the switch, the engine came to life immediately. He listened to the low hum of the Ferrari's powerful, perfectly tuned motor for a moment, then put the car in reverse and backed out of the parking stall, reaching for the garage ticket he'd left on the dashboard. The garage, he noticed as he headed for the exit, was almost empty now. He glanced at the gold watch on his left wrist. It was later than he'd thought.

As he pulled out of the garage onto Arlington Street, he was still wondering what could have brought his father to town. Business, no doubt. Quentin Deverell lived for Intercontinental Oil, the family business, as Collin referred to the corporation his father had founded and built into a global giant over the past thirty years. He expected the same total devotion from each of his many employees, and from his identical twin sons, Collin and Justin. It had been their father's idea, sending the twins to Harvard, and then to the Harvard Business School. It was Quentin Deverell's most fervent dream that one day his sons should rule side by side over the empire he had created. For Justin, it had been easy: Justin, like their father, had the blood of the boardroom flowing through his veins. He couldn't wait to occupy a seat on the board of directors. Collin, on the other hand, had never shared their enthusiasm. He had never quite been able to picture himself locked away in an office all day, pushing papers and making deals. He did not think of himself as a businessman. He had only accepted the idea of the Harvard Business School because he knew how much it meant to his father, and because he was not yet sure what he wanted to do with his life.

There had been a time he had believed his future was in the world of sports, in fencing. It was a passion he had felt the first time he took a foil in his hand at the age of fourteen, much younger than most professional fencers begin their training. He had taken an interest in it first as a hobby, then later as a possible career. His first coach, a *maître d'armes* from Paris, had seen a natural ability in Collin Deverell and filled his head with thoughts and dreams of Olympic gold. As he grew older, Collin's love of fencing prevented him from giving one hundred percent of himself to his father's plans for his future. Furious, Quentin Deverell had put an abrupt end to the training, insisting that his son's future was in the boardroom, not on the tournament circuit. But Collin had persisted, and soon had a new coach, a former gold medalist from Milan who also saw promise in his young protégé and encouraged his ambitions. With his encouragement, Collin had gone from local to national tournaments to the international level of competition. He had developed a rather flashy style that combined the best elements of the intellectual, defensive French style learned from his original coach with the aggressive, offensive Italian game taught by his new mentor. By the time he was eighteen, he had won several major tournaments, including a world championship. He had been preparing for the Pan-American Games when his father suffered a heart attack. Knowing how much it meant to his father that he and Justin pull together and concentrate on the family's business interests, Collin had shelved his plans to go for the gold and concentrated on his studies, not wishing to upset his father or cause him further concern. That had been four years ago, and still Collin wondered what his life would have been like today had he continued to pursue that dream. Would he have found what he was looking for, or would he still feel the confusion, the uncertainty he was feeling at this moment? If only, he thought now, he could be more like his brother.

Though Collin and Justin were identical twins, and it was virtually impossible to tell them apart physically, one had only to spend a few moments with them to recognize the striking differences in their personalities. Collin was outgoing, flamboyant, daring, and enjoyed nothing more than poking fun at his twin brother's serious, uptight, ultraconservative ways. Though they were only twenty-three, Collin often complained that his brother behaved like a very old man, while Justin would refer to Collin as "childish." There had never been any doubt in Justin's mind that he would one day follow in their father's footsteps, that he would hold a high rank within the upper echelons of Intercontinental Oil. Collin, on the other hand, had never been so certain about his future. He could not imagine himself an executive, even within his own father's company. He possessed the heart and the spirit of the true adventurer, and wanted something he had yet to find. Excitement. Challenge. For a while, fencing had been the answer. Nothing else had made him feel so alive, so exhilarated. And while his dreams of capturing the highest award possible in the game had been dashed, he had never been able to turn his back on it completely. He still played, almost every day, whenever he could find someone willing to take him on. Unfortunately, most of the fencing enthusiasts he had met at Harvard were amateurs and offered little challenge for a world-class player such as himself.

Crossing the river into Cambridge on the Harvard Bridge, he glanced up at the gray, overcast sky. It looked as if Boston would finally get that snowstorm the forecasters had been predicting for the past three days. He switched on the car radio and fiddled with the dial until he found a station broadcasting the local news. "Damn!" he muttered under his breath as the announcer predicted five to eight inches of snow by morning. A traveler's advisory had been issued by the National Weather Service, the announcer was saying. And Collin had plans for the weekend. Important plans. A snowstorm would definitely put a damper on them. He promptly switched the radio to an album station and adjusted the volume. Then he reached up and loosened the muffler wound around his neck. It had been a long day, and he was glad it was over, even if the coming storm did manage to ruin his weekend.

He drove into the darkened tunnel leading down into the parking garage under his apartment building and parked the Ferrari in his assigned space. He switched off the radio and the ignition and got out of the car, locking the door before he strode off to the elevators. As he rode up alone in the elevator to his floor, he looked at his watch. He would have to put in a call to his father at the Ritz-Carlton as soon as he got in the door. Quentin Deverell was a man who did not like to be kept waiting, even by his own son. He tugged at the muffler until he pulled it off his neck, then unbuttoned his coat. A small smile played on his lips as he thought about the art history major from Radcliffe who was coming over to cook for him tonight. She was quite a work of art herself, he thought. If she were to spend the night. . . . Maybe the possibility of a snowstorm wasn't such a catastrophe after all.

The elevator doors opened and Collin stepped out of the car, walking briskly down the corridor to his apartment, keys in hand. As he let himself into the apartment, the first thing he noticed was that the light was on in the living room. Concerned at first—he knew he hadn't left it on himself—he suddenly remembered: he had given Laura the spare key yesterday so she could let herself in if he were not home when she arrived. Of course—that was it. She'd probably decided to come early and surprise him. Well, he had a few surprises in store for her, too. He turned and opened the closet door, smiling in anticipation of the night ahead.

"Hello, son," said a familiar voice from behind him as he started to hang up his coat. "I was beginning to think you'd decided not to come home tonight."

Collin jerked around. Framed in the doorway leading to the living room, Quentin Deverell, at fifty-three, was an imposing figure of a man, tall, with the same lean, athletic build and sharp, angular features as his sons. His thick hair, combed straight back off his face, was the color of gunmetal, and his eyes were slate blue under winged brows. He was a man of presence, even in his most relaxed moments. A man accustomed to total obedience from everyone around him, including his wayward son. *He's the chairman of Intercontinental Oil, but he's also my father*, Collin thought fondly.

"How did you get in?" he asked casually as he hung his coat in the hall closet.

Quentin Deverell smiled. "Your superintendent let me in," he said. "That shouldn't surprise you, Collin. I *do* pay the rent for this little pleasure palace of yours."

Collin smiled, closing the closet door and turning to face him again. "Does he also keep a log of my comings and goings—and a detailed account of everyone I entertain?"

"I don't need anyone to keep tabs on you, Collin," Deverell responded with a chuckle. "I know you. I know your habits—and your tastes. Remember?"

"Only too well." Collin paused momentarily. "What brings you to Boston, Dad?"

Deverell smiled. "Do I really need a reason to drop in on my sons from time to time?"

"No," Collin said slowly, "but when you *do* drop in, as you put it, it's usually for a specific reason. Am I being called on the carpet again?"

"Not at all."

"Then what *is* the reason for this visit?" He couldn't have come at a worse time, Collin thought as he walked past his father into the living room, a large, spacious room filled with Regency furnishings and prints of hunting scenes adorning the walls. Laura would be here soon, and he could hardly be the suave, seductive host with his father in attendance.

"Your graduation."

Collin smiled. "That's four months away, Dad," he responded. "Are you that eager to chain me to that desk in the office you're readying for me?"

"Be serious, Collin," Quentin Deverell said crossly. "The company is your future, yours and Justin's. Your legacy."

"I'm sorry, Dad," Collin said softly. "I don't mean to make light of it. I know how hard you've worked to make Intercontinental Oil what it is today, and I know how you feel about keeping it in the family. I'm just having a hard time imagining myself pushing papers day after day, that's all." He walked over to the bar in one corner of the room. "Can I buy you a drink?"

Deverell nodded. "Scotch and soda." He paused for a moment, looking around the room. "It still amazes me, the difference in your taste and your brother's. You're like a throwback from another time. Justin's apartment is so starkly modern that it looks like something from the twenty-first century."

"It looks antiseptic," Collin said flatly as he poured the drinks. "I have a hard time believing anyone actually lives there."

Deverell accepted the glass his son was offering him. "I always believed twins—particularly identical twins—were supposed to be close," he said slowly. "Closer than other brothers and sisters."

"I honestly don't think Justin's capable of being close to anyone, Dad," Collin said frankly. "As far as I know, he's never even made it with a woman—"

"That's quite enough of that, Collin," his father retorted sharply. "Your brother prefers to concentrate on his future for now, that's all—something I wish you would give serious thought to doing."

Collin frowned. The same old song and dance, he thought. There were times he wished he didn't care as deeply about his father as he did, didn't care about winning his respect and admiration. It would be so much easier to think only of himself, of what he wanted. "I'm trying, Dad," he said quietly.

"Justin and I had lunch at Apley's," Deverell was saying. "I do wish you could have joined us."

"I was at the gym. I didn't even know you were in town." Collin seated himself on the couch across from his father and drew one leg up, his knee almost to his chest, sipping his drink, waiting for Quentin's response.

"Fencing again?" There was clear disapproval on Deverell's face.

"It's not interfering with my studies, if that's what concerns you," Collin said easily. "I think I can safely say I'm still in the top third of my class."

"Collin, I do realize how enthusiastic you've always been about it. God knows the instruction was expensive enough," Deverell said with a sigh. "And I *am* proud of how well you've done." He paused, looking at the numerous awards displayed on one wall of the apartment, along with the weapons, and his son had them all, from the beginner's French foil to the more complicated épée to the most impressive of all, his elaborate saber. "But we both know your place is at Intercontinental Oil, with myself and your brother."

Collin smiled wryly. "If you want the truth, Dad, I think Justin would be much happier if I were to stay out of the business altogether."

"I don't believe that for a minute," Deverell said, shaking his head. "Justin has known right from the beginning that I expect both of you to be actively involved with the company. He's accepted it, as I wish you would."

Collin thought about it for a moment. "But couldn't that be considered having too many chiefs and not enough Indians?" he asked, trying to make his voice light.

Quentin Deverell frowned. "The two of you don't spend much time together these days, do you?" he asked, dismissing his son's last remark.

"He has his life and I have mine," Collin pointed out, finishing his drink. "We really don't have very much in common, except for seeing the same face looking back at us from the mirror."

"I know, and it disturbs me," Deverell admitted. "After all, one day the two of you will be running the company together—"

Collin's laugh was mirthless. "Do you really want your kingdom divided, Dad?" he asked. "You know perfectly well that Justin and I are about as compatible as oil and water."

"How well I *do* know," Deverell said, drawing in his breath in resignation. Almost from the beginning, when they were small children, he had realized the striking differences in his twin sons' personalities.

Even as children, Collin and Justin had not been close. They were so alike in their physical appearance that only their mother, Deverell's socialite wife Francesca, had been able to tell them apart, and it had not always been easy for her. Yet they were so different in their personalities and attitudes that it was hard to believe that they were brothers, let alone identical twins. They had arrived quite unexpectedly, a month before their anticipated due date, while Francesca Deverell was touring Intercontinental Oil's drilling operations in South America with her husband. Born in a Venezuelan hospital in Caracas, it had been evident from the moment they were delivered that any and all similarity between them ended with their remarkable physical resemblance. Collin, the firstborn of the two, had emerged from his mother's womb squalling with indignant rage, while Justin, born four and a half minutes later, had made a rather calm entrance into the world.

As infants, the differences were always there. Collin was impatient and temperamental, demanding his bottle and his feedings and howling with rage if someone did not respond immediately. Justin, on the other hand, was not a fussy baby. Even at that tender age, there was a serene kind of dignity about him. He was quiet and easy to care for. By the time they were three years old, it was clear to Quentin and Francesca Deverell that their sons were twins in body, but not in spirit. Collin was a handful, even then, while Justin was almost too quiet. "I think this one got all the nerve," Quentin would tell his wife as he dragged Collin out of his study or reprimanded him for raiding the kitchen and driving the cook to distraction. "Justin's going to be the scholar, but Collin—Collin's going to be a bit of a troublemaker."

By the time they were six, Justin had been reading for two and a half years and was still unusually quiet and reserved for such a young child. Collin had been directly responsible for the resignation of three nannies, the last of whom parted describing her young charge as "an unholy terror." He had set off the security alarm system in the main house an average of twice a week, had fed a small rubber ball to one of the guard dogs, and had broken his arm falling out of the tree outside their bedroom window while staging a jailbreak. As they grew older, the differences between them were even more pronounced. Collin was restless and adventuresome, while Justin was studious and controlled. Those differences caused them to drift further and further apart over the years, until there was no closeness between them at all. At the age of eighteen, they were spending as little time together as possible. Though both boys were extremely intelligent and showed remarkable potential, only Justin was making any great academic achievements. Collin had been expelled from almost every private school in Manhattan, and the reports from his instructors and counselors were always the same: "Collin Deverell is uncommonly bright and has the potential to become an outstanding student, but he has exhibited a tendency to being unruly and difficult, with a total lack of respect for authority." His mother felt certain that it was just a phase he was going through and that he would eventually outgrow it, but his father had been genuinely concerned. After all, he reminded his wife, according to the right of primogeniture—which determines which twin born to a ruling monarch will be next in line to the throne—Collin, as the firstborn of their sons, was the natural successor to his position as chairman of Intercontinental Oil.

"But you are not a king, and this is not a monarchy," Francesca Deverell pointed out on more than one occasion. "Does it really matter if Collin decides he does not want to follow in your footsteps? After all, Justin is far better suited to it—"

"Francesca, we have two sons," Quentin Deverell responded, weary from fighting what had been apparent almost from the start. "It is only right that they should share in the responsibility for the company as well as in their inheritance."

"But Collin isn't cut out to be an executive, darling," his wife told him. "Don't try to make him into something he's not. Let Justin run the company. Perhaps Collin could have an equal amount of stock, a seat on the board of directors—"

"And allow my son to throw away his future dashing around the world playing Errol Flynn?" Deverell asked incredulously. "No—I won't hear of it!"

"But if it's what he wants—"

His look silenced her. "I don't believe even Collin knows

what he wants at this point," he said stiffly. "But I do think it's time he began to accept responsibility."

Collin's lack of interest in his legacy had bothered Quentin Deverell for more years than he cared to admit. While his brother had spent most of his life preparing for the role for which he had been born, Collin had resisted assuming that responsibility with equal determination. Justin worked hard, studied hard. Collin, on the other hand, had discovered the opposite sex early on and devoted himself to exploring as many amorous pursuits as possible. His vacations were spent traveling throughout Europe, making countless sexual conquests along the way. Quentin Deverell had been disturbed by reports he'd received from friends and associates who had spotted Collin in the casinos of the French Riviera during his previous summer vacation. It appeared to Quentin Deverell that his son was becoming something of a globe-trotting Romeo, but it was the gambling streak Collin had developed that bothered his father most. Deverell tried to tell himself that things would change in time, that as Collin matured, his priorities would change. They didn't. Quentin had the feeling that subconsciously, Collin still resented him for abruptly ending his career as a world-class fencer. If only he could make his son see that the thrill of a spirited duel, the lure of the blackjack tables and the roulette wheels, were no match for the risks and the gambles of the boardroom. If only Collin would open his eyes and see that this was where he truly belonged. If only, Quentin Deverell thought sadly, his sons could see that Justin's cool logic and Collin's penchant for risk-taking could make them an unbeatable team in the oil community. There would be no stopping them.

Pulling off his mask, Collin picked up a small white hand towel from a nearby bench and wiped the perspiration from his face. "You're not much of a challenge anymore, Farnsworth," he taunted. "I think I could take you with one hand tied behind my back."

"I don't doubt it for a moment," Derek Farnsworth said breathlessly as he put down his foil and pulled off his glove.

Collin laughed. "I—" He stopped short as he saw Justin enter the gym. "Damn," he muttered under his breath. "What does he want?"

Derek Farnsworth grinned. "That's what I like to see—brotherly love," he quipped. "I have an idea—why don't you take *him* on?"

Collin made a wry face. "Taking Justin on in a duel would be like swatting flies," he insisted. "Squash is his game. No chance of spilling any blood there."

Farnsworth shook his head. "I think I'll leave you two alone to discuss whatever it is that's brought your dear brother down here among the commoners." He collected his things and headed for the locker rooms.

"Collin," Justin addressed him as he approached. "I thought I'd find you here."

Collin tossed his towel over his left shoulder casually. "I thought I was safe here—you've never liked this place."

Justin Deverell ignored his brother's sarcasm. "I didn't come here to trade insults with you," he responded curtly.

"True to form—you never would enter into a competition you had absolutely no chance of winning," Collin remarked, picking up his glove and gauntlet from the bench. "All right, why are you here?"

"Father called this morning. As usual, he was unable to reach you," Justin said coldly. "What do you *do* with yourself?"

"I sure as hell don't sit home waiting for the phone to ring," Collin answered. "What's up?"

"He wants us to fly down for the weekend," Justin said, looking around the gym disdainfully. "They're having guests out on the Sound, people he thinks we should meet."

"Grooming us for the succession again, is he?" Collin asked tightly. "One has to give him credit. He never stops trying."

"In your case, perhaps he should," Justin commented. "It would seem he's wasting his time."

"Maybe you're right," Collin agreed. "But I doubt either of us will ever convince him."

Justin stared at him for a moment. "You really don't have any interest whatsoever in the company, do you?"

"Did I say that?"

"You don't have to. Your actions speak for themselves," Justin said disapprovingly. "Don't you think he can tell? Don't you think he knows you'd rather be spending your time jetting all over Europe with a saber in one hand and a woman in the other?"

"Then why doesn't he let it go?"

"Maybe he has more concern for your future than you have yourself," Justin replied.

Collin studied him thoughtfully for a few seconds. "I've never refused Dad anything and you know it," he said, trying to control his mounting anger. "I've gone along with all of his plans for my life. I'm here, aren't I?"

"Somewhat halfheartedly, but yes, you are here," Justin conceded with reluctance in his voice.

"Then get off my back!" Collin snapped. With that, he turned on his heel and walked away, leaving his brother staring after him.

Collin adored the Deverell estate at Sea Cliff, overlooking Long Island Sound. He had grown up here; his happiest memories were of this house. Even now, he still loved roaming the estate late at night or in the early hours of the morning. He liked to walk alone on the wooded, perfectly tended grounds that surrounded the magnificent English Tudor-style mansion, with its manicured gardens, man-made waterfall, and balustrades of stone. He liked to remember what his childhood here had been like, skipping rocks on the pond, terrorizing the servants with his endless pranks, the long talks he'd had with his mother, discussing the doubts and fears he'd had, first as a child, then as he approached manhood. He had always loved both parents—even when his father was at his most overbearing, his love was never doubted—but Collin had always felt closest to his mother.

It was odd how the genes seemed to have been divided in the case of himself and his twin brother, he thought now, staring up at the clear, star-filled June sky. Justin had inherited their father's fierce ambitions, his cool British reserve. Collin was more like his mother. He had been born with all the intensity and passion of his mother's Italian heritage, and he wouldn't have wanted it any other way. Justin was unable to show his feelings, but Collin had never been able to control his. He felt everything more intensely than his brother, whether it was love, physical passion, anger, or grief. *Passion is a weakness*, his father had said more than once. But a lack of it, Collin reasoned, was a living death. He was a passionate man, physically and emotionally, even if commitment wasn't in his vocabulary.

It is good to be home, Collin thought. Good to have the long years he had spent at Harvard, preparing for a life he wasn't sure he really wanted, behind him at last. Though his father was already making plans for installing Collin and Justin in their offices at Intercontinental Oil, Collin had made up his mind to have a talk with him before the week was over. He wanted to tell his father that he was not ready to assume his role as heir apparent just yet, that he wanted—no, *needed*—to take some time to get away, to think about things. Maybe he'd go to Europe, enter a few tournaments, hit the casinos, relax for a month or two. Maybe it would help him to put things into perspective. He was still having doubts. He was a part of Intercontinental Oil because his father wanted him to be a part of it, but was that enough? he asked himself. Was it enough to make him tie himself to the company for the rest of his life, perhaps missing out on a life that would make him happy?

"You were unusually quiet during dinner," observed a familiar voice from behind him.

Collin turned. Francesca Deverell stood in the doorway, silhouetted by the bright light streaming through the French doors from the music room. At forty-nine, she was a stunning woman, tall and slender with the bearing of one born to nobility. Her dark, luxuriant hair and dark eyes were clearly evident of her Florentine ancestry. Again, a balance, he realized. Though he and Justin had inherited their sharp, angular features from their father, their dark coloring was clearly their mother's.

He managed a slight smile. "I needed some time alone—to think," he said in a weary tone.

"Obviously." She came closer. "I would think it would come as a relief to you, to finally have your education completed and out of the way."

"Now comes the hard part," he said quietly.

"Telling your father you don't want to join the company," Francesca concluded.

Collin looked at her, surprised. "How did you know?"

She gave a little laugh. "I know you, my darling."

"I'm that obvious?" he asked.

"Yes, you are." She touched his arm affectionately. "I've always loved you and your brother equally. I think you know that. Unfortunately, I could never get as close to Justin as I did to you." She paused. "He always held back—with everyone. But you . . . you were always so transparent. I had only to look into your eyes to know what you were feeling. A man who wears his heart on his sleeve, I believe it's called."

"Does Dad know?" Collin asked.

"Your father sees only what he wishes to see," she answered. "He believes he's doing what's best for you by pushing you into the executive suite."

"And what do you think?"

She smiled patiently. "What's important is what you think," she told him. "What do you want to do with your life?"

Collin drew in a deep breath. "I wish I knew," he sighed.

"Don't you think it's time you found out?"

Collin nodded. "He's been counting on this since the day we were born, you know."

"No one knows it better than I," she said, putting her hands on his shoulders. She looked up into his eyes as she spoke: "Talk to him, Collin. Tell him how you feel. Tell him you're not ready. Don't commit yourself to a future you don't want out of a sense of duty to your father.''

"There's more to it than duty, Mother," he said quietly. "I want him to respect me. I want him to be proud of me. I need that from him.''

"You must also respect yourself," Francesca reminded him. "To be truly happy, you must put your own needs and desires first. Besides, your father will always be proud of you—no matter what.''

"Maybe he's right. Maybe I do belong there," he said slowly.

"Listen to me, Collin. Your father and I are flying down to Caracas next week to observe the offshore drilling operations there. Why don't you think it over while we're away and have a long talk with him after we return? Perhaps by then . . .''

Collin smiled, embracing her gently. "What would I do without you, Mother?''

She looked up at him with love in her eyes. "I don't intend to give you the opportunity to find out," she said softly.

"Are you sure no one is around?" The slim blonde following Collin up the wide oak staircase looked concerned.

"I'm absolutely certain," Collin assured her. After getting her this far, he had no intention of letting her slip away now because she was afraid someone might walk in on them. He had spotted Fallon Merritt on the cover of a top fashion magazine at a Manhattan newsstand four months ago as he was coming from a visit to his father's offices and had been immediately captivated by her lush blond hair, wide green eyes, and exquisite face. Her body had enticed him even more. Determined to meet her, he'd used his family's connections to gain an introduction. It had taken him almost three weeks to persuade her to come to Sea Cliff with him for the weekend. She had not been enthusiastic about sleeping with him in his parents' house, but he had assured her that they would not be arriving home from South America unexpectedly. "My father's trips are often extended, but never cut short," he said with certainty as he led her upstairs to his bedroom. "I even dismissed the servants for the weekend so we could be alone. You're not going to disappoint me now, are you?"

She shook her head. "Of course not."

He guided her into the room and closed the door. Then he pulled her into his arms and kissed her hungrily as his hands slowly roamed up and down the length of her body, caressing her through the sheer fabric of her lightweight summer dress. He started to lift her skirt, but she pulled away abruptly. "Aren't you going to close the drapes?" she asked.

"What for?" he asked, amused.

She looked at him. "Well . . . you know."

"I like to be able to see what I'm doing," he said in a teasing voice.

"Please, Collin." She was obviously uncomfortable with the idea of going to bed with him in the harsh light of day.

"All right," he agreed reluctantly. He crossed the room, a large, impressively decorated suite done in rich fabrics and colors, and drew the heavy velvet drapes until the room was in total darkness. "Better?" he wanted to know.

"Much."

He took her in his arms and kissed her again, this time unzipping the back of her dress as he did so. He pulled the dress off her shoulders and pushed it down over her slim hips until it fell to the carpet around her feet. Then he removed her slip and undergarments and cast them aside. His mouth came down on hers, hard and demanding, as his hands explored her body. He slipped one hand between her legs and fondled her until she began to squirm at his touch. "Undress me," he muttered in her ear as he pressed himself against her.

She nodded mutely and started unbuttoning his shirt. He cupped her breasts in his hands and teased her nipples with his fingertips as she unbuckled his belt and unzipped his pants, pushing them down his muscular legs so he could step out of them. Already he was erect with desire. She began stroking him, arousing him even further. Then, abruptly, he pushed her down on the bed and lay on top of her, kissing her as he let his hands move over her nakedness. He started kissing her neck, her shoulders, gently licking her nipples as his mouth moved lower, over her belly to the delta of soft, pale hair covering her pubis. Preparing her with his stroking fingers, he began to kiss her lightly, at first softly, gently, then with a growing insistency. As she became more aroused by his expert manipulations, she began to squirm again, trying to pull away from him. He grasped her buttocks in his hands and held her down to the bed as he continued his assault on her with his mouth and tongue. He did not let up on her until she cried out, begging him to stop. Then, he reared over her, launching himself into her, riding her mercilessly. She clung to him, digging her nails into his shoulders as he took her, swiftly, silently.

He was exploding inside her at the moment the door burst open and a stream of blinding light sliced through the darkness. He looked up, startled. Justin stood in the doorway, his face dark with anger. "I should have expected this!" he snapped. "You could at least have the decency not to bring your conquests here." He snatched up the dress lying at his feet and thrust it at the young woman angrily. "I think you had better go now."

Collin sat up. "Just a damn minute now—"

"It's all right, Collin," Fallon cut in quickly, pulling the sheet up over her breasts. "If the two of you would just leave me alone long enough to dress . . ."

Collin looked up at Justin. "The least you could do is knock before entering my bedroom," he snapped.

"It could have been avoided if you hadn't found it necessary to turn the phones off," Justin said coldly. "Everyone has tried to reach you. I've been calling since early this afternoon. Where, may I ask, are all the servants?"

"I gave them the weekend off." Then Collin saw something in his brother's face, something he had never seen there before and could not identify. "Why have you been trying to reach me? Is something wrong?"

"You're damned right something's wrong," Justin said bitterly. "While you've been carrying on here, there was an explosion on one of the rigs down in Venezuela—" He stopped short, at a loss for words for the first time in his life.

Collin looked at him, suddenly filled with a growing sense of unease. "Mother and Dad—" he began.

Justin shook his head, taking a moment to find his voice again. "They're dead," he said finally. "They're both dead."

Caracas, Venezuela, June 1976

The Intercontinental Oil jet landed at the Simón Bolívar Airport in Maiquetia, thirteen miles from Caracas, just before dawn on a hot, humid summer morning. The press was out in full force, assaulting Collin and Justin with questions about the explosion and the deaths of their parents as they made their way through the mob to a waiting car. Justin attempted to answer their questions, but Collin pushed past them forcefully, not bothering to conceal his resentment. Why couldn't they just go away and leave him alone to deal with his loss? Why did they have to swarm around like a bunch of goddamned vultures circling over the desert, waiting for their prey to finally die?

"You could have said something," Justin told him when they were alone in the back of the limousine. "We do have our image to think of—"

"I don't give a damn about our image—or the company's," Collin snapped back, staring through the tinted glass at the calm Caribbean. "Mother and Dad are dead, Justin—that's all that matters now."

Justin sank back against the seat and turned away from his brother. "There's no use trying to talk to you, is there?"

"Not now," Collin answered without hesitation. "I'm not in the mood to argue with you or anyone else."

"Odd," Justin said coldly. "I thought you were always in the mood for an argument."

"Leave it alone, Justin." Collin's tone held an unmistakable note of warning that made Justin back off immediately.

The remainder of their journey into Caracas was made in silence, each of them preoccupied with his own thoughts. Collin found himself trying to recall the last time he had been there. It was two years ago, and Quentin Deverell had decided it was time his sons began familiarizing themselves with Intercontinental Oil's many operations and holdings throughout the world. There were the oil fields in Texas, of course, and the drilling going on in Alaska, as well as the latest acquisition, a large number of leases in the South China Sea, but the offshore operations in Venezuela were by far the ones of which Quentin Deverell had always been proudest. It was here, he had told his sons more than once, that Intercontinental Oil had been founded in 1946. It had always seemed somehow appropriate to him that his children had also been born here.

Soon Collin caught sight of the remnants of what had been, two days earlier, the largest offshore drilling operation in the Southern Hemisphere.

Collin would have liked to bury his parents on the grounds of the estate at Sea Cliff, but his father's attorneys had patiently explained that this was not possible, due to some zoning regulation, so Justin had made all the necessary arrangements to have them buried at a cemetery in nearby Sands Point. Justin had taken care of everything. Collin had not been able to even think about taking part in those necessary rites of death. At first his mind had not been able to accept the reality that they were really gone. Just one week earlier he had had that heart-to-heart talk with his mother, had made his decision to tell his father he wanted no part of the company. Now, *he* was the new chairman of the board.

He still couldn't believe it, even though he'd heard it from his father's own attorneys. His father had left the chairmanship to *him*. Knowing how he felt, his father had still done it. Forced his hand.

He looked at Justin, who was lost in his own thoughts. What was he thinking right now? What was he feeling? He had to be disappointed. Probably angry as hell, too. The company was Justin's life—literally. He lived for it. He had expected to take their father's place as board chairman. Hell, he'd earned it. Yet he'd shown no emotion at all when the attorneys revealed the contents of the will. No angry outburst, nothing. Why? Collin wondered. What had been going through his mind at that moment?

What had been going through their father's mind when he'd had that will drawn up?

It had taken Justin and Intercontinental Oil's attorneys several days to unravel all the red tape involved in transporting the bodies of Quentin and Francesca Deverell back to the United States, and then only with the aid of a high-ranking official from the American embassy in Caracas. Collin had not been involved in the legal procedures at all. He spent his days on a small boat, staring at the rig's wreckage for hours at a time. He talked to the men who had survived the disaster, looking for answers, trying to explain to himself what had happened. The offshore drilling had been going on here for years. Years. What had gone wrong this time? Why had it happened? What could have caused the explosion? The authorities had not been able to provide him with satisfactory answers to his questions. It was, they pointed out, something they might never be able to explain.

"What does it matter now?" Justin asked irritably when Collin brought it up over dinner one night. "They're dead. They're gone, the rigs are gone—"

"I want to know *why* they're dead!" Collin persisted. "I want to know why that explosion happened! I want to know how it could have been averted, how all those lives—including our parents'—could have been saved!"

"There's no point," Justin said wearily, throwing his napkin down on the table, clearly annoyed with his brother's stubbornness. "It just doesn't matter anymore."

Collin stared at him for a moment. Right from the beginning, from the moment he had arrived at Sea Cliff to tell Collin about the explosion, it seemed to Collin that Justin had been unnaturally cold, dispassionate. True to form. He had handled everything calmly, almost too impersonally. Collin had wondered more than once if his brother really cared at all that their parents were dead. But now it seemed that Justin was fighting for his self-control, fighting with everything he had to maintain that cool, composed image of his. Suddenly Collin felt sorry for his brother. But much as he wanted to reach out to Justin now, something deep within his soul held him back.

Can over twenty years of hostility be erased overnight? he wondered. *Can it ever be erased completely?*

On a hot summer morning in mid-August, Collin walked alone on the grounds at Sea Cliff, lost in thought. It had been six weeks since they returned from South America, six weeks since his parents were buried at Sands Point. Six weeks since he had seen or heard from Justin. They'd parted after the funeral service and neither of them had attempted any form of contact with the other since. Collin suspected that Justin had to deal with his grief in his own way, on his own time. He thought about what their mother had told him, just before she left for Caracas: she had never been able to get close to Justin as she had Collin; he had always held a part of himself back. Perhaps, Collin thought now, his brother was afraid to let go, afraid to show his emotions. Maybe Justin wasn't the cold, unfeeling man Collin had always believed him to be. *With Mother and Dad gone, maybe I should try to close the gap between us,* he thought. *Make peace. Is it possible that we could find some kind of closeness between us after all these years?*

Collin knew that his place was at Intercontinental's offices in Manhattan helping Justin pick up the pieces and hold the company together in the wake of their father's death, but he still was not able to face that responsibility. Not yet. Though he felt he owed it to his father, he was unable to bring himself to take part in the survival of something he still held responsible for his parents' deaths. Justin would condemn him for being foolish and irrational, but Collin was unable to control how he felt.

He wandered through the large rooms of the mansion, gazing at the priceless antiques and paintings, staring absently at the personal effects of his mother and father that were still scattered throughout the house, remnants of lives that no longer existed. He took his mother's jewelry from the wall safe in the bedroom and held it, as if trying to summon up her spirit. He sat in the suede-covered executive chair in his father's study, surprised to find that it still smelled of his after-shave and cologne. He studied the large world map on the wall, dotted with bright-colored pins indicating Intercontinental's various holdings all over the world. *My father's kingdom*, he thought sadly. The kingdom he had built from the ground up, his legacy to his two sons. The kingdom that had destroyed him. *Why?* Collin asked himself again. *Why did it have to happen?*

It had taken Collin almost a month to bring himself to have the maids pack away his parents' clothes and other personal items. It seemed so final somehow, seeing the boxes filled with all that remained of his mother and father, of their lives there, being carried away to storage. *It's like having to say good-bye all over again*, he thought as he watched the last box being taken away. All that was left now were his memories—and Intercontinental Oil, a giant he would have to face eventually, one he would have to come to terms with.

Fencing is often compared to chess in that it is extremely demanding mentally, and is essentially a battle of wits in which the fencer must trick his opponent into anticipating his offensive move in one direction, then surprise him with an attack to another part of the target area. The expert fencer must be intelligent, patient, quick-witted, and fast on his feet, able to detect and then exploit his opponent's weaknesses. For Collin, it was second nature. His first fencing coach, Jean-Michel Perrin, had claimed that if anyone were truly born to the sword, it was Collin Deverell. "You have the makings of the true champion," the *maître d'armes* had proclaimed. Though Collin had given up his dreams of pursuing it professionally, he still gave as much of himself to it as he could, finding it an excellent way to blow off steam, especially now, when his world had become so unbearable, and he was so tormented by indecision. If he had waged war with his opponents in the past, he was now doing battle with his own soul. He wielded the foil as though it were a mighty sword and he were defending his very life with it.

Now, fencing with an old college chum at the Santelli Salle d'Armes in Manhattan, he felt as though he were performing a ritual of exorcism. He launched his attack with a long forward lunge, his sword arm fully extended. His opponent made a parry, deflecting the blade of Collin's foil before launching his counterattack. Collin responded with a riposte, defending himself against the assault. The challenger, sensing his uncontrollable fury, backed off, attempting once again to deflect the blade Collin directed at the upper portion of his trunk.

"Take it easy, will you, Deverell?" The other man was clearly intimidated by Collin's unusually aggressive attack, and unnerved by his strange mental state. What had gotten into him? he wondered as he continued to defend himself. He knew that Collin Deverell's parents had died recently, but his were not the actions of a man in mourning: they were the actions of a man consumed by rage.

Now Collin launched his final—and most spectacular—attack. Appropriately called a *flèche*, the French word for arrow, he initiated it with a sudden start, running full tilt at his opponent, catching him off guard with no time to think or react. The other man got out of the way as quickly as he could. Collin's foil plunged forward, hitting the wall, bending and snapping in half. In his fury, he swung backward, catching his opponent's sword arm with the razor-sharp tip of the broken foil. It ripped through the fabric of the immaculate white jacket, and in an instant, the other man's upper arm was covered with blood. Collin, suddenly alarmed, threw down the broken foil and, without a word, ripped the fabric away from the open wound. There was a deep gash in his friend's arm, but it was bleeding so profusely that he was unable to see how deep it went. "Come on," he said tightly, "I'll take you to the hospital."

The other man gave a weak laugh. "Don't be ridiculous," he protested. "It's just a flesh wound. Bandage it up, and—"

"This is no flesh wound," Collin said, looking up at him. "You're going to need stitches." It was, he realized, the first time he had ever injured anyone, even in his most aggressive moments.

What's happening to me? he asked himself.

If the depth of Collin's interest in his birthright had been in question before, there was no longer any doubt in his mind: he wanted no part of Intercontinental Oil. He had always doubted his suitability for the future his father had mapped out for him, but now he was absolutely certain that he did not belong in the executive suite. His father had devoted his entire life to the company, and in the end his creation had destroyed him. His brother had given it the same total devotion, and the result had been a life that had no room for anything or anyone else. They had never controlled the company: it controlled them. Collin knew that it could never control him. He would not allow it.

Collin knew that Justin had been burning the proverbial midnight oil at the office lately, combating the rumors that flew on Wall Street that Intercontinental Oil was facing collapse as news of Quentin Deverell's death sent its stock prices plummeting. He knew that he should be there, working with his brother to save everything his father had fought so hard to accomplish, but he couldn't. He had not been able to force himself to go near the company's headquarters since they returned from Venezuela. Instead, he continued to deal with his deep sense of loss by pushing himself to the limit—in fencing, in driving at breakneck speeds in the Ferrari, in a long series of one-night stands with beautiful women he barely knew and never saw again once he had been to bed with them. He drank too much and slept too little. He knew he was on a collision course with self-destruction but seemed unable to control himself.

If only something would take away the pain. . . .

"Don't you think it's time you put all this foolishness aside and started accepting your responsibilities to the company?" Justin stood in the living room of his ultramodern condominium at the Trump Tower, watching Collin pour what little remained in a bottle of scotch into a glass at the bar. It was the first time Collin had visited his brother or spoken to him since the funeral. Now, as Collin looked absently around the room, with its stark furnishings, abstract paintings, and bronze and black accents, he wished he had not come.

"Responsibilities to the company," Collin repeated slowly, biting off each word as though he were tasting a bitter fruit.

"It was Dad's intention that we work together, that we run the company together," Justin said carefully, staring down at the floor.

"It seems to me that you'd be perfectly happy to go on ruling over Dad's little petroleum empire all by yourself," Collin said sarcastically, hunting through the cabinet for another bottle of scotch.

"I would," Justin admitted without hesitation. "I've always felt I was better suited for the chairmanship than you ever could be."

"Well, at least we agree on one thing," Collin said with a wintry smile. "Got any more scotch around here?"

"No, and I think it's just as well. You've had enough," Justin said crossly. "Collin, we owe it to our father . . ."

Collin looked up at him and grinned. "Funny . . . I never thought of you as someone with such a great sense of duty."

"And I never thought of you as a coward," Justin responded.

Collin swung around to face him, his brown eyes blazing with anger. "You're way out of line," he said warningly.

"Am I?" Justin's manner was as cool and composed as always. "It seems to me that you're running away from your obligations these days. Not your style, as I recall."

"My first obligation is to myself, little brother," Collin snapped.

"From what I hear, you're not even living up to that very well."

Collin shook his head. "What do you expect?" he wanted to know. "Before they left for Caracas, I had a long talk with Mother. I told her how I felt, that I didn't want to disappoint Dad, but I didn't feel I really belonged at Intercontinental Oil. I was waiting for him to get back, to tell him I wanted out—"

"Do you think it was ever easy for me?" Justin exploded, the first real show of intense emotion Collin had seen his brother exhibit since they were small children. "I felt like I was always forced to take second place to you—in the company *and* in Dad's affections! No matter what I did or how hard I tried, you always came first with him—"

"That's not true!" Collin insisted.

"Oh, but it is—it always was," Justin shot back. "You were the firstborn, even if it was only by four and a half minutes. You were the one who was being groomed to succeed him. I always resented you because you were first in his heart! You know, the more daring and rebellious you were, the more he admired you. He was convinced that you, the risk taker, were perfect for the role of chairman of Intercontinental Oil. I used to wish I could be more like you, that I could do the things that came so naturally to you, but I couldn't seem to shed my own natural cautiousness. I always wished he'd leave you alone, let you go off after your fencing championships and your gambling ventures and your women. I tried so hard to prove to him that I was the one who should be his eventual successor, but I had to work twice as hard, give twice as much of myself, just to make him see that I was ready to give myself to it one hundred percent! I had to make it my whole life, while you were jetting all over the world, living the good life! And for what? Where did it get me?''

''You're running the company—just as you always wanted to do,'' Collin said darkly.

''Only because you haven't seen fit to take your place there,'' Justin said, swirling the half-melted ice cubes around in the bottom of his glass. ''When the will is read—''

''When the will is read, we'll have to make some decisions of our own,'' Collin finished quietly. ''Until then, things will remain as they are now.''

''And after?'' Justin asked.

Collin frowned. ''I wish I knew.''

Collin had not been as surprised by Justin's open admission of resentment as he had been by the length of time it had taken to surface. As he drove back to Sea Cliff late that night, he found himself surprisingly sober, unable to stop thinking about the things Justin had said. Though he'd always been able to sense his twin brother's resentment of him, it had never occurred to him that Justin had ever yearned to be like him. Collin always believed that Justin found his behavior deplorable, that he considered Collin irresponsible and unpredictable, and that their father had felt exactly the same way, yet they had both admired him in their own way. Justin had envied his willingness to take chances. His father had considered that trait an asset in business. *You discover something new every day*, Collin thought dismally.

''We always had to share everything, didn't we,'' Justin had said with a mirthless laugh. ''Only you were the favorite son as far as Dad was concerned. Did you ever realize how far he was willing to go to make certain your future was tied to Intercontinental Oil's? He was so damned afraid your penchant for fencing and gambling would get in the way of his plans for you—God, it makes me sick!''

The sound of a car's horn brought Collin back to the present abruptly as he realized he'd crossed the yellow line dividing the lanes. Blinded by the headlights of the oncoming car, he grasped the wheel and swerved to avoid a head-on collision. He pulled over to the shoulder of the road and tried to catch his breath. It had been close. Too close. But his thoughts were still on Justin, on their conversation at the Trump Tower. If only their father had seen how they felt, had seen Collin's need for independence, for a life other than the one Quentin Deverell had planned for him, and Justin's need for their father's acceptance, his recognition. Justin had always longed for that special closeness with their father, had dreamed of following in his footsteps. Collin had felt the need to escape that world, to find that special something he knew it would take to make him happy. Their father, good as he'd been to them, had been blind to those needs, attempting to force Collin into a role for which he was not suited, shoving Justin into his brother's shadow, a position he found unbearably unacceptable. Collin was sure his father had believed he was doing the right thing for both of his sons, but he realized now just how well his mother had understood her husband. What was it she had told him? His father saw only what he wished to see. He was a good man. He had been a good father, always. But his single-minded determination to make Intercontinental the biggest and best at all costs had made him blind to the pain his children were going through. It made Collin wonder what their lives would have been like if things had been different. If Justin had been born first. . . .

"You know, I feel your body next to mine, I can see you lying here beside me, yet I have the feeling that you're a thousand miles away." The woman in Collin's bed was stunning, with an aristocratic face, an almost perfect body, and a magnificent mane of dark red hair that hung down to the middle of her back. She was staring at him with wide, heavily-lashed blue eyes as she traced tiny circles on his chest with the tip of her index finger. "Your body has been more than willing, but I suspect your heart isn't in it."

Collin lay on his back, arms folded behind his head, staring blankly at the ceiling. "I've got a lot on my mind, that's all," he responded quietly.

"Give me a chance and I'll take your mind off your troubles, darling," she said in a low, suggestive voice.

Collin rolled over to face her, smiling for the first time. "Think you're equal to the challenge?"

Her eyes met his. "I'm sure of it." She kissed him full on the mouth, running her fingers through his hair. He returned her kisses hungrily, his hands sliding down the length of her silken body, caressing her breasts, her buttocks, then crushing her body against his own. She pulled away from him suddenly, breaking his grasp, as she began kissing his neck and shoulders, running her tongue over the lean, muscular contours of his chest. She savored the strong, masculine scent of his flesh as if it were the most expensive perfume as her lips moved lower, down over the taut, toned muscles of his midsection and abdomen, down over his groin to the thatch of thick, dark curls from which his penis rose like a hard, firm, quivering arrow, throbbing with expectation. Taking it in one hand, she began kissing it repeatedly, first the tip, then down along the swollen shaft to his scrotum and back up again. She took the tip of it in her mouth and sucked at it lazily, gradually drawing more and more of into her hot mouth, taking as much of it as she was able to accommodate, sucking with increased intensity as her expert fingers caressed his testicles. Soon he began to moan with pleasure. He looked down at her as she worked on him. He could only see the back of her head. The room was in darkness, except for a stream of light coming from a narrow opening in the heavy velvet drapes, and when the light hit her hair, it seemed to turn a dozen shades of red, ranging from bright orange to the multitude of shades of autumn leaves to the deep, dark red of an Irish setter's coat. He reached down and put his hand at the back of her head, pushing her down to him, trying to force himself deeper within her mouth, her throat. His hips moved up off the bed as he began thrusting, his excitement growing. Abruptly, he grabbed her and rolled her over on her back, entering her with such force that she cried out. He started thrusting again, moving deeper and faster inside her, taking her swiftly, wordlessly, coming to an explosive orgasm. Then he fell off her, breathing heavily.

She turned to look at him, smiling as she traced the muscles of his upper arm with her fingertips. "Well?" Her voice was soft and low. "Have I succeeded?"

Collin didn't hear her. He had already shut her out.

No matter where he was or what he was doing, Collin found himself thinking about his last conversation with Justin, about all the frustration and resentment that had surfaced that night at the Trump Tower, about how different their lives might have been—how different their relationship as brothers might have been—had they each been allowed to realize their own dreams and ambitions rather than living out their father's dreams for them. They might have been closer. They might have been brothers, real brothers, instead of rivals. So much could have been different.

Collin was certain of only one thing: he was never going to find out what he really wanted unless he could put some distance between himself and the past, the unpleasant memories. He would never know what it was he wanted if he became his father's successor and attempted to live his father's dream. In the months since the explosion in Venezuela, he had become increasingly restless. As much as he loved the estate at Sea Cliff, he had begun to feel the need to get away, to find what had eluded him up until now, to establish some sort of direction in his life. He knew he had to do something. It was hell, not knowing where he belonged or what he wanted to do with himself. He thought about it long and hard, and finally reached a decision he felt would have a profound effect on him and his brother.

The next day, he went to see Justin again.

* * *

Standing outside the fifty-story Intercontinental Oil building in Manhattan's financial district, Collin was suddenly hesitant to go inside. He stared up at the impressive glass and steel tower, that monument to the incredible ambition and determination of his late father, seemingly ablaze in the setting sun, and he asked himself one last time if he were doing the right thing. *I have to believe it's right—for both of us,* he thought. *It may not bring us any closer, but it could right the wrongs that have been done in the past.*

He entered the building and strode across the vast lobby, enclosed in floor-to-ceiling glass with gray marble floors and gigantic potted trees throughout. As he headed in the direction of the bank of the elevators that would take him to the executive suite on the fiftieth floor, a uniformed security guard greeted him with a smile and a tip of his hat. " 'Evening, Mr. Deverell.''

"Good evening.'' Collin smiled to himself as he stepped into the empty express elevator and the doors closed behind him. The poor man probably didn't know which Mr. Deverell he was. No one had ever been able to tell them apart on sight alone.

As he entered the reception area outside his father's—now his brother's—office, Justin's secretary looked up, appearing mildly confused. "Mr. Deverell, how—'' she began, flustered.

He managed a smile. "I'm Collin Deverell. My brother is expecting me, I believe,'' he said helpfully.

"Of—of course,'' she stammered. "I'm sorry I—it's just that we haven't seen you around here since—''

"It's okay,'' he said pleasantly. "Is it all right if I go in?'' He gestured toward the door.

She nodded. "Certainly.''

As he entered the office that had once been his father's, he discovered that Justin had not changed a thing. Everything was exactly as Quentin Deverell had left it: the furniture, the antique desk which really wasn't Justin's style, the paintings, mostly Italian Renaissance selected by their mother. Justin was on the phone. He looked up as Collin entered, unsmiling, and motioned to him to sit down. Collin started across the room, pausing for a moment to take in the extraordinary view of lower Manhattan. To the southwest, the majestic twin towers of the World Trade Center rose above the skyline like twin pillars, gleaming in the dim light of a dying sun. Beyond, ships leaving New York harbor headed out to sea. It was spectacular, he thought now, taking a seat across from his brother. No wonder their father had wanted his office in this precise location. Collin smiled to himself, suddenly realizing that Quentin Deverell was not a man to be moved by a view, any view. If this spot had been selected for the view, then it had been his mother's choice.

Justin replaced the receiver and looked at Collin for a moment. "You've avoided this building as if it were a leper colony for the past four months," he said icily. "What brings you here now?"

Collin knew what he was thinking, and was not surprised by his brother's defensiveness. Justin thought he was here to claim his right to succeed their father as chairman. Collin put him at ease by getting right to the point. "I want out," he said bluntly.

"Out?"

"Out of the company. Completely," Collin explained. "I'm not cut out to be an executive. I never was. I want it to be a clean break. That's the only way—for both of us."

"I agree, but exactly what are you proposing?" Justin asked carefully. He leaned forward, not concealing his interest. Arms on the desk, he pressed his fingertips together pyramid-fashion and waited for Collin to go on.

"A deal," Collin answered finally. "A trade-off, if you will."

"Involving what?" Justin wanted to know.

"You want Intercontinental Oil. I don't. I want no part of it—not now and not in the foreseeable future," Collin admitted. "What I do want, however, is the place at Sea Cliff. I want the property, the artworks, and Mother's jewelry. In return, I'm prepared to sign over all of my stock in Intercontinental Oil.''

Justin stared at him as if he did not believe what he was hearing. ''That's it?'' he asked. ''That's all you want?''

Collin smiled wearily. ''Isn't that enough?''

Justin nodded slowly. ''And the personal assets?''

''Divided equally, as they wanted them to be,'' Collin answered without hesitation. ''Everything else will be carried out according to the will. Agreed?''

''Agreed.'' Justin got to his feet, smiling with relief. He looked as though a tremendous burden had been lifted from his shoulders as he extended his hand to his brother. ''You have yourself a deal.''

Collin shook his hand, realizing as he did that it was the first time in their twenty-three years that they had been able to truly agree on anything, the first time they'd managed to work out a problem to their mutual satisfaction.

He thought about it as he left the building and climbed into the Ferrari. *I wish I could have been everything you wanted me to be, Dad*, he thought sadly. *But I can't. I'm sorry I've disappointed you, but I have to find my own way. You're gone now, but Justin will carry on what you started.*

It's time for me to get on with my own life.

San Francisco, August 1978

Ashley Gordon stood on the curb at the foot of California Street, waiting for a cable car to pass. There wasn't a cloud in the sky, and the sun seemed brighter than usual, and hotter than was typical for the mild San Francisco climate. She brushed a strand of her long dark hair away from her face and reached down to smooth the front of her white linen dress. She stole a quick glance at her watch. Ten forty-five. Good, she was early. She dashed across the street against the light and headed for the Embarcadero Center, eight and a half acres of innovative, ultramodern architecture, malls and plazas, sculptures and unusual fountains, restaurants and shops, and galleries, one of which had given her her first exhibit a year and a half earlier. That night, she thought with deep satisfaction, had changed her life.

Across the mall to her left, a group of tourists gawked at the Vaillancourt Fountain, a unique sculpture that had on occasion been described by its many critics as "Stonehenge unhinged," and "dynamited debris." It was the first fountain she had ever been able to walk through without getting wet, she thought with mild amusement. A smile came to her lips as she watched a young couple—lovers, obviously—holding hands as they followed the steppingstones across the reflecting pool and darted playfully in and out of the fountain's enormous, oblong arms, laughing at the sound of the water drumming in a steady rhythm on the outside of the sculpture, startled by the unexpected spouts of spray. It made Ashley recall with fondness the first time she had come here, two years earlier. She'd just arrived in San Francisco, eager to make a new life for herself, eager to make this city her own. She'd been alone the first time she came here, but she had not spent much time alone since.

Ashley walked briskly back along the plaza in the direction of Market Place, the sidewalk café at the Hyatt Regency, still thinking about how her social life had become intertwined with her career, how the contacts she had made in her private life had served to further her professional ambitions. She liked to think she was sophisticated enough to use whatever resources were available to her to realize her dreams and mature enough to cope with whatever that might involve. She had not come here with a large trust fund to sustain her while she was waiting for that first triumph, but she had been smart enough to realize that there was nothing wrong with using the social connections she'd made through the art world to gain entry into the world to which she was eager to belong. The rich, influential men she had met during her two years in San Francisco found her beautiful, charming, and witty. They enjoyed being with her. And more important, they knew the right people. Some of those men had been her lovers, but Ashley had never compromised herself. She'd never slept with a man solely for the purpose of advancing herself as an artist. When she became involved with a man, it was because she was attracted to him. If he was socially prominent or influential in the art world, she was certainly pleased that he shared something so important to her, but she'd often spent passionate nights with wonderful men who knew very little about art.

She seated herself at one of the tables at Market Place, gazing across the court at the nearby street fair where an unusually large group of tourists browsed through the merchandise on display—macramé, leather goods, musical instruments, pottery, handmade jewelry, paintings, and sculpture—purchasing items directly from the craftsmen themselves. Normally, the crowd did not begin to gather until around noon. The street fair brought back memories for Ashley, memories of that first summer in San Francisco, of a time when she had sold her own works at the street fair, paintings she'd done over a period of three years while still living in the Napa Valley. Those sales had sustained her financially, had seen her through that first summer. They had sold well, but it was the sale of one painting in particular that actually launched her career.

Michael Anthony. Ashley would never forget his name—or anything else about him. He was one of the most attractive men she had ever met. Tall and slender, with thick, blue-black hair and piercing blue eyes, he had the strong, finely chiseled features of a face on a Roman coin, and a dazzling smile. He was thirty-seven, with the natural charm and grace of one who was to the manner born. She'd found him different from anyone she'd ever known, certainly different from the men she'd grown up with in the valley. He was handsome in the most refined and sophisticated of ways, not at all like the outdoorsmen she was accustomed to, men like Sam Cavelli and his friends. He had seemed more interested in the artist than in her works that mild August afternoon, but he'd noticed her talent enough to buy her favorite painting—the one she'd worked hardest on, the one of the men working in the vineyards near St. Helena—and expressed an interest in launching her career.

They'd had dinner that night, and were together almost every night after that. Michael had been Ashley's first lover, and she'd found him surprisingly tender and considerate. He'd released physical passions she hadn't known she was capable of. He had been enchanted with her, or so he'd said then, so much so that he had bankrolled her first exhibit. That show had been an unqualified success, bringing Ashley recognition and success beyond her wildest expectations. The local critics called her "the most promising landscape artist to come along in years," and her paintings had brought prices she would never have dreamed possible for a neophyte artist like herself. She was ecstatic. She and Michael had a wonderful, intimate celebration that night in her apartment, making love with an intensity neither of them had ever known before. That was the night Ashley found out about Michael's wife.

Oddly enough, she had not been angered by the discovery that he was married. A part of her had always suspected it, but she'd never been able to bring herself to ask. Subconsciously, she did not want to know. And now, in a crazy kind of way, she was actually relieved. In the weeks prior to the exhibit, he had become increasingly demanding, making Ashley restless and dissatisfied with the relationship. Admitting that he was married had diminished his emotional stranglehold on her, but he'd had no choice but to tell her the truth. He was playing with fire, he'd told her, since his wife's family had all the money. Her father owned the company for which he served as senior vice-president. Ashley had been calm, but she insisted they could not go on seeing each other. He'd resisted, of course, continuing to call her and coming to the apartment even though she never let him past the front door.

Since Michael, there had been others. In the past few

months, her name had appeared in the society pages and in the gossip columns more frequently than it had in the art critics' reviews, always linked to the names of San Francisco's most attractive and eligible men.

Now, as her thoughts returned to the present, she looked across the plaza at a group of artists setting up paintings in a display, attempting to attract the crowd. She realized it was time that she too returned to her one true passion—her work.

"Ashley!" A familiar female voice cut through her thoughts. She looked up and saw Mara Cortlandt, owner of a new gallery that had just opened in the Nob Hill area, approaching her table.

"Mara!" She greeted the older woman with a warm smile. "How prompt you are! I've been looking forward to talking with you. . . ."

Ashley's apartment was located on an upper floor of a new, ultramodern high-rise building in the heart of San Francisco's artistic community, Telegraph Hill. Overlooking the bay from North Beach, Telegraph Hill is an entrancing, quiet residential area comprised mostly of narrow alleys and frame houses dating back to the 1920s, when the predominantly Italian residents were replaced by a more bohemian crowd that moved into the inexpensive housing they found there, setting up housekeeping and devoting their time to writing, painting, or pursuing other creative endeavors. Then in the 1950s came the beatniks—and with them, a more chic, moneyed class moved in, renovating and transforming many of those old homes into spacious apartments. As a result, the rents shot up to dazzling heights, thus keeping out the "undesirables." The few high-rise buildings in the area had been built in recent years, supposedly part of a master plan to enhance the area.

From the bedroom that Ashley had transformed into a studio, the view of the bay was spectacular. The morning sun provided the ideal lighting for her painting needs. She filled the room with her easels, canvases, and other art supplies. On the walls were framed newspaper clippings, glowing reviews of her work by the area's leading critics, and many of her favorite pencil and charcoal sketches. The room always smelled of oil paint and turpentine because there was always a work-in-progress on one of the easels. There were numerous objects in the room that had, at one time or another, served as subjects for her paintings: a beautiful antique enameled vase she'd found at a small shop in Chinatown, now filled with lovely silk flowers; a wicker basket that had been immortalized on canvas, painted overflowing with an appealing array of fresh fruits; and two porcelain dolls dressed in finely detailed turn-of-the-century attire. The most disorganized room in the apartment, it was also the room Ashley loved best, the one in which she spent most of her time.

Now, as she prepared a tempting al fresco breakfast for two out on the terrace, enjoying the soft, warm breeze coming in from the bay, she reflected on how different her life now was from what it had been in the valley. How drastically her life had changed since the day she summoned up the courage to leave the only world she had ever really known and to seek a new and better life in a city so different from St. Helena it might as well have been Paris or Rome. Though she would never have admitted it to anyone but herself, there had been many times—too many times— during those first critical months in San Francisco when she had been afraid she might actually fail. Those early months had been the most difficult, most frightening time of her life, in spite of Michael's emotional and financial support.

She pushed those thoughts from her mind as easily as she pushed the heavy curtain of hair back away from her face and paused to scrutinize the perfectly set table—the gleaming crystal and china, the spotless flatware, the crisp white tablecloth—and the carefully prepared breakfast of eggs Benedict, slices of ripe peaches ready to be splashed with cold champagne, and freshly squeezed orange juice. When she was convinced that everything was perfect, she walked barefoot, wearing nothing but a sheer, dark blue nightgown, into the darkened bedroom. The man who had spent the night with her was still sleeping soundly, facedown on the bed, the sheets pulled up about his muscular shoulders, his thick, sandy-brown hair tousled from tossing and turning in his sleep—and from a night of ardent lovemaking. Smiling to herself, Ashley crossed the room silently and shook him gently. "Daniel." She spoke his name in a voice barely above a whisper. "Daniel . . . it's time to get up."

"Hmm?" He stirred slightly but did not open his eyes.

"Come *on*, Daniel!" she urged, shaking him more forcefully the second time. "You have to be at your office in an hour and a half!"

He grunted again. Ashley shook her head disapprovingly. In the two months they had been lovers—she'd met him at one of her exhibits—she had yet to be able to get him out of bed on the first call. She got off the bed and went over to the windows, opening the drapes slowly, allowing the brilliant early morning sunlight to flood the room. Still he did not move. She went back to the bed and pulled the pale blue satin sheets away from his naked body in a last-ditch attempt to rouse him. As she reached out to shake him again, he rolled over suddenly and grabbed both of her wrists, pulling her down on the bed. "Daniel!" Ashley shrieked, surprised. "Damn you! You were awake all the time!"

"Of course I was," he growled, kissing her deeply. "I just wanted to see how far you'd go to get me up." With one swift motion, he reached down and pulled her nightgown up to her waist. He kissed her again as his fingers probed between her thighs, caressing her with a firm insistence.

"Daniel!" she gasped. "The eggs—"

"Forget about the eggs," he muttered, kissing her neck.

"Don't you want breakfast?" Ashley began to giggle.

"Only if you've changed your name to breakfast." He pulled the nightgown down off her shoulders as his lips moved across her breast.

"Daniel, stop it!" she said as he started kissing her exposed nipple.

He paused and looked up at her. "Now, that's not what you really want, is it?" he asked with a suggestive grin.

"I thought you had to be at your office at nine," she protested weakly.

"I find it very hard to think of anything else when I'm lying here with you, looking as you do right now." He started touching her again.

"Daniel . . ." Finally, she stopped fighting the inevitable and lay back, enjoying what he was doing to her with his hands and his mouth and his splendid body.

Ashley's parents never visited her in San Francisco, but this did not surprise her; she'd long suspected that only death itself could tear them away from the Napa Valley. She could not get away to visit them with any great frequency, what with her work and her exhibits and her extremely full social life, but she spent a relaxing weekend with them as often as she could manage. The people who had been a part of her life there for as long as she could remember, some of whom she had grown up with, treated her differently than they had before. They regarded her with awe, as though she were not the same person. *Actually, I'm not*, Ashley thought, aware that she had in fact changed a great deal in the past two years. But she liked to think that all the changes had been for the better.

Even her parents, proud as they were of her accomplishments, of her successes and triumphs, behaved differently toward her now. They tried not to show it, but she had noticed it immediately. It seemed as if they did not know what to say, how to talk to her now. Their own daughter. *It'll pass in time*, Ashley assured herself. *We've just been apart too long.* Privately, however, she wondered if the distance between them had been more than just a matter of miles.

"I'm still your daughter, Papa," she tried to reassure her father once. "That hasn't changed. It's never going to change."

"Isn't it?" Tony Giannini asked, unconvinced. "Already, you're different. You look different. You talk different. More important, you *act* different. You're a hotshot artist now, a big celebrity. I look at you and I ask myself, 'Whatever happened to my Abby?' She's gone. My sweet, stubborn Abby is gone and this slick society girl's taken her place."

Ashley laughed, enveloping him in a fierce bear hug. "I haven't changed all that much, Papa," she insisted. "I'm older now, and maybe a little different on the outside—I've gained a bit in the way of street smarts, but that's all a part of the survival game in San Francisco—but in my heart, I'm not so different."

"I always hoped you'd stay the same sweet, unspoiled girl you were before you left us," Tony admitted with a twinge of disappointment in his gravelly voice.

"No one stays the same forever, Papa," Ashley said gently.

"I can see that," he said quietly, extricating himself from her embrace. He reached down to the chair behind him and brought up a copy of a recent issue of a San Francisco newspaper, folded to show a photograph of Ashley at the opening of a new Nob Hill restaurant with Daniel Redmond. The caption hinted of a "red-hot affair" between the celebrated artist and the well-known corporation lawyer. "Is this true, Abby?" he asked. "Are you—involved—with this man?"

She hesitated for a moment. "That would depend on what you mean by involved, Papa," she said carefully.

"Are you sleeping with him, Abby?" Tony asked bluntly.

She didn't answer right away, tempted for a moment to lie. But she knew it would do no good. Her father knew her too well; he would be able to sense it immediately. "Yes, Papa," she answered finally, avoiding his eyes. "Yes, I am."

"Why, Abby?" he asked, pain in his eyes. "These men you involve yourself with, do they make promises? Do they tell you they will marry you? Do they help you with your career?"

Ashley paused for a moment, thinking of Michael. "No," she said slowly. "They never promise me anything. I don't want them to."

"Then *why*, for God's sake?"

She forced a slight smile. "Papa, things are different in San Francisco than they are here," she said, attempting to explain her actions to him. "Life's not as simple as it's always been for us. People don't just get married and live happily ever after anymore—not even here, to be perfectly honest. They don't always spend their lives with the first person they fall in love with. They don't always get married even when they are in love. It's—"

"—exactly why I never wanted you to go to San Francisco," he cut in gruffly. "I never wanted to see you live your life in the fast lane. I never wanted to see success spoil you."

"It hasn't spoiled me," she insisted. "Just because I've changed . . ."

"You've cheapened yourself." Tony Giannini's voice was harsh. "You give yourself to all those men. . . . Every time I see a San Francisco newspaper it's somebody different. You're out dancing until dawn, going to all those parties and openings. I ask myself, Is this the same girl who wanted to devote herself totally to her painting?"

"I *have* devoted myself to my art," Ashley said emphatically. "But the social scene is important to someone in my position. I have to meet certain people—"

"Do you have to sleep with them to sell paintings?" her father growled, not bothering to conceal his displeasure.

"*No!* Papa, I can't justify it—I can't even explain it—not so you would understand, anyway," she said wearily. "I know you don't approve—that you never will approve—but please, allow me to live my own life."

Tony shook his head, his eyes downcast. "How could I stop you, girl?" he asked. "You're not exactly living next door."

"I love you and Mama with all my heart," she said softly,

putting her arms around his neck. "I don't expect you to understand, but . . ."

He nodded. "I can't live your life for you, Abby," he conceded. "Your mama and I tried to bring you up right, to give you a set of values, but you have to make your own mistakes, pay the price just like the rest of us. Whatever you do, it won't make us love you any less."

Ashley hugged him tightly. "The last thing I ever wanted to do was disappoint you, Papa."

As she drove back to San Francisco, Ashley was still thinking about that conversation. It was the most open communication she had ever had with her father. She had always wanted his approval. And no matter what happened, whatever else she was or would become, that one fact of her life would never change. Ashley Gordon or Abby Giannini, she was still his daughter, their daughter, and she was grateful for the values they had instilled in her, the strength she had inherited from her courageous Italian ancestors who had abandoned the security of their homeland to seek a new life in a strange world. Though she was sure that neither of her parents realized it, it was that strength and determination of her Tuscan ancestors, which flowed through her veins just as surely as their blood did, that had enabled her to pursue her own dreams, to accept the challenge and the risk. She was fiercely proud of that heritage.

Crossing the bay on the Golden Gate Bridge with the top down on her convertible, the sun felt warm against her face, the wind invigorating as it whipped through her hair. She wished her parents had not seen the San Francisco newspapers, wished they had not read the things that were being written about her. She wished she could keep from them those aspects of her new life she knew would upset them. The gossip columnists had a real gift for making things sound much more sensational than they really were. They made her relationships—she hated the word *affair*, it sounded cheap and dirty somehow—sound shallow and superficial. Ashley shook her head. She had had a number of lovers, it was true. She had been to bed with men she did not love, did not expect to have a future with. That hardly made her unique in this day and age. But she had never given herself to a man she did not care for at all, a man she was not attracted to, at least in a physical sense. Her relationships had not endured because in each case, she had quickly realized that the man was not what she was looking for, what she needed. The magic had not been there, and she was not willing to settle for less. She wanted it all—success, money, recognition, and yes, love. And she would have it, one way or another. But this incident with her father made her realize that she had to find a way to keep her life as Ashley Gordon separate from the world in which she had grown up, the world in which her parents still lived and Abby Giannini still existed.

Ashley Gordon and Abby Giannini, she discovered, could not coexist.

San Francisco, April 1979

The Hyatt Regency, at 5 Embarcadero Center, is San Francisco's most architecturally unique hotel. Rising seventeen floors above the rose-brick edge of the Center at Market Street, its ultramodern design provides a striking contrast to the rococo clock tower of the nearby Ferry Building. The hotel's structure is shaped much like a giant pyramid, two sides forming a right angle while the third sweeps inward in graduated steps similar to those ancient Egyptian monuments, serrated with long rows of balconies hung with ivy, jutting out from the face of the structure. Inside, twin escalators extend up from the ground level to a sweeping central court of the Portman-designed atrium lobby. This area is ringed with balconies doubling as corridors for each of the upper floors, extending up to the glass roof at the top of the building, from which daylight filters down in a soft, almost eerie glow. The court's centerpiece is *Eclipse*, Charles Perry's huge circular sculpture, perched atop a smooth black marble fountain. Scattered throughout the atrium are containers of flowers and greenery, caged birds and seating areas, and live music is featured almost nonstop.

In the Equinox, the Regency's revolving rooftop restaurant, which offers a spectacular view of the city—particularly at night—Ashley attended a fund-raising dinner with Scott Nelson, the scion of a wealthy and prominent San Francisco political family. She had been seeing him for almost six months, and enjoyed his company, but tonight, as she stood at the windows near their table, staring absently at the twinkling lights across the bay, she was not enjoying herself. She might have been able to, she thought resentfully, if Scott had not been so preoccupied with accommodating the press. She felt as though she had been posing for photographs from the moment they stepped off the elevator. Not that she minded being photographed, of course, or seeing those photographs in the newspapers. Except for her concern about her parents' reactions to the things being printed about her, she enjoyed being pursued, being something of a celebrity. But tonight, she was exhausted and cross with Scott for insisting upon attending the dinner. It had been a long, grueling day and she was not up to smiling for the cameras while trying to eat her dinner. When she suggested he come alone—or bring someone else—he had been petulant. This was important to his career, he had pointed out, and if she were going to be a part of his future, she would have to become accustomed to making public appearances with him. *His future—the nerve*! she thought angrily. *How dare he make an assumption like that!* She had never said she expected to be a part of his future—or even that she wanted to be! He had taken it for granted, just as he'd begun to take everything about their relationship for granted. After tonight, she decided, she would definitely be seeing less of Scott Nelson.

He had been totally unsympathetic to her feelings when

she complained about the manner in which the photographers had intruded upon their dinner, taking pictures of her as she ate, pictures she knew would be most unflattering. "The Nelsons have always maintained high visibility," he reminded her. "It's good for the political image."

"You're an attorney," she said pointedly, letting him know how annoyed she was.

"Not for long," he responded. "Dad's been priming the pump with the party leaders in Sacramento. It looks like I'm their choice for state attorney general in '80. We have to put up with this sort of thing—"

"Maybe you do, but I don't," she cut in angrily.

"If you're going to be my wife—" he started.

She stared at him incredulously. "I don't know where you ever got the idea that I wanted to be! I wouldn't marry you, Scott Nelson, if you were the last man on the face of the earth!"

"Ashley, people are staring." His voice was low, pleading.

"Let them stare, dammit!" she snapped. "I don't know how you could assume such a thing without even mentioning it to me. What am I to you, Scott—window dressing for your political campaign? I don't recall either of us ever using the word love. You've certainly never brought up the subject of marriage . . . so what gives?"

"Please, Ashley." Scott looked around the room wildly. No doubt in search of his father, Ashley thought resentfully. "We need to talk—"

"You're damn right we do!"

"I promise—when we leave here, we'll talk about it. But please don't make a scene . . ."

She nodded. "I won't embarrass you in public, if that's what concerns you," she assured him. "But I think you should know now that there's very little you could possibly say to smooth things over between us."

"You don't understand," he said evenly.

"No, Scott. *You* don't understand—and I don't think you

ever could,'' she responded. Without another word, she turned and walked away, leaving him staring after her.

Now, as she stood at the windows, staring into the night and trying in vain to control her anger, she was suddenly aware that she was not alone, that someone was standing next to her. She turned slowly to her right. The man at her side was tall and slim, with thick, wavy blond hair, intense blue eyes, and an intelligent face. He was smiling at her. ''Trouble in paradise?'' he asked casually.

''What business is it of yours?'' she asked.

''None, really, but you weren't making any secret of it a few minutes ago, so I figured it was safe to ask,'' he said amiably.

She gave him a suspicious look. ''Are you a reporter?''

''Hardly,'' he answered with amusement in his voice. ''Since we haven't met, allow me to introduce myself, Miss Gordon. I'm Brandon Hollister. Scott and I are with the same law firm.''

''He doesn't have to send his friends to plead his case,'' she said tightly.

Brandon Hollister laughed. ''Hold it—I said we're with the same firm,'' he reminded her. ''I didn't say we were friends. The truth is, I never liked him very much.''

''I'm not sure I like him very much either,'' she admitted.

''That's not the way I hear it.''

''Oh? And just what have you heard?''

''That you and he are headed for the altar.''

''Apparently I'm the last to find out,'' she said, turning back to the windows.

''That shouldn't come as a surprise, under the circumstances,'' he said.

''What circumstances?'' She didn't really care, but since he was there, she asked the question. After all, this situation wasn't his fault.

''How did you meet him?''

She thought about it for a moment. ''His father arranged

the meeting," she said slowly. "It was after one of my exhibits . . ."

"Exactly," Brandon said, taking a long swallow of his drink. "You see, Ashley—may I call you Ashley?—Stanford Nelson arranges everything for his son. Word has it that the elder Nelson had his eye on the White House the day his firstborn son came into the world. Everything he does, he does with one goal in mind: to eventually install his boy there, to see him become president. It's all quite simple. Scott Nelson gets the best of everything—the best clothes and cars, the best schools. He's wormed his way into the best law firm in town . . . even though he's a second-rate attorney . . ."

"And just how do I figure into his plans?" Ashley wanted to know.

"That's easy. The senior Nelson wants you for his son's wife," Brandon answered.

"What?" She couldn't believe what he was telling her.

"It's the truth," he insisted. "Stanford Nelson thinks you would make the perfect icing on the cake, so to speak. You're a celebrity in your own right, you have the personality, and God knows you're beautiful. Your name and your face are well known around here."

"And Scott? How does he feel about all this?" she asked carefully, barely controlling her anger.

Brandon shrugged. "Who knows? Regardless of how he feels, he'll always do as his father says." He paused. "His father pulls all of the strings—Scott's, and everyone else's who's connected with him, with his future. I strongly suspect that if he ever does make it to Pennsylvania Avenue, it'll be his father who's really running the country."

"So if his father decided he should get married . . ."

"When his father gives the command, Scott obeys," Brandon said simply. "I sometimes wonder if he's capable of thinking for himself."

"Of all the nerve!" She turned abruptly and pushed her way through the crowd, headed for the table where Scott and his father sat talking with two reporters. Brandon followed her, unable to stop her and not sure he really wanted to. "Scott, I want to go home," she announced.

"Certainly, darling," he said amiably. "In a little while."

"I want to go now," she said sharply.

"I can't leave just yet, sweetheart—"

"Then I'll take a taxi," she said promptly.

He got to his feet. "She has been busy—she needs her rest," he told the group at large. Then he turned to Ashley again. "I'll call you in the morning."

Her eyes met his. "Don't bother," she snapped. The two journalists looked shocked. Stanford Nelson's face was dark with rage but he said nothing.

"Ashley—" Scott began.

"Good night, Scott—or rather, good-bye." She turned on her heel and walked out.

Brandon Hollister followed her to the elevators. "Wait a minute!" he called after her. "Where are you going?"

"I'm going home," she said.

"But the evening's just getting started!"

"As far as I'm concerned, it's over." Impatiently she rang for the elevator again and again.

He slipped his hand between hers and the panel. "That's not going to bring it any faster," he said, clearly amused by her fiery temper. "Look, I can drive you home if you like . . ."

"I *don't* like," she told him. "I can take a taxi." The doors opened and she stepped into the empty car. Brandon followed her.

"Just because you've had it with Scott is no reason to take it out on me," he said as the elevator doors closed and the car began its descent.

"I'm not taking anything out on you. I just want to be alone, that's all."

"Then let me drive you home. I'll take you to your door and go without an argument. That's a promise," he said.

She turned to face him, her dark eyes blazing with anger. "What is it with you, anyway?" she demanded hotly. "You tell me all these things and now you want to take me home. What are you after?"

"Does everyone have to have an ulterior motive?"

"No, but people usually do—so what's yours?"

"Mine?" he asked. "I saw what was happening and I didn't like it. Scott and his father were using you. I thought you should know about it. If I had known what a nasty temper you have, I might not have been so quick to say anything. Here I am, trying to rescue a damsel in distress, and she turns out to be a fire-breathing dragon in disguise!"

"Very funny." The doors opened and she pushed past him, crossing the lobby in a quick, angry stride. He followed her to the escalators.

"My offer to drive you home still stands," he told her as they walked out to the street.

She looked up at him. "You're certainly persistent, aren't you?"

"I just don't think it's safe for you to be out alone at this time of night—taxi or no taxi," he said simply.

She threw back her head and laughed. "You have to be kidding! San Francisco is the one place in the world where a woman is safe on the streets after dark!"

He knew what she was referring to. "I'm not so sure about that."

"I can take care of myself," she insisted.

"Oh, I'm sure you can," he said agreeably. "But for my own peace of mind, will you stop protesting so much and let me be the gentleman I was brought up to be?"

She studied him for a moment. "A gentleman—that would be a refreshing change of pace," she said haughtily.

"Well?" He was waiting for her answer.

She smiled. "Oh, all right," she said finally. "Far be it for me to keep a white knight from doing his noble duty."

"I thought you were going to take me straight home," Ashley commented in a suspicious tone as Brandon guided her through a dimly lit cocktail lounge toward a booth in the far corner of the room.

"Okay, so I lied. Sue me," he said as they sat down.

"I will. Can you recommend a good attorney?"

"Touché," he responded with a grin. "Just have a drink with me—one drink—and I'll confess everything. Then, if you still want me to take you home, I will."

She looked at him for a moment. "And how do I know I can believe you?"

He grinned. "Would a white knight lie?"

"He would if he were only pretending to be a knight," she said, beginning to enjoy herself—and Brandon's company—in spite of her anger at having been used by Scott and his father.

"There's no substitute for the real thing, I assure you," he said earnestly.

He's absolutely right, she thought as the waitress approached the booth to take their order. "I'll have a glass of white wine," she told her.

"Vodka and tonic," Brandon said quickly. As the waitress moved out of earshot, he turned to Ashley again. "When I told you all of those things about the Nelsons, I did have an ulterior motive," he said in a low voice.

She smiled. "Now, why doesn't that surprise me?"

"I told you I never liked the guy," Brandon reminded her.

"And?"

"And I hated like hell to see him marry you."

"Why? Why should you care?" she asked.

"For one thing, I knew he wasn't really in love with you," he said in a serious tone. "I knew it was all engineered for political reasons, that you were supposed to complete his public image. And for another"—he hesitated for a moment—"I wanted a chance to get to know you better myself."

She looked up. "We don't know each other at all."

"And we'd never have gotten the chance if he'd had his way," he said quietly. "When I saw you there tonight, when we started talking—I can't explain it. I just knew I couldn't stand back and let you end up with that creep.'

"That's very gallant of you," she said in a teasing voice.

"What I'm trying to say is—"

She laughed. "I know what you're trying to say, Brandon Hollister," she assured him. "But I believe I forgot to say thank you."

"No thanks necessary," he said quickly. "Didn't I tell you? That's my other occupation."

She raised her eyebrows questioningly. "Other occupation?"

He nodded, his face serious. "I'm only an attorney by day," he said darkly. "By night, I go around saving damsels in distress."

Ashley laughed aloud. "Well, I must say that you're very good at what you do, Sir Brandon," she told him. "And may I also say that I'm very happy that you chose to rescue me."

He looked at her. "Happy enough to have dinner with me tomorrow night?"

She smiled. "Yes, I believe I am."

"Do you like Donatello's?"

"It so happens that it's my favorite restaurant in all of San Francisco," she replied truthfully.

"Excellent! You see? Already we have something in common," he pointed out.

Ashley only smiled knowingly. She had the distinct feeling that they had more in common than a preference for a certain restaurant.

"I come from wine country," Ashley told Brandon as they walked the darkened streets in the direction of her apartment building. "My father owns a vineyard there."

More than once in the past year, Ashley had regretted that lie, but no more so than she did at this moment. She wasn't ashamed of her heritage. Her ancestors were proud, passionate people who lived and loved with an intensity most of the people she'd met here in San Francisco would never be capable of. Her father had been right all along. The world Abby Giannini had longed to be a part of was glamorous, yes, but populated by selfish, shallow people who judged you by your pedigree and your bank balance rather than who you were. But now, she was caught in the lie created by a starry-eyed young girl desperate to be accepted, and not quite sure how to get out of it without looking like an idiot.

"Oh," Brandon responded, his face lighting with recognition. "A vinter's heiress."

"Not exactly," she said uneasily. "He only grows the grapes. He doesn't make the wine." Then she added, "He wants to start a winery, of course, but that's still on the drawing board."

"I've been out to Napa and Sonoma a few times," he said then. "It's beautiful. It must have given you plenty of landscapes to paint."

Ashley nodded, smiling. "More than a few." She paused. "Where are you from, Brandon? You don't sound like a native Californian. Something about your voice . . ."

He laughed. "I'm not," he admitted. "I'm from New York City, originally. I moved out here after I finished law school. My father wasn't too crazy about the idea. He wanted me to join his corporation, but . . ." His voice trailed off.

"Why didn't you?" Ashley hoped she wasn't out of line.

Brandon shrugged. "I guess you could say I just don't like the way he does business. We don't see eye to eye on things," he said, avoiding her gaze.

Ashley had the feeling he did not want to talk about it, so she did not pursue it further. "What made you decide to come all the way to San Francisco?"

He drew in his breath. "For one thing, it was the best offer I received. For another, I was feeling the need to put some distance between myself and my life in New York."

Kindred spirits, Ashley thought.

"What about you?" he was asking, almost as if he had read her mind. "What made you leave the wine country?"

"I too had to put some space between myself and my former life," she answered without hesitation. She had never expressed those feelings to anyone else before and was surprised to be doing it now. She felt comfortable with Brandon in a way she never had with any of the other men she'd known. She felt as though she could talk to him, and that he would understand her. "And then there was my painting. As beautiful as the Napa Valley is, I knew I didn't want to go on painting landscapes the rest of my life. I wanted to experience the world beyond the valley, to experience *life*—and transfer that experience to my canvases."

Brandon smiled. "I really think we should send Scott Nelson and his father a thank-you note," he said promptly.

"For what?" she asked, perplexed.

He grinned. "For being the biggest prize shits in the city, of course," he replied. "If they hadn't been, we might never have met."

Ashley laughed. "I like you, Brandon Hollister," she told him. And to herself, without really knowing why: *I think I've been waiting all my life for you.*

Monte Carlo, August 1979

Collin Deverell, a dashing figure in his immaculate white dinner jacket, emerged from his Rolls-Royce Phantom and entered the casino with his characteristic long, quick stride. Passing the first of the grand rooms without so much as a pause or even a glance, the rooms where casually dressed tourists happily played the slot machines to an upbeat jazz tempo, he strode purposefully past the stern-faced sentinels guarding the entrance to the Salles Privées, the private rooms. Here, Collin thought as he stepped into the gilded, opulent splendor, here, the legendary glamour of Monte Carlo truly existed. Here, the popping lights of the slot machines and the mad jazz beat were replaced by a soft, rosy glow and a mellow waltz. Men and women in formal attire spoke in low, hushed tones as they clustered around the roulette tables. The air seemed charged with electricity, the intoxicating aura combining with the irresistible lure of gaming and playing and betting to weave a spell to which Collin had never been immune. His world, he thought with satisfaction. So much more his world than the boardroom could ever be.

He made his way through the crowd to the cashier, where he bought twenty thousand dollars' worth of chips. *Just for starters*, he thought, as he was given two hundred large black chips, each of them worth five hundred francs. He took them and picked his way through the crowd again, taking a seat at one of the tables. He stared thoughtfully at the chips stacked neatly on the green baize for a few moments, then asked the croupier to put ten on twenty-one black.

"Rien ne va plus," the croupier announced to the group, indicating that no more bets could be placed. Collin looked on in silence as the wheel was spun and the ball began its rollicking dance of luck. As the wheel slowed to a stop, the ball skipped around for only a moment before coming to rest on twenty-one black. Collin smiled to himself. So the evening was going to get off to a good start. An omen? he wondered.

The croupier attended to the other players, making sure all their bets had been placed, then turned to Collin again. "Will you stay on twenty-one, monsieur?" he asked.

Collin nodded, rubbing his chin as he stared at the wheel. The croupier gave it a spin. This time, the ball landed on twenty-three. Collin drew in his breath and shook his head. Next, he bet on twenty-four black. And won. He let it ride. His hunch paid off again.

"Don't you ever play the red?"

The voice addressing him was soft, feminine, and very definitely French. He turned. To his right stood the most beautiful redhead he had ever seen, tall and voluptuous, with enormous blue eyes and full, sensuous lips. Her hair was like a lion's mane, lush and full and cascading down her bare back. She wore a strapless, low-cut gold lamé gown that left little to the imagination.

"Never," he said with an easy smile. "Call it superstition. Red's never been lucky for me."

Her eyebrows arched questioningly. "Never?" she asked in a cool voice.

"Never—in roulette, that is." He reached out and took her hand, pressing it to his lips.

She withdrew slowly and took the chair next to his. The other players placed their bets. Collin decided to let it ride on twenty-four black. He turned to look at the woman beside him. "Not playing?" he asked casually.

She shook her head. "I am only a very interested spectator," she told him. "I've been playing blackjack in the Salles des Amériques all evening—and losing consistently, I am afraid."

He glanced sideways as the wheel was spun again. "How much did you lose?" he asked.

"Thirty thousand francs," she admitted, slightly embarrassed.

"The *unité de mise*?" he asked, shaking his head disapprovingly. "I'm surprised. I would have thought you to be a bit more reckless."

She frowned, her eyes fixed on the roulette wheel. "The will is there, but the francs, I am afraid, are not."

"I see." Collin studied her for a few seconds, then took a stack of his own chips and placed them in front of her. "Will that help?"

She looked at him with a feline smile. "But how will I ever be able to repay your generosity?"

He smiled back. "I'm sure you'll think of a way."

Collin beckoned to the attendant, instructing him to buy him another hundred chips. Between them—himself and this exceptionally beautiful redhead whose name he did not know—they had managed to lose more than twice what he'd started with. But he was not ready to admit defeat. Not yet. This time, he thought defiantly, he would go for broke. All or nothing, on one number. He took the chips the attendant brought him and placed his bet.

The woman at his side stared at him in disbelief. "Are you crazy?" she asked in a tone that was urgent but barely above a whisper.

Collin grinned. "It *has* been rumored on occasion," he responded, clearly unconcerned.

"That's fifty thousand francs!" she gasped.

"Give or take a few, I think."

"*Rien ne va plus,*" the croupier said in a strong, clear voice.

All eyes turned to the wheel as it was spun. Collin leaned forward in anticipation. The wheel began to slow down. The ball did a few hops and then a wide roll, finally coming to rest on the number Collin had chosen. A gasp rose from the crowd. The woman's lips moved but no sound came out as she attempted to mentally calculate his winnings. All the numbers paid off at thirty-five to one. She stared at Collin in disbelief. "Do you realize—" she began.

He gave her a knowing smile. "Yes, I do," he said in a low, suggestive voice as his hand came to rest on her thigh, exposed by the high slit in the side of her gown. "And I do think it calls for a celebration."

"I don't believe I caught your name," the woman said casually as she and Collin walked arm in arm through the ballroomlike lobby of the Hermitage, where Collin was staying, the sound of their heels clicking on the snow-white marble floor echoing through the opulent and unusually deserted entrance.

"I didn't throw it," he responded.

She looked at him, confused. "I do not understand—"

He smiled. "No—of course not," he said. "My name, if it really makes a difference, is Collin. Collin Deverell."

"That is a nice name, Collin Deverell," she said, smiling. "You are British?"

He shook his head. "American."

"Not a tourist, certainly." The elevator doors opened and he stepped aside so she could enter.

"No," he said with a slight shake of his head as he stepped in behind her and the doors closed. "More like a semi-resident."

"Where do you live when you are not here?" she asked, genuinely interested.

"Wherever I happen to be," he answered without hesitation. It was the truth. He had left New York six months after settling with Justin and had not been back. "For a while, it was Rome. Then it was the Aegean islands—the Cyclades. After that, Paris. And now here."

"How long have you been in Monte Carlo?"

The doors opened and he led her out of the elevator and down the corridor to his suite. "A long time," he said as he pulled his key from his pocket and unlocked the door. "A year, give or take a few months."

She giggled. "You do not remember?"

"I haven't really thought about it." He led her into the room, closed the door, and took her in his arms. "I've always had other, more important things on my mind," he murmured, as his mouth sought hers in the darkness. "Like right now . . ."

She returned his kisses eagerly as he slowly unzipped her dress and pulled it down to expose her lush, full breasts. He was still kissing her as his hands moved slowly, deliberately, over her satiny skin, his thumbs making small circles over her nipples. They were hard with longing. Her breathing became labored as he began to tug at them, forcefully enough to arouse her, but without causing her pain. He lowered himself to his knees as he peeled the gown down over her hips, pulling it down to her ankles. Underneath, she wore nothing but a black lace garter belt and black seamed stockings. He pulled her forward, his face nuzzling close, kissing her, licking her. She began to moan as she grasped his head with both of her hands and held him there, pressing herself to his mouth. He kept licking, sensing her excitement, until she was about to climax. Then he withdrew abruptly.

"Don't stop!" she gasped.

"Patience, *chérie*," he said in a low voice as he got to his feet, never taking his hands off her. He scooped her up in his arms and carried her over to the bed, her shoes falling off as he did so. He never took his eyes off her as he undressed hastily and joined her on the bed. His mouth was hot and demanding as he kissed her hard on the mouth, his hands moving up and down the length of her body, savoring her nakedness. Then he began kissing her neck and her shoulders, descending to her breasts slowly, gradually. He nuzzled her breasts, first one, then the other, back and forth, licking her nipples until they were wet and hard with desire. Then he took one of them into his mouth and began to suck at it fiercely as she writhed and moaned beneath him. Again, he moved back and forth, from one to the other, until she begged him to stop. He pulled away, sliding down on the bed to finish what he had started on the floor. He parted her thighs and buried his face in her pubis, licking and sucking at her until she was crying out and gasping for breath, then stopping again abruptly.

"My God!" she rasped, clutching at him. "Don't stop! Please, don't stop!"

He smiled but said nothing. He bent his head to lick at her once again, deliberately avoiding that spot he knew he would have only to touch to bring her to orgasm. He pulled away from time to time, blowing at her thick red pubic hair, then nuzzling her again before he resumed his intent licking. She begged him to keep going, to let her come, but he seemed intent upon prolonging the inevitable for as long as possible. Finally, convinced that she had had enough, he dragged his tongue over her swollen clitoris, bringing her to a sharp, convulsive orgasm the moment he touched her there. She screamed out, but he pinned her down to the bed, covering her mouth with his own, muffling her cries of ecstasy. As she lay trembling beneath him, he looked down at her and smiled. "Now it's my turn," he said with a wicked grin.

She nodded slowly, still trying to catch her breath. He lay back on the bed expectantly as she rolled over and took his organ in both hands and started caressing it, gently at first, then with more pressure. He was so hard and erect that she thought he would surely come in her mouth as she began to suck at him. She did not realize, even after what he had done to her, just how able he was to control his own desire. He lay back, arms folded behind his head, summoning up every bit of self-control he could muster, insisting that she keep working on him. Finally, unable to hold back any longer, he began to thrust his hips as he reached down and held her head so that she could not pull away. Suddenly he grabbed her roughly, rolled her over on her back, and got on top of her, launching himself inside her just as he exploded, his body rigid on top of hers. Finally he went limp, burying his face in her breasts. When he finally did catch his breath, he pulled himself up and smiled at her in the darkness. "Well worth waiting for, don't you think, Mademoiselle—" He stopped short, realizing she had never told him her name.

"Danielle," she said, stroking his chest. "My name is Danielle."

They made love again and again, until the sun rose over the Mediterranean and they were both too spent, physically and mentally, to try again. Then they lay in each other's arms for a long time, and when they finally regained their strength, they took a shower together and Collin ordered room service. Later that morning, he told her he would be leaving Monte Carlo before nightfall and sent her away.

With half of his winnings.

As Collin stood on the deck of his rented yacht, the *Baronne*, watching Monte Carlo disappear in the distance, he had no idea where he would go next. He had only decided to leave early that morning, after his night of wild lovemaking with Danielle. While he had enjoyed her in bed, enjoyed having a woman with whom he could do as he wished, someone who would cater to even his most unorthodox desires, he made it a rule never to spend more than one night with the same woman. The last thing in the world Collin wanted was to become involved—with anyone. Caring meant leaving oneself wide open to be hurt, he had determined after losing his parents, and he did not need that kind of pain to complicate his life. He would never give himself the opportunity to care.

He smiled to himself as he leaned on the yacht's railing, his hair ruffled by the morning breeze. He doubted Danielle would even give him a thought. She would be so busy throwing away her share of the winnings from the night before at the casino that he would be the last thing on her mind. Somehow, he could not imagine Danielle as a woman who cared too much about losing a lover. For a woman who looked as she did, who was as uninhibited as she had been, there would always be another man waiting in the wings.

How long had he been living like this? How long had he been wandering the globe aimlessly, never staying in one place for long, never making any commitments, never forming any emotional attachments? How long could he continue to live this way? How long before he began to feel the need for familiar surroundings? How long before he began to think about going home? He had not been back to Sea Cliff in over two years. He had not even thought about it in almost that long. He had not been able to face the memories it held for him. When he left New York, his only thought had been to get as far away as fast as he could.

He'd ended up in London, where he stayed for only a week. He had driven from London to Scotland and lived a secluded existence there for almost a month. Then, restless and eager to find some excitement, he'd gone on to Deauville, and from there to Paris. Collin adored Paris. He had walked the streets for hours at a time, lost in thought. He'd prowled the museums there, indulging the great love of art he had inherited from his mother. It had been painful for him at times, because every time he paused to admire a favorite painting of Francesca Deverell's, he found himself seeing her face, hearing her voice. He took in the Folies Bergère and explored the Left Bank and artists' haunts in

Montparnasse. He enjoyed the French women but never for more than one night. When he finally decided to leave Paris, he chartered the *Baronne* and sailed the Mediterranean, ending up in Greece. For a while, the easy, relaxed lifestyle of the villagers on the small Aegean islands had been immensely appealing to him, as were the passionate and tempestuous Greek women. But, predictably, he was stricken with wanderlust once again, and set out for Rome. The Eternal City had not been eternal for him, and he soon traveled northwest to the Italian Riviera. He'd stayed little more than a month before moving on, returning to Paris. Afterward, he'd returned to the *Baronne*, anchored in the harbor at Marseille, and cruised the Mediterranean, stopping in Nice, Sardinia, Crete, Cairo, Tangier, and Gibraltar. But the lure of Monte Carlo had been irresistible, and he had set anchor in Monaco early in October.

Now, more and more, he found himself thinking of home, of what it would feel like to return to the States, to New York, after having been away so long. He wondered if anything had changed since he'd been away. He wondered how his brother was getting along, and idly, he wondered if Justin were living up to the high standards their father had set for everyone connected with Intercontinental Oil. Did Justin even know he was gone? he asked himself. Did he give a damn? Justin probably had not been to Sea Cliff since the day the papers were signed, finalizing their agreement. He had never cared for the place. Justin had always preferred Manhattan, preferred his apartment at the Trump Tower.

Collin thought about it. By God, he did miss his home! He missed all the familiar objects, the familiar surroundings. He even missed that cold-blooded son of a bitch brother of his. Impulsively, he went below to find the captain, to tell him there would be a change of plans. They would not be sailing east. They were going to Marseille. The long journey was over.

It was time to go home.

* * *

The Concorde came to a final stop on the runway at New York's Kennedy Airport. Collin looked at his watch: 3:00 A.M. He did not anticipate a long wait in customs at this ungodly hour. He had only one suitcase and nothing of significance to declare in spite of the length of time he had been away. He had always believed in traveling light, and chose to leave most of his clothes behind. He smiled to himself. The crew members aboard the *Baronne* were probably having a field day with his expensive silk shirts and gold cuff links. Hell, they'd earned it; they'd put up with his bad habits longer than most people would, in spite of his tremendous wealth. Wealth his father had always believed commanded a certain deference and respect. Wealth that had never quite compensated for Collin's characteristic unruliness.

Collin got to his feet and slung the heavy canvas carryon bag over his left shoulder as the other passengers began to file out the front exit. He waited until everyone else had disembarked from the supersonic jet, in no rush to get home. Sea Cliff had survived over two years without him; it would survive a few more hours. The last one off the plane, he strode into the terminal and looked for the closest immigration booth. As he approached, he took out his American passport and offered it to the inspector with a cordial smile. The man studied it for a moment, then looked up at the tall, uncommonly attractive man before him.

"Welcome home, Mr. Deverell," he said as he stamped the passport and returned it. "I see you've been away a long time."

Collin nodded. "Too long. It's good to be back," he said as he put the passport back in his carryon and walked away. The immigration officer studied him as he headed for customs, curious as to why he was dressed as he was. Jeans, expensive black leather boots, and a royal blue sweater. In August? He shook his head. In his many years working for immigration, he'd seen them all. But never anyone quite like Collin Deverell.

Collin heaved the carryon onto the customs table and

looked around impatiently. Not that he was in a hurry, but he did not want to spend an entire morning in customs. He'd done it too often in the past. Where the hell were the customs inspectors? he wondered. Had they all decided to take a coffee break at the same time? He pursed his lips thoughtfully, about to call out, when the uniformed officer appeared and stepped up to the counter. "Welcome to New York," he said cordially as he opened the bag and searched its contents meticulously. Then he looked up at Collin. "Isn't it just a bit warm for wool?" he asked suspiciously, eyeing Collin's attire.

Collin shrugged. "It was cool in Paris when I left," he said in a casual tone. "But I'll be damn glad to get out of these things as soon as I get home."

The customs inspector nodded, then looked around for a moment, his expression a puzzled one. "Where's the rest of your luggage?" he wanted to know.

"I haven't any," Collin answered truthfully.

The inspector looked at the passport lying on the counter in front of him. "You've been out of the country since January 1977," he noted aloud, "and this is all you're bringing back with you?"

Collin nodded, his face innocent. "Only brought the important things," he replied.

The inspector shook his head. "In other words, nothing to declare," he concluded.

Collin grinned. "Afraid not," he said as he slung the bag over his shoulder again.

"All right." He put a chalk mark on Collin's bag and waved him on.

Ten minutes later Collin was in a taxi bound for Sea Cliff. He leaned back and smiled to himself as he reached down inside his sweater and drew up the solid gold chain with the gold medallion dangling from it. The same medallion he'd picked up at the antique auction in Paris for the equivalent of four thousand American dollars. The medallion he hadn't bothered to declare in customs. It bore the image of the phoenix, that mythical bird of Arabic legend who was reborn of its own ashes. He almost laughed aloud. In all his years traveling throughout the world, he had never been able to resist trying to outwit the customs officials by smuggling in his acquired treasures. Not that he couldn't afford the duty tax, of course—he simply couldn't resist the challenge.

And so far, he had never been caught.

Until now, Collin thought as the taxi passed through the magnificent iron gates at the Deverell estate, he had not known how good it would be to come home, to the only real home he had ever known. Until now, he had not realized how much he really did miss this place. He leaned forward in anticipation, gazing up at the English Tudor mansion, relieved to find that it looked exactly as he had left it. A part of him had harbored an irrational fear that it might have changed in his long absence, that it might somehow be different.

The taxi slowed to a stop at the entrance to the main house. Collin paid the driver, adding a generous tip, and climbed out of the car, the carryon still on his left shoulder. Climbing the stairs, walking along the balustrades, he paused, looking around in the predawn dimness. His staff had done a good job of looking after the place in his absence. He was pleased. He made a mental note to see that they were rewarded for it as soon as possible.

As he entered the house, he was met in the reception hall by one of the maids. "Mr. Deverell!" she exclaimed, surprised to see him. "When did you arrive?"

"Just now," he said, taking the bag off his shoulder.

"But no one told—" she began, confused.

Collin laughed. "They couldn't. I didn't let anyone know I was coming," he told her. "It was a last-minute decision. There wasn't time to phone or cable my arrival time."

"How was your trip?" she asked, taking his bag. "Did you enjoy Europe?"

"About as much as it's possible to enjoy Europe," he answered, looking around. "Where's Henry?" Henry Harrison was the Deverells' major domo, and had been running the household since Collin and Justin were small children.

The maid paused for a moment. "I believe he's in the kitchen, sir," she said, not sure.

Collin nodded. "Find him. Tell him I'd like to see him in the study," he instructed.

She nodded. "Yes, sir."

Collin walked down the long hallway to his father's study. *My study*, he corrected himself mentally. He stopped in his tracks abruptly and looked around. Something was definitely different. Something seemed to be missing. But what? He thought about it for a moment. Of course—the Renoir! Had someone moved it? he wondered. Everyone on his staff knew better than to touch those paintings without his express permission. They all knew that the paintings, his mother's paintings, were priceless, and that they were not to be moved for any reason unless he specifically ordered it.

He stalked angrily into the study and what he saw—or more precisely, what he didn't see there—made him freeze in his tracks. The paintings! All six of the Italian Renaissance paintings that had always hung in the study were gone! He ran out of the study and up the wide staircase to his bedroom. The Monet was also gone. He ran frantically to the bedroom that had once been occupied by his parents. The Cézanne was gone too! "Henry!" he shouted at the top of his voice as he ran back down the hall to the top of the stairs. "Henry, where the hell are you?"

"Right here, sir," Henry Harrison answered in his familiar British accent as he came into view in the entrance hall. "Is something wrong, sir?"

"Damned right something's wrong!" Collin snapped. "The Renoir . . . the Cézanne . . . the Monet—they're gone! All of the goddamned paintings are gone!"

Harrison looked puzzled. "Of course they are, sir," he responded calmly.

"Where the hell are they?" Collin demanded angrily.

"I'm afraid I don't understand," Harrison began, looking genuinely confused.

Collin gripped the railing until his knuckles went white. "*You* don't understand! *I* don't understand—and I would like to know where they've gone, *if* you don't mind!"

Harrison shook his head, still perplexed. "You sold them sir," he answered slowly. "The men came and took them away six months after you left."

Collin stared at him in disbelief. Someone had stolen all of his paintings right under the noses of his household staff! But how?

New York City, September 1979

At his offices in midtown Manhattan, Anton DeVries, a special investigator for the insurance company holding the policy on the Deverell art collection, studied the reports on the desk in front of him. Three weeks ago, he had been sent out to Sea Cliff, on Long Island, to look into the reported theft of a number of paintings worth several million dollars. When he arrived, Collin Deverell told him that over a million dollars' worth of jewelry belonging to his late mother had also been discovered missing from the safe. Deverell had explained that he had been in Europe for the past two and a half years, and had returned to find that the paintings had been taken away in broad daylight, under the watchful eyes of his staff. But in talking with each member of the household staff, DeVries began to wonder if the younger man were not just a very good liar. Everyone—from the major domo, a man who had been with the family for well over twenty years, to the maids to the groundskeepers—was under the impression that the paintings and jewels had been sold, and Henry Harrison had told him how the men who came to collect the items had produced a bill of sale signed by Collin Deverell himself.

"Are you sure it was his signature?" DeVries had asked.

It would not have been the first time a robbery was pulled off in this brazen fashion.

"I was—at the time," Harrison admitted nervously. "I was so sure . . . I thought I would be able to recognize his signature anywhere, but . . ."

"Mr. Deverell was so distraught over the deaths of his parents," one of the maids recalled. "That was why he went away, you know. I suppose he couldn't live with the memories."

Distraught. So much so that he'd spent the last two and a half years abroad. DeVries got to his feet and stood at the window behind his desk, staring blankly at the traffic on Madison Avenue, fifteen floors below. The maid believed Collin Deverell had felt the need to get away from the memories the house held for him. Had he also found the memories of the paintings and jewels, which he claimed were his mother's great passions, too much to bear at the time? Could he have sold them on an impulse, then decided he wanted them back? No . . . only a fool would try a stunt like that. And whatever else he was, DeVries was sure that Collin Deverell was no fool. None of it made any sense. Collin Deverell did not need the money. His sale of his Intercontinental Oil stock to his twin brother back in 1976 had made him a multimillionaire. Still, young Deverell's penchant for gambling and risk-taking were legend. Had he managed to get himself into some kind of trouble that necessitated the sale of the paintings? Was he now trying to bail himself out of some kind of trouble by declaring the items stolen?

No, it didn't make any sense at all. DeVries had checked out each member of the Deverell household staff thoroughly and was convinced that none of them could have been involved in this. But Collin Deverell himself was another matter. Something didn't ring true. DeVries had checked out Deverell's story. He had at least been telling the truth about that. He had been everywhere he claimed to have been in the past two and a half years. He had spent a great deal of money in the course of his travels, it was true. He had also lost a great deal of it gambling. But he was far from poverty. Collin Deverell was still an extremely rich man.

So he didn't need the money. He didn't want to give up the paintings and jewels, he had insisted: they were his mother's, and he would never have parted with them willingly. Yet all the signs pointed to his compliance in the sale of those items. Anton DeVries decided he had to find out for himself what had happened at the Deverell estate while Collin Deverell was away. He had to have proof that the paintings and jewels were indeed sold and that Deverell himself had done the selling.

His secretary came to the door. "Mr. DeVries, Collin Deverell is here to see you," she announced.

DeVries hesitated for a moment, then nodded. "Send him in," he said quietly.

A moment later, Collin Deverell walked through the door, tall and tanned and indecently handsome, dressed in light gray slacks, a white silk shirt buttoned low, revealing an unquestionably expensive gold medallion hanging around his neck. Over one shoulder he carried a navy sports jacket. He entered the office silent, unsmiling, and came forward without hesitation. "I came to find out what you're doing to locate my stolen paintings," he said, dispensing with unnecessary amenities as he pulled up a chair.

DeVries studied him for a moment. DeVries himself was forty-five, of average height and slightly overweight, with a receding hairline and a spare tire around his middle. He never thought about his appearance until he compared himself to someone who looked like Collin Deverell, and then he had to admit—if only to himself—that he was slightly resentful. "I'm still looking into it," he answered carefully.

Collin did not bother to hide his displeasure. "I'm sure you're aware that the longer it takes, the less likely we are to ever find them," he said sharply.

We. DeVries nodded. "It can't be helped," he pointed out. "These paintings have been missing—gone—for almost two years. By now, there's no way of knowing where they've been taken. Probably Switzerland."

"Why Switzerland?" Collin asked.

"Because, Mr. Deverell, Switzerland has a good-faith purchase and protection law," DeVries explained.

Collin looked at him. "Meaning exactly what?" he wanted to know.

"Meaning," DeVries said slowly, "that if a purchaser says he bought a work of art in good faith, the Swiss government will allow him to keep it, even if it actually is stolen. It happens quite often, actually." He sat down at the desk. "A valuable painting is purchased, a large insurance policy is taken out on the work, then the owner arranges its theft so he—or she—can collect on the policy. The painting is sold to a private party—frequently in Switzerland—and the original owner profits twice."

Collin stared at him for a moment. "You believe I stole my own paintings," he said flatly.

"I'm not drawing any conclusions—yet," DeVries assured him. "I prefer to wait until I've completed my investigation."

"Meanwhile, my paintings and jewelry could be anywhere," Collin said.

"Everything that can be done is being done," DeVries insisted.

"I see." Collin got to his feet. He studied the other man for a moment, his dark eyes blazing with fury. "Thanks— for nothing!" He turned on his heel and stormed out of the office, leaving DeVries staring after him.

And wondering again if Collin Deverell were guilty.

Collin was still burning with rage as he drove back to Sea Cliff that afternoon. Racing along the Long Island Expressway at least twenty miles over the posted speed limit, he thought about his meeting with the insurance investigator, unable to believe that the man could seriously consider the possibility that he had staged the theft of his own property just to collect on a lousy insurance policy. Dammit, he didn't need the money, and those paintings meant everything to him. No matter how it looked, did the man really think he was stupid enough to try such a thing, especially with all of the servants around? Did DeVries really think if he had been behind this, he would have allowed his own staff to think he'd arranged the sale? Only an idiot would have handled it so badly!

The sound of the police car's siren cut through his thoughts. He glanced up at the rearview mirror and saw the New York Highway Patrol car coming up behind him. He slowed down, bringing the Ferrari to a stop on the shoulder of the highway. The patrolman parked behind him, got out of his car, and came forward. "Are you aware you were going twenty-two miles over the speed limit?" he asked.

Collin nodded. "Guilty," he admitted.

"Your license, please."

He took out his wallet, removed his New York driver's license, and gave it to the patrolman. The officer studied it for a moment, then looked up at Collin.

Collin grinned. "Driver's license photos always look like hell, don't they?" he asked, attempting to ease the tension.

The patrolman nodded. "This isn't the first time you've been caught speeding, is it, Mr. Deverell?" he asked, looking at the license again.

"No, I'm afraid not," Collin confessed. "But it *is* the first time in a few years. I've been out of the country—"

"I'm going to have to give you a ticket," the officer told him then.

Collin nodded. "I'm familiar with the procedure," he said as he took the license and tucked it back into his wallet.

Fifteen minutes later Collin was back on the highway, headed for home. And dwelling, once again, on the situation there. Did whoever had done this really think he would get away with it? he wondered. It was the work of an amateur; he was convinced of that. A professional would have been more careful. A pro would have made sure everything was done correctly. A pro would have tied up all the loose ends. Couldn't that investigator see that?

* * *

In fact, DeVries had thought of it. He had thought of little else, especially after Collin's unexpected appearance at his office. Something was definitely amiss here, he thought as he reviewed the reports again and again. By all indications, young Deverell had disposed of a fortune in artworks and jewels. It appeared that he was attempting to collect on the insurance, yet in DeVries's conversations with him, Collin Deverell had not once mentioned the policy or the money. He talked only of his chances of recovering his property. Of course, that could be a front. It wouldn't be the first time he'd encountered a distraught owner desperate to have his artworks returned, only to discover later that that same person had engineered the theft. Still, Collin Deverell had not merely been upset. He had seemed obsessed, as if the items that had been taken were in some way symbolic to him. If he weren't telling the truth, the man was an incredibly good actor.

DeVries was intrigued by the story of the Deverell dynasty, of how Quentin Deverell had made his fortune in the oil industry by the time he was twenty-three, how he had struggled and fought and manipulated his way to the top, making Intercontinental Oil one of the giants of the industry. He was also intrigued by the fact that Collin Deverell and his brother Justin were identical twins, that no one could tell them apart by appearance alone. He found it curious that Collin and Justin Deverell were at odds with each other, that they had never been close in the way that brothers—and especially identical twins—normally were. Not once, in all of their conversations, had Collin Deverell ever mentioned his brother, yet DeVries knew that Collin Deverell had obtained full ownership of the paintings and jewels as part of a settlement with his twin brother, an agreement that left Collin with the family stronghold on Long Island and his brother with full control of the company. That information had come to him in the course of his investigation. Why, he wondered, had Collin Deverell willingly given up his share of a company that was worth billions, a company that was sure to make him staggeringly wealthy in the years to come, trading it for paintings and jewels that were certainly valuable but nowhere near as valuable as his Intercontinental Oil stock? DeVries had discovered that it had been Quentin Deverell's intention, before his sudden death three years ago, to name Collin, not Justin, as his successor to the chairmanship of Intercontinental Oil. Yet Collin had walked away from the company without a backward glance. Why? DeVries asked himself.

He reached for the phone on the corner of his highly organized desk and dialed a number. "Yeah—DeVries here," he identified himself. "I need some information . . ."

Collin was alone in the library. He stood in front of the fireplace, looking up at the portrait of his mother, so elegant and beautiful in her Dior gown. So regal. She had been twenty-eight when that portrait was completed, and she looked like a young queen about to ascend to her throne. And in his mind he remembered the warm, passionate woman she had been in life, a caring, devoted mother who always placed her children above all else. It was odd how easy it was for him to reconcile the grand lady in her designer gowns and priceless jewels with the woman in slacks and sweaters who had romped with him on the grounds, a rollicking, playful mother who had made such a fuss over the crayon drawings he had made for her as a small child, drawings of things she had only pretended to be able to identify. She had been like a lioness protecting her cubs when the press attempted to invade their privacy. And Collin had loved her as much as he would ever be able to love anyone.

His father. Quentin Deverell had been another story. He had been the disciplinarian of the family. He was strict and unyielding, but Collin had never doubted his love for his children. His fondest memories of his father were of that giant of a man who had hoisted him up on his shoulder and carried him through the halls of the mansion. The man who had taught him to ride and to handle a gun. The man who promised him he was going to have a wonderful life ahead of him. It was the only promise his father had not been able to keep, Collin thought unhappily.

He reached up and took the ceremonial saber from its place on the wall and hefted it in his hands. He remembered the day Jean-Michel had given it to him, predicting that he was going to take the gold in fencing at the upcoming Olympics. The same day his father had arrived in Nice to drag his son home to resume his studies. It was then that Collin had realized that his father was never going to stand for his pursuing a future as a professional fencer. It was then that his dreams had been shattered. Collin had forgiven his father, of course, but he had never stopped wondering what might have been.

He glanced up at the spot where his father's favorite painting, a Piero della Francesca, had hung. If he could get hold of whoever had taken it—and his other paintings—right now, he believed he could kill that person with his bare hands. His rage was such that he was not sure he could control it. He had almost lost control when he met with that insurance investigator. Angry as he was, he knew he could not allow that to happen again. He had to be careful in his dealings with DeVries. He needed this man, needed him on his side. *Don't antagonize him*, Collin told himself. *Don't make him more suspicious than he is now.* Much as Collin hated to admit it, he needed DeVries's help.

Three months passed. Anton DeVries had conducted a thorough investigation into the alleged theft at the Deverell estate, and though he believed Collin Deverell's story, believed he had not been involved in the theft, the evidence against him was most incriminating. Though DeVries's highly developed instincts, which had served him so well in the past, told him that Collin Deverell was in no way involved in the sale of the paintings and jewels, everything pointed to fraud against the insurance company that had hired him to look into the matter. His employers were not going to accept his theory that Deverell had been set up unless he could provide them with concrete proof. What they were going to accept, however, was the information he had collected, including the bills of sale that had been verified by handwriting experts as bearing the signature of Collin Deverell.

DeVries thought about it long and hard before he even considered talking to Collin Deverell. He had always prided himself on being a thorough man, on being able to look beyond the obvious, being able to find even the smallest bit of evidence needed to solve a case. But this time he had the feeling that something was missing. Something important. Something that would help him uncover the truth. Something he could not give a name to.

He retraced his steps from the moment he had entered the case. He had spoken to Collin Deverell, of course. He was convinced he'd obtained as much information from Deverell as he was ever going to get. He had investigated each member of the household staff thoroughly, and they'd all come up clean. He had spoken to each of them separately, and their stories had not conflicted. They were telling the truth as they saw it. He had looked into Collin Deverell's background and put together a mental portrait of a man who was unusually intelligent, daring, straightforward, and a bit of a gambler at heart, but not a thief. Not a man who would commit fraud.

He had wanted to speak with Justin Deverell, but the first time he called he was informed by a secretary at Intercontinental Oil that Mr. Deverell was in Singapore on business and was not expected back for three weeks. The next time, he was in Houston, another business trip. The third time, he was vacationing in the Virgin Islands. It appeared to DeVries that Justin Deverell was avoiding him. Why? he wondered. He had checked into the activities of the second Deverell twin, and found that he was clean. It seemed that Justin Deverell literally lived for Intercontinental Oil. If he had a social life, no one knew anything about it. He divided his time between his office and his Trump Tower apartment, and was seldom seen in public. He did take a vacation once a year, but he traveled alone and spent his leisure time alone. It was intriguing, DeVries thought. Collin and Justin Deverell were both loners, each in his own way. Two men, identical in physical appearance, worlds apart in personality and lifestyle, neither of whom had been in New York at the time of the theft. He checked the available handwriting samples of Justin Deverell. Their signatures were as alike as their faces. It was uncanny. DeVries decided to speak with one of his superiors about it.

"I'm convinced, Frank," he said. "I don't believe Collin Deverell had anything to do with it. I think you would have had to kill him to get those paintings away from him. I think the sentimental value was more important to him than the dollars-and-cents value."

"Are you suggesting the twin brother could have been the one?" the other man wanted to know.

DeVries shook his head. "I don't know what to think. Justin Deverell was out of the country at the time. And why the hell would the chairman of the board of an outfit as big as Intercontinental Oil want to steal paintings and jewelry he gave his brother in exchange for control of that company? It doesn't make any sense."

"Nothing about those two makes any sense," Frank Howard said slowly as he looked over DeVries's report. "On one hand, you have Collin Deverell, clearly the rebel of the family, a brilliant student with little or no interest in the family business, who's been into every kind of mischief possible since he was very young—speeding tickets, illegal gambling, you name it. On the other hand is Justin Deverell, who's also bright and the most private kind of man you could ever imagine. Few friends, no serious romance in his life—ever. An almost obsessive dedication to the company. Doesn't that sound a little strange to you?"

"Everything about this case sounds strange," he muttered, rubbing his eyes tiredly.

"The handwriting experts say guilty, but you still believe his story," Howard concluded.

DeVries nodded. "He's convincing—and I don't think

anyone could be that good an actor,'' he stated. "Handwriting experts or no handwriting experts.''

"So what do we tell our client?''

"We tell them we have no proof,'' DeVries said without hesitation. "We tell them the servants believed Deverell sold the paintings, but we have no proof. I'm going to recommend they pay off the policy, though I don't believe it will give Deverell much satisfaction.''

"One thing, Anton—have you told Deverell anything?'' Howard asked then. "Does he know about the handwriting verification?''

DeVries shook his head. "Not yet. But he will. Soon.''

"If this handwriting expert is so sure, then why do you believe my story?'' Collin stood against a wall of bookshelves in the library, looking at DeVries warily.

"Is there some reason why I shouldn't?'' DeVries asked.

"No,'' Collin said carefully. "It's the truth. I wouldn't have sold those paintings at any price. But you wouldn't understand why, so why should you believe me when your so-called evidence all points to fraud? I don't think your client's going to be very happy with you.''

DeVries ignored his cockiness. He wasn't sure he wouldn't react the same way if placed in the same situation. He handed Collin a photocopy of the report from the graphologist. "I'm putting my ass in a sling,'' he said. "The insurance company could charge fraud—and they'd probably win.''

Collin studied it for a moment, then looked up. "So why aren't you giving it to them? What's in it for you?'' he asked suspiciously.

DeVries was annoyed with Collin Deverell's attitude, but it made him even more convinced that Collin was telling the truth. "I don't like to make mistakes, Mr. Deverell,'' he said slowly. "I'm not in this business to send innocent people to prison. I think you were set up. I don't believe your theory that this was the work of amateurs.''

"Oh?" Collin looked at him coldly. "And what, may I ask, is your theory?"

"I believe whoever was behind this knew exactly what he—or perhaps they—were doing. I think someone would like to see you go to prison for the theft of your own property. Any ideas who that might be?"

Collin looked down at the handwriting samples in front of him. He had an idea, all right, but he wasn't going to share it with DeVries or anyone else.

This was something he had to take care of himself.

Collin had not wanted to believe that his brother could possibly be involved. Even when the suspicion first arose, when Henry Harrison told him about the signed bill of sale he had seen, he had deliberately pushed the thought from his mind. Whatever else Justin was—or wasn't—the one thing Collin had always been certain of was that his brother was not a thief. Even after what the insurance investigator had revealed to him, he had hoped he was wrong. He had not confronted Justin immediately. Instead he began looking into his brother's activities since he had become chairman of the board of Intercontinental Oil. When Collin left New York, almost three years ago, the rumor on Wall Street was that the company was in trouble. The death of Quentin Deverell had placed Intercontinental Oil on a shaky foundation. Collin, wondering if the company could possibly be in serious trouble, decided to look into the matter. What he discovered was shocking. Before his death, their father had taken out several large loans to finance the expansion of his holdings in Venezuela and the South China Sea. Delays in drilling operations in Caracas had placed him in serious financial difficulties. That, Collin learned, was the reason for his parents' ill-fated trip to South America. That was why they went, and that was why they died. His father had been pushing his crews to the limit, apparently at the expense of the safety of all concerned. When Justin took over the company, what he found himself faced with was a dying giant. What he had done to save it, Collin thought resentfully, was unforgivable. He intended to have a showdown with Justin.

Then he would go to DeVries.

"Did you really think you'd get away with it?" Collin demanded hotly, thrusting the handwriting analysis in front of his brother. The confrontation was taking place in the privacy of Justin's living room at the Trump Tower. Justin sat on the black suede couch, calmly sipping a brandy, while Collin prowled the room, a time bomb about to detonate.

Justin looked at the paper dispassionately, then up at his brother. "I don't have the slightest idea what you're talking about," he responded in a cool voice.

"The hell you don't!" Collin snapped. "Who else could duplicate my signature so closely that it could even fool a handwriting expert? Who else—if necessary—could have gained access to the main house without arousing the suspicion of the staff? Who else had the motive—"

"Motive?" Justin laughed aloud. "Why on earth would I want to—"

"Cut the crap, Justin!" Collin roared. "I know all about the troubles the company's been facing. I know how deeply in debt Dad was at the time of his death. I also know—finally—why they were in Venezuela, and why they died."

Justin frowned, looking down at the empty glass in his hand. "Then you know why I had to do it," he said finally.

"No, dammit, I don't!" Collin shouted. "There's no good excuse for what you've done! Those paintings—and Mother's jewels—belonged to me! It was part of our agreement! You had no right to just take them!"

"I had to do whatever was necessary to save the company," Justin said firmly. "It wasn't enough, of course, but it was a start. It's what they would have wanted. You know that."

"You're not concerned with what they would have wanted," Collin said acidly. "You're only concerned with finally being in charge, with getting what you always wanted. You've tasted power, and now it's a sickness with you. You'll do anything to get it, to hold onto it. But mark my words, brother, you're not getting away with this!"

Justin looked up. "What are you going to do?" he asked hesitantly.

Collin studied him for a moment. "I don't know—yet," he said truthfully. Then he turned and walked out, slamming the door in the wake of his anger.

Alone in the elevator, Collin leaned against the wall, trembling with rage. He knew what he wanted to do. He wanted to turn Justin over to DeVries and the insurance company—and the police. But even as he considered it, he knew he would never go through with it. Whatever else he was, whatever else Justin had done, they were still brothers. He might gain some satisfaction from punishing Justin for what he had done, but that victory would be short-lived. His parents would not have wanted this. He did not want it, in his heart. Besides, he had more important things to think about.

How he was going to get his property back.

Big Sur, November 1979

"Hold still, Brandon," Ashley scolded, looking up from her sketch pad. Brandon was perched on a wooden railing overlooking the Pacific Ocean at the Julia Pfeiffer Burns State Park, and behind him the view was spectacular. "If you keep moving, I'm never going to finish this!"

"I can't help it! I have a cramp in my leg and I'm about to fall backward into the ocean." His voice was pleading. "Is that what you want—to get rid of me?"

"Don't be ridiculous!" She smiled, thinking to herself that nothing could be farther from the truth. She took a deep breath. "Okay, I know when I'm licked—take a break. Ten minutes."

"You're all heart," he teased as he hopped down from his perch. "How about an hour? I've never been here before, you know. I'd really like to do some sightseeing."

"Later. You promised I could do your portrait, remember?" Ashley put down her pad and charcoals and stood up as he approached.

"I know, but I thought you'd do it the same way you do your landscapes—with photos and slides, in your studio. I didn't think I was going to become a living statue," he grumbled.

"A photo isn't good enough for a portrait, at least I've never thought so," she told him, wiping her hands on a small towel. "I want to capture the real you."

He grinned, taking her in his arms. "Well, why didn't you say so?" he asked in a playful tone. "I'll be more than happy to oblige. In fact I thought you'd never ask!" He kissed her longingly.

Ashley withdrew, smiling up at him. "That's not what I was talking about and you know it, Brandon Hollister," she said, laughing.

"You said you wanted the real me. Well, this is about as real as I get," he insisted, refusing to release her from his grasp. "Unless . . ."

Her eyes met his. "You promised," she reminded him.

He stared at her for a moment, then let her go. "A promise I'm sorry I ever made," he said hoarsely. "I want you, Ashley—God how I want you!"

"We agreed to give it time," she said carefully. She wanted him just as much as he wanted her. But she had purposely kept him out of her bed in the months they had been seeing each other because she had sensed the night they met that he was different from any of the other men she had known. Special, very special. She wanted more from Brandon Hollister than a one-night stand or a short-term affair. She wanted him one hundred percent. She wanted a future with him. And some deeply buried instinct had told her, right from the beginning, that making herself inaccessible to him sexually would only make him want her more.

Stalling would give him time to allow her access to his heart, to make him love her as she had come to love him. *I want you for keeps*, she thought as she gazed up at him. *I want it to be all or nothing.* They were close to making that emotional commitment, very close. Soon she would be able to give herself to him as she had wanted to all along.

"What do you want to do this afternoon?"

She thought about it for a moment. "I'd like to take in some of the shops in town," she answered finally. "The Galerie, the Big Sur Bazaar—and maybe when we get back to the Ventana Inn, we could check out the gift shop there?"

He nodded, taking his camera from its case. "I think turnabout really is fair play," he said promptly. "I've been posing up there for almost two hours." He pointed to the railing. "Now you have to reciprocate."

Ashley laughed. "That sounds fair enough," she agreed with a nod of her head. "Where do you want me?"

Brandon grinned. "Do you really want to know?"

She threw her towel at him. "Be serious!"

"I've never been more serious in my life." He adjusted the lens as she climbed up on the railing and struck a whimsical pose, her long hair billowing in the soft breeze like a great dark banner.

"How's this?" she wanted to know.

"Perfect." He raised the camera to his face and adjusted the lens again. "Beautiful, really beautiful," he declared.

She smiled. "Thank you."

"I was referring to the scenery," he said flatly.

"Brandon Hollister, you definitely do not know the way to a woman's heart!" she cried out in mock anger.

"Don't move!" he commanded. "Wait a minute—could you lift your skirt just a bit higher?"

"Make up your mind," she said menacingly. "Which is it? Do I sit still or do I move the skirt?"

"Pull it up . . . just a bit. Show the knee. You know, cheesecake," he said, fiddling with the camera again.

"How corny!" Ashley dutifully lifted her skirt to reveal her knee.

"Maybe just a little bit higher," he said slowly, peering through the viewfinder.

She pulled it up almost mid-thigh.

"Just a little bit more . . ."

She put her hands on her hips and glared at him. "If I pull the damn thing any higher, no one will develop this film," she joked. "There are laws, you know, Mr. Big-Time Lawyer!"

He looked up over the camera and grinned. "I have my own darkroom," he said simply.

"Oh!" Her mouth dropped open in surprise. "So that's it! That's how you get your kicks, right?"

"I have never taken a pornographic photo in my life!" he declared indignantly. "Of course, there's always a first time—if you're interested in being my model . . ."

"You're terrible!" Ashley started to laugh.

"That's it!" he exclaimed. "That's exactly what I want!" He shot several pictures in rapid succession as Ashley rocked on the railing, laughing heartily, head thrown back in abandon, cheeks flushed as the breeze blew her skirt up over her legs.

"You know," Ashley said as she climbed up onto the top rail and teetered for a moment as she balanced herself, "when I was a child, I used to walk on the top rails of the fences surrounding the vineyards. I was pretty good at it, too. I could outlast any of the boys." She started to walk, putting one foot in front of the other carefully, extending her arms to maintain her balance.

Brandon put down his camera. "Be careful, Ashley," he said with uneasiness in his voice. "You could fall . . ."

"Nonsense," she scoffed. "I told you, I'm an old hand at this—" Suddenly her foot slipped. Her body lurched wildly as she struggled to regain her balance. Brandon raced forward, catching her in his arms as she dived toward the stone walk in front of him. He held her close for a moment, their hearts racing, and stroked her hair. She looked up at him, her dark eyes shining. Their gaze held for a moment, then he kissed her deeply. "I was so afraid," he whispered, kissing her hair.

"*You* were afraid," she gasped. "You should have been in my position."

He looked down at her. "I don't know what I would have done if anything had happened to you," he said softly. Then he kissed her again.

"I knew you wouldn't let it," she breathed. "I knew it all along."

His lips were on her neck. "I love you, Ashley. I think I've loved you all along."

"You're only saying that because we're both so damned scared," she insisted, clinging to him tightly.

"No . . . no, I'm not," he said, nuzzling her ear. "I do love you."

"And I love you," she admitted hesitantly.

"Let's go back to the inn," he muttered against her neck. She giggled. "That's not fair!"

"What's not fair?"

"You. You wouldn't use my weakened state to take advantage of me, would you?"

"You'd better believe I would, pretty lady," he growled. "Well . . . what's it going to be?"

Her eyes met his again. She gave him a wicked smile. "I suppose I should thank you for saving my life . . ."

The Ventana Inn, on the Pacific Coast Highway, is a luxurious wilderness resort built on a thousand-acre oceanfront ranch, high in the mountains overlooking the Pacific. Opened four years earlier, it fulfilled a need for lodgings worthy of the wild, magical Big Sur countryside. The resort's forty guest rooms, housed in natural-wood buildings with slanted roofs, seem to blend in with the landscape perfectly. The interiors are done in either blue or yellow color schemes, with wall-to-wall carpeting color-coordinated to the patchwork quilt bedspreads from Nova Scotia. The walls are a blend of cedar paneling and white stucco, and many of the rooms have either very high ceilings or wood-burning stoves. Each room has a terrace or balcony overlooking the ocean, dressing rooms, and luxurious baths. Other luxuries include a ninety-foot heated outdoor pool and three outdoor Japanese hot baths equipped with multiple jets where guests can soak in the nude, one for men only, one for the ladies, and the third for the more uninhibited mixed crowd. The inn boasts a first-rate restaurant which, like everything else here, is rustic in decor. The raw cedar interior is airy, with heavy beams, a huge stone fireplace, and cedar tile floor. The tables are redwood, the chairs cane and bentwood, and the overhead globe lamps rattan-shaded. Baskets of ferns, potted plants, and fresh fruits are scattered throughout.

As Ashley lay in Brandon's arms in the large, comfortable bed in her room, spent yet deliciously fulfilled after an afternoon of the lovemaking she had denied herself for too long, she suddenly realized that the sun was setting, that they had missed lunch and were probably going to miss dinner as well if she did not wake him soon. She looked up at him, sleeping peacefully, his thick, honey-blond hair rumpled, and she asked herself why she had waited so long. She had believed she was doing the right thing in postponing the inevitable, the consummation of their love, but now it seemed so unnecessary. She knew, she believed without the slightest doubt, that he loved her. Not only because he had said so, but because she had felt it, felt it when he took her in his arms, felt it when their lips met and their bodies fused together, becoming one. The magic had been there all along—if only she'd realized it! It had existed between them from the moment their eyes met, that night at the Equinox, when he foiled Scott Nelson's plans to use her to further his political ambitions. *I wanted to make love with you then, you silly, wonderful fool*, she thought as she traced his profile with the tip of her finger. *I've wanted to make love with you every time we've been together in the past seven months.*

Brandon opened his eye and smiled at her. "Well?" he asked, looking at her questioningly.

She smiled back. "Well what?"

"Any regrets?"

She kissed his chin. "Only that it took us so long to get here," she said simply.

"Not my fault," he reminded her, stroking her hair. "I was more than willing. I just couldn't talk you into it."

She studied him for a moment, her smile changing to a frown. "I was afraid," she confessed.

He looked puzzled. "Of what?"

"That once we made love, you'd get disenchanted with me and we wouldn't last." She avoided his eyes. "Silly, huh?"

"Silly, yes," he agreed. "I thought you knew I was in love with you."

"You never said anything . . ."

He rumpled her hair. "I'm not very good at putting my feelings into words."

She pulled herself up on one elbow and looked at him, surprised. "A lawyer who's not good with words? Unheard of!" she teased, her mood changing abruptly.

"That's different and you know it," he pointed out. "I can argue a case or put together a contract or a will, I can clown around and make a fool of myself, but I've never told a woman I loved her before. It was harder than I expected it to be."

She kissed him again. "I guess we're in the same boat, then," she decided. "I wanted to tell you how I felt so many times, but I couldn't quite get the words out."

He chuckled softly. "You? At a loss for words? Now that's hard to believe!"

"Don't make fun of me, Hollister," she chided him as she sat up and grabbed a pillow in both hands, unaware that the movement had caused the sheets to fall down around her waist, exposing her breasts. "I'm trying to tell you how much I love you, and you're making jokes!"

"I'm sorry, darling, it's just that I can't imagine you not saying exactly what's on your mind," he said, amused. He reached up and seized the pillow from her, tossing it aside. He grabbed both of her wrists and pulled her down to him.

"But as the saying goes, actions do speak louder than words . . ."

Ashley giggled. "Don't you ever get tired?"

"Sure," he admitted, tangling his fingers in her hair. "But never at a time like this."

She pulled away from him. "I don't think I've got the energy to keep up with you right now," she told him. "I'm hungry. Famished, in fact."

"Hungry?" He stared at her, unable to believe it. "How can you be hungry at a time like this?"

She laughed. "Easy. Lovemaking always leaves me ravenous," she said, tossing her head back, shaking her hair away from her face.

"Oh." He gave an exaggerated groan. "Okay, give me time to take a shower and I'll take you to dinner. But I think I should warn you now. If sex makes you hungry, you'd better learn to control your appetite or you'll weigh three hundred pounds six months from now!"

Ashley sat on the balcony outside their room, watching the first rays of dawn break the blanket of darkness that seemed to cover the earth. Out on the ocean, a whale leaped from the water, causing a giant wave as he reentered the surf. Ashley didn't notice. Her mind was on other things. More important things. She had no idea how long she had been sitting there, staring into the darkness. Restless and afraid she might wake him, she had left Brandon sleeping soundly in the bedroom and had come out here to think, to try to come up with a solution to her problem.

She had lied to Brandon. She had led him to believe that she was the daughter of a wealthy Napa Valley landowner. She'd led him to believe that she came from a moneyed family, as he did. She had never told him the truth, that her father did not own the vineyards, that he only worked there. She had created an elaborate fairytale childhood to go with her new life, her public image. Somehow it had seemed right when she had first arrived in San Francisco, but now she was caught up in her own lie, wondering how to confess the truth to the man she loved. She did love Brandon. She loved him as she had never loved anyone in her life. Brandon was the embodiment of everything she had ever wanted, everything she needed. He was rich. He was dedicated and he worked hard. But Brandon had given her something much more important: love. He loved her, flaws and all. He had seen her at her worst and it had not changed his feelings for her. *I made the world's worst first impression, and still he keeps coming around*, she thought as she remembered that first meeting. *But how will he feel when he finds out I've been less than honest with him? Will we survive that as well?* She knew there was only one way she was going to find out. *I'll tell him*, she promised herself. *Soon. But not now. Now is definitely not the right time.* She had to face the truth: she was a coward. She did not want to break the magical spell of their newly consummated love. Not yet.

He had survived her unholy temper and her sometimes outrageous behavior. He had endured her erratic habits, her frequent abrupt decisions to end an evening early because she'd come up with an idea for a painting she wanted to do and felt the need to get to a sketchbook as quickly as possible. He'd put up with her adamant refusal to go to bed with him even though they had both wanted it all along. *He'll understand this, too*, she told herself. *I know he will. He loves me. The truth won't change that.* But the unspoken fear she harbored was that he would not understand why she had lied to him. Would he not be able to trust her after he found out? Would he cease to believe anything she told him? *You're being irrational*, she told herself. *It's not that important.*

Not to Brandon, maybe, but his parents might be another story.

They had breakfast on the balcony, and Ashley fed bits of her croissant to the ravens who landed on the railing, begging for food. "If you let them, they'll eat all of your breakfast," Brandon warned in a teasing tone.

She looked at him. "I'm only taking your advice," she

said indignantly, breaking off another piece of the croissant for one of the hungry birds.

He looked at her as he sipped his coffee. "My advice?" he asked.

"Of course," she said. "You're the one who told me if I didn't learn to curb my cravings for food after sex, I'd weigh a ton after being with you for a few months."

"That's not exactly what I said," he corrected her. "I told you that you would weigh three hundred pounds in six months."

"Same difference," she insisted. "Give or take a few hundred pounds and a few months one way or the other." She stood up, drawing her green silk robe around herself. She wore nothing underneath, and in the bright morning sun, the fabric was almost transparent.

"Come over here," Brandon growled, aroused by the sight. He extended his arms, beckoning her to come.

Ashley grinned. "Now what have you got in mind, you wicked man?" she purred.

"Come over here and I'll show you."

"Is it safe?" she asked.

"No, as a matter of fact, what I have in mind isn't safe at all," he admitted. "But when have you ever been concerned about being safe?"

"You know me too well." She stepped forward, coming to a stop directly in front of him. "Remember, Hollister, we're in a public place. Semipublic, anyway."

"I know full well where we are." He reached up and untied the sash on her robe, letting it fall open. His hands moved slowly over her breasts, full yet firm, stroking her nipples with his fingertips until they became erect. Then he raised his head to suck at them, first one, then the other, while she held his head in her hands and stroked his hair. When he finally released her, his hands slid down between her legs, caressing her, fondling her until she could stand it no longer. She lowered herself to his lap, straddling him, pushing his robe open to reveal his swollen organ, ready for her. She lowered herself slowly, feeling him enter her. Her mouth came down on his hungrily as she wrapped her arms around his neck, her hips gyrating as they came to a quick but explosive orgasm together. Then she lay her head against his shoulder, trembling, and he held her close for a long time, both of them silent, not feeling a need for words. Finally, Ashley broke the silence. "Darling, I hope this isn't going to ruin everything between us, but—" she stopped short.

"But what, sweetheart?" he murmured.

"I'm hungry."

They spent Thanksgiving together. Ashley made excuses to her parents, telling them she was getting ready for an exhibit and could not get away for the holiday. She was not ready to tell them anything about Brandon yet. She wasn't sure what Brandon had told his parents when he telephoned them in New York. He did not seem to want to talk about them—he almost never mentioned them to her—and she did not want to press him for an explanation that, as far as she was concerned, was unnecessary. They were together constantly during the four-day weekend, and most of that time was spent in bed. Brandon, gentle, conservative Brandon, was surprised at times by her lack of sexual inhibitions, but the more time they spent in bed together, the more adventurous he became. "You're a sex maniac, you know that?" he teased her.

She gave him a suggestive smile as her hands explored his body. "You bring out the worst in me, that's all," she told him.

"I'd hardly call it the worst," he said. And they would make love again and again.

The following Monday, Brandon left for Los Angeles on a business trip. "I wish you'd change your mind and go with me," he told her at the airport. "I'm not looking forward to being away from you, lady."

"It's only for two days," she reminded him. "And I'll be waiting for you, waiting to welcome you home royally."

"Still—" he started.

"You're going to miss your plane," she pointed out as the other passengers began filing through the gate. "Now, go! I have things to do here while you're away."

"Like what?"

"It's a surprise," she insisted. She wasn't lying. *It will come as a surprise when I finally tell you*, she thought as she watched him disappear into the crowd.

When she left the airport, she drove out Highway 101, that familiar route she'd traveled so many times over the past three years, to the Napa Valley. She spent most of the afternoon sitting under the same old oak tree she had sat under so many times over the years as she pondered the landscape. Now she was lost in thought as she looked down at the vineyards. Her past. Her heritage. It was a part of her, just as her painting was a part of her. If Brandon loved her as much as she believed he did, he would accept it. He would accept her reasons for the lie she'd lived with for so long. She decided then and there that she would tell him everything as soon as he returned from L.A.

Everything.

"And that's about it," Ashley concluded. She stood by the fireplace in her living room, dressed in black slacks and an emerald-green turtleneck sweater. "I made it all up when I came here because I wanted acceptance. My real name is Abby Giannini—not Ashley Gordon. My father does not own the finest vineyards in all of the Napa Valley. He works in them, works for someone else. I don't come from a wealthy family. In fact it was damned hard just making ends meet! You know, there were times I had to boil the bones of rabbits shot by some of the men there in the winery to make the substance I needed to treat my homemade canvases. I hated it, but I always knew I'd make it if I kept trying. I'll understand if you're angry with me and want to end it right here, but that's where I come from and I'm not ashamed of it—"

"Hold it!" Brandon put down his drink and got to his feet, clasping his hands on her shoulders. "In the first place,

I'm not angry, and in the second, you have nothing to be ashamed of.''

"Then you're not angry that I lied to you?" she asked.

"Angry? I'm relieved!" he laughed. "When you said you had something important to discuss with me, I thought you were going to say that we had to end it, that you're married with a husband and a couple of kids lurking around someplace!"

"Husband? Kids?" She gestured expansively. "Look around. Have you ever seen a husband and kids in all the times you've been here?"

"Of course not!"

"Then where, pray tell, would I be hiding them?" she wanted to know. She started to laugh, feeling as though a tremendous weight had been lifted from her shoulders.

"I don't know, maybe another home somewhere—" He shrugged.

"Oh, come now!" Then her eyes softened. "You're sure you don't love me any less now that you know the truth?"

He kissed her tenderly. "Ashley, I fell in love with you, not your pedigree," he assured her. "But there is one thing . . ."

"What?" she asked carefully.

"I would like to meet your parents. I'd be willing to bet they spend a lot of time worrying about a wild child like you," he said cheerfully. "I think I should reassure them that you're in good hands."

Her smile was wicked. "Boy, am I in good hands!"

Ashley did not telephone her parents to tell them she was coming—or that she would be bringing Brandon with her. She wasn't sure how or what to tell them about her relationship with him. They loved each other, yes. They were lovers in every sense of the word. But they had made no commitments to each other beyond the admission of that love. She wasn't sure yet what the future held for them, so how could she answer the questions she knew they were going to ask?

As it turned out, she needn't have worried. To Ashley's surprise, Brandon and her father seemed to hit it off right away. "Do you think Papa really likes him?" Ashley asked her mother when they were alone in the kitchen, putting the finishing touches on the special dinner Lucia had insisted upon preparing for them. She could see them from the kitchen window, talking on the back porch, but she couldn't hear what they were saying. "They've been out there for a long time—"

Lucia Giannini laughed. "You worry for nothing, *cara*," she told her daughter. "Tony likes your young man. Trust me. I've been married to him long enough to know when he's putting up a front and when he's not. Your papa is not a good liar."

Ashley turned to look at her. "What about you, Mama?" she wanted to know. "What do you think?"

Her mother smiled. "I think you've done well for yourself." She paused. "You are in love with him, aren't you?"

Ashley smiled. "Yes, Mama, I am. Does it show that much?"

Lucia nodded. "It's written all over your face." Then she asked, "Do the two of you have . . . any plans?"

Ashley shrugged. "Not yet. We've been taking things one day at a time," she said carefully. "Maybe one day . . ."

Lucia smiled and embraced her. "If it's meant to be, Abby, it'll happen."

Ashley hugged her mother tightly, blinking back tears. She realized now that it had not been Brandon's reaction to her confession that had troubled her. She had been bothered by her own guilt at having pretended to be something she wasn't. Her parents, her life here . . . they were nothing to be ashamed of. Her mother and father were good people, strong people with good, solid values. They had brought her up with those values. She was strong because of those values, and their love.

I'll never be ashamed of who or what I am again, she thought.

* * *

"What did you and Papa find to talk about for so long?" Ashley asked as she and Brandon walked through the vineyards in the twilight. "I didn't think you'd have that much in common."

Brandon grinned. "We have one very important thing in common," he told her. "You. It seems we both love you, even if it's not in the same way."

"You told him that?" Ashley asked, surprised.

"Of course I did," he answered, fingering one of the vines absently. In the dying light, his blue eyes seemed to sparkle. "He asked me what my intentions toward you might be, and I told him."

Ashley's expression was a mixture of astonishment and anger. "I cannot believe he would actually ask you anything like that, or that you would answer . . ."

"There was nothing wrong with the answer I gave him," Brandon insisted. "And as for his asking, I wasn't surprised. I wasn't surprised at all. I expected it. Your father's a very old-fashioned man. I like that. Sometimes I wish my own father had values."

She was still annoyed. "Papa knows how I feel about that," she said in an irritated tone. "I can't believe he would embarrass us like that!"

Brandon grabbed her shoulders and looked down at her, their eyes meeting suddenly. "Easy," he urged. "Don't blame your father entirely. I was as much to blame for the intimacy of the conversation as he was. Maybe more so."

She stared at him for a moment, not sure she understood. "I don't get—"

"You see, darling, I'm old-fashioned myself in some ways. I had a specific reason for wanting to come here today, to meet your parents," he confessed with a sheepish grin.

Ashley was getting impatient. "Stop talking in riddles, Brandon," she demanded. "What could you possibly have to discuss with my father?"

"You," he said simply. "I came to ask his permission to marry his daughter."

She looked at him, stunned beyond words. "You—what?" she asked, not sure she'd heard correctly.

He placed his hand under her chin and lifted her face to his, kissing her tenderly. "I love you, lady," he said softly. "I want to marry you. Your father gave us his blessing. Now all I need is your answer. What's it going to be?"

Her lips were moving but no sound was produced at first. "How could you do this to me?" she asked finally.

He looked confused. "Do what to you?"

"Tell him before you told me!" She wrapped her arms around his neck and kissed him hard.

"Is that a yes or a no?" he asked, pretending innocence.

"It's a yes, you wonderful idiot!" she cried happily. *"Yes!"*

New York City, December 1979

"I have a confession to make," Ashley told Brandon as the taxi departed from Kennedy Airport. "I thought you wanted to keep the news of our engagement from your parents."

He looked at her. "Why on earth would I want to keep it a secret from anyone?" he asked, genuinely surprised.

She shrugged. "I don't know," she said with a sigh. "It just seemed to me that you were avoiding breaking the news to them. You didn't seem too anxious to call them, or—"

He laughed. "And you thought I didn't want to tell them about you?"

"Well, that's how it looked," she admitted.

He put his arm around her. "For the record, Ashley, I am not hiding you or what I feel for you from anyone. In fact, give me a chance and I'll shout it from every rooftop in Manhattan. I'll buy time on television. I'll—"

"Hold it!" Ashley laughed. "You don't have to go that far. I'm convinced. I swear I am."

"Then why the doubts?"

Ashley shook her head. "I just couldn't figure out why you kept putting off telling them. I would have bet we wouldn't be here now if your mother hadn't pressured you to come to New York for Christmas. You didn't act like you wanted to tell them."

He held her close. "I didn't, but it's not what you think," he insisted. "I told you, my father and I—well, we don't see eye to eye on things. There are problems between us. I don't want you dragged into the middle of it. That's all."

She looked up at him, her face suddenly serious. "If I'm going to be your wife, I want to share everything with you, good or bad," she said simply.

He smiled and kissed her forehead. "You're absolutely right," he conceded. "How did I ever manage without you all these years?"

"I have no idea," she said, snuggling against him, "but you'd better never try in the future."

Brandon's parents lived in an elegant brownstone town house in the East Seventies. "They also have a place at Montauk," Brandon told her as they entered the reception hall, followed by the Hollisters' butler, who carried their luggage. "I always preferred it to the town house, but my mother likes to be here—in the middle of things."

Ashley didn't respond. She was looking around, admiring her impressive surroundings. She had known the Hollisters were rich, but she'd had no idea just how rich until this moment. The blatant opulence of their home spelled money—big money. And somewhere in the back of her mind, Abby Giannini was breathlessly taking it all in, comparing it to her own childhood home. But Brandon wasn't happy here, she reminded herself. He had left this place, these people. *I don't have to compete with any of this. There's no contest as far as he's concerned. Besides, what do they have that we won't have ourselves eventually?*

"Brandon, darling!" A female voice broke through Ashley's thoughts as a fashionably dressed brunette who looked to be in her late forties or early fifties came from another room, smiling, her arms extended. "I was so afraid you'd call to cancel at the last minute—as you have for the past two years."

"Not a chance, Mother," he assured her. "Not this time. I have a special reason for coming." He turned to look at Ashley.

Ashley held her head high as she came face-to-face with Brandon's mother, Claudia Hollister, for the first time. The woman was so poised and elegant in her Valentino suit with good diamonds sparkling from her earlobes. Her hair was short and perfectly styled, not a hair out of place. Her green eyes were glacial as they met Ashley's. "Oh?" she asked, forcing a smile as she looked up at her son again.

"Ashley wanted to meet my parents," Brandon announced.

Claudia Hollister looked over at Ashley again.

"Ashley, this is my mother, Claudia Hollister. Mother, I'd like you to meet Ashley Gordon."

Claudia Hollister's face registered recognition. "The artist?" she asked.

Ashley nodded. "Unless there are two of us," she said, keeping her voice light.

"I've seen your work, and may I say that I'm an admirer," Claudia said then, her voice suddenly warming. "I especially like your landscapes."

"Thank you." Ashley accepted the compliment gracefully. *Maybe they won't eat me for dinner after all*, she mused.

"Your father should be here shortly," Claudia said, turning to Brandon again. "He was delayed in a business meeting."

"A business meeting," Brandon repeated her words tightly. "I suppose it's all business as usual, am I right?"

Claudia looked at him for a moment, then at Ashley, then back at Brandon again. "I don't think we should discuss this in front of Ms. Gordon, darling."

"Please—call me Ashley," she said quickly. *Discuss what in front of me?* she wondered.

Claudia nodded. "Ashley—and you must call me Claudia," she insisted, her voice suddenly tense. "I'm sure you two must be absolutely exhausted from your trip. I'll have Mason show you to your room, Ashley, if you'd like to freshen up a bit . . ."

Ashley nodded. "Thank you, I would." What was that exchange between those two all about? she wondered. Brandon had said there was some bad blood between himself and his father, that he didn't agree with some of his father's business practices, but she had the feeling that there was more to it than that, much more.

"Claudia and I saw your exhibit at one of the galleries. What was the name of that place, dear?" Bradley Hollister, an impressive man in his late fifties, with thinning salt-and-pepper hair and strong, blunt features, sat beside his wife in the library, a look of confusion on his face as he tried to remember the location of an exhibit of Ashley's paintings. "It was in San Francisco, two years ago. Your name was just becoming known in the art world. One of Claudia's friends had bought one of your landscapes and Claudia was determined to acquire one herself. Unfortunately, by the time we saw the exhibit, the landscapes had all been sold."

"Mother's friends," Brandon confided, leaning close to Ashley, "are a group of harpies who sit around all day dissecting everyone who is not one of them. And on occasion, they'll even sharpen their talons on each other."

"Brandon!" Claudia Hollister looked horrified. "We do nothing of the kind!"

"They've changed since I've been in San Francisco?" he asked, surprised. "As I recall, they all went in for blood sports."

"Perhaps we sometimes comment on those who don't live up to certain standards . . ."

"Which usually includes most of Manhattan," Brandon finished.

Ashley looked at him. She had never seen Brandon so cold, so merciless. His parents seemed to be going out of their way to be polite to her, but he seemed ill-at-ease and annoyed with both of them. What could possibly have happened between them to make him so bitter? she wondered. He'd barely spoken five words to his father since his arrival, and the tension between him and his mother appeared to be growing by the minute.

"Where are you from, Ashley?" Claudia asked pleasantly. "Originally, I mean?"

Ashley smiled. "California. I've lived there all of my life. I come from St. Helena—in the Napa Valley. It's not far from San Francisco."

"Wine country," Bradley Hollister concluded. "Your family's in the wine business?"

"Yes."

"I recall reading somewhere that your father owns vineyards in the valley," Claudia remarked. "A rather large one, if memory serves me."

Ashley hesitated for a moment, tempted to lie again. She changed her mind abruptly. *To hell with them*, she thought defiantly. *If Claudia and her pack of society vultures want to pick me apart at their next get-together, let them. I'm proud of who I am.* "That's not exactly true," she said finally. "My father doesn't own the vineyard. He works there. He picks the grapes when they're ready to be harvested. He works in the winery when he's needed."

Bradley and Claudia Hollister exchanged glances, but said nothing in response. Ashley could almost read their thoughts. *So much for getting their approval*, she thought as Brandon spoke up. "I think now is as good a time as any to tell you why I've brought Ashley here to meet you both," he said then. "We're getting married. She wanted to meet my parents—and hopefully, get your blessing."

"And what about you, Brandon?" Bradley Hollister asked, regaining his composure. "Do you also want our blessing?"

Brandon looked at his father. "It would be nice, but not really necessary as far as I'm concerned."

Ashley looked at him again, puzzled. To say that there was bad blood between Brandon and his parents was like saying World War II was a minor international incident! No wonder he hadn't wanted to come!

Before Brandon could respond, Mason, the Hollisters' butler, appeared in the doorway. "Dinner is served," he announced in a stiff, formal tone.

Must be fun working here, Ashley thought silently.

"Something smells great," Brandon commented as he and Ashley followed the Hollisters into the elegant formal dining room. "Wonder what it is?"

Ashley looked up at him and forced a smile, dropping her voice so that only he could hear. "Sacrificial lamb?" she whispered.

"Bradley, we simply cannot allow this marriage to take place." Claudia Hollister and her husband were alone in the library late that night, discussing their son's wedding plans. She had been ready to accept Ashley into the family with open arms—until the stupid girl so blatantly advertised her less than desirable background! "We have to put a stop to this madness of Brandon's right here and now!"

Bradley Hollister looked at his wife, amused. "You were sweet enough to send a diabetic into a coma until she told you her father picked grapes for a living. Why the sudden change of heart—as if I didn't know?"

Claudia turned on him in anger. "Are you trying to tell me, in your typically subtle way, that you approve of this marriage?" she demanded hotly.

Hollister looked up at her and responded in a calm voice. "No, of course not. She's hardly in Brandon's league," he conceded. "But we're hardly in a position to influence our son one way or the other. I think he made it clear the day he left us to make a life for himself in San Francisco that he wanted no interference from us whatsoever."

"So you're going to just sit back and let him make the biggest mistake of his life?" Claudia asked incredulously.

"I didn't say that. But for us to make any kind of open protest now would just push him right into her arms," Hollister reasoned. "It would be the worst move we could possibly make."

Claudia leaned forward, supporting herself on her hands, which she had placed firmly on his massive mahogany desk. Her heavy gold bracelets clattered as they slid down her wrist. "Just how do you suggest we handle it, then?" she demanded.

"They'll be here a few days. He has promised to stay for Christmas," Hollister reminded her. "I'll put in a few calls to some of my people out on the West Coast and see what we can find out about Ms. Ashley Gordon. Then we'll take it from there."

Claudia scowled at him. "And suppose your people don't find anything we can use? The girl does seem scrupulously honest . . . which, may I remind you, is hardly the kind of woman you need to have our son confiding your 'business' secrets to!"

"Relax, Claudia," he urged. "Have I ever failed to get the dirt on anyone before?"

She looked at him. "No," she said slowly. "But—"

"If they can't find anything, then we'll just have to come up with something on our own." Hollister paused, allowing a small smile to play on his lips. "Still, I can see why Brandon's so infatuated with her. She is a splendid-looking young woman. Someone like that could make a man lose his head."

Ashley lay awake, unable to will sleep to come even though she was bone-tired. She and Brandon had been in New York for three days and she had the feeling that his parents would stop at nothing to evict her from his life—permanently. Oh, they were pleasant enough to her. Cordial with an icy undertone, she thought dismally. Just looking Claudia Hollister in the eye gave her a sharp chill. She was beginning to wonder if it might not have been wiser for her to have kept her mouth shut, at least for now. It wasn't necessary to justify herself to the Hollisters. They didn't need to know where she came from or what her father did for a living. *It's none of their business*, she thought resentfully. *I'm marrying Brandon, not his whole family. He accepts me for what I am, and that's all that matters.*

She got out of bed and walked over to the windows. Staring up at the full moon that hung over the towering skyscrapers of Manhattan, she suddenly wished she had not come, had not talked Brandon into bringing her to meet his parents. *He isn't any happier here than I am*, she thought. *He didn't want to come. He only did it for me. And now we're both miserable.*

Ashley decided she could not tell Brandon how she felt, of the hostility that was being directed at her like a physical force, assaulting her nonstop. His parents had been careful to be most pleasant to her in his presence. It was obvious to Ashley that they did not want him to know, that they had not expressed their feelings about her or their marriage plans to him openly. To tell him would only make matters worse, she reasoned. He's angry enough with them now. *I have nothing to gain by driving the wedge between them even deeper, and it would only hurt him more. I have to get through the next few days. We'll be going home soon, and hopefully it'll be the last I'll see of them for a very long time.*

If I'm lucky.

"What the hell are you trying to pull, Dad?" Brandon demanded angrily, his eyes blazing as he faced his father squarely. They were in the library, and Bradley Hollister had insisted they talk privately, with the doors closed.

"Keep your voice down, son, or she'll hear you," Hollister urged in a hushed tone. "Everyone will hear you."

"I don't give a damn who hears me!" Brandon snapped. "You know, Dad, you've pulled some pretty low stunts in your time, but this has to be the worst thing you've ever done! You just couldn't leave it alone, could you?"

"Your mother and I only want what's best for you—" Hollister began.

"Sure you do! You've proven that time and time again, haven't you? Everything you've ever done was what was best for me. Your little empire—that was all created for me, wasn't it?"

"I had hoped you would take it all over one day, yes . . ."

"Now, that's what I call a truly concerned father!" Brandon's eyes rolled upward in disbelief. "Your idea of looking out for me—and now this!"

"This woman is nothing more than a tramp, son—"

"Don't 'son' me!" Brandon shouted, shaking his head furiously. "All you care about is keeping me from marrying Ashley or anyone else who might find out the truth about you and your 'business interests,' someone who might be honest enough to blow the lid on your operations. Well, you don't have to worry about that. I wouldn't tell Ashley or anyone else. I'd be ashamed to admit it to anyone, just as I'd be ashamed to tell Ashley what you're trying to pull right now."

"You can't deny that she's been rather . . . promiscuous . . ." Hollister started.

"I don't give a damn what she did with her life before I knew her," Brandon informed him coldly. "I know for a fact that she's been with no one but me since the night we met, and that's all I care about. I'll thank you to stay out of our private affairs." He started for the door, then stopped and turned to his father again. "We'll be leaving in the morning. I want to get married as quickly as possible—if Ashley'll still have me, now that she knows who her in-laws will be!"

He walked out, leaving Hollister with the realization he'd made a mistake.

True to his word, Brandon and Ashley were married immediately upon their return to San Francisco. He wanted to take her on an extended honeymoon, suggesting a Caribbean cruise, but Ashley insisted they stay home and just enjoy those magical days of being newlyweds. "We have to find a house," she told him in bed the night they were married. "We can't go on living here in my apartment."

"We could," he said, kissing her neck. "There's plenty of room for the two of us. Besides, I'd be happy living in a closet if it meant I'd be closer to you."

"If it were just the two of us, this apartment would be fine, but . . ." she began hesitantly.

He stopped what he was doing and looked at her. "But what?" he asked. "Is your mother moving in with us or something?"

"Not exactly." She paused. "I haven't been feeling very well lately, so I went to see Dr. Edwards before we went to New York. I've been waiting for the right time to tell you, and—"

"And what?" He was so heady with desire that it still wasn't sinking in.

She took a deep breath. "I'll just ask you what he asked me," she said finally. "Would you like a boy or a girl?"

He stared at her as though he'd been struck. "You're . . . you're . . ."

Ashley laughed. "The word is *pregnant*, darling, and yes, I am. Almost six weeks, according to Dr. Edwards."

"How?" he asked, stunned.

"The usual way, silly!" She kissed him playfully. "I hope you're happy about it."

His face broke into a grin. "Of course I'm happy about it!" he insisted. "I'm just surprised, that's all. I didn't have any idea . . ."

"Neither did I," she admitted. "I thought it was salmonella or something."

"But I thought—I mean, I just assumed that you were on the pill . . ."

"I can't take it," she said. "Some hormone problem. Even the low-dose ones made me feel awful. I use a diaphragm, but things happened so fast between us at Big

Sur—it was so unexpected—I forgot about it. Pretty dumb, huh?"

"Not dumb—wonderful," he insisted. "Big Sur . . . you think it happened at Big Sur?"

"I'm sure of it. It's the only time I ever forgot," she said with certainty.

Suddenly, he enveloped her in a bear hug and kissed her with renewed eagerness. "This is the best wedding present you could possibly have given me," he told her. "The very best . . ."

They bought a house on Nob Hill, a spacious old home with large, airy rooms and a solid construction Brandon insisted just didn't exist in most newer homes. It was in need of some repair and a paint job, but Ashley was thrilled at the prospect of supervising the needed work herself. *It's going to be fun to fix this place up and decorate it ourselves*, she thought as she roamed through the large, empty rooms. *When we're finished, it's going to be a real home. Our home.*

The seasons melted into one another. Winter became spring and spring became summer as Ashley's pregnancy became more and more obvious. They hired local workmen to come in and repair the leaky roof, the faulty plumbing, and the ancient, worn-out electrical wiring. From early in the morning until late in the evening, the house was filled with carpenters, painters, plumbers, and electricians. Brandon worried that Ashley was trying to do too much, that she was putting in too many hours, but she insisted she had never felt better. "I'm doing exactly what I want to be doing," she assured him. "I rest when I need it and I haven't missed a meal since we started." She patted her enlarging stomach and laughed. "Do I look undernourished to you?"

"Just make sure you follow Dr. Edwards's orders to the letter," he said firmly as he rested his hand on her swollen abdomen. The baby gave a sharp kick. "I want a healthy baby, and it would be nice if his mother were in good health too."

"Don't worry about me. I come from very strong stock," she said confidently. "Just promise me this house will be finished by the time our son is born."

He raised an eyebrow. "Our son?"

"Of course it will be a boy," she said with certainty. "A son . . . for you."

He kissed her gently. "I'd be just as happy with a little girl who would be the spitting image of her mother," he told her.

"Maybe, but this baby is a boy."

Ashley refused to even consider hiring a professional decorator. She was an artist, and this house was going to reflect her own style, the personal preferences of herself and her husband. She selected the wallpaper, taking great care in the choice of each pattern and color. She haunted the local antique shops and picked up wonderful and unique pieces at auctions and estate sales. For the kitchen, she chose hand-painted ceramic tiles in deep colors and a restaurant-model refrigerator with large doors of unbreakable glass, and a black, restaurant-style stove that Brandon described as "ugly" but did not strongly object to after Ashley pointed out how practical and functional it would be. "I'm Italian, darling," she reminded him. "Most Italian women love to cook." She did not have to remind him that she was an excellent cook. The countertops, at her insistence, were made of butcher block, and in one corner she installed a Lucite stepladder that was to be adorned with the green plants she adored.

She insisted that the walls in Brandon's den be covered not with wallpaper, but with dove gray corduroy for a warm feeling. She bought him a large antique desk from England and had floor-to-ceiling bookshelves built in. She found a wonderful old globe on an intricately carved stand at another estate sale, as well as her silver, china, crystal, and table linens, buying them all for a fraction of what they would have cost originally. Three of the walls in the enormous living room were covered in white silk, and the third became a giant canvas on which Ashley painted a magnificent mural from slides she'd brought back from that fateful weekend in Big Sur. The couch and chairs, treasures she'd found at an auction, were recovered in rich fabrics in shades of gray and mauve. She found an antique crib and matching chest of drawers for the nursery, and decorated the room in delicate shades of blue, pink, and yellow. "Just in case," she told Brandon when he saw it for the first time. "Later, when he's older, we can have it redone."

The rooms she spent the most time on were the master bedroom and her studio. For the studio, she chose one of the larger bedrooms, one in which she would have the morning sun, since she did most of her work early in the morning. She had it painted stark white and the hardwood floors refinished. For a worktable, she selected a large, antique oak drawing table with drawers in which she could store her paints, palette, and brushes. A second easel was added next to the one on which she usually worked, holding a large white board she used for projecting the images from the slides she took of landscapes, seascapes, or other scenes she wanted to paint. In one corner she installed a large, sixteen-drawer apothecary cabinet in which she would store additional supplies—pencils, inks, paints, and the like. She bought a large table to be used for framing her work, a mat cutter, screen printing equipment, and an eighteen-drawer flat cabinet for storing mat boards, paper, and finished prints. The walk-in closet was filled with framing supplies and, on one side, a rack for finished paintings. *The studio I always wanted*, she thought with satisfaction as she surveyed the finished room.

For the master bedroom, she elected to paint the walls herself, using the colors of the sea: the blues and greens of the water, the pinks and beiges of the sand and the seashells. She bought a king-size brass bed and white wicker furniture and had a plush comforter and shams custom-made in fabric reflecting the colors of the walls. She also had the pale blue-green silk drapes custom-made, with matching fabric on the cushions on the wicker chair at her dressing table and the stool she kept in one corner of the room. The walls in the adjoining bath were covered with large mirrors and all the faucets replaced with brass ones. *This house is us*, Ashley thought happily as she walked through each of the finished rooms.

They moved into the house in mid-July. Though Ashley never admitted it to Brandon, she was glad it was over, that the house was finished at last, for her energy had begun to wane in recent weeks. It seemed to her that her body's natural rhythm had begun to slow down, most of her once abundant energy being channeled into the new life she had created and nourished in her womb. Sometimes she would wake in the middle of the night and lay on her back with her hands on her bulging belly, taking joy in the movements of the baby inside her, eagerly awaiting his arrival.

Soon, she thought happily. *Very soon now.*

She went into labor late in the afternoon on a Friday in early August. At first she did not realize what was happening, in spite of all the books she had read and the Lamaze classes she and Brandon had taken. The pains were erratic and concentrated in her lower back. They felt like mild cramps. She became increasingly restless and nervous, and after an hour or so, she began to time the pains. They were twelve minutes apart. She kept timing them. *This is it*, she thought. When they were ten minutes apart, she phoned Dr. Edwards. "I'll meet you at the hospital," he told her. Then she tried to reach Brandon. He was in a meeting. "This is Ashley," she told his secretary. "Please tell Brandon to meet me at Bay Memorial Hospital."

She drove herself to the hospital in spite of the promise she'd made to Brandon weeks earlier that she would take a taxi if she went into labor when he was not home. She pulled over to the side of the road when the pains became too sharp. When she finally arrived at the hospital, an attendant was waiting outside for her. She was immediately taken to the labor room, where Dr. Edwards joined her. She was lying on her back in bed when he entered, wearing a green surgical scrub suit. "How do you feel, Mrs. Hollister?" he asked pleasantly.

"Like a beached whale," Ashley replied, breathless from the last wave of pain. Each contraction was getting stronger. "How long do you think it's going to take?"

"I'll have a better idea after the examination," he told her. Assisted by an obstetrical nurse, he did a quick pelvic exam.

"Well?" Ashley asked anxiously.

"Not long," he promised. "I think we'll be going to the delivery room very soon now."

"Not until my husband gets here!"

He smiled patiently. "I'm afraid these things just don't wait, Mrs. Hollister," he told her. "If he's not here by the time we take you to delivery, one of the nurses will see that he joins us when he does arrive."

At that moment, the door opened and Brandon entered, rushing to her side. "I came as soon as Beverly told me," he said, taking her hand. "How do you feel?"

"I've changed my mind," she said lightly. "Let's send it back."

Brandon stayed with her until Dr. Edwards determined that she was ready to deliver, then followed a nurse to a room where he was given instructions to scrub up and get into one of the traditional green surgical suits. The next time he saw Ashley, it was in the small, antiseptic delivery room. Even in her condition, wracked and contorted with pain, her face and hair damp with perspiration, she was beautiful. He held her hand and wiped her face with a damp cloth and talked to her in a soothing voice as he attempted to assist her during labor. After seeing what she had to go through, he decided he wouldn't blame her if she never wanted any more children. *It's true*, he thought. *Women can endure so very much more than a man ever could.* He lowered his face to hers. "I love you," he whispered.

"I love you, too," she gasped. "You know, this is a hell of a lot harder than conception was."

He rolled his eyes upward. How very like her the comment was.

He looked up at the clock as Dr. Edwards urged Ashley to give that final push. Nine-thirty in the evening. She had been in labor almost eight hours. Now it was almost over. The long months of waiting were almost over.

His thoughts were interrupted by a thin squeal. He looked down at the other end of the table. Dr. Edwards was holding up the baby, red and covered with his mother's blood. "Outdoor plumbing," the obstetrician declared. "You have a son."

Brandon looked down at Ashley. Her face was glowing.

Marrakesh, August 1982

At first glance, one might think the Djemaa El Fna, the heart of traditional Marrakesh, is merely a tourist domain, jammed with numerous taxis and rickety souvenir stands. To be sure, there are plenty of tourists to be found there— both foreign and Moroccan—but they pour into the square along with the locals for one purpose: to enjoy this open-air entertainment center. In the course of a single afternoon, one might buy native clothing, have a meal of Moroccan specialties, hear a Moslem holy man deliver a passionate sermon, see a man swallow fire or drink boiling water, have his or her fortune told, or try one's luck at a nearby shooting gallery. In all but the chilliest months, a troup of colorfully dressed Gnawa dancers are around, ready to go into action at the approach of any prosperous-looking man or woman.

Collin Deverell, dressed in gray pants and a pale blue shirt, the gold medallion he always wore glistening in the dying sunlight, picked his way through the crowd, pausing for a moment to watch as a middle-aged man—a tourist, no doubt—tested his bowling skills by attempting to knock over a number of packs of cigarettes at the end of a chalk line drawn on the tarmac. The man roared with laughter when every pack toppled over and he was given his prize—a pack of cigarettes. Collin shook his head and walked on, only halfheartedly aware of the human circus around him, with its variety of mystics, native musicians, street-corner orators, and peddlers. His mind was on other things.

As he walked back to his hotel, the Hotel des Almoravides on Djenan Lakhdar, he was lost in thought. It had taken him almost three years to locate each of his stolen paintings and the jewels that had belonged to his mother, but he had done it, thanks largely to the list of names DeVries had given him, names of those parties who had supposedly purchased his property legitimately. His journey to recover them would begin here, in Morocco, in Marrakesh. The Renoir was here, in the possession of a man named William Harrington. *But not for long*, Collin promised himself. He would do whatever was necessary to recover each painting, every piece of jewelry. And once it was done, he would decide what to do about Justin.

Justin. He still found it difficult to believe that his brother could possibly sink so low, that he could have resorted to stealing those things that meant everything to Collin to save the company. What was even harder to believe was that Justin could literally have sold his soul to hold on to Intercontinental Oil. Collin had always known that his twin brother was ambitious, but he had not realized just how ambitious until now. In the course of Collin's search for answers, for information that would lead him to his stolen property, he had uncovered information that was so shocking he was still finding it difficult to believe. Justin's larceny had only been the beginning, and he had not acted alone. It seemed that while Collin was in Europe, the situation at Intercontinental Oil had quickly worsened. Justin, far from the businessman Collin had once thought him to be, had apparently gotten in over his head. He had secured financial assistance from the worst possible sources, men who were rich and powerful through crime syndicate connections. He had allowed them to buy into the company, and now they were taking over, bleeding it of its remaining assets. Through the underground, that network of reliable sources of information concerning criminal activity in New York, Chicago, and other major cities, Collin had been able to determine that the syndicate had plans for Intercontinental Oil—and for his brother. Collin told himself he did not care what happened to the company, and that Justin had made his proverbial bed and had to lie in it, but a part of him still felt that he had somehow let his father down. *When will the ghosts ever stop haunting me*? he asked himself.

He reached into his pocket and took out a slip of paper, unfolding it and reading it yet again. On it was an address. He had located the elusive William Harrington, but finding him was only the beginning. Once found, he had to determine a way to get to the man, to get his painting back. The journey ahead of him was a long one, he realized now.

Long . . . and very dangerous.

The next morning, Collin had breakfast at a small sidewalk café in the medina, a traditional Moroccan breakfast of mint tea, toasted bread, and a handful of olives. He was too nervous, too preoccupied to give much thought to food. He had to come up with a plan to get the Renoir back, and do it as quickly as possible. Harrington was not going to surrender the painting to him on demand, of that he was certain. And if the man found out he was in Marrakesh, he would be on his guard. No, Collin had arrived in Morocco three days earlier knowing that the only way he was going to get his property back was to get it the same way Justin had—by stealing it. But how? he asked himself. He was a lot of things, but he had never been a thief. He had never stolen anything in his life and he was not sure how to go about it now.

He looked up as a large crowd made its way through the narrow streets outside the café, remembering now that he had arrived in Marrakesh at the time of the Moussem of

Sitti Fatma, a colorful festival held annually in honor of a local saint. The city had turned into a gathering of thousands setting up camp at a place believed to be holy and filling the streets with almost nonstop shows featuring dancers, jugglers, acrobats, and storytellers. A fantasia, it was called by the locals. Though non-Moslems were not permitted to approach the saint's tomb, everyone was welcome to participate in the endless merrymaking. Collin did not feel festive at the moment, or he might have enjoyed it tremendously. For a man who had traveled the world in search of fun, of excitement, it would have seemed a most promising opportunity, but now, all he could think about was getting back that which already belonged to him.

He signaled the waiter. "How much?" he asked in Arabic as he pointed to his plate.

The young waiter smiled and rattled off a price in rapid Arabic. Collin stared at him for a moment, then pulled out some dirhams and gave them to the young man. "Keep the change," he said, fumbling for the correct Arabic phrase.

The young man looked at the coins, then grinned broadly, nodding and expressing gratitude in words Collin could not understand. He could only guess their meaning by the expression on the waiter's face. *What did I do—give him a twenty-dollar tip*? he wondered as the waiter walked away.

By early afternoon, Collin was standing outside the walls surrounding Harrington's magnificent villa on the outskirts of the city. *It's a goddamned fortress*, he thought dismally as he peered through the heavy iron gates, watching the armed guards patrol the grounds as dogs—half a dozen vicious-looking Dobermans—were turned loose inside the high walls. Harrington must have been afraid that U.S. agents would come looking for him here. William Harrington had, until his retirement four years ago, been one of the more ruthless and powerful members of organized crime. It was said that he had been involved in some international arms deals that had attracted more than a little attention from the Justice Department. When the evidence against him began to accumulate and he realized there was no one working on the case who could be bought with syndicate "blood money," he had supposedly fled here, to Morocco, where he could avoid extradition. *The bastard's not taking any chances*, Collin thought ruefully. *Damn—if only I were not so stupid as to come here without a definite plan in mind.*

He had no idea at this point how he could possibly gain access to the Harrington stronghold.

The solution to his problem came to him unexpectedly that evening at the casino set in the gardens by the luxurious Mamounia Hotel. He decided to immerse himself in Marrakesh nightlife on the outside chance that he might meet someone who knew William Harrington or knew of a way he could make a contact inside the walls of the mansion, someone who could unwittingly provide him with the information he needed to develop some kind of plan, a course of action. He had not counted on meeting Harrington's own daughter at one of those exotic Moroccan nightspots, or on the fact that she would be so intensely attracted to him.

Samantha Harrington was twenty-two, tall and blond with a stunning figure and a shy, unassuming manner. She was breathtakingly beautiful and unbelievably naive. *What's she doing in a place like this?* Collin wondered. *She can't be his daughter*, he thought, amused, as they talked over a drink at his hotel. *He probably stole her as a baby from one of his victims. God, she doesn't even look like the son of a bitch!* As they talked, as she looked at him with obvious longing in her immense blue eyes, a plan began to take form in Collin's mind. Samantha was the key to Harrington's villa. Make her fall for him, take her as his lover, and he already had his foot in the gate! *I can think of more painful ways to get inside*, he thought as he asked Samantha if he could see her again. "I have a feeling that Fate meant for our paths to cross, *chérie*," he said as he reached across the table and took her hand.

She smiled demurely. "Do you really believe in Fate?"

His eyes met hers. "I do now," he answered truthfully.

* * *

Samantha Harrington, Collin decided, must have led a sheltered life in Morocco. She must have led a sheltered life in New York, for that matter. She lacked the worldliness, the coldness that was so much a part of the man who had once been a powerful part of the syndicate. She seemed to Collin to be as far removed from William Harrington's world as anyone could possibly be. She was quiet and unpretentious, almost old-fashioned. A child-woman who obviously had had little experience with men. *The men she met were probably afraid to touch her*, Collin thought wryly. *Harrington would chop their balls off and throw them to the jackals.*

Collin saw Samantha every day. They always met in town, sometimes for lunch but often early in the morning, and were together until late at night. She never asked him to take her home or call for her there. She was always brought into town by Harrington's driver, and the car was always waiting to take her home at night. Collin finally decided the only way he was going to get her to take him to her home was to lead her to believe that he was serious about her and their relationship. To do that, he reasoned, he would have to convince her he was falling in love with her. *No time like the present*, he thought as he waited for her at their usual meeting place.

He spotted her as soon as she emerged from the car, tall and bronzed, her long golden hair swinging about her shoulders as she walked across the street to the little sidewalk café where he was waiting. She wore navy blue linen slacks, a sheer white blouse, and a heavy silver choker around her neck. *She is beautiful*, Collin thought as he got to his feet. *Too bad she has a monster for a father.* "Good morning, *chérie*," he greeted her, taking her hand. He bowed slightly, pressing her hand to his lips.

She smiled, and he saw the color come to her cheeks, then fade away instantly. "Good morning, Collin," she said in her familiar low, soft voice. "I'm sorry I'm late. Have you been waiting long?"

He shook his head. "You are well worth the wait as far as I'm concerned," he assured her, smiling warmly.

"You're too sweet," she said, embarrassed by his flattery. "I'm afraid I overslept. It was almost three when I finally got home last night."

"I hope I didn't get you into any trouble," Collin said carefully. The last thing he needed now was to arouse Harrington's anger—or his suspicion.

Samantha shook her head. "No. My father's away right now. He'll be in Tangier for the next week or so."

Collin looked at her, trying to conceal his surprise. This was an unexpected bonus. Harrington away from the stronghold, his daughter making herself available to Collin whenever he wanted to see her . . . it could not have worked out better if Collin had planned it that way. "Good," he said finally. "I'm glad. And I'm especially glad that your father's going to be away for a while. That will give us more time together."

She giggled. "How could we possibly spend any more time together than we do now?"

His eyes met hers. "There is one way . . ."

The sun was setting when Collin took Samantha back to his room at the Hotel des Almoravides. She had been hesitant at first, but Collin had used all of his charm to persuade her that it was only right that they make love. "How can I show you how I feel about you if you won't let me make love to you?" he had asked as he kissed her longingly in the shadow of the Koutoubia mosque's minaret. He had kept kissing her until her doubts and concerns began to dissolve in the heat of her awakened passion.

Now, alone in the hotel room, he took her in his arms and kissed her again. "Don't be afraid," he whispered as he stroked her hair. "It's going to be wonderful, you'll see."

"I love you, Collin, but—" she stammered nervously.

"But what?" He started kissing her neck.

She hesitated for a moment. "I've never done this before," she said finally. "I've never been with a man before."

Collin was not surprised. Harrington probably guarded

his daughter even more closely than he guarded his stolen treasures. Or tried to anyway. "I'll be gentle, Sam, I promise," he told her as he fingered the small buttons on her blouse. "I won't do anything you don't want me to do, all right?" Slowly, he unbuttoned the blouse and pushed the fabric away from her breasts. Then he unhooked the front of her lacy bra and cupped one of her breasts in his hand. "Beautiful," he whispered as he caressed it gently, his lips coming down on hers again. She was trembling. "Relax," he whispered as he scooped her up in his arms and carried her over to the bed. He finished undressing her slowly, whispering endearments as he stroked her flesh tenderly. He shed his own clothes much more quickly, then lay down beside her, taking her in his arms. He held her, caressing every inch of her body as he kissed her repeatedly. She really was beautiful, he thought as he felt himself growing hard with desire. "Relax, *chérie*," he urged in a low voice as he ran his fingers lightly over her breasts, making tiny circles around her nipples with his thumb. He lowered his head to her left breast and took the nipple into his mouth. He sucked gently at first, taking time to arouse her, then more forcefully, drawing the nipple up to a wet little point. He moved to the other breast as he insinuated one hand between her legs and began to stroke her there. She clamped her thighs together involuntarily, but he pried them apart gently and continued to fondle her. He could feel a dampness there, but knew she was not ready yet. "Let me kiss you there," he whispered as his fingers continued to touch and excite her.

She shook her head violently.

"Just once, baby," he urged gently. "If you don't like it, then I'll stop. Promise." Without waiting for her answer, he slid down on the bed until his face was directly above the mound of soft golden hair covering her pubis. Parting the seashell pink lips with his fingers, he lowered his face to her and kissed her. Then again and again. Finally, when he was convinced she was ready, he began licking her, nibbling at her lightly with his lips, careful not to use his teeth.

He could feel her trembling as he continued to lick at her, though he was not sure if she was trembling out of fear or out of excitement. She did not try to stop him, so he persisted until she began to squirm at his touch. He held her down as she writhed against his insistent mouth, finally bringing her to a sharp orgasm, not stopping until her back arched and she cried out in release.

His own body was throbbing with desire, but Collin sensed she was not ready to be taken, not yet. He stretched out beside her and slid his right hand between her legs. She jerked away at first, but he held her close, whispering his declarations of love as he put one, then two fingers up inside her. He rotated his fingers slowly, all the while urging her to relax. "Feel it," he whispered as he guided her hand down to his erect penis. "I want to put it in you. Now."

"Not yet," she begged.

"It will hurt a bit, but only for a minute," he promised. "Easy, baby . . . let me give you my love." He eased himself on top of her, pinning her down to the bed as he entered her, slowly, patiently. She cried out, but Collin stroked her hair and kissed her again and again. "Relax," he urged. "Just lie back and let me love you . . ." He began to move inside her, deeper, faster, feeling his own excitement growing until he finally exploded inside her. He fell limp on top of her, lying there until his breathing returned to normal.

"Are you all right?" he asked finally.

Samantha nodded, smiling contentedly. "I'm glad it happened, darling," she said softly. "I wanted to make love for so long—from the night we met—but I had never done it before and I wasn't sure . . ."

He pulled himself up on his elbows and looked down at her in the darkness. "It's sometimes difficult the first time, but it gets better. It's going to be wonderful. You'll see," he assured her.

She looked up at him, and her eyes were bright, shining. "I'm sure it will," she said, fingering the medallion around his neck. "You are so very patient . . ."

You have no idea, he thought.

* * *

Collin did not like having to use Samantha to gain access to her father's fortress. Samantha was young and vulnerable and she was in love with him. He hated what he had had to do to her, but there had been no other way. She was the only means available to him to regain what was his. He tried to justify his actions by reminding himself that Harrington had taken something that belonged to him, so it was right that he take what was Harrington's. *But she's not a painting or a piece of jewelry*, he thought dismally. *She's a living, breathing human being. A warm, sensitive young woman who's being used—and when she finds out, it could destroy her.*

He had not entered into this wanting to hurt anyone. He had only wanted what was rightfully his. *But now I'm no better than they are*, he thought. But he did not stop, did not consider turning back. He had come too far to let his conscience stop him. He continued to see Samantha, continued to let her believe he was in love with her. Samantha had quickly overcome the fears she had experienced the first time he took her to bed, and was now not only willing but eager to make love. Whether they were having dinner at the best restaurant in town or prowling through the souks or enjoying Marrakesh's nightlife, Collin knew that he had only to look at her in that special, private way to get her to go back to the hotel with him. He knew that he could have her now, any place and any way he wanted her. He exerted his sexual influence over her by taking risks only a madman would take: leading her into dark alleys or other secluded spots where he would slip his hand under her top and fondle her breasts, or open her blouse just enough to enable him to suck hastily at her nipples for a few minutes, or put his hand between her legs and stroke her until she was wet with longing. Just enough to make her hungry for more. He possessed her body and her soul, and he knew it was only a matter of time before Samantha would enable him to get past her father's goons and into the villa.

Time was running out, he reminded himself. Harrington was still in Tangier but would be returning soon. Collin had to get into the villa and get the Renoir before Harrington returned.

It happened unexpectedly. Samantha phoned him at the hotel early one morning to tell him the car had broken down and their driver would not be able to bring her into town. Collin was pleased: this was the opportunity he had been waiting for. "Why don't I come and get you?" he suggested, keeping his tone casual.

"I don't know . . ." she began, uncertain.

What was she worried about? Collin wondered. Her father was still in Tangier. "You *do* want to be with me, don't you, darling?" he asked, letting her know he was concerned by the tone of his voice.

"Of course! But—" She hesitated for a moment. "All right. I'll inform the guard at the front gate. Come up to the main house. I'll be waiting for you there."

"I'll be there in an hour," he promised.

His mind was racing as he drove to the Harrington villa. Once inside the house, he had to locate the painting. Then he had to find a way to get it out without letting her know what he was up to, without tipping off the guards. He thought of the dogs that guarded the grounds. *They'd rip me to shreds*, he realized dismally. Again, he cursed himself for not having come here with a definite plan in mind, for not having thought things through more carefully.

When he arrived, he was admitted by a uniformed guard at the gate who informed him that he was indeed expected and should go straight to the villa. As he drove up the long paved driveway, he looked up at the magnificent Mediterranean-style villa. It had to have at least forty rooms. *It could take all day to find a painting in this place*, he thought. *And then it would be easy to get lost.* He parked the car and went to the front door. A Moroccan houseboy let him in and escorted him to the library, where he was told to wait. Collin smiled to himself. Samantha was probably still trying to decide what to wear. Her enthusiasm for a new dress or a pair of shoes was almost childlike. He didn't mind waiting. *It'll give me time to think, to come up with a plan*, he told himself.

The door behind him opened. "So, *chérie*, you're finally ready—" As Collin turned, he stopped short, realizing he was facing not Samantha but her father, the notorious William Harrington. He was taller than Collin had imagined, with a full head of white hair and a stern, hawklike face.

"Good morning," Harrington said coldly. "I'm afraid my daughter won't be joining you today. You see, she's just left for Paris."

"She didn't mention it on the phone—" Collin began.

"She didn't know about it until half an hour ago, when I insisted she go." Harrington seated himself at his great leather-topped antique desk. "I know all about your relationship with my daughter . . . and I do *not* approve."

"Samantha's old enough to make up her own mind—"

"You can drop the charade," Harrington cut him off harshly. "I know who you are and why you're here, Mr. Deverell. I know that you've been using my daughter to get into my home. But you came here for nothing. I paid a very large price for the Renoir—and I have every intention of keeping it."

"It belongs to me!" Collin raged. "It was stolen!"

"Not according to the bill of sale," Harrington countered.

"A forgery!" Collin snapped.

"One that will hold up in any court of law," Harrington reminded him blandly.

"I don't think you'll get within fifty miles of any court of law anywhere, Harrington," Collin challenged.

"I won't have to," Harrington told him. "You see, Mr. Deverell, my people have been watching you from the moment you arrived in Marrakesh. My eyes and ears are everywhere. I know that you took advantage of my daughter, that you seduced her and used her to get what you wanted. For that alone I am more than willing to kill you."

It was at that moment that Collin was struck by the sudden, mind-smashing certainty that that was exactly what

Harrington intended to do. He lunged forward almost involuntarily, only to be stopped by Harrington's bodyguard, a mountain of a man who slammed him to the floor with one hand. As he struggled to his feet, he was grabbed by two other men. The first advanced on him as he struggled to break free from the other two. The monster drew back and smashed a fist into his stomach. Collin doubled over, his eyes rolling back into his head. The men released him as he fell to the floor, unconscious, barely breathing.

The huge man turned to William Harrington. "What do you want us to do with him, boss?" he asked.

"Dispose of him," Harrington said coldly. "But not too quickly. I want his death to be as slow and painful as possible."

Collin opened his eyes slowly. At first he didn't know where he was. *So this is what hell is like*, he thought, dazed. He tried to pull himself up, but his right arm would not support his weight. *It's broken*, he thought as it gave way under him. *The sons of bitches broke my arm*. Squinting, he looked up at the white-hot sun. Hot . . . unbearably hot, he thought, his mind clouded by pain. He could feel sand beneath him. He was out in the desert, of that much he was certain. He tried to crawl, using only his left arm to drag himself forward, but his body felt incredibly heavy. He tried to look around, to get some idea of exactly where he was, but his eyes refused to focus and he had a throbbing headache. His throat felt dry, as though he'd swallowed a ball of cotton. He had no idea how long he'd been lying there, but there was no doubt in his mind as to how he had gotten to where he was: Harrington's goons had brought him. Harrington wanted him dead, and it looked as though he might get his wish.

Collin looked up at the sky again. Even though his vision was blurred, he could see large birds circling overhead. Vultures—or was it just a hallucination? Watching and waiting. The sight filled Collin with rage—and with a fresh determination to survive. *You might win, you bastard*, he thought angrily. *I might not get off this goddamned desert alive. But if I do,*

I'm making you a promise now. I'll get you and all the others. Including my dear brother. I'll get you if it's the last thing I do.

And then he lost consciousness again.

Ouarzazate, Morocco, September 1982

Collin could feel himself drifting in and out of a dreamlike state, never fully regaining consciousness. He was only dimly aware of the fact that he was no longer lying on sand. There was no heat, no broiling sun, no blinding light. Only a cool, comforting darkness. He had the vague feeling that he was floating on a cloud of soft, refreshingly cool silk. From time to time he felt something cold and wet against his face, something he could not identify. His mind was dazed, his body numb. He had no idea where he was or how long he had been there. *Am I dead?* he wondered before drifting off into the darkness again.

When the fog finally lifted and he became fully conscious, he found himself in unfamiliar surroundings. He was in a bed, in a small, bare, dimly lit room, and he was alone. He tried to sit up but found he was unable to move. His right arm was in a cast, but he felt no pain. His head felt heavy. With his left hand, he reached up and touched his temple gingerly. His head was bandaged. *How did I get here?* he wondered again. Who had brought him here? Who bandaged his wounds and set his broken arm? How had he survived out there on the desert? He knew the answer to that one: he had survived by sheer will. He could not die—would not die—because he still had a score to settle. Unfinished business that could not be left to chance alone. He had to take his vengeance against the man who had stolen from him, tried to kill him.

The door opened at that moment and a man entered, a tall, dark man who looked to be in his late fifties or early sixties, possibly not Moroccan but definitely of Arab heritage, with strong, sharp features. His hair—what Collin could see of it beneath his turban—was black and very curly, just beginning to be flecked with gray, and his complexion was swarthy. He was dressed in the traditional loose-fitting cotton robe, and he carried a large silver basin filled with water, which he placed on the small table beside the bed. Collin tried to speak, but his lips and tongue would not obey his brain, and he strangled on his own words. The man took a glass of water and held it to Collin's lips, offering him a drink. Collin sipped slowly, then attempted to speak again, this time managing to thank the man in phrase-book Arabic.

The man looked at him, and his black eyes twinkled with amusement. "I speak English," he said with a heavy accent.

Collin stared at him for a moment. "How . . . how did I get here?" he asked finally.

"I brought you here." He took a damp cloth from the basin, wrung it out, and wiped Collin's face.

"How long have I been here?" Collin wanted to know.

"Almost two weeks," the man said quietly. "You have been asleep for a very long time. You would perhaps like something to eat?"

Collin nodded, suddenly realizing he was very hungry.

"I will attend to it. It will not take long." He started to rise from the chair, but Collin reached out and grabbed his arm.

"Wait!" he said urgently. "You have to tell me—"

The man smiled patiently. "You are in no condition to talk now," he said firmly. "Later, when you have regained your strength, I will answer all of your questions. For now, you must rest and concentrate on your recovery. We have a long road ahead of us, my friend. A most dangerous one. You will need all of your strength and courage to see you through the days ahead." He got up and walked to the door. "I will return shortly. Do not try to get out of bed.

You are not ready yet.'' He left the room, closing the door behind him.

Collin stared at the door for a long time, thinking. *We have a long road ahead of us.* That was what he had said. *We.* The man had saved his life, was nursing him back to health. Why? Collin wondered.

What could he possibly want from me?

"You are a survivor,'' the man noted with approval in his voice as Collin ate a hearty meal. A week had passed since he regained consciousness, and his strength was returning more and more with each passing day. "It is a good sign.''

"A good sign for what?'' Collin stopped eating and faced him squarely. "In the past week you've made frequent references to the difficult task ahead of us and all that we must do, and I don't even know who you are or why you saved my life!''

"You are most impatient,'' he observed. "A trait you will have to learn to curb in the weeks ahead. To answer your questions, my name is not important. You probably could not pronounce it anyway. You may call me Blackjack. As for my reasons for collecting you from the desert, you could call it concern for a fellow human being.''

"But there's more to it than that, isn't there?'' Collin concluded.

Blackjack hesitated for a moment. "Yes, there is,'' he said finally. "A great deal more.''

Collin nodded slowly, taking a bite of the grilled *kefta* his host had prepared for him. It was made of ground meat with savory spices, including chili peppers, and was hot and delicious. "Well,'' he said carefully, "if I owe anybody, it's you. How can I repay the debt?''

"By doing what you set out to do when you came to Morocco.''

Collin looked at him in frank amazement. "You know about that?'' he asked, putting down the skewer of meat.

Blackjack nodded. "I know who you are and why you came here, and why the man called Harrington wanted you dead,'' he said bluntly. "I have been watching you, almost since you arrived. I saw them take you from his villa. I followed them out to the desert, and when I was certain that they had gone, that I would not be seen, I took you away. And brought you here.''

"Why?'' Collin demanded, stunned by the man's revelation. "Why should you care if I get my painting back from Harrington or not?''

The man smiled. "You are not the only one with a score to settle,'' he said quietly. "I, too, have an ax to grind, as you Americans put it. A score to settle against Harrington and his kind.''

"Why do you need me to do that?'' Collin asked.

"It is not only that I need you—we need each other,'' he corrected. "You are young and very determined. Courageous but foolish. I am too old to fight the battle that must be fought, but I have the knowledge and the skills to give you the edge you will need to win our battle.''

"I don't get it.''

"You will,'' Blackjack promised him. "You see, Collin, there is only one way to beat men like this William Harrington, and that is to beat them at their own game.''

"Their own game?'' Collin wasn't sure he understood.

"They are thieves. They operate above the law,'' Blackjack reasoned. "To stand any chance of winning against them, you must also become a thief. You must learn to operate above the law, as they do.''

Collin shook his head emphatically. "But I don't know how—'' Blackjack held up a hand to silence him. "I, my friend, will show you how,'' he promised.

Though Blackjack spoke little of himself and his reasons for wanting vengeance against Harrington in the weeks that followed, Collin was able to determine from what little the man had said that Blackjack had once been a very successful thief himself, stealing paintings and other valuables, working in a partnership with one of Harrington's underlings. At some point, he had been cheated out of a great deal of money and went to prison after being framed by Harrington and his goons. By the time he was released from prison, he was too old to return to the only life he had ever known, and Harrington's people, dealing in the white-slave trade in Morocco, had sold his fifteen-year-old daughter to a brothel in Tangier. Blackjack had originally wanted to kill Harrington, but he found it impossible to get near the man. For years he had been watching and waiting, hoping to make connections with someone who hated the man as much as he did, someone who had been burned by Harrington as he had. He had said that he knew he'd found that person when Collin arrived in Marrakesh. "I suppose I should not feel as I do," Blackjack told him as they talked one night in front of a roaring fire in the main room of Blackjack's house, "but I was pleased when you took his daughter as you did. It made me think of my daughter, and I felt as though she had been avenged."

Collin stared into the fire, his eyes half closed. "I'm not proud of the way I used Samantha," he said quietly. "It's not her fault, the things her father's done. To be perfectly honest, I don't think she even knows what kind of man he is."

"But the sins of the father are visited upon the sons— and the daughters," Blackjack reasoned.

"Maybe," Collin said with a nod, "but that doesn't make it fair, does it?" He got to his feet, prowling the room like a caged animal. He was thinking not of Samantha, but of himself and his brother, growing apart because they had had to pay for their father's mistakes.

Blackjack looked at him. "You are now an amateur playing a professional's game, Collin. You must learn to think with your head and not your heart if you hope to survive in our world," he warned. "There is no place for a conscience in this business."

Our world. Collin drew in his breath. Was it his world, really? Could he become the man he would have to become in order to accomplish his goal? Not his goal, *their* goal. Blackjack, the man who had rescued him from an almost certain death out there on the Sahara and brought him here to Ouarzazate, on the desert's edge, looking after him as he recovered from the ordeal, had an even more powerful motive for seeking revenge than he did. Collin thought of Blackjack's daughter, an innocent teen-age girl sold into prostitution by those bastards. Blackjack had looked for her when he was finally released from prison, but his efforts to find her had been in vain. He told Collin that he discovered she had been sold to a wealthy Frenchman and no one at the brothel knew where the man had taken her. And if they did, they weren't talking. Collin shook his head. He thought of the long, difficult journey that had brought him here, the quest that had nearly cost him his life. He thought of his father and mother and the senselessness of their deaths, and of Justin, obsessed and ultimately corrupted by power, and he realized he would never find peace within himself unless he finished what he'd set out to do. He turned to Blackjack.

"When do we start?"

"The most important thing to remember, the one thing you must never forget, is that there is no margin for error here," Blackjack told Collin. "One mistake can be your last."

Collin felt as though he were in training for the Olympics. They worked from dawn until dusk every day, seven days a week, keeping up a Spartan regimen that even a superbly conditioned athlete like Collin found difficult. He learned how to disconnect a burglar alarm and crack a safe. He mastered the various methods for breaking and entering. He learned forgery and memorized the various types of security systems. Blackjack showed him how to use a scaling ladder and string a cable which would enable him to gain access to high-rise offices and apartments. Blackjack was a tough, demanding instructor who insisted Collin repeat each maneuver until he could do it swiftly and precisely, and in Collin he discovered a most promising pupil who was quick-witted, agile, and fearless.

After dinner each evening, they talked for hours about what they had done that day and what they would be covering the next day. Blackjack taught Collin everything he knew, and Collin learned a great deal more. His athletic ability and perfect balance and coordination made him a natural as a cat burglar, and his imagination and daring showed the promise of a truly gifted con artist. "You have both the ability and the motivation, Collin," Blackjack told him. "You can do it. You are the man who will beat the masters at their own game." Collin would often lie awake at night, thinking about how far he had come and how far he had yet to go. When he came to Morocco, he'd made the mistake of coming without a definite plan in mind. He had underestimated Harrington, an error in judgment he would never make again.

The dummy was hanging from the rafters in the small, dilapidated shed at the back of the house. There was no electricity there, but plenty of light streamed in from every direction through the wide gaps between the boards of the shed. Collin studied the dummy. It wore a suit with ten pockets, and a bell was attached to each pocket. "The pockets are filled with money and jewelry," Blackjack explained. "The trick is to empty all ten pockets without ringing any of the bells."

Holy shit, Collin thought. Aloud he asked, "I'm going to be picking pockets?"

"Possibly," Blackjack answered with a nod. "You must be prepared for anything."

Collin thought about it for a moment. *If you're going to do it, you might as well go all the way*, he decided. The first time, he rang the bell on the first pocket. The second time he was more careful. He made it to the fourth pocket. He tried again and again until, by the end of the day, he was able to empty all ten pockets without ringing any of the bells.

"You are taking to this life quickly," Blackjack told him that night. "You learn fast, much faster than any of the pros I have known."

Collin grinned. "I'm a quick study," he said simply. He sat on a colorful handwoven rug in front of the fireplace, staring into the fire as he recalled something his father had once told him: *Whatever you do, whether it's business or pleasure, always strive to be the best. That's what the Deverells are all about.* Collin smiled to himself. *Well, Dad, for once I'm taking your advice,* he thought, *though I doubt this is what you had in mind.* The idea made him laugh aloud.

"What's so funny?" Blackjack asked.

Collin told him. "You and I have our work cut out for us," he said. "When we're through, I have to be the best damned thief in the business."

"Now comes the real test of your ability," Blackjack told Collin over breakfast one morning. "You are ready to return to Marrakesh."

Collin looked at him, surprised. They had been working, and working hard, toward a common goal for months, and it had always seemed light-years away. Now that the time had actually come, it all seemed to be happening too fast. "Are you sure?" he asked carefully.

"I have not the slightest doubt," Blackjack said with absolute certainty. "If I were not sure you are equal to the task ahead of you, there is no way I would send you to what would be certain death for you if you were caught. The only thing that has kept you safe up until now is their belief that you died out on the desert."

Collin nodded. "So when do I leave?"

"Tomorrow morning, very early. It is almost five hundred kilometers to Marrakesh from here," Blackjack answered. "That leaves us with less than twenty-four hours to make our plans."

" 'Our'?" Collin asked. "Are you going with me?"

Blackjack shook his head. "No. When you leave here tomorrow, you will be completely on your own," he said gravely. "You will have only your wits and the skills you have learned here to see you through. But there is much I can tell you about Harrington, about his compound, that will help you."

Collin frowned. *My baptism by fire,* he mused.

* * *

"There are always at least six armed guards on the premises at all times," Blackjack told Collin as they studied a layout of the Harrington compound together. "And dogs. At least a dozen dogs, all trained to attack to kill." He paused. "You can forget about using the main gate. It will not be possible."

"What about the wall?" Collin asked. "I could go over it, and—"

"And the dogs would rip your throat open before you traveled twenty yards." Blackjack shook his head. "No, it will not work. You must find a way to get past them, stay beyond their reach. Think, Collin. You are alone now, with no means of defending yourself if caught. What is the best route to take?"

Collin stared at the diagram for a long time. "Here," he said finally, pointing to a specific area on the layout. "There's a large tree right here, midway between the wall and this balcony at the back of the villa. If I can use the rope, I can swing over to the balcony and enter through the master suite."

Blackjack looked at him. "You are aware of the distance involved?"

Collin nodded. "At least thirty yards. A piece of cake."

"You can see no other way?"

"Nope," Collin said with finality. "This is my only chance."

"You have learned well," Blackjack said approvingly. "The master suite, as it happens, is connected to Harrington's vault."

Collin looked at him. "Vault?"

Blackjack nodded. "A very large walk-in vault. That is where he keeps his valuables—money, jewels, papers. Your painting may even be there."

"In the vault?" Collin asked.

"Harrington has in his possession many stolen works of art," Blackjack explained. "I should know—I stole many of them personally. He does not always place them on display where they might be easily recognized. Some of them are stored until he can find a way to dispose of them or move them to another location.''

"Then my painting may not even be there," Collin concluded.

Blackjack shook his head. "I would be willing to bet any amount of money that it *is*," he said. "Harrington went to the trouble to try to kill you to keep you away from the villa. He now believes you are dead. That painting must be somewhere in the villa, if not on display, then in the vault."

Collin nodded. "If it's there, I'm going to find it."

He slept fitfully that night. He was up well before sunrise the next morning, unable to eat, unable to think of anything except the task ahead of him. *One wrong move could be your last.* The words echoed through his mind as he studied the layout of the Harrington stronghold one last time.

"Remember . . . do nothing to arouse suspicion," Blackjack told him as he climbed into the Jeep his friend had placed at his disposal, preparing to leave for Marrakesh. "They must go on believing Collin Deverell is dead. You must wear the robes and turbans I have given you until the time comes for you to make your move. Everyone—and I mean everyone—must think you are one of the locals. Talk to no one. Allow no one to get a close look at your face."

"Don't worry," Collin told him. "I won't be in Marrakesh long enough to be seen by anyone."

"*In sha allaah*—God willing—I will see you tomorrow night," Blackjack said, handing him a rucksack containing everything he would need.

Collin put it on the seat beside him. "You bet." He paused. "Look, if I ever owed anybody anything, it's you. I don't know if I ever thanked you for saving my hide, but I'm doing it now."

"The success of your journey is all the thanks I wish, my friend," Blackjack said honestly.

"I know that," Collin responded with a nod. "But just in case something happens that I can't come back here right away, that I have to take flight, I promise you—I'm going to find your daughter. And when I do, I'll send her back to you, one way or another."

Blackjack managed a smile. "I believe you mean that, Collin," he said in a strained voice.

"Damned right I do," Collin shot back with a grin. "I'm going to nail those bastards—for both of us."

Blackjack watched him drive away, and for the first time in many years, he allowed himself the luxury of tears.

Allah had answered his prayers.

It was just past midnight. The villa was in darkness, except for a few lights in the downstairs rooms. William Harrington, Collin had learned, was in Paris for his daughter's wedding. *I wonder if he sold Samantha to the highest bidder*, Collin thought as he perched on the high stone wall, concealed by the branches of the tree he intended to use for his airborne entry to the main house. He instantly dismissed the guilt he had felt where Samantha was concerned. *Learn to think with your head, not your heart. There's no room for a conscience in this world*, he reminded himself. He looked on in silence as the guards passed directly under his perch. In the distance, he could hear the dogs barking. As soon as the guards were far enough away, he would make his move.

He waited for what seemed an eternity. *Patience*, he told himself, *you have to learn to be patient.* At last he was convinced it was safe. He slid a long rope with a large, four-pronged hook off his shoulder and took it in both hands, grasping it firmly as he swung it out, allowing the hook to catch on a heavy limb jutting out toward the balcony. He gave it a hard jerk to make sure it was secured there. *Good*, he thought. *Got it on the first try.* Then he grabbed it firmly and leaped from the wall, swinging swiftly across the courtyard, coming down squarely on the large balcony outside the master bedroom suite. Hearing the sound of voices approaching, he crouched low behind the balustrades, peering out at the guards passing by for the second time. "Damn!" he muttered through clenched teeth. If only he could think of a way to distract them.

After they were gone, he carefully disconnected the burglar alarm as Blackjack had showed him, picked the lock, and entered the bedroom. It was in total darkness. The safe was on the opposite side of the room. As Collin started to cross the room, he was startled by the sound of an animal chattering. He jumped backward. In a cage near the window was a mongoose. Harrington and his cronies entertained themselves by pitting a mongoose against a cobra and betting on the outcome, Blackjack had told him. It seemed that Harrington had a mongoose that had never been defeated. "Shut up," Collin whispered, annoyed at the creature's sounds. Then he heard another sound coming from the hallway. Voices. Quickly, he ducked behind the heavy drapes on the French doors. The bedroom door opened and two men entered, both carrying guns in shoulder holsters. From his hiding place, Collin could see that one was holding a small device that looked like a remote control switch.

"I don't know why Mr. Harrington insists we check out the vault every night," one of the men said to the other. "I mean, what are the chances of anyone getting in here?"

"Slim and none," the other replied with a harsh laugh. "But you know the boss. He doesn't take unnecessary chances." He pressed a button on the device in his hand. A red light flashed on and it made a high-pitched whistling sound. The large steel door, until now concealed behind a massive curtain, immediately swung open. Collin peered through a small opening in the drapes. The two men were going inside. He could see the Renoir leaning against one wall inside the vault. He cursed under his breath. He'd learned how to crack every kind of safe imaginable, but how was he going to get that vault open after the goons were gone without that device? It was impossible, he thought. Then he remembered something Blackjack had once told him: *It is never really impossible. Improbable, perhaps. Difficult, certainly. But never really impossible.* His mind was racing. He would have to find something with which to duplicate that sound. But what? It would have to be exactly the same sound, since the door to the vault was obviously operated electronically by that precise pitch. Harrington certainly was not a man to take unnecessary chances, he thought ruefully. Collin could feel his own heart beating wildly inside the wall of his chest. *When are they going to leave?* he wondered.

Finally, the two men came out of the vault and closed the door with the same electronic device they had used to open it. Laughing and talking as they did so, they drew the curtain and walked out, closing the door but not bothering to turn out the lights. As soon as they were gone, Collin came out of hiding and began looking around for something he could use to duplicate the sound the men had used to open the vault. The mongoose ran back and forth in its cage, making strange noises as it watched Collin warily. *There has to be something here*, he thought furiously. Then he spotted a bottle of wine and two crystal goblets on the table beside the bed. In his mind, he saw his mother, years ago, entertaining him and Justin as children by pouring wine into her crystal goblets and running her finger around the rim of the glass to produce a low whistling sound. He took a deep breath and retrieved the bottle and one of the goblets. He poised himself in front of the vault and uncorked the wine, filling the glass. Then he ran his finger slowly around the rim. It wasn't quite right. *Too much wine?* he wondered. Hastily, he took a long swallow of the wine. *God, how does Harrington drink this stuff?* he wondered. It tasted like gasoline. He tried again. Still not exactly right. He drank some more of the wine. *If I don't get it right soon, they're going to find me passed out in the floor*, Collin thought. He held the goblet in front of him and ran his finger slowly around the rim again. This time it produced a familiar, high-pitched tone. Collin held his breath as the huge door swung open, revealing the contents of the vault. *Bingo!* he thought as he hurried inside. He took a knife from the rucksack he'd brought in on his back and hesitated in front of the Renoir. He hated to do this, but there was no other way he could get it out safely.

I'll have it reframed when I get back to New York, he promised himself as he cut it from its frame and hastily rolled up the canvas, tucking it into the rucksack. As he started to exit, he stopped, catching sight of several large stacks of currency on one shelf just inside the doors. He thought of Blackjack, of how Harrington and his people had cheated his friend. He took as much of the money as the rucksack would hold and ran out of the vault.

Suddenly the shrill sound of an alarm filled the room, and Collin froze in his tracks, realizing to his horror that he'd made that first and possibly fatal mistake: he had forgotten to disconnect the alarm in front of the vault. His eyes scanned the room furiously, coming to rest on the cage holding the mongoose. A smile came to his lips as he raced forward, certain his problem was solved. "Maybe you've got a real mission in this life after all," he muttered under his breath as he fumbled with the latch on the cage.

When the two men, accompanied by two armed security guards, ran into the room moments later, Collin was gone. "It's not possible that anyone could have been in here," one of the men insisted. "There's no possible escape. If he went out the windows, the dogs would have had him by now."

"Here's the culprit," one of the guards announced, scooping up the mongoose crouched on the carpet in front of the vault. "He set off the alarm."

"Who the hell left his cage open?" one of the men demanded.

"It was probably an accident. No doubt it wasn't tightly latched when he was fed this evening," the guard said, amused, as he returned the mongoose to its cage. "No harm done."

"No harm done!" another of the men gasped. "That goddamned alarm scared the shit out of me!"

"You could stand to lose a little more," the guard chided. "Let's go."

Outside the walls of the compound, Collin was speeding away in his Jeep, relieved. It had been close. Too close. But as he drove off in the direction of Ouarzazate, he thought about what he had done, and he was exhilarated. For him, life had been a constant search for the great adventure, the ultimate challenge. Finally, tonight, he had found it. And it was only the beginning. He had a long way to go, a great deal to do. And he had the feeling he was going to enjoy matching wits with the masters, challenging them and ultimately outwitting them.

He thought about how he had released the mongoose from its cage to throw them off, and he wondered what they thought when they found the animal roaming around in Harrington's bedroom. He started to laugh uncontrollably.

It was true. There was only one way to beat these men: beat them at their own game!

San Francisco, December 1985

The past five years had been good to Ashley. Her marriage to Brandon had flourished, as had her career. She had gained some measure of recognition on an international level, and there was talk of the possibility that she might soon be doing an exhibit in London. Brandon had become a full partner in his law firm and was getting some interest from political power brokers. "I wonder what the galleries in Washington are like?" Ashley asked idly over dinner one night. "I may be doing most of my work there in the next few years."

"Don't call the movers just yet," Brandon cautioned her, grinning. "They're only expressing an interest. No one's made any offers so far."

"But they will," Ashley said confidently. "These men are not stupid, darling."

Ashley knew that Bradley and Claudia Hollister had never stopped trying to drive a wedge between them, but she no longer let it bother her. *I'm lucky they live on the other side of the country*, she told herself. *My in-law troubles are all long-distance affairs.* She knew that Brandon had little contact with them by phone, that he never visited them in New York, and that their letters often went unanswered. "They're your parents," Ashley had reminded him. "Don't you think you should at least try to patch things up with them?" For herself she was glad she did not have to see them or hear from them, but she knew that whatever had come between Brandon and his father still troubled him deeply, and for his sake, she felt she should urge him to resolve it. But Brandon seemed uninterested.

"Some things are just plain unpardonable," he told her, not offering an explanation. In the years they'd been married, he had never told her exactly what had come between him and his parents, and she had never pressured him to tell her, but she often wondered what could have been so serious that he had never gotten over it. Knowing the Hollisters, it could have been just about anything.

Their son, Robert, who had been named for Ashley's brother, was now five years old and the image of his father. He had Brandon's thick blond hair and intelligent blue eyes. He was tall for his age and athletic, and he'd inherited his father's quick mind and sense of humor. "I couldn't have done a better job of duplicating you if I'd been a Xerox machine," Ashley often quipped.

Brandon had built a tree house for Robert in an enormous oak tree in their backyard, and Ashley could see him playing there from the windows of her studio. Sometimes she would stop whatever she was doing and stand at the window, watching him climb up the homemade ladder leading to the tree house or playing with his collie pup, Chaser—so named because of his penchant for chasing cars—or swimming in their backyard pool, and she would marvel at the miracle she and Brandon had created. *My masterpiece*, she thought, filled with a satisfaction she had never known before. Brandon's parents had never seen their grandson, except in photographs, but Robert had spent a great deal of time with Ashley's mother and father and adored them. He would sometimes spend a week or two at a time in the Napa Valley when Brandon was off on business and Ashley was preparing for an exhibit, and he came home filled with enthusiastic accounts of the harvest or the process by which wine was made, or any one of a hundred stories his grandfather had told him about his ancestors in Tuscany. "Wouldn't it be fun to live there, Mommy?" he had asked more than once. "To be there all the time?"

"I'm sure it would be, darling," Ashley agreed.

Now, standing before her easel, staring thoughtfully at the blank canvas, she was about to begin a painting she had wanted to do for a long time: a portrait of her son. He was growing up so fast, she thought wistfully. She wanted to capture the innocence of his youth on canvas before it was lost to her forever. "Sit still, Robert," she told him as he squirmed on the stool on which she'd posed him.

"How long do I have to sit like this?" he asked, bored.

"For a while," she answered. "You want to surprise Daddy, don't you?"

"Couldn't we just go to the store and get my picture taken in one of those booths?" he wanted to know. "They only cost fifty cents."

Ashley wrinkled her nose disapprovingly. That wasn't art. It wasn't even good photography. "I think your father would like this much better."

"Maybe you could take a picture of me and use it—like you do for your other pictures," he suggested, shifting around on the stool impatiently.

"Robert, please sit still," she pleaded.

"I have a Charley horse in my leg—" he began, rubbing his calf emphatically.

Ashley shook her head, suppressing a smile. "You're just like your father," she told him, remembering the time she'd tried to sketch Brandon at Big Sur. "He couldn't sit still either, and I've never asked him to pose for me again. Is that what you want?"

Robert grinned. "Yes!" he exclaimed happily.

"Okay, you win," she conceded with a wave of her hand. "Go on outside. I'll find one of your recent photographs." She watched as he hopped down off the stool and ran for the door, and she was filled with a love so powerful it threatened to choke her. There had been a time when she had been absolutely certain she would never have children. She wanted a career, and was convinced that it would be enough to make her happy. How wrong she had been! Brandon and Robert had completed her life in ways even painting never could. The love she felt for them made her whole, made her fully alive. Without them, nothing else would matter quite so much.

"I have to fly to Denver for a few days," Brandon told Ashley. They were walking along the beach, hand in hand. Robert ran ahead of them with Chaser at his heels, searching for seashells.

She looked at him. "Thursday's our anniversary, in case you've forgotten," she reminded him. "We do have plans—"

He nodded. "I know," he said quietly. "Believe me, honey, I'd get out of going if I possibly could, but there's no way. I've been handling this client exclusively for the past two years. Sending someone else in my place is out of the question."

"But—"

He stopped walking and grasped her shoulders. "I don't want to go. I have to go," he explained. "The matter in question is just too important to be put off, even for a day. I know how you feel. I feel the same way, but . . ."

She couldn't hide the disappointment in her dark eyes. "I understand, or at least I'm trying to," she said with a sigh. "You know, when I married you, I promised to love and honor, in sickness and in health—and in spite of demanding clients. But sometimes . . ."

He kissed her forehead. "I'll make it up to you—Scout's honor," he promised. "I'll be home on Friday. Maybe we'll

send Robert out to see your folks and take a drive down to
Big Sur, just the two of us, stay at the Ventana Inn . . .''

Her eyes narrowed in mock anger. "Think you can bribe
me, Hollister?" she asked.

"Well . . ." he began, eyes cast upward innocently.

"Well, you can." She encircled his waist with her arms.
"You have yourself a date. Just make sure you're here on
Friday to keep your promise, or I'll make you think you're
living in a monastery!"

He grinned. "Why, of all the women in San Francisco,
did I have to fall in love with such a nut?"

She kissed him. "You just couldn't help yourself," she
teased. "You always were a sucker for a damsel in distress."

Ashley rolled over in bed, her right arm extended, searching
for her husband. When she did not find him, she woke with
a start, having forgotten for a moment that he was in Denver. She sat up in bed, running one hand through her hair
as she pushed it back away from her face. She hated it when
he had to be away for any length of time. She hated sleeping
alone. "I've grown accustomed to your face," she would
tease Brandon. "After all, hugging another body is much
more fun than hugging a pillow." Often, when she was
asleep, she would toss and turn until she found him, wrapping her arms around him and taking comfort in the closeness they shared in those intimate moments, shutting out
the rest of the world as easily as they closed the bedroom
door. *The romance isn't dead in our marriage*, she told herself. *If
anything, it's stronger than ever.*

She picked up his pillow and hugged it tightly. Ashley
smiled to herself, happily anticipating their weekend at Big
Sur. He was such a romantic, that husband of hers. How
many men actually thought of taking their wives to the place
where they'd made love for the first time to celebrate an
anniversary? *Most of them probably couldn't*, she thought wryly.
*Who wants to spend a romantic weekend in the back seat of a '67
Chevy?*

She looked at the telephone on the night table, tempted for a moment to call him at his hotel. It would be eight o'clock in Denver; he was probably having breakfast right now in his suite. She reached for the phone twice, but changed her mind at the last minute each time. He might have already left, she told herself. When the phone rang unexpectedly, she jumped, startled. She snatched up the receiver. "Hello?" she snapped irritably.

The familiar voice on the other end was clearly amused. "My, aren't we crabby this morning! Did I wake you?"

"Brandon!" she gasped. "You must have been reading my mind!"

"What?"

"I was just lying here, thinking about calling you," she told him. "How's Denver?"

"Twenty-nine degrees and snowing," he answered. "I've been thinking—how would you like to fly up here and meet me on Thursday evening? We could drive out to Aspen or Vail—"

"Nothing doing!" she told him. "You promised me Big Sur, and I'm holding you to it!"

"You're sure you wouldn't want to change plans?" he asked. "I know you've never been to either place before."

"I've never been on skis before," she declared, laughing. "I'd probably end up wrapped around a tree somewhere!"

"I think you could be a marvelous skier if you'd give yourself a chance," he disagreed. "You've got the balance, the coordination . . ."

"What I *don't* have is the nerve," she confessed. "Let's just drive down to Big Sur, where I can do something I know I'm good at."

There was a pause on the other end. "You're absolutely right, now that I think about it," he said finally. "I think I discovered your real talent at Big Sur."

Ashley laughed. "I'm sure you're not referring to the portrait I did of you."

"No, not exactly."

"How's the meeting going?" she asked, changing the subject abruptly.

"Couldn't be better. If all goes well today, I could be home by Thursday after all," he told her.

"That's wonderful!"

"I know. I miss you, sweetheart," he said then.

"I miss you, too. And so does your son." Ashley swung her legs over the edge of the bed and onto the carpet as she pulled the wayward strap of her sheer green silk nightgown back up over her shoulder. She cradled the telephone on one shoulder as she talked. "I'm afraid I still haven't gotten the hang of maneuvering those remote-controlled speed-boats you bought him for the pool."

Brandon laughed. "Are you still planning to take him out to St. Helena on Friday?"

"If you're coming home Thursday, I just might take him Thursday morning," she responded in a suggestive tone. "That way we can have a real anniversary celebration, just the two of us . . ." Her voice trailed off, the implication clear.

"Hmm . . . with an offer like that, I think I'll just have to make sure all goes well here today," he said. "I doubt I'll be able to concentrate on business while I'm thinking about what's waiting for me at home."

Ashley laughed. "Just be sure you let me know what time you're coming in so I can be at the airport to meet you."

"I will," he promised. "I'd better run now, or the meeting will never get started today, let alone finished."

"Right," she agreed. "Love you."

After he had hung up, she sat, still holding the receiver in both hands. "Oh, do I love you, Brandon. Come home to me soon, my darling," she whispered.

Ashley stood in front of her easel, staring at the unfinished seascape she had been working on. No matter what she did, it just didn't seem to work. *Maybe I just need to put it away for a while and work on something else*, she thought, frustrated. *Or maybe I need to burn it and get it over with. I've wasted too much time with it already.*

The truth was, she had not been able to concentrate on that painting or any other all afternoon. She had driven Robert out to her parents' place early that morning, and with both Robert and Brandon gone, the big house seemed empty and unbearably lonely. She'd found herself putting down her palette and brush from time to time and going to the window, expecting to see her son climbing up to the tree house, or she would go downstairs to Brandon's den or into the kitchen. *How did I ever stand living alone?* she asked herself, amused by her own behavior.

She checked the time. In another two hours, she would be leaving for the airport. Brandon's flight was due in at six, but she liked to leave early in case the traffic was heavy or she was unavoidably delayed for some other reason. She took a shower and dressed, and as she stood in front of the full-length mirror in the bedroom, she found herself suddenly aware of just how much she had changed since she left the Napa Valley, nine years ago. In her mind, she saw the young Abby Giannini standing beside her in the mirror, a fresh-faced girl in jeans and those wonderfully comfortable peasant shirts she'd always worn, a far cry from the stylish Ashley Gordon-Hollister in her designer clothes, displaying a dramatic flair that was entirely her own. Ashley's love of bold colors, dramatic styles, and fashionable hats would have been out of place in the vineyards but was entirely appropriate at the center of the San Francisco art world. It was a symbol, she decided. A decidedly different look for a woman who's come a long way in nine years. Nine years that seemed like a lifetime.

Her thoughts were interrupted by the shrill ringing of the telephone. She picked it up hastily, almost afraid to answer, afraid it would be Brandon, telling her he was going to have to stay in Denver another day. "Hello?"

"Ashley—I'm glad I caught you at home. I thought you might have left for the airport already." The voice on the

other end was that of her artist's representative, Melanie
Masters.

"No yet, but soon."

"That's why I thought I should try to get you now,"
Melanie said. "I know you have plans for tonight, and I
thought you might want something else to celebrate when
you break out the bubbly."

"You have a check for me," Ashley guessed.

"Better than that," Melanie said. "It's definite now,
Ashley—you're going to be doing a one-woman show in
London at the end of March."

Ashley paced back and forth nervously in the busy terminal
at San Francisco International Airport. Traffic on the Bay-
shore Freeway had been unusually heavy and she'd arrived
later than she had planned, but the reservation clerk at the
airline ticket counter informed her that the flight on which
Brandon was booked had been delayed by a snowstorm over
the Rockies. Though both Ashley and Brandon were basically fearless fliers, she always worried when he had to fly
at this time of year. So many of the eastern states were
getting snow in large amounts. Sleet and freezing rain made
travel hazardous, even by air. She looked at her watch. The
flight was now almost an hour late. *What could be keeping them?*
she wondered.

She couldn't wait to tell Brandon the news Melanie had
delivered that afternoon. London! Ashley had never been
out of the country before. This, she promised herself, was
going to be the honeymoon they had never had. Of course
Brandon would be going with her: it had never occurred to
her to go without him. Certainly the firm could spare him
for a couple of weeks! They would have a wonderful time,
even though for her it was going to be a business trip. She
had briefly considered taking Robert along, but decided that
he would be much happier here, staying with her parents.
They would not have much time together, except at night,
and he was usually fast asleep by nine-thirty. Perhaps when

he was older, when he could enjoy it more. Perhaps by then, they would be going to Paris or Rome or Amsterdam. . . .

She looked at her watch again. She decided to check with the clerk one more time. As she headed for the counter, fifty yards away, she was intercepted by Harry Wilcox, the senior partner in Brandon's firm. "Harry—what are you doing here?" she asked, surprised. "Brandon told you I would be picking him up, didn't he?"

There was a look on Wilcox's face that she did not quite understand. "Sit down, Ashley," he said quietly.

She felt a growing panic inside without understanding why. She shook her head emphatically. "The plane's late, Harry," she said. "I was just going to ask—"

He grabbed her shoulders. "Sit down!" he commanded sharply.

"No, Harry." Her voice was barely above a whisper. Something was wrong. She didn't want to hear what he was going to say.

He wouldn't let go of her. "There's been an accident, Ashley." His words struck her like hammer blows. "The plane . . . it went down in the Sierra Nevadas . . ."

"Brandon . . ." She began to tremble violently. *No . . . this can't be happening*, she thought, her mind racing. *We're going to Big Sur for the weekend, for our anniversary. It's going to be just like it was the first time. We're going to have that honeymoon we never had in London. He's going to be so proud of me when I tell him about the show. We'll try to have another baby . . . maybe a little girl this time.* Then she looked up at Harry Wilcox's troubled face. *No . . . this can't be happening. Not to us. Not now.* "Harry, please . . ." she begged. "No . . ." Tears streamed down her cheeks, smearing her mascara. Her eyes stung but she felt nothing.

"There was a crash," Wilcox said in a strained voice as Ashley broke away from him. "There were no survivors."

She turned to look at him, her eyes glazed like those of a frightened animal. She started shaking her head, unable to accept the reality that was assaulting her. "No . . ."

"He's dead, Ashley," Wilcox told her as he stepped forward. "Brandon's dead."

Her hand flew to her mouth, her terror rendering her speechless. Wilcox reached her just as she collapsed, catching her in his arms. She didn't hear the announcement being made over the PA system, nor was she aware of the reactions of the distressed people around her.

It's all just a bad dream, she thought just before the world went dark.

St. Helena, December 1985

"I still can't believe he's really gone." Ashley stood at the kitchen window, watching her father and Robert out in the small backyard behind the cottage. "I've been going through all the motions, making all the arrangements, and in my mind I know I've lost him, but my heart just can't accept it." She turned to face her mother, wringing her hands nervously. "I don't even know how to tell Robert his father is gone. I know it's going to be the most difficult thing I've ever had to do. Driving out here this morning . . . I kept thinking about it, kept trying to find the right words. But there are no right words, no easy way to tell him his father's—" She stopped short, unable to say the word, unable to say that Brandon was dead. Somewhere in the back of her mind she'd convinced herself that if she did not say it, did not put the reality into words, then it had not really happened.

Lucia Giannini frowned, sensing her daughter's pain and knowing of no way to ease her suffering. "Would you like your papa or I to tell him?" she asked then.

Ashley shook her head. "Thank you, Mama, but no," she said wearily. "It should come from me. I should be the one to tell him. Robert's just now beginning to realize what it means to die. I remember how upset he was when his guinea pig died last summer. He's going to need me." *And I'm going to need him*, she was thinking.

"When will you do it?" her mother asked, concerned.

"Today. As soon as possible. I've put it off too long already," Ashley said, her gaze still fixed on her son, scampering at his grandfather's side out in the yard. "I should have come out here immediately when I got back from Lake Tahoe." For the past two days, she had been going through all the painful but necessary rituals of death—making funeral arrangements, selecting a casket, finding a cemetery plot since they didn't own one already—but she'd been functioning much like a somnambulist, going through all the motions without really being aware of what she was doing or what was happening around her. It was as though some primitive survival instinct deep within her had taken over, propelling her through the seemingly endless, unbearably painful process. She knew she had sent his parents a telegram, unable to face speaking to them but did not really remember doing so. She had only a vague recollection of her talk with the undertaker. The one thing she had not yet been able to do, the one thing she knew she must do, was break the news to her son, to make him understand that his father was never coming home. She stood watching him for a few seconds longer, then drew in her breath and pushed open the screen door, stepping out onto the back porch. "Robert," she called out to him.

He looked up, grinning broadly when he saw her. "Mommy!" he cried out excitedly, racing toward her. "Is Daddy with you?"

Now came the hard part.

"I don't understand, Mommy." Robert looked up at her, his small face clearly troubled, his bright blue eyes shining with tears. "You said Daddy would be home today, that—"

"I know, darling, but there was an accident." She brushed an errant lock of his thick blond hair away from his face. "Your daddy was coming home. He was on a plane, flying home to us. I was waiting for him at the airport. But there was bad weather—a snowstorm—and something happened. They don't know exactly what yet, maybe they never will. The plane crashed, and Daddy was killed."

Robert did not yet fully grasp the meaning of death. "He's never coming back?"

Ashley reached for his hand. "No, darling, he's not." She paused. "Do you remember when your guinea pig Harold died a while back?"

He nodded.

"Remember how we all went out in the backyard and Daddy dug a hole and we had a funeral for him?"

"Uh-huh."

"We all took turns telling each other what a good guinea pig he was and how much we loved him, and then we put him down in that hole and Daddy covered him with dirt. Do you remember that?" she asked.

He nodded again.

"That's how we're going to say good-bye to Daddy now," Ashley said softly. Her voice cracked, but she summoned up all the strength she could muster. "We're going to have all of our friends, everybody who loved Daddy around us, and we're—"

"No!" Robert shook his head furiously. "I don't want to put Daddy down in the ground! I don't want to say good-bye! I want my Daddy!" He began to sob uncontrollably.

Ashley held him close, stroking his hair as he buried his face in her dark blue wool jacket. "I know, darling, I don't want to say good-bye either," she told him. "I didn't want to ever say good-bye to your daddy. But sometimes we don't get a choice. Sometimes we can't always have things the way we'd like them to be." Putting him through this was tearing her apart. *That's it, baby*, she thought. *Cry. Let it all out. Give in to your pain.*

And maybe, when it's all over, I can give in to mine.

* * *

Ashley stood before the casket as it was about to be lowered into the ground, clutching her son's hand. She was dry-eyed and self-possessed, determined to be strong for Robert. He needed to be able to draw upon her strength, now more than ever. *I can't stop living, much as I want to*, she told herself. *I have Robert to think about.*

She gazed up at the clear blue sky, thinking it somehow obscene that it should be such an unusually beautiful day, that life should be going on as usual around her when her world had just been destroyed. That she should be burying her husband on such a beautiful December afternoon that looked and felt more like April or May. A tear escaped from the corner of her eye and rolled down her cheek, undetected behind the veil of the wide-brimmed black hat she wore. She looked down at Robert standing straight and silent at her side in the dark blue suit his father had chosen for him just a month earlier. Brandon was always so proud of his son, she thought sadly. He had such wonderful dreams for Robert. *Now he won't even get to see his son grow up, find out what kind of man he would become. He won't be able to do all of the things he always wanted to do for him.*

She felt her mother's hand touching one of the shoulders of her black wool suit, and she turned to give Lucia a reassuring glance, as if to say, *I'm going to be all right, Mama— I promise.* Her father stood at her mother's side, and Ashley saw tears in his eyes as well. Tony Giannini, who had never shed a tear in the presence of anyone since the day his own son died, thirty years ago, was crying now for the son-in-law he had come to love as his own. Ashley had loved him even more for the way he had accepted Brandon into the family with open arms, even before they were married. He was loved, she thought as her eyes scanned the large group at the gravesite. But then, he was that kind of man. Her eyes came to rest on the Hollisters, standing a few feet away, refusing to acknowledge the rest of the group, except, of course, for their grandson. She recalled now their arrival in San Francisco, insisting that their son be buried in New York, at the family plot on Long Island, and how furious they had been when she refused to even consider it. Ashley had known instinctively that Brandon would not have wanted that. He had intended the distance between himself and his parents to be a permanent one, she was sure of it. He'd made his home—their home—in San Francisco, and she was convinced that this is where he would want to be buried.

"It's your fault we've never been able to see our grandson!" Claudia Hollister's accusations still raged through Ashley's mind as she looked at her mother-in-law now. "You poisoned Brandon against us. After he married you, he never even answered our letters." But that wasn't true and Ashley knew it. Brandon had not kept in touch with them because he had not wanted to. How many times had she suggested he take Robert and visit them in New York, just the two of them? She had not bothered to tell Claudia that. It no longer mattered, and she knew the woman would not believe her anyway. Later, when things had settled down, when Robert had adjusted to the reality of his father's death, she would write to the Hollisters, offering to let Robert visit them during the summer months if they wished. He would be starting school next year, she reminded herself. But there were always the summer vacations. She would not dream of keeping him from them, though she was troubled by whatever reasons Brandon might have had for doing so. She looked down at her son, and she was grateful to have him. *He's my reason for going on now*, she thought.

Her thoughts returned to the present as she realized the service had ended. The minister was offering his condolences. She shook his hand. "Thank you," she said quietly. "It was a beautiful service." She saw no reason to let him or anyone else know that she had not heard a word of it. She glanced over at the Hollisters, but decided not to attempt to speak to either of them.

Her parents came up to her as the minister walked away. "We were planning to go home tonight, Abby," Tony Giannini said in a low voice, "but if you need us, we can stay . . ."

Ashley shook her head. "I'll be all right," she assured him, then impulsively, she reached out and hugged each of her parents tightly. "It means everything to me, just having you here now."

"Are you sure . . ." her mother began.

She nodded, fighting back her tears. "What I really need right now is to be alone for a while."

Ashley was not sure how she had managed to get through the days following the funeral. She had not been sleeping well, and spent most of her nights curled up in the bay windows in Robert's bedroom, watching him sleep, there to comfort him when he was awakened by the nightmares that had tormented him since his father's death. She had not been able to surrender to her own pain, her own need for emotional release, because she felt she had to be strong for her son. She and Robert had been locked away in the house, cut off from the outside world, since the day Brandon was buried. They saw no one, and Ashley had refused to even answer the telephone. She had sent the cleaning lady away, telling the woman that her services would not be needed for a while. She had not gone near her studio since the day her husband died. *What good would it do*? she asked herself. *All I could paint now is death.*

Not a day passed that Ashley did not relive, detail by detail, the day of the crash. She had insisted upon going up on the mountain near Lake Tahoe where the plane had gone down, insisted upon identifying her husband's body herself, even though Harry Wilcox had offered to go in her place. "This is something I have to do myself, Harry," she'd told him. "If I don't see him, I'm never going to believe he's really gone."

"You'll see him at the funeral home," Wilcox pointed out. "This is going to be hard enough for you, Ashley. To see him like that—"

"I'm going, Harry." And that had been the end of that.

She was glad, however, that Wilcox had insisted upon making the trip with her. It had been a more difficult experience than she had anticipated. The bodies had been brought down from the mountain, some of them on stretchers, some—the more mutilated ones—in jute bags. When she was first taken to her husband's body, she had not recognized him. Wilcox had sent for dental records to identify him. The sight had made Ashley physically ill, and she was taken to a makeshift infirmary where members of the rescue team were being treated for exposure to the extreme cold. As she lay on a cot, her head spinning, she told herself that maybe it wasn't Brandon, that maybe he was still alive somewhere. . . .

"Call the hotel in Denver, Harry," she had begged Wilcox. "Call the Brown Palace. Maybe he's still there. Maybe he missed his flight—"

Wilcox grabbed her shoulders roughly, attempting to snap her out of her hysteria. "He's not in Denver, Ashley," he said harshly. "He's not at the hotel. He's dead. Everyone on that flight is dead now!"

"No!" She shook her head furiously. "That's not him! I'm sure it's not! I would know my own husband, Harry—"

"Ashley, you have to get hold of yourself," he urged. "You have to face it. Brandon is dead!"

"No!"

But the dental records had confirmed it.

Why did this have to happen? Ashley asked herself now. Why did it have to be Brandon? Why did he have to be on that particular flight? And then it hit her. He was on that flight because of her. He had not planned to come home until Friday. He had wrapped up his business in Denver and taken an earlier flight because she had wanted him to, because she had wanted to have him home on their anniversary.

She'd made reservations for the weekend at the Ventana Inn. She had forgotten all about it. They'd made such wonderful plans, she thought, bitter at the injustice of it all. They'd had such a bright future ahead of them. *It's not fair*, she thought resentfully. *It's not fair!* For the first time since the crash, she began to cry, to really cry, at last allowing the tears to come freely, at last giving in to a moment of weakness, surrendering to the pain that consumed her.

Suddenly, she was aware of the insistent ringing of the doorbell. She hesitated for a moment, thinking that if she waited, whoever it was would go away. But when the bell continued to ring, she finally pulled herself together, wiping her eyes as she descended the stairs to the reception hall. She opened the door slowly. "Mrs. Ashley Hollister?" asked the tall, thin, redheaded man on the doorstep.

Ashley had never seen him before. "Yes," she said carefully.

"This is for you. Have a good day, ma'am." He turned on his heel and walked away.

Ashley stared after him for a moment, inflamed by his cheerfulness at a time like this. Then she closed the door and looked down at the paper in her hand. It looked like a legal summons of some kind. She opened it and read it hastily. It didn't make sense at first, and she'd had to read it again before she finally realized what it was all about. "Those bastards," she said slowly as the heart-stopping reality hit her. "Those cold-blooded bastards!"

She ran to the phone in Brandon's den and called Harry Wilcox. "I know you're a corporate lawyer, Harry, but I need your help," she said in an urgent, terrified voice as soon as he came on the line.

"Take it easy, Ashley," he told her. "Calm down and tell me what's wrong."

"How can I calm down?" she shouted. "Those vile, heartless—"

"Who, Ashley?" Wilcox asked, trying to make sense of what she was saying.

"The Hollisters!" she raged. "Brandon's parents are suing for custody of Robert!"

Fifteen minutes later, Ashley, acting against Wilcox's advice, confronted Bradley and Claudia Hollister in their suite at the Pacific Plaza. "You wasted your time coming here," Bradley Hollister coldly informed her at the door. "Whatever you have to say should be handled through our attorneys.''

''What I have to say to you, you wouldn't want your attorney to hear!'' Ashley snapped, pushing past him, stalking into the suite.

Claudia emerged from the bedroom wearing a terry robe, a thick towel around her head like a turban. ''Bradley? What—'' She stopped short as she spotted Ashley. ''What are you doing here?''

''I came to tell you that you are *never* going to take my son away from me,'' Ashley stammered, trembling with a rage she could barely control. ''Never.''

''I think that's for the courts to decide,'' Hollister said evenly as he closed the door.

''I'm his mother! What makes you think you can just waltz in here and take him away from me?'' she demanded angrily.

''Oh, come now,'' Claudia said venomously. ''With a history like yours—''

''Shut up, Claudia!'' Hollister snapped crossly. ''Our attorneys—''

Ashley turned on him furiously. ''Your attorneys what?'' she asked, her eyes narrowing suspiciously.

''I refuse to discuss anything with you,'' Hollister said evenly. ''I suggest you get yourself an attorney, and when you do, have him contact ours.''

''I have an attorney,'' Ashley snapped. ''And I'm putting you on notice—both of you. I don't care how much money you have or how many high-priced lawyers you send after me. Send an entire platoon if you like! You are not getting Robert away from me!''

''Our grandson is all we have left of Brandon—'' Claudia began.

''You lost Brandon a long time before that plane went down,'' Ashley said harshly.

''Thanks to you,'' Claudia retorted.

''Oh, no,'' Ashley said, shaking her head emphatically. ''I tried to get him to stay in touch with you. I urged him to take Robert to New York to visit you. He didn't want to! He didn't even want to talk about you—either of you! I don't know what you could have possibly done to him to make him feel as he did, but now that I see the two of you for the monsters you really are, I'll bet it didn't take any effort at all!''

"Now just a minute, young lady—" Hollister began.

"He told me he left New York because he needed to put some space between himself and you. He said he wouldn't join his own father's firm because he didn't like the way you conducted your business affairs. I used to think he was wrong to keep Robert away from you, but now I see why he felt as he did!" Ashley was burning with rage as she spoke, unable to contain herself any longer. "He didn't want you to be a part of our son's life—and I'd respect his wishes to the end. You are never going to do to Robert whatever it was you tried to do to Brandon!" She started for the door.

"Wait a minute," Bradley Hollister called after her.

She stopped in her tracks and turned to face him. Her eyes were dark with rage as she met his gaze, but she said nothing, waiting to see what his next move was going to be.

"This could all be settled out of court if you would just listen to reason," he told her. "We're going to win this case, I'll tell you that right now. We can't possibly lose. If you were to turn our grandson over to us now, I'd be willing to make things easier on you. I'd be more than happy to give you generous visitation rights, plus a large cash settlement—"

"Cash settlement?" Ashley stared at him incredulously. "You bastard! My son is not for sale—at any price!"

He took a deep breath. "Then we'll see you in court," he said sternly.

"No, Mr. Hollister," she said with a shake of her head. "I'll see you in hell." And she turned abruptly and walked out.

* * *

"Are you telling me they might actually win this case?" Ashley sat across the desk from Harry Wilcox in his luxurious oak-paneled office overlooking San Francisco Bay.

"I'm saying we should be braced for one hell of a fight," Wilcox said carefully as he looked up from the papers spread out on his massive desk. "The Hollisters have a lot of influence, even here. They have their millions to back them up, not to mention some of the most brilliant legal minds in the country."

"And that's all that matters when the custody of a small child is being decided?" she asked, unable to believe it. "How much money someone has or how many high-priced attorneys he has in his hip pocket?"

"No, of course not." Wilcox genuinely liked Ashley Hollister and knew that Brandon—who had been like a son to him—would never have wanted his parents to raise his son, no matter what. Though Brandon seldom spoke of it, Wilcox knew there was a good deal of bad blood between himself and his family. Now he felt an obligation to protect Brandon's widow from what promised to be a very messy legal battle and at the same time do whatever he could to help her retain custody of her child. It was not going to be easy, but he would give it his best shot.

"Then what are you saying, Harry?" she asked. "Please—don't sugarcoat it. I have to know what to expect. Can they take him away from me?"

Wilcox hesitated for a moment, then nodded. "Yes. It could happen," he said finally. "Ashley, I know Bradley Hollister's reputation well enough to know that he's not bluffing when he threatens to bring out the heavy artillery. This is a man who did not become as powerful as he is today by making empty threats. He intends to drag you through the mud if he has to."

"How—" she began.

"He's been digging into your past," Wilcox said, slightly embarrassed. "He knows about the rather colorful reputation you had around here before you married his son. He

also has the names of every man you were ever involved
with.''

"Were," Ashley said slowly. "That's the key word here,
Harry. *Were*. There hasn't been anyone else in my life since
the night I met Brandon.''

"Are you telling me the truth, Ashley?" he asked, his
eyes meeting hers.

Her temper flared. "Yes, I am—and if you don't believe
me, you can go straight to hell with the rest of them!" she
snapped.

"Take it easy," he said quickly. "I had to ask you that.
I had to be sure before I could prepare our case. I always
felt you and Brandon had a solid marriage, but one can
never tell.''

"I loved Brandon. I was never unfaithful to him in the
time we were together, and I think he was always faithful
to me," she said with finality.

He studied the beautiful young woman sitting across from
him in her charcoal gray wool suit, her dark eyes blazing
with anger, her face flushed at the insinuation that she might
have cheated on her husband. Whatever else Ashley Hollister was or might have been, he was sure of one thing: she
loved her son and would fight to the death to keep him. But
then, he thought, disturbed, it might very well come to that.

"I think you should be prepared, Ashley," he began. "Hollister is ready to make you look like a tramp in that courtroom. Your reputation may well be ruined when it's over.''

"I don't give a damn about my reputation, Harry. The
only thing that matters now is Robert's welfare," she responded without hesitation.

"One may depend upon the other," he told her. "If Hollister and his lawyers prove you an unfit mother in the eyes
of the court, you could lose him.''

"I don't even want to think about that possibility," she
said sharply.

"We have to think about it," he insisted. "We have to
be ready for whatever they throw at us. It's going to be

hard on you. You're going to have to sit in that courtroom and listen to them air all your dirty linen. You're going to have to face them and defend yourself when they try to make you look like some cheap whore—''

Ashley got to her feet. "I can face anything, Harry," she assured him, "except losing both my husband and my son."

Ashley sat motionless at the front of the courtroom, with Harry Wilcox at her side. He had told her to expect it to be messy, but that had been in the nature of an understatement. *It's like the old Salem witch hunts*, she thought as she listened to the testimony given by Bradley and Claudia Hollister, who made her appear to be a fortune hunter out to get her hands on their son's inheritance. "She used her influence over our son to keep him away from us," Claudia testified, giving a performance worthy of an Academy Award. She looked and sounded like an angel. No, not an angel, Ashley thought. That's sacrilegious. "After he married her, he cut himself off from us completely. He never called or came to visit, never answered any of our letters. He wouldn't even allow us to see his son—our only grandchild!" She looked at the judge pleadingly.

The bitch, Ashley thought angrily.

"She kept him from returning to New York and heading up the legal department at Hollister International," Bradley Hollister told the judge. "I suppose she was afraid we might see through her little scheme. She knew that one day Brandon would inherit everything—and that, I am convinced, is what she was really after. She never loved our son, she cheated on him almost from the day they were married."

Ashley leaped to her feet. "That's a lie and you know it!" she exploded.

"Mrs. Hollister!" the judge shouted. "Mr. Wilcox, if you cannot control your client, she will be held in contempt of court!"

"Ashley." Wilcox touched her elbow. "Sit down. Don't let them get to you. This is exactly what they want you to do," he said in a low voice.

She sank back down into her chair. "I couldn't help it, Harry," she said, dropping her voice to almost a whisper. "They're lying. I know it and they know that I know it."

"The important thing is that we prove to the court that they're lying," he pointed out. He reached out and gave her hand an encouraging squeeze. "The war's not over yet."

She sat in stunned silence, barely able to contain her anger, as some of her former lovers took the stand and swore under oath that they had slept with her during the five years she was Mrs. Brandon Hollister. "They're lying," she told Harry Wilcox. "Every one of them is lying. I wonder how much this sideshow is costing Bradley Hollister?"

The hearing lasted two days. On the second day, Harry Wilcox attempted to destroy the distorted image of Ashley created by the Hollisters and their attorneys. "Your Honor," he addressed the judge, "Mrs. Hollister had no reason to make for herself a marriage of convenience. She certainly didn't need whatever her husband's inheritance might have been. Ashley Gordon-Hollister is successful in her own right, a celebrated painter whose works have received national acclaim and are currently being shown in various parts of Europe as well. And may I also point out that her success came before her marriage to Brandon Hollister . . ."

He tried to break the witnesses who had testified for the Hollisters, tried to expose their lies. Each of them clung stubbornly to his story. "They've really been coached," he told Ashley. "Their stories are so airtight they could hold water."

"Things aren't looking too good for us, are they, Harry?" she asked him as they left the courtroom at the end of the second day.

"Well—" he began hesitantly.

"Don't lie to me, Harry," she insisted. "I have to know. What do you think is going to happen now?"

"I think they've done a lot of damage," he said truthfully. "But until the judge gives his decision, we won't know for sure just how badly we've been hit."

Ashley stared at him, unable to accept the fact that Robert could be taken from her, that the one thing Brandon never wanted might actually happen.

I can't let it happen, she thought stubbornly.

The judge's decision came surprisingly fast. "It's a bad omen, isn't it?" she asked as she and Wilcox climbed the stairs to the courthouse entrance.

"Now, Ashley, don't expect the worst until it actually happens," he cautioned her.

"I think it's already happened," she said dismally.

Bradley and Claudia Hollister were already in the courtroom when Ashley and Wilcox entered. Bradley Hollister did not look at her, and his wife did so only long enough to give her former daughter-in-law a confident smirk. *I'd like to wipe that smile off her face*, Ashley thought angrily. *In fact, I'd like to wipe her face off completely.* She said nothing, keeping her anger in check. She seated herself next to Harry Wilcox and did not move until the judge entered and they were instructed to stand. As they seated themselves again, the judge began to speak.

"I have given the matter of the custody of the minor child, Robert Brandon Hollister, a great deal of consideration," he began. Ashley didn't hear the rest. She could tell by the way he looked at her, the tone of voice in which he spoke now, that she had lost. Suddenly his voice seemed far away, as though it were in a distant tunnel somewhere, and the room began to spin wildly. She grabbed Wilcox's arm, feeling as if she were falling. In her mind, she was at the airport again, and he was telling her that Brandon was dead. The judge was saying something about Robert's best interests. "*. . . they have proven that they are both willing and able to give the child the kind of stable home life he needs at this time in his life . . .*" Oh, God, no! she thought, reeling. *This can't be happening—not again!*

"Mrs. Hollister, it is the order of this court that you surrender the child to Mr. and Mrs. Bradley Hollister no later than noon on Friday, the fifteenth of February,'' the judge was saying.

He's been bought and paid for too, Ashley thought frantically. Before Wilcox could stop her, she was on her feet, shouting angrily at the judge. ''You can't let this happen!'' she screamed. ''Don't you see what they're doing? Or are you also on Bradley Hollister's payroll?''

''Mrs. Hollister!'' the judge snapped. ''I warned you before of the consequences of another outburst of this nature!''

''Ashley!'' Harry Wilcox was at her side, trying to coax her back into her seat. She pushed him away forcefully and turned on the judge again. ''What are you going to do to me?'' she demanded. ''What can you possibly do to me that you haven't done already?'' She turned and ran out of the courtroom, ignoring the outraged voice of the judge as he called after her.

Harry Wilcox found her leaning against the wall outside the courtroom, trembling violently. ''Ashley, I don't even know what to say to you,'' he began in a quiet tone.

''It's not your fault, Harry,'' she responded in a quivering voice. ''You did all that anyone could, under the circumstances. How could you know that Hollister owned everyone in that courtroom but you and me?''

The doors opened then and Bradley and Claudia Hollister appeared, smiling triumphantly as they approached. ''I'll come for Robert at noon sharp on Friday,'' Claudia informed Ashley in a cool voice. ''Please make certain that he's ready on time. We'll be flying home to New York and I would not want to get to the airport late.''

''You witch—'' Ashley began, clenching her fist. Wilcox grabbed her arm, afraid she might physically attack the other woman.

''You should have realized that you never stood a chance,'' Claudia taunted her, thoroughly enjoying her moment of victory.

''I'm not finished with you yet,'' Ashley informed her in a menacing tone.

''Oh, but you are. When we leave here, I don't expect

we'll be seeing each other again," Claudia told her, making it clear that visiting Robert would be out of the question.

"No, I'm not finished. Not by a long shot," Ashley insisted. "When I *am* finished, you're going to wish you'd never started this."

She walked out of the courthouse, leaving them staring after her.

"Remember what I told you, sport," Ashley said as she knelt in front of Robert on the azure blue carpet in his bedroom, straightening the front of his shirt. "No matter how bad things look, we can put up with anything as long as it's temporary."

"What's temp-rerry, Mommy?" he asked, his face streaked with tears. He had cried himself to sleep the night before, and there was nothing Ashley could do to give him any comfort.

"Temporary? That means not forever. For a little while," she said, fighting back her own tears. "That means that no one will ever be able to keep us apart for good."

"I don't want to leave you at all, Mommy," he said. "Why do I have to go with them? I don't know them. You say they're my grandpa and grandma, but I don't know them."

"They're your daddy's mother and father," she said. "You never saw them before because they live so far away from here. But they love you. They really do. To them, you're all that's left of your daddy, their son." As much as she loathed Bradley and Claudia, she couldn't frighten Robert more than he was already by telling him what kind of people they really were. She had to try to put his mind at ease until she could find a way to get him back.

"If they love me so much, why are they doing this to me?" he asked. "Why are they taking me away from you?"

"I wish I could explain it to you, darling, but the truth is, I don't understand it myself." She smoothed his hair once more and forced a smile. "It won't be for very long. You'll see."

"Are you going to make me go?"

She stared at him for a moment. She couldn't make him understand that she had no choice in the matter. He thought he was being punished for some reason. He didn't understand, couldn't understand, and it tore Ashley apart to have to send him away like this. "I'd never let you leave me if I had a choice," she told him truthfully as she wiped his eyes with her handkerchief. "I don't have any more to say about it than you do. Not this time."

"But you're my mother. You always tell me what to do." He looked like a small, frightened animal who'd been cornered.

Ashley took a deep breath. "There are some people in this world who even tell mothers what to do," she said, trying to keep her voice from breaking. "Sometimes, anyway. And this, my darling, is one of those times— unfortunately. They're wrong, but there's nothing I can do about it—yet."

"But you will come for me, won't you?" There was an urgency in his voice that made Ashley want to run away with him, as far and as fast as she could go. *I don't care if I have to be on the run from the law the rest of my life*, she thought. *But that's no life for you, Robert. There has to be a better way.*

The sound of the doorbell cut through her thoughts. "They're here," she said gravely, taking her son's hand and leading him down the staircase. She opened the front door to find Claudia Hollister and two uniformed policemen on the doorstep.

"This isn't necessary," she said quietly.

"I think it is," Claudia disagreed. "I wanted to make sure you didn't try anything foolish."

"They're frightening Robert," Ashley said in a low voice. 'Or doesn't that matter to you?"

"Of course it matters," Claudia insisted. "The court sent them."

"I'm sure," Ashley said. "His suitcases are packed. They're upstairs—"

"He won't be needing them," Claudia said quickly. "I intend to buy him all new clothes when we get home."

"His home is here!" Ashley snapped. Then she lowered her voice. "He has a few favorite things that he won't part with."

Claudia looked at her for a moment, then nodded. She turned to one of the policemen. "Could you please get the child's luggage?"

He nodded. Ashley gestured to the top of the stairs. "It's the first door on the right."

He returned with the two large suitcases quickly. Claudia took Robert's hand but he recoiled. "I don't want to go with you," he said stubbornly.

"You have to go with me," Claudia said firmly. "Besides, you'll love living with us in New York once you get used to it. I'm having your father's old room redone just for you, and—"

"I don't want to go with you!" Robert shouted angrily, pulling away from her again. "I want to stay here with Mommy!" He clung to Ashley, shrieking. "Please don't let them take me, Mommy! Please!"

Ashley looked at Claudia with unmasked hate in her eyes, then knelt down in front of her son. "It won't be for long, baby—I promise," she whispered. "Just remember how much I love you. Don't ever forget that, no matter how it might seem sometimes."

Claudia grabbed his hand roughly, and it was all Ashley could do to keep from attacking her, policemen or no policemen. She kissed Robert good-bye, then stood in the doorway and watched until they were in the car and had disappeared down the street. Then she closed the door and leaned against it, tears flowing freely down her cheeks. The look on her son's small face as he was being torn from her arms had had the impact of a bullet in the heart. A bullet would not have hurt as much, she thought, feeling as though her whole world had fallen apart. She wished she could have scratched that vile woman's eyes out. She wished she could kill them both, Claudia and her all-powerful husband, with her bare hands. *One way or another, I'm going to find a way to get you back, baby*, she thought, filled with a fresh determination. *And when I do, they're going to pay for what they did to your father—and now to us.*

I'm going to destroy them both.

Paris, October 1986

An armed security guard patrolled the cavernous headquarters of the Ferrand-Bessèges Jewelers on the rue François, the sound of his heels clicking on the marble floors echoing throughout the empty store. Convinced that all was secure, he settled down into a chair at the back of the massive room. It was filled with glass display cases that were now empty, since at night all of the jewels were taken to the enormous walk-in vault at the rear of the building. Settling in to take a nap, he counted his blessings that his supervisor would not be coming by tonight. His boss was in Lyon for the week and would not be coming around to check up on him as he usually did. If he ever found him taking a catnap on the job—*merde*! He didn't know why the boss had to be so strict. Nothing ever happened around here. It was like spending the night in a mausoleum.

In the vault, Collin was thinking exactly the same thing. He sat on the floor in one corner of the locked chamber and leaned back against one of the walls that was lined with drawers of various sizes holding jewels of varying proportions. He stared into the darkness as he took deep breaths from the oxygen mask clamped over the lower half of his face. He had been in there only a matter of hours, but he felt as though he had been buried alive. *A place like this could give a mole claustrophobia*, he thought as he reached into his pocket and drew out the elaborate diamond and sapphire necklace that had been his father's twentieth wedding anniversary gift to his mother. It had taken him almost three years to finally locate it: the necklace had been sold and resold twice, finally ending up here, in the vault of one of Paris's most prestigious jewelers. It was the last piece to be recovered. He studied the necklace, remembering the last time his mother had worn it, the night they'd had their heart-to-heart talk, just before she and his father left for Caracas. That night was still as clear in his mind as if it had been yesterday. *It's finally going back where it belongs*, he thought triumphantly.

He stashed the necklace in his rucksack and put down the oxygen mask just long enough to slip the straps of the sack up over his shoulders and secure it there. Feeling a little light-headed, he quickly put the oxygen mask to his face again and breathed deeply. This had been his most challenging scheme to date. It had taken him days to figure out exactly how he was going to get into the vault and hide there until after the store had closed. Obtaining the things he needed hadn't been easy, even though Blackjack had told him where to look. He had visited the jeweler many times in the past week, each time donning a different disguise. During those visits, he had been able to determine that the vault was almost never left unattended for any length of time. It was operated by a time lock that locked automatically at closing time and opened the same way just before the store opened each morning. If he got into the vault, he realized he would have to be prepared to spend the night there, since even he would not be able to get it to open before its designated time. It had taken time and a great deal of thought, but he had finally come up with a plan he was convinced would work.

Earlier that day, he had entered the store in another of his disguises, his dark hair concealed under a dark blond wig. His cheeks were fleshed out by foam sponges, and he wore green contact lenses to conceal his brown eyes. He was dressed fashionably, presenting himself as a man of wealth, a man who could easily afford the prices of the jewels here, and he spoke French with a German accent. He sauntered around, eyeing the jewels in the cases as the two available salesmen attended to other customers. When no one was looking, he slipped a small, cylindrical object from his pocket and pulled the pin, tossing it behind a case in one corner of the room. Immediately, the contrivance began to emit smoke and sparks of fire. Within seconds, the smoke alarms sounded, their shrill warning alarm deafening. Everyone rushed for the exit, including Collin. He looked at his watch. He would have just enough time to get back to his hotel and get ready for phase two of his plan.

At precisely five that afternoon, he returned to the store, this time posing as an electrician. He entered the offices at the rear of the store dressed in stained overalls that made him appear at least fifty pounds heavier than he actually was. This time, he wore a dark, curly wig and bushy mustache, and his nose as well as his cheeks had been fleshed out by the foam sponges. He carried a large toolbox. "I think it's probably just a short," he announced in fluent French as he went through the motions of checking out the wiring and fuse boxes. As soon as he was able to slip away unobserved, he took a chunk of dry ice from his toolbox and planted it in one of the fuse boxes. Then he took out a can of soda and opened it, pouring it slowly over the dry ice. Predictably, it began to smoke profusely. "I think you'd better clear the place," he announced to the manager. "We may have a problem here. I'll get it put out, but I'm going to have to ask you to lock up until I can get back here tomorrow with some help and more tools."

As the personnel prepared to leave, Collin pretended to be collecting his tools. When no one was looking, he slipped into the vault and hid there until he heard the sound of the massive door closing, engulfing the chamber in darkness. Then he removed the wig, mustache, and sponges, stashing them in the toolbox. He peeled off the overalls to reveal his black turtleneck sweater, pants, and leather jacket. His rucksack was strapped to his back under the jacket. Moving quickly, he took out a flashlight and began searching the drawers until he found what he was looking for. Once it was in his possession, he settled down for the long night ahead of him, taking a sandwich and thermos from his toolbox and eating by the light from his flashlight. He had checked his watch periodically, knowing precisely how long the air in the vault would hold out. When the end of that time period drew near, he took a small oxygen tank and mask from the toolbox and tried to make himself as comfortable as possible, anxiously anticipating his next move: how he was going to make his escape when the vault opened the next morning.

Collin's thoughts returned to the present. He took a quick look at his wristwatch. Six A.M.—the vault would be opening in another hour. It was time to get ready. When the massive door swung open at seven, there would not be a moment to waste. Outside, the manager and at least two security guards would be waiting to enter the vault and remove the jewels that would be taken out to the display cases for the day. He would have to move quickly, taking them by surprise and not giving them a chance to go for their guns until he was able to get far enough away from them to make his escape.

He had thought it all through carefully. Every detail had been taken care of, every possible problem anticipated. If he had learned anything from Blackjack, he had learned to be thorough. Expect anything, his mentor had told him repeatedly. As he put down the oxygen mask and took a pair of high-topped roller skates from the toolbox, he smiled to himself. *I'm learning*, he thought with satisfaction. *I'm definitely learning, old friend.* He took off the scuffed shoes he wore and slipped on the skates, lacing them up tightly. *Nothing like a good set of wheels for a fast getaway*, he thought with mild amusement. He was sure as hell going to surprise them when they opened that door.

For the next hour, he kept a close watch on the time. *Not a minute to spare*, he kept telling himself. *The minute that door opens, you've got to be ready to move—fast!* He took frequent deep breaths of the oxygen that had sustained him throughout the night and struggled to keep a clear head. *No margin for error here*, he thought. *It's like Blackjack always said: one mistake can be your last.* He wondered how Blackjack was doing. He had not seen his friend and mentor in almost three years, since the morning he left Morocco for the last time, but he knew that Blackjack was probably following his activities through the media. His escapades had made headlines on four continents over the past two and a half years, though no one was aware of his true identity. He wondered how Blackjack was enjoying the money he had given him, the money he'd taken from William Harrington's vault, and he hoped his friend knew he had not given up the search for his daughter. He had not turned up anything definite yet, but he fully intended to keep the promise he had made to Blackjack the morning he drove off to Marrakesh.

Six fifty-nine. Collin put the oxygen mask to his face for the last time and took one final deep breath before putting it aside and rolling the black wool ski mask down over his face. He pulled on his leather gloves as he began the final countdown: *Ten . . . nine . . . eight . . . seven. . . .* He could hear the huge tumblers clicking as the combination was sought out automatically. *Six . . . five . . . four. . . .* He drew in his breath as he got to his feet and moved toward the door. *Three . . . two . . . one. . . .* As the huge door swung open, Collin launched himself forward, shooting past the startled manager and security guards, racing toward the front of the store.

"What the hell . . . !" The manager's face went white. He looked as though he were about to go into cardiac arrest, but Collin didn't notice. He was racing through the store at lightning speed, headed for the glass double doors leading out to the rue François. The guards ran after him. "Stop or I'll shoot!" one of them called out to him as he drew his gun. He fired once, but Collin kept moving.

Here goes nothing, Collin thought as he lifted his arms, crisscrossing his forearms in front of his face as he raced headlong at the glass doors. He closed his eyes, hearing the sound of shattering glass as he plunged through the doors and out into the street. He never stopped moving. He heard the shrill sound of the burglar alarms as he streaked down the street. Now he was being pursued by what appeared to be an entire platoon of gendarmes, all shouting and firing, but none of them hitting their mark. *Thank heaven for lousy marksmen*, he thought as he made a sudden turn and dashed into a dark alley, where he hastily shed his jacket and ski mask, changing into a gray jacket over his sweater and slacks. He discarded the jacket, mask, and skates, and stashed the rucksack in a large canvas flight bag. He walked out into the street casually, making his way to a small shop half a block away, where a shopkeeper was watching the police search the area thoroughly.

"What's going on?" he asked in French.

"Someone robbed the jewelry store," the man said, nodding in that direction. "Apparently he was hiding in the vault when they opened this morning and took them completely by surprise. The thief must be insane."

Collin agreed, nodding.

Checkmate, he thought as he walked away.

That same afternoon, Collin arrived at Charles de Gaulle Airport, waiting to board a TWA flight to New York. The necklace was secure in a small chamois bag hanging from a heavy string around his waist inside his trousers. Once again, he was prepared to match wits with the customs inspectors, and there was not the slightest doubt in his mind that, as always, he would triumph. It had become so easy that he no longer considered it a challenge. *It's like riding a tricycle long after you've excelled at motorcycles*, he thought, amused, as he headed for a newsstand.

At the newsstand, he bought himself a small package of mints. The bitter coffee he'd sipped during his long night in the vault had left a terrible taste in his mouth. He unwrapped one and popped it into his mouth. As he started to leave the shop, he caught sight of that day's issue of *Le Monde* on the newspaper rack. The front page carried an account of the daring robbery at "a prominent Right Bank jewelry store.'' *Might as well see what they're saying about me*, he thought as he took a copy and paid the cashier. *Maybe I should start a scrapbook.* He found himself a seat near the gate where he would be boarding his flight and settled down to read the article.

He found it amusing that, once again, there were no leads as to the identity of the man who had hidden in the vault overnight, but that the main suspect in the case was a man the French police now believed had been posing as an electrician in order to gain entry to the vault. They were perplexed by the discovery that only one piece of jewelry had been taken from the vault. *I never take what isn't already mine*, Collin thought, reading on. *That's the difference between myself and my dear brother.*

He sat alone in a row of empty seats on the plane bound for New York. He'd been surprised that customs had not been checking luggage more carefully on the possibility that whoever had taken the necklace in Paris might have tried to leave the country with it. *But then, who would be so foolish?* he thought. As he finished his dinner, he decided that he really was happy to be going home. He had been away far too long this time. Over the past three years, he had spent little time at Sea Cliff. After he left Morocco, he had gone to Rome, where he'd located the Cézanne and the Monet. Another painting had been traced to Geneva. After that, he'd returned to Sea Cliff for six months before leaving for South America, where he'd tracked down several pieces of his mother's jewelry. He had hopped from Caracas to Bogotá to Montevideo to Rio de Janeiro. After that, it had been on to London. And then Madrid. And Biarritz.

He told himself how wonderful it would be to be able to go home to Sea Cliff and just take life easy for a while, but even as the thought crossed his mind, he knew he would never actually do it. No, there was too much yet to be done, too many scores left unsettled. Justin had betrayed and cheated him. But even worse than that, Justin had sold out. He had taken the company their father had built from the ground up, taken the power that he'd inherited, used it, abused it, and then allowed organized crime to move in and take over. Syndicate bosses were stripping it of its assets, taking all that they wanted, and when it was over, Intercontinental Oil would be nothing more than a shell, a shadow of the company it had once been. Though Collin had never wanted the power within the company his father had been willing to give him, he was beginning to think he might have handled that power much better than Justin had. *At least it's not too late to right the wrongs my brother's done*, he thought as he drained his wineglass and the flight attendant took his tray away. Already, he had begun to develop a plan to regain control of the company—and bring down the crime bosses in the process. Trouble was, it was a difficult and dangerous scheme, one he could not possibly pull off alone. *If only Blackjack were here*, he thought. But Blackjack was too old and his health too poor to take an active part in the wild plot Collin had in mind. He needed someone as young and as agile and fearless as himself, someone who had as much reason to want to bring down the bosses as he did himself. Someone who could be trusted. Finding that person, he conceded, was not going to be easy. Those who had a beef against the mob did not generally advertise it.

He was exhausted but found sleep impossible. He read the newspaper he'd bought at the airport from first to last page, then signaled one of the flight attendants. "You wouldn't happen to have a current issue of *The New York Times* on board, would you?" he asked. "I've been away for a very long time and I'd like to catch up on what's going on at home."

The young woman was pretty and blond, in her late twenties, but Collin had too much on his mind to give her more than a casual smile. "As a matter of fact, I bought a copy before I left New York for Paris," she told him. "It's yesterday's issue, though . . ."

"Close enough," Collin said quickly.

She nodded. "I'll get it for you."

So much has been going on; I wonder if I'll even recognize Man-

hattan when I get there. He read the newspaper, surprised by all that had happened in his absence. The renovations on the Statue of Liberty had been completed and the monument reopened in July. Airport security had been tightened due to terrorist attacks against American citizens traveling abroad, particularly after the United States' raid on Libya in April. *Uh-oh*, Collin thought. *Getting past customs at Kennedy may not be as simple as I expected it to be.* He decided he would have to be extremely careful this time.

He flipped to the section covering arts and entertainment. On the first page was an article about Ashley Gordon-Hollister's upcoming exhibit at a well-known Madison Avenue gallery. Ashley Gordon-Hollister. Collin stared at the photograph for a long time. Even if she had not been such an incredibly beautiful woman, she would have fascinated him. Bradley Hollister's former daughter-in-law. She had been married to his estranged son. After Brandon Hollister's death last year, Hollister and his wife had sued for custody of her young son and won. *Probably had the entire San Francisco legal system on his payroll*, Collin thought ruefully. Of all the men he had vowed to get revenge upon, Bradley Hollister was at the top of Collin's list. Hollister ran the syndicate like the awesome power machine that it was, swallowing up legitimate businesses and corporations through which he could conduct his illegal operations without arousing suspicion—and launder his less-than-clean assets. Collin remembered him well. He'd attempted a takeover of Intercontinental Oil when Quentin Deverell was still alive and, Collin suspected now, had been a major contributor to his father's financial problems. As far as Collin was concerned, that meant Hollister had killed his parents just as surely as if he'd caused the explosion on that oil rig. But as much as Collin hated him, he suspected that his former daughter-in-law hated him even more. *There's a woman with good cause to want to see Hollister ruined*, Collin thought, intrigued. *A woman I'd like to meet. I wonder how much she knows about her late husband's illustrious family?*

As the 747 began its descent to Kennedy Airport, Collin

fastened his seat belt and leaned back, mentally preparing himself for whatever might happen in customs. He reached down and touched the leg of his trousers where the chamois bag hung securely. He took a deep breath. *I've come this far. I can make it the rest of the way without getting caught.*

Collin took out his passport as he approached the immigration booth. The inspector took it from him and flipped it open to Collin's picture, staring at it briefly, then looked up at the tall man in the black sweater and trousers and gray jacket with the bulky carryon bag slung over his left shoulder. Then the inspector punched up some keys on his computer. He studied the screen for a moment, then nodded and handed the passport back to Collin. "Welcome home, Mr. Deverell," he said with a friendly smile.

Collin nodded. "Thank you."

He walked on to customs, positioning himself in line behind a short, grossly overweight woman in a bulky mink coat and a tall, thin man wearing a monacle who had three large suitcases to be checked out.

"What do you mean, I have to pay duty on this?" the fat woman raged, waving her hands furiously as the customs inspector took five bottles of expensive French perfume from one of her bags and placed it out on the counter. "These are gifts!"

"You have to include gifts, ma'am. It says so right here on the declaration," the inspector tried to explain, pointing it out on the reverse side of her customs declaration. "This perfume is a hundred and fifty dollars an ounce if it's a penny."

"I'm going to write my congressman about this!" she screeched indignantly.

The man smiled pleasantly. "Please feel free to do so if you think it will help, ma'am," he responded, returning her passport to her.

The man in front of Collin seemed to have enough luggage for a family of six. Collin stood behind him, growing more impatient by the minute as the customs inspector searched each piece, turning up nothing of any interest. Finally, he was allowed to leave. Collin gave a deep sigh of relief as he hoisted his carryon up onto the counter. The inspector recognized him immediately. "Welcome home, Mr. Deverell," he greeted Collin cheerfully. "Long time no see."

"I've been traveling a great deal," Collin said wearily. "And very anxious to get home."

"I can understand that," the inspector said agreeably. "I think with everything that's going on over there now, I'd be more than a little skittish about traveling in Europe."

Collin forced a smile. "I just pretend I'm French or Swiss or German," he said lightly.

The inspector grinned. "Not a bad idea." He placed a chalk mark on Collin's bag without even looking inside. "Just one, as usual?"

Collin nodded.

"Again, welcome home." The man waved him on.

Collin's whole body sagged with relief as he slung the bag over his shoulder again and made his way through the busy terminal to the main exit. He had worried for nothing! But then, he had not expected to encounter a customs inspector who knew him. *Fate's smiling down on me again*, he thought as he pushed his way through the crowd to the taxis outside.

He was heading for an empty taxi when he collided with a woman bound for the same cab. She grasped the door handle firmly and looked up at him, her cheeks flushed and her dark eyes flashing angrily. She looked to be in her late twenties or early thirties, with long, lush dark hair and a lovely face. She wore a black fox-trimmed wool ensemble he'd seen among Pauline Trigère's fall designs in a recent magazine layout, and her face was partly shadowed by the large black fox hat she wore. *My God, she's even more beautiful than her photographs!* he thought, recognizing her immediately.

"I believe I was here first," she said sharply as she opened the door and put one foot inside the cab.

He smiled. *So this is Ashley Gordon-Hollister*, he thought, intrigued. "Far be it from me to argue," he said pleasantly, holding the door for her. He took her luggage and carried it over to the trunk, helping the driver pile it inside. As the cab drove away, he realized that she had not even bothered to thank him. He shrugged it off and got into the next taxi to arrive, giving the driver his address. But as the taxi maneuvered through the heavy traffic on the parkway, he was still thinking about that brief encounter with the lovely young woman he'd just read about. He knew he would be seeing her again.

New York City, November 1986

Ashley walked alone up Fifth Avenue, oblivious of the crowds around her. Her gray wool cape flapped wildly about her in the cold fierce wind that swept down between the skyscrapers, but she took no notice of it. She paid no attention to the glittering displays in the windows of the stores, elegant Christmas displays that served as the first sign of the impending holiday season in Manhattan. Ashley's thoughts were still on the meeting she'd just come from, a conference with the attorney she'd retained to handle her appeal. She'd agreed to this one-woman show in New York because she'd felt it would give her a chance to marshal her forces, to take the Hollisters on once again in the legal arena, get the original ruling overturned, and regain custody of Robert, but her attorney had not been so optimistic. He explained that he'd gone over all the records, all the transcripts of the first hearing, and was surprised by the strength of the case presented by the Hollisters and their attorneys. She had a chance of getting the San Francisco ruling overturned, yes, but at best it would be a slim one. Though Ashley had been tempted for a moment to find herself another lawyer, she finally decided against it because she realized that any attorney she consulted would probably tell her exactly the same thing. Besides, he'd agreed to take the case even though the odds were against them because he believed she deserved to get her child back, and Ashley was convinced she could do a lot worse than Elliott Morgan. She'd talked at length with Harry Wilcox that morning, and he had been satisfied that the attorney was more than capable of acting in her best interests.

She turned the corner at Central Park South, glancing absently at the limousines parked at the entrance of the Plaza and walked on quickly to an apartment building halfway down the block. As she entered the lobby and headed for the elevators, she nodded to the uniformed doorman who held the door for her. She squeezed into a crowded elevator just as the doors closed and drew in a deep breath. She hadn't been fully aware of the cold when she was outdoors, but now, in the cramped space in the elevator, sandwiched between two other tenants and wrapped in her heavy winter cape, she felt unbearably hot. She rode up to her floor in silence, eyes downcast, avoiding eye contact or conversation with others in the elevator. She did not know any of these people and was not up to small talk.

As she stepped out of the car on the tenth floor, she fished through her small black leather handbag for her keys. She let herself into the apartment and closed the door, then pulled off her elbow-length black kidskin gloves and removed the black fox hat she wore. As she removed her cape, she looked around the apartment for a moment. It was beautifully decorated, a blend of Regency and Louis XV, done in shades of blue and green, but it wasn't her. *But then, how could it be?* she asked herself. She'd moved in just last week, having sublet the place from another painter, a former client of Melanie Masters who was now doing a series of exhibits all over Europe, after which she would be spending a year at Cap d'Antibes. Ashley had sublet the apartment for that year, although she hoped she would not be needing it nearly that long. *If all goes well*, she thought, *Robert and I will be going home in a few months.*

She sat down on the couch and took off her black suede boots, then carried them into the bedroom. As she opened the closet door to put them away, she caught sight of herself in the full-length mirror on the inside of the door. The windblown hair, the flushed cheeks, in the wine-colored flannel suit she'd found in mint condition at a vintage clothing store, she was still a stylish woman. People still described her as beautiful, but Ashley felt as if she were nothing more than a shadow of her former self. She still looked the same, still dressed with the same theatrical, highly individual flair, but something was definitely different. Perhaps around the eyes . . . no amount of makeup could enhance her dull, lifeless eyes. In her mind, she could hear Brandon saying, ''The most beautiful thing about you, Ashley, is the sparkle in your eyes.'' *They haven't sparkled in a very long time, Brandon*, she thought sadly. *If only you were here, darling. . . .*

She took off the jacket with its exaggerated shoulders and black velvet lapels and hung it on one of the heavy wooden hangers in the closet. The blouse she wore underneath was made entirely of white lace with a high, Victorian neckline and small pearl buttons. She remembered the first time she had worn it. She and Brandon were having a romantic candlelight dinner at home; Robert had been visiting her parents in St. Helena. She'd worn the blouse with a full-length black velvet skirt and two strands of freshwater pearls, her hair hanging loosely around her shoulders. Brandon had remarked that though the style was very Victorian, the sheerness of the lace was very sexy. Ashley remembered his comment, and for her meeting with Morgan, she'd kept her jacket on.

She crossed the room to the windows. Her bedroom overlooked Central Park, and as she gazed down at the park entrance at the corner of Fifth Avenue and Central Park South, she saw a group of children running down the street, bundled in their warm winter clothing. Thinking of her own son, she felt as though her heart were being ripped from the wall of her chest. Robert, her darling, wonderful son, was just blocks away at the Hollister town house on East Seventy-eighth Street, and she had not been permitted to see him or even speak to him on the phone since her arrival in New York. She'd called Claudia Hollister twice, and each time Claudia had refused to let her visit her son. He was making a difficult adjustment, Claudia had informed her coldly, and seeing her could only make matters worse.

Ashley hugged herself tightly, trembling with rage. She knew perfectly well that Robert's emotional adjustment had nothing at all to do with Claudia's refusal to let her see him. Claudia was just being vindictive. The woman had never been able to accept that she and her husband had driven Brandon away from them long before he had even met her. *This is how she plans to get even with me*, Ashley thought as she stared absently at the pedestrian traffic at the edge of the park.

She sank down onto the bed, taking the framed photograph of Brandon and Robert from the night table. She recalled the day it was taken. They'd been picnicking at the beach, and Brandon was giving Robert a piggyback ride in the sand, with Chaser running along at their heels. When she snapped their picture, she'd been standing only a few feet in front of them and they were charging right at her.

Ashley blinked back tears. Only a year ago, their lives had been so different. They'd been on top of the world. Brandon was still alive, their careers were soaring, *they* were soaring. They'd all been so happy. And now Brandon was gone, she hadn't seen Robert in well over six months, and her whole world had suddenly fallen apart. Once, she'd had it all. But now it took a monumental effort just to get from one day to the next.

The Mason-Gilling Gallery was on Madison Avenue just north of East Seventy-fourth Street. The first time Ashley had gone there with Melanie Masters to discuss her upcoming exhibit with the gallery's owner, the walls were adorned with brightly colored landscapes from an exhibit featuring the works of top Colombian artists. She'd only glanced absently at the paintings as she made her way through the gallery to the office at the back of the building. She would have been able to appreciate the quality of the art had her mind not been on other things, but that particular afternoon her thoughts had been on the same thing they were on every waking moment of every day: her son and how far she would be willing to go to get him back.

Now, as she entered the gallery again, the first thing she noticed was the barren walls. *Barren like my soul*, she thought dismally. Her paintings were on the floor, stacked up against the walls in groups of three or four. She paused for a moment to look through them. There were the seascapes of the California coastline at Big Sur and Carmel, two of San Francisco Bay, six of her early landscapes of the Napa Valley and the winery. The paintings brought back memories, some sweet, some painful. Most painful.

"We haven't had time to hang them yet. I'm sorry."

Startled, Ashley's head jerked up abruptly. The owner of the gallery, Diana Gilling, a tall, reed-thin blonde in her late thirties, stood in the doorway of the office, dressed in an emerald-green suit and navy silk blouse.

"They just arrived this morning," Diana explained.

Ashley forced a smile. "I'd hang them myself if I thought it would ensure the success of the exhibit," she responded as she straightened up, smoothing her calf-length raspberry suede skirt.

Diana laughed. "You have absolutely nothing to worry about," she said confidently. "Take my word for it—this show's going to be a smashing success."

"I hope so. I have butterflies as big as elephants," Ashley admitted, looking down at the paintings again.

"Perfectly normal," Diana reassured her. "I've never met an artist who wasn't at least slightly nervous just before an opening. You're going to be a big success in New York, just as you've been on the West Coast. As a matter of fact, your work is already drawing attention. I've already had a call from a gentleman who just happens to be one of the most influential art patrons—not to mention one of our most enthusiastic collectors—and he's very interested in your work.''

''Oh?'' Ashley was surprised—and intrigued.

Diana nodded. ''He owns a rather impressive collection of masterpieces: Monets, Cézannes, Renoirs, Picassos—''

Ashley gave a little laugh. ''And he's interested in my work?'' she asked. ''A man who owns a collection like that?''

''You could be just as famous one day,'' Diana suggested. ''That's what he's banking on.''

''Only after I'm dead,'' Ashley said quickly. ''Everyone knows artists don't become famous until after they're dead.''

Diana paused for a moment. ''It's good to see you smile, Ashley. I think it's the first time I've seen you do so,'' she said finally. ''I know you've had some personal problems in the past few months . . .''

''Everything will work out,'' Ashley said tightly. ''Right now, I just want to concentrate on making the most of this show.''

Diana Gilling didn't respond. She just stared at Ashley for a moment, wondering if she'd somehow offended her. She watched as Ashley looked through the stacks of paintings once more, and she wondered how Ashley could keep her mind on the upcoming exhibit—or anything else, for that matter—with all the turmoil in her private life. What Diana didn't know, couldn't know, was that Ashley's work, and its potential to help her in her battle to get her child back, was the only thing that kept her mind off her troubles.

The only thing that kept her sane.

Though Ashley's days in Manhattan were busy and full, with interviews and preparations for the opening of her one-woman show, her nights were long and unbearably lonely. Though she had several acquaintances in the New York art world, and Melanie—who was her only close friend as well as being her artist's rep—was in town for the exhibit, she seldom accepted any of the invitations she received to dinner or shows. She spent most of her evenings alone at her apartment, leafing through her photo albums and wishing she could somehow turn back the hands of time. Looking at the photos of Brandon and Robert brought back all of those wonderful, painful memories. It always left her depressed and made her cry, but she was unable to stop, unable to make herself put the albums away. *I must be a masochist*, she thought darkly. *Why do I keep torturing myself like this?*

"You have to either put it all behind you or drag the Hollisters back into court again and fight it out," Melanie had told her more than once, and was now telling her again over lunch at La Côte Basque.

"Easier said than done," Ashley said with a weary shake of her head. "You've got two kids of your own, Mel—how would you feel if some judge took them away from you and you couldn't even visit them?"

"I'd fight back," Melanie answered without hesitation.

"I've already seen an attorney here in Manhattan," Ashley told her, glancing absently around the crowded restaurant at the Lamotte murals of the Basque coast and harbors. She drew in a deep breath. "He's agreed to take the case, but I have the feeling he's not terribly optimistic about my chances of winning an appeal. This could be my last chance to get Robert back."

Melanie sipped her wine thoughtfully. "It seems to me that if you can't regain custody, you could at least get the court to order the Hollisters to allow you visitation rights."

Ashley shook her head. "Not when the judge is in Bradley Hollister's hip pocket," she said gloomily. She put down her fork. "If only I could prove it . . ."

"Careful." Melanie regarded her warily. "If you're considering something foolish . . ."

"Don't worry," Ashley said, frowning. "I'm not about to do anything stupid. Not after coming this far."

"You have a great deal going for you now, Ashley," Melanie reminded her.

"I don't have my son. I don't have my husband," Ashley responded flatly.

"No, you don't," Melanie conceded. "But you do have your career, something you've worked hard to achieve. And you do have a chance to get Robert back."

Ashley's eyes met Melanie's. "That chance, Mel," she said evenly, "is the only thing that keeps me going. If I lose that, too, I don't know what I'll do."

Ashley walked alone in Central Park, bundled against the sharp winter winds in a silver fox jacket and matching hat. She walked every day, even on the coldest days, and did at least an hour of yoga each night on a mat on her bedroom floor. She'd taken it up right after she left St. Helena for San Francisco, because she'd discovered it relieved the tension in her muscles that came from standing in front of her easel for long periods of time. Now, she walked and performed her yoga routines in the same way she painted and did everything else in her life: with a vengeance. Everything she did, every move she made was done with a barely controlled inner rage that consumed her like a great flame. Every waking moment was spent in search of release from her torment, a never-ending search for a way to dispel the darkness from her soul. But no matter what she did or how hard she tried, nothing helped. Nothing gave her any real relief. Nothing, but nothing, took away the pain.

Ashley drew her jacket tightly around herself as she walked. Her cheeks stung in the bitterly cold wind. It was an unusually cold day, even for New York in late November. She watched as a group of children in brightly colored ski jackets and knitted caps raced toward the Wollman rink, skates in hand. The sight of those happy-go-lucky children brought tears to her eyes. In her mind, she saw Robert that winter she and Brandon took him to Lake Tahoe the week between Christmas and New Year's. Robert had so enjoyed that vacation. Brandon had taught him to ice skate. Ashley had never been on skates in her life and had been afraid to try, despite her husband's encouragement.

"I've never skated before, Brandon," she'd confessed as

she helped Robert lace up his skates. "There's not much opportunity to learn in the valley."

"There's nothing to it," Brandon had insisted. "I used to skate at the Rockefeller Center rink every winter when I was a kid."

Ashley sighed softly. It was the only time in all the years she'd known Brandon that he'd ever mentioned any positive childhood memories. She'd always wondered why—until Brandon's death, when the Hollisters had shown their true colors.

She looked up, catching sight of a plump, gray-haired woman leading a small boy by the hand several yards ahead of her. Ashley's heart nearly stopped. "Robert!" she called out. "Robert!" Neither the child nor the woman responded. Ashley raced forward, stopping dead in her tracks as the boy turned and she got a closer look at his face. *It's not Robert*, she thought, her whole body sagging with the tremendous weight of her disappointment. *My God, it's not Robert*.

She stood there stock-still, watching as the woman and child disappeared in the distance. She drew in her breath, realizing at that moment that she could not go on like this, tormenting herself this way.

She had to see her son.

Ashley was trembling as she got out of the taxi in front of the Hollisters' elegant three-story brownstone on Manhattan's Upper East Side. She had not been there since she had come with Brandon just before they were married. She had not seen the Hollisters since they had left San Francisco after taking custody of Robert. *I have to face them sooner or later*, she told herself. *They're going to find out soon enough why I'm really here. They might as well hear it from me*.

She paid the cab driver and stood on the curb, preparing herself as if for battle. She took a deep breath, pulled her shoulders back and her back straight, then turned back to the town house. Galvanized by her fierce determination to be reunited with her son one way or another, she pushed

open the heavy wrought-iron gate and marched purposely
up the sidewalk to the front door. She rang the doorbell
impatiently until the door was finally opened by Mason, the
Hollisters' major domo. He smiled, his eyes lighting with
recognition when he saw her. "Good day, Miss Gordon—
uh, Mrs. Hollister," he greeted her warmly, stepping aside
so she could enter the reception hall.

*They obviously don't discuss the skeletons in their closets in front of
the staff*, Ashley thought as she pulled off her black gloves
and looked around. "Is Claudia—Mrs. Hollister—in?" she
asked.

"Yes, madam, she is," Mason replied in his stiff, formal
manner. "I believe she's in the library. I'll tell her you're
here."

"Thank you, Mason."

As he disappeared down the long corridor, Ashley opened
the front of her silver fox jacket, suddenly feeling uncomfortably warm. *Where's Robert?* she wondered, looking up the
stairs, hoping for a glimpse of her son. It had been over
eight months since he was taken from her that afternoon in
San Francisco, and not a day had passed in that time that
she had not wondered if he was all right, if he'd adjusted to
his new life, if he still believed she would keep her promise
and come for him. She had worried that he might be suffering. She was even more concerned now, as she surveyed
the marble and crystal glamour around her. She'd forgotten
how beautiful the Hollisters' home was, and how cold and
loveless. *It's not a home, it's a goddamned museum*, she thought,
troubled.

"What are you doing here?"

Ashley's head jerked up abruptly. Claudia Hollister stood
on the landing, a look of disdain on her face.

"It's good to see you, too, Claudia," Ashley responded
dryly. "I've come to see Robert," she added as Claudia
descended the stairs.

"Out of the question," Claudia snapped. "May I ask
who the hell let you in here?"

"Mason did," Ashley replied. "You know, Claudia, you

really should let your people know who gets in and who doesn't.''

"I intend to," Claudia said coldly. "You'll have to leave—now."

Ashley steeled herself against Claudia's glacial stare. "Not until I've seen my son," she said evenly.

"Then I'll have you removed—"

"Mommy!"

Both of them looked up. Robert was at the top of the stairs, beaming at the sight of his mother. He raced down the staircase as fast as his small legs would carry him and flew into Ashley's arms. "I knew you'd come, Mommy!" he cried, burying his face in her neck. "Even when Brad and Claudia told me you were gone, that I'd never see you again, I knew—"

Ashley looked at Claudia, amused. "He calls you Claudia?" she asked.

Claudia stiffened. "He says we're not his grandparents, that they're at the winery," she said nervously. "Your fault, of course."

"What did you expect?" Ashley demanded. "You're strangers to him!" She turned to Robert again, kissing his forehead. "I'd never forget you, baby," she murmured.

"I think you'd better leave," Claudia insisted firmly.

Ashley ignored her. "Are you all right, darling?" she asked softly as she lowered him to the floor and knelt in front of him.

"I am now, Mommy," he said, hugging her tightly. "Am I going with you?"

"I think you should leave," Claudia said again.

"Not this time, sport, but soon," Ashley promised. "Very soon. You have my word on it."

"Will you leave now, or must I call the police?" Claudia demanded impatiently.

Ashley looked up at her for a moment, then got to her feet slowly. "I'm going," she said carefully, struggling to keep her anger in check. "But I'll be back."

Claudia's eyes met Ashley's, and her gaze was ice cold. "It won't do you any good," she said sharply.

Ashley returned her stare. "We'll see," she said quietly, "we'll see." She kissed her son good-bye, turned, and walked out.

Sea Cliff, Long Island, November 1986

Collin sat on the overstuffed couch in the massive, oak-paneled library at the Deverell estate, reading the morning newspapers. All of the New York City newspapers were delivered to him daily, and he read them all religiously, first page to last, especially since his return from Paris, since that chance meeting with Ashley Gordon-Hollister at Kennedy Airport. Now, as he reclined on the couch, dressed in jeans and a bulky gray sweater, finishing his morning coffee and the *Daily News* simultaneously, he was intrigued by the photograph of the beautiful woman staring back at him. Intrigued by the memory of that hot-tempered woman he'd encountered that day at the airport. Intrigued by the guts she'd displayed in publicly announcing her intentions to do legal battle with the Hollisters once again for custody of her young son. Collin admired her spirit. *Maybe I've found myself a partner after all*, he thought as he studied the photograph.

Putting down his coffee, he got to his feet and went over to the desk. He carefully cut out the photograph and accompanying article. Taking a large brown envelope from one of the drawers, he emptied its contents onto the desk. More clippings. Everything he'd been able to accumulate on Ashley Gordon-Hollister. Clippings from both New York and San Francisco newspapers, from the gallery guides and artists' magazines. In the past few weeks he'd managed to accumulate a great deal of information on the lady. *I probably know as much about her as her own mother does*, Collin thought, satisfied. The opening of her one-woman show was only a week away, and he was going to be there. He had the feeling that Fate had intervened the day they collided at that taxi stand, that they were meant to meet, to forge an alliance, an alliance that would enable both of them to achieve their objectives. Maybe she didn't know everything about her ex-father-in-law's business interests, but Collin was willing to bet she knew enough about the Hollisters to make cultivating a relationship with her worthwhile. He smiled as he stared thoughtfully at one of the photographs. Knowing this woman, he decided, would be worthwhile even if she weren't a Hollister, even if her family connections weren't so vitally important to his cause.

He put all the clippings back in the envelope and returned it to the drawer. Automatically, he took his keys from his pocket and locked the drawer. He'd never had a problem with servants prying into his private papers, but he saw no reason to place temptation in their paths. In his world, there was no one who could be trusted completely, no one he could confide in—except Henry Harrison. The houseman was his only confidant, the only other person in the world besides Blackjack who knew what he was doing and why. Harrison knew because Collin had often found it necessary to enlist his aid in carrying out some of his schemes. Collin wasn't sure the older man approved of his methods, but Harrison was not one to pass judgment: he just discreetly looked the other way.

Collin went to the built-in bookshelves on one side of the room. Removing one specific volume from its place on the shelf, he released a concealed lever. The entire wall panel moved to one side, and Collin stepped inside a small, darkened room behind it as the panel moved back into place. The hidden chamber was now bathed in a dim, eerie green glow emanating from several computer terminals lined up against one wall. He'd installed them here—where even his own household staff would not be aware of their existence—over a year ago. His computers' memory banks contained vast amounts of data he'd accumulated over the past four years involving key members of organized crime—from business activities to personal information—as well as the names and assets of companies owned or controlled by the syndicate.

At first, Collin had been amazed at how many supposedly legitimate businesses and corporations were underworld-connected. The syndicate was like a giant octopus, and its tentacles of power seemed to be everywhere. They owned giant conglomerates and mom-and-pop-type businesses alike. They employed two-bit hoods and had policemen, attorneys, judges, and high-level politicians on the payrolls. They controlled automobile dealerships and insurance companies, retail stores and wholesalers, restaurants and theaters, and many publications. An illegal operation hiding behind a deceptively legitimate front, Collin thought as he pondered the data on the screen. It was staggering.

He had used documents and other information he'd stolen from the homes of some of those upper-level syndicate men to assemble a profile of sorts of the underworld and its members. Collin was a firm believer in knowing as much as possible about his adversaries before the attack. *Learn their weaknesses—and their strengths*, he told himself. That was where Ashley Gordon-Hollister would come in handy, or so he hoped. She'd been married to Hollister's son. Surely she knew something about Hollister's operation—but how much? There had been bad blood between Hollister and his only son for several years before the younger Hollister's death. Why? Did it have anything to do with the syndicate?

Whatever Ashley Hollister knew, Collin intended to make use of it—and of her. After all she'd been through, she had to hate Hollister as much as he did. Probably more. He felt she was someone he could trust with the knowledge of his secret life and the details of his plans. She could be a big help to him. As a thief, he'd been able to operate alone quite successfully, but for what he had in mind now, two heads were definitely better than one. Two bodies as well, in many cases, he conceded reluctantly. Though he was certain his cat burglar days were far from over, his overall game plan called for something even more complicated: a con game, a means of accumulating evidence against Hollister and his lieutenants. Much of what Collin had in mind couldn't be accomplished alone. Ashley was a beautiful woman with a score to settle, and if there was one weakness common to most men, it was a beautiful woman. Collin smiled to himself. As his father always liked to say, the chain was only as strong as its weakest link. In time, Collin would find the syndicate's weak link.

And he would bring the underworld's most powerful group to its knees.

At his office in Manhattan, Anton DeVries read and reread a report he'd received from Interpol three days earlier. A report concerning the theft of a diamond and sapphire necklace from Ferrand-Bessèges Jewelers in Paris. Law enforcement officials had been puzzled, not only by the theft itself—which they described as imaginative, daring, and carried out in broad daylight in full view of the manager and half a dozen security guards—but also by the fact that only one item had been taken. The thief, they suspected, had been in the vault all night. He'd had ample time to take whatever he wished. There had been jewels in the vault worth a king's ransom, yet their thief had taken only one necklace. And it was not even the most expensive one, they reported, puzzled. He had made his escape on roller skates. Roller skates! Who would even think of such a thing?

DeVries felt like a bloodhound who'd just picked up the scent. Over the past few months he'd read countless reports coming out of Interpol headquarters in Paris concerning a rash of similar, daring robberies taking place across four continents. Interpol claimed the thefts were the work of a ring of flamboyant cat burglars. DeVries had a theory of his own. He'd been bothered by a growing suspicion over the past six months that was now an overwhelming feeling of certainty. He took another file from the cabinet next to his desk and looked it over carefully. There it was: a diamond and sapphire necklace worth a quarter of a million dollars. He was sure now that he'd been on the right track. There was no burglary ring. There was only one man, one brilliant, resourceful, very determined man.

Collin Deverell.

The blade of his saber flashed brilliantly as Collin darted about with lightning speed, his opponent struggling to fend off his frighteningly aggressive attack. Normally, Collin would have given all of himself to his game; it would have been the only thing on his mind. But today his body functioned while his mind was elsewhere. He was thinking about a telephone conversation he'd had that morning with William McNichol, who had been general manager of Intercontinental Oil for as long as he could remember. Once he and Justin were grown, McNichol ended up on friendlier terms with Collin than with Justin, perhaps because Justin had that irritating tendency to keep everyone at arm's length. Now McNichol was being kept uninformed intentionally, despite his position within the company. To Collin, the reasons were obvious.

McNichol had phoned Collin because, he explained, there was no one else he could turn to with his suspicions. "I think your brother and some of the board members have in mind the liquidation of the company," he'd said, concerned.

"Liquidate?" Collin couldn't hide his surprise. "Is the company in such bad shape financially that it can't be saved at all?"

"Bad shape?" McNichol's laugh was hollow. "Collin, Intercontinental's problems could have been solved—until your brother brought in those friends of his, whoever they really are. They've been stripping the company, transferring assets—"

"Transferring assets?" Collin interrupted. "What the hell for?"

"That's just it. I don't know for sure," McNichol admitted. "Justin's deliberately kept me in the dark about it. I wouldn't have known anything, had I not stumbled onto it when I was checking out some discrepancies on the computer.''

"What kind of discrepancies?" Collin asked carefully.

"Minor things. Funds unaccounted for, stock transfers, things like that." The man was clearly concerned. "When I saw what was happening—"

"Exactly what *is* happening?" Collin wanted to know. "How are they doing away with Intercontinental's assets?"

"Transferring large blocks of stock, moving assets to other corporations—dummy corporations if my hunch is correct." McNichol paused for a moment. "It's incredible what they've been doing. It's like watching a flock of vultures pick a carcass clean."

"Why did you call me?" Collin asked in a cautious tone. "What is it you want me to do—or more accurately, what do you think I can do?"

"I don't know, Collin," the other man had answered truthfully. "I just didn't know where else to go with this. I certainly couldn't go to Justin, and it's getting more and more difficult to tell who on the board—or even on the upper-executive level—can be trusted."

"Unfortunately, my position within the company ceased to exist ten years ago," Collin reminded him. "I don't even hold stock."

"I thought you might be able to find out something from Justin . . ."

"I'm afraid that's not possible either," Collin responded solemnly. "I haven't seen my dear brother in some time, and I suspect that's the way he likes it."

"I know you washed your hands of Intercontinental Oil when your parents were killed, Collin," McNichol began hesitantly, "but I can't believe you'd just sit back and allow everything Quentin worked for be destroyed like this."

"I'm not really in a position to do anything, Bill," Collin reminded him. "But give me time to think about it. Maybe with the two of us working together, I might be able to come up with something."

Collin's thoughts returned to the present abruptly as he

launched an offensive attack against his opponent. He was glad Bill McNichol had called him first. The man's hunch had been correct: going to Justin would have been a mistake, and there was no one on the present board of directors who could be trusted. No, Bill McNichol had done the right thing. Though Collin could not tell anyone, not even his father's most trusted executive, he did have something in mind. He was relieved to still have someone inside the company from whom he could obtain information.

Bill McNichol had been right about something else, too: regardless of his personal feelings where Intercontinental Oil was concerned, there was a part of him that could not, would not, allow him to simply stand back and watch all that his father had worked so hard to achieve be destroyed by his brother's ineptitude. Collin could not let almost thirty years of his father's life be for nothing.

I owe him that much, he thought dismally.

Three days later, Collin telephoned William McNichol at home. "Can you get me a computer printout of all the data you told me about?" he asked.

There was a momentary hesitation on the other end. "Of course," he said finally. "I'll bring it by tomorrow evening, if that's convenient."

"I'll make it convenient," Collin said quickly. "Come around eight-thirty."

"Could we make it nine?"

"Fine." Collin paused. "I know I don't have to tell you this, Bill, but I don't think you should mention this conversation to anyone."

"I wouldn't even consider it."

"Will you have a problem in getting the printout without arousing suspicion?" Collin asked, scribbling some notes on a yellow legal pad as they talked. He didn't want to, but he could always break into the offices after hours to get what he needed.

"No problem," McNichol assured him. "After all, in

spite of your brother's efforts to keep me out of these matters, I am still the company's general manager."

"A general manager who's being excluded from most of the intracompany activity," Collin added gravely. "Face it, Bill, my brother's treating you like a mushroom these days. He's keeping you in the dark and feeding you a lot of shit."

"That's not far from the truth," McNichol admitted reluctantly.

"Justin's a goddamned fool," Collin said then, glancing over the notes he'd made. "That's about the best explanation I can offer at this point."

As he replaced the receiver on its cradle, Collin thought about it. He wished he could offer Bill McNichol some sort of reassurance, but he couldn't. He belonged to a world where no one could be trusted, where only a loner had any real chance of survival.

And in the end, it's only that end result that counts, he told himself as he switched off the lamp on the desk and went upstairs to bed.

"As you can see, they're bleeding us dry," William McNichol told Collin as they looked over the computer printout together. "Assets are being transferred on a daily basis and the stock is being bought up by a select few. And oddly enough, Justin is not among those few."

Collin stared at the printout for a long time, rubbing his chin thoughtfully. "Isn't this sort of thing illegal?" he asked at last.

"Only if the stock is being obtained under fraudulent circumstances," McNichol answered. "If that were the case, it would be a matter of calling for an inquiry through the Securities and Exchange Commission."

Collin turned to look at him. "But it isn't the case?"

McNichol shook his head. "Not so far as I know," he said darkly. "I wouldn't swear to it, of course—under the circumstances, anything is possible—but it appears that they're obtaining their blocks of Intercontinental stock through perfectly legal channels."

Collin frowned. "These people have a way of making everything they do *appear* legal even though it usually isn't," he said tightly.

"You might claim you were swindled by your own brother and take legal action," McNichol said grimly. "But by the time you could drag him through the courts and get back your share of the company—which would be a long shot—they'd have more than enough time to strip the company completely." He took another printout from his attaché case and spread it out on the desk as Harrison entered the room with a heavy silver tray laden with sandwiches and coffee for the two men. "Take a look at this—" He stopped short when he saw Harrison.

"It's all right," Collin assured him, running a hand through his hair in frustration. He took a sandwich from the tray and offered McNichol one. The older man shook his head. "As you can see, Collin, large blocks of stock have been acquired by each of these men over the past six months. If they keep it up, by the end of the year these six men will be in control of Intercontinental Oil. Even Justin will be out."

Collin bit into his sandwich and chewed slowly as he studied the printout. "Interesting. My dear brother's being shafted by his own people and doesn't know it," he muttered.

"Exactly, but I doubt he'll believe it if we tell him," McNichol said, reaching for the coffee. "For an intelligent man, he's been surprisingly naive where these people are concerned."

"Maybe I could call their bluff . . . ask the SEC for an inquiry anyway," Collin suggested.

McNichol shook his head. "It wouldn't work."

"But it might shake them up a bit," Collin went on. "The last thing my brother's business associates want is to call attention to themselves. If I were to go to Justin and make the threat, it just might be enough to force them to keep a low profile for a while. It would buy us a little time, don't you think?"

McNichol sipped his coffee. "What good will that do?" he asked, still not convinced.

"Maybe none at all," Collin admitted. "But it could give us enough time to come up with a better idea, time I'm going to need to figure this out."

"If you need anything at all—"

Collin forced a smile. "You'll be the first person I'll call," he assured the older man. "You can count on that."

McNichol got to his feet. "Keep the printout," he said as he placed his attaché case on the desk and snapped it shut. "I have my own copy."

Collin nodded. "Thank you for calling this to my attention, Bill," he said as he walked McNichol to the front door.

The other man frowned. "I just hope it's not too late to do something about this," he said gravely.

"Me, too." Collin opened the door. He hesitated for a moment. "Be careful, Bill," he cautioned. "These people are dangerous. If they suspect anything at all—" He stopped short. "They *can't* suspect. We have to make certain they don't."

William McNichol looked puzzled by his statement but did not question him about it. "They won't," he assured Collin. "I've been general manager of this company for over twenty-six years. I know how to handle it. They'll never suspect a thing."

"Don't call me from the office," Collin warned. "No one must know we've had any contact at all. Understand?"

The older man looked at him, opening his mouth as if he wanted to say something, then changed his mind. He shook his head. "I'll be in touch," he said, shaking Collin's hand.

Collin leaned on the balustrades, watching as McNichol descended the steps and made his way to his Mercedes. The man was worried, that was obvious.

And so was he.

"Your heart's not in it," Melanie Masters diagnosed over the crème brûlée she was having for dessert at Le Cirque.

Ashley looked up from the mocha cake she'd been picking

at with her fork for the past twenty minutes and gave Melanie a tired smile. Her dark eyes were shadowed by the wide brim of the scarlet hat that matched her cashmere peplum jacket. "It's that obvious?" she asked.

Melanie nodded. "It's that obvious," she said, concerned. She leaned forward, the light reflecting off the gleaming gold greyhound pin she wore on the lapel of her Chanel cavalry twill suit. "I hope," she began, dropping her voice almost to a whisper, "you can at least fake a little enthusiasm for the opening. All the top art critics in Manhattan will have their eyes on you that first night."

Ashley raised a hand to silence her. "Don't worry about me, Mel. I'll be on my very best behavior," she promised. "I'll have that smile painted on if I have to."

Melanie smiled patiently. "I hope that won't be necessary," she said, smoothing back a lock of her short, reddish-brown hair that peeked from beneath the black velvet cloche she wore. Her dark brown eyes reflected sympathy for Ashley's predicament. "Your work was always so important to you."

"A lot of things were important to me," Ashley said gravely. "It just happens that my work is all I have left."

"You're going to need money—a great deal of money—if you're to go on battling your in-laws," Melanie reminded her. "This exhibit could be very important to that battle from a financial standpoint."

Ashley's laugh was hollow. "You must be expecting all of the paintings to sell," she said, keeping her voice light.

Melanie lit a cigarette. "Most of them already have," she announced with a sly smile.

"What?" Ashley looked up, confused. "What do you mean, most of them have already sold? The paintings haven't even been shown yet . . ."

"I just found out myself this morning. It seems that Diana arranged a private showing for that collector she told you about," Melanie explained. "Apparently he's absolutely fallen in love with your work and has reserved all but six of the paintings for himself."

"Who is this . . . patron of the arts?" Ashley wanted to know.

"His name is Collin Deverell." Melanie flicked her ashes into an ashtray. "I'm told he's quite rich—a philanthropist, Diana says. Rumor has it he owns one of the most impressive collections in the world."

"How much?"

"What?"

"How much did the paintings bring?" Ashley asked impatiently.

"Two hundred fifty thousand dollars."

Ashley couldn't mask her surprise. "He's willing to pay that much—"

"As I said, he obviously has a great deal of admiration for your work," Melanie said, pleased. She scooped up the last of the crème brûlée and finished it.

"He must be madly in love with it to buy a quarter of a million dollars' worth of paintings," Ashley speculated, still quite stunned by the news. She straightened up in her chair and shook her head, trying to absorb the reality.

"That should make you very happy," Melanie said promptly.

"Oh, it does," Ashley assured her. "It also makes me a little self-conscious."

"Why?"

"I don't know. I suppose it's because no one's ever made such a large investment in my work before. Except—" She stopped short, thinking of Michael Anthony, who had literally bankrolled her career those first months in San Francisco. "I suppose it doesn't make any difference—as long as he's buying the paintings."

"No, it doesn't," Melanie said emphatically. "And you, my dear, should be very pleased with yourself. How often does a painter—even a very successful one—sell almost all of her paintings almost a week before her exhibit opens?"

Ashley smiled weakly. *I can only hope my luck holds out*, she thought.

* * *

Collin stood on the fire escape outside Ashley's bedroom window, dressed in black pants and turtleneck sweater. He hesitated for only a moment before picking the lock on the window. Raising it carefully, he swung one leg inside, then the other. Perched on the windowsill, he looked around for a moment, then slid inside. The room was in total darkness except for the dim light from the street lamps below filtering through the sheer curtains that billowed in the soft, cold breeze. This, he realized at that moment, was the first time in his years as a professional thief that he'd victimized someone not connected with the syndicate, someone who did not have something that belonged to him. *It's necessary*, he reminded himself. He had to learn as much as he could about this woman before they met again, before he approached her with a proposition that would make her his partner. He had to know just how much, if anything, she knew about Bradley Hollister and his so-called business interests. He had to know as much as possible about the woman herself if he intended to trust her with his own secrets.

He searched the drawers in her night table first and found an address book and a few letters, along with a photo album. No surprises there. The letters, he found upon closer inspection, were from her parents in California. The photos were candids of her husband and son. He went to the dresser. Nothing important there, either. It was odd, he decided. Normally, a home reflected the life and the personality of those who lived there, but this apartment was as barren and impersonal as any he'd ever seen. It seemed that whoever lived there did not really live, but simply existed, as if the soul were a blank canvas, lacking any real depth or feeling. *She's dead and doesn't know it*, he thought, oddly disturbed by the discovery. There were none of the little things that were normally present, even in a home that had not been occupied for long—pictures on display, little personal effects, items to which the inhabitant was especially attached. *I've seen hotel rooms that were more personal*, he thought as he rummaged through her drawers.

He found nothing that would indicate to him what kind

of woman Ashley Gordon-Hollister really was, what she was like or what she might once have been like. He opened her lingerie drawer and took out a sheer raspberry silk nightgown. As he held it up and stared at it speculatively, he thought about the woman who wore it. *This is as personal as you get, isn't it, Ashley?* He fingered the off-white lace trim. More than once, he'd wondered what she looked like under those stylish clothes of hers. Now he wondered what she must look like in that sheer, provocative nightgown. Ashley Gordon-Hollister was a very attractive woman, and Collin had to admit—if only to himself—that his interest in her went beyond making her his accomplice. In his mind, he saw her as she'd looked that day at Kennedy Airport— cheeks flushed, dark eyes flashing. A woman with spirit. Collin wondered what she must be like in bed. A tigress, probably. Dismissing the thought abruptly, he put the nightgown back in the drawer and closed it, going on about his business.

In twenty minutes he'd managed to search the apartment from top to bottom but found nothing of any real significance, nothing that revealed anything important about the woman who lived there. The woman he'd chosen to be his partner. Collin finally gave up. As he climbed through the window to the fire escape, his gaze swept over the room one last time. There was, he decided, only one way he was going to find out what he wanted to know about Ashley Gordon-Hollister, and that was going to be from the lady herself.

Face-to-face.

"You're not even dressed yet!" Melanie stood in the doorway, dressed in an oversize gray jacket over a slim black skirt. "Ashley, we're expected at the gallery in one hour!"

"Relax," Ashley said quickly, letting her into the apartment. She looked down at her black silk robe. "All I have to do is get into my dress and we can leave."

"You're smiling," Melanie observed, dropping her small handbag on the couch. "At least I can be thankful for that."

"It wasn't as difficult as I expected it to be," Ashley

admitted as she disappeared into the bedroom. She raised her voice so Melanie could hear her. "All I had to do was remind myself that this exhibit, and specifically the patronage of one Mr. Collin Deverell, will bankroll my custody battle." There was a brief silence. "You know where the bar is, Mel, if you'd like a drink—"

"I think I'll pass," Melanie said without hesitation. "There's going to be plenty to drink at the gallery, and I do have to keep a clear head tonight."

"Will the mysterious Collin Deverell be there?" Ashley asked.

"I don't really know," Melanie answered. "I would think so, considering the size of his investment in your work."

"Good." Ashley opened her closet and took out the dress she'd bought especially for the exhibit opening. "I'd like to meet him." She paused. "What were you able to find out about him from Diana?"

"Not much," was Melanie's reply. "It would appear that no one knows very much about the man. He pretty much stays to himself."

"Someone must know something." Ashley opened her lingerie drawer and stopped short. Something was wrong . . . different. She couldn't put her finger on it, but something was definitely different. She had the uncomfortable feeling that someone else had been here, in her bedroom. Someone had been in these drawers. She checked her jewelry case. As far as she could tell, nothing was missing. She didn't have time to check everything thoroughly, but she would certainly do so when she returned from the gallery tonight.

"Only the most basic information," Melanie was saying. "Collin Deverell is one of the identical twin sons of Quentin Deverell, founder—and until ten years ago, chairman of the board—of Intercontinental Oil. He's one of the ten richest men in the country, not to mention one of the most attractive and eligible bachelors in New York." She paused, looking at her diamond-encrusted wristwatch. "Ashley, I hate to press you, but—"

"One more minute, Mel," she called out. "That's all I need."

Minutes later, Ashley emerged from the bedroom, wearing a red silk jacquard dress with a four-strand pearl and ruby choker and large ruby earrings. Her dark hair was full and loose, but anchored above her ears by antique tortoise-shell combs. "Shall we go?" she asked with a forced cheerfulness in her voice. "I'm dying to meet my new patron."

The Mason-Gilling Gallery was crowded. As Ashley and Melanie entered, photographers clustered around them, flashbulbs popping continually in their faces. Across the room, Diana Gilling, who had been chatting with a *New York Times* art critic, waved them over. Ashley pushed past the reporters forcefully and, followed closely by Melanie, made her way through the crowd. "I was beginning to wonder if you'd decided not to put in an appearance at your own opening," Diana said in a low, half-joking voice as Ashley reached her side. "This, my dear, is Rance Bascomb of the *Times*. Rance, may I present Ashley Gordon-Hollister and Melanie Masters."

"It's a pleasure to meet you both," the man said pleasantly as he shook hands with both women. "And may I also tell you, Mrs. Hollister, how much I admire your work?"

Ashley favored him with her most dazzling smile. "You most certainly may, Mr. Bascomb," she told him. "You'll get no objection from me."

While Melanie engaged in a serious conversation about the important new painters on the international art scene with Bascomb, Diana patiently introduced Ashley to each of the other critics present. "Is he here?" Ashley whispered as they maneuvered through the crowd.

"Who?" Diana looked puzzled.

"Collin Deverell. I'm very eager to meet him."

Diana shook her head. "I haven't seen him, but then, he doesn't show for too many openings," she admitted. "When he's interested in a new artist, he generally arranges to buy whatever he wants before the show. I get the feeling he hates crowds.''

"Oh." Ashley felt oddly let down.

"But," Diana continued, "there are plenty of people here tonight who are dying to meet you. Come—I see Harriet Ambrose over there . . ."

Weary from all the introductions and attempts to make small talk with all the so-called important people who had turned out for her first plunge into the New York art world, Ashley finally managed to extract herself from Diana's protective grasp. As she wandered through the gallery, inspecting each of the paintings exhibited, someone handed her a glass of wine. Her dark eyes scanned the room, searching the faces of each of the men, wondering if any of them could be the mysterious Collin Deverell. If he'd bought almost all of her paintings, why wouldn't he come to find out if the exhibit were a critical success?

She paused in front of one of the paintings, a landscape depicting the richness and color of the Napa Valley as she had known it when she was growing up there. She sipped her wine thoughtfully, trying to imagine what Collin Deverell must look like. Melanie said he was attractive. Ashley knew without asking that he had to be very rich. She envisioned a tall man in his late forties or early fifties, with a stern, serious face and piercing eyes. Dark hair, just beginning to go gray. Intelligent, aristocratic. Oil rich. Melanie had told her that he was one of the most eligible bachelors in New York, so she knew at least one thing about him: there was no Mrs. Deverell.

"I take it you have a special fondness for that particular painting." A very distinct masculine voice cut through her thoughts.

Startled, Ashley jerked around. Standing to her left was a tall, lean, well-built man who appeared to be in his early thirties, with thick, wavy brown hair that curled around his ears and strong, angular features. His eyes were brown and very intense, and Ashley thought he looked positively dashing in his black tuxedo. But it was his smile that held her attention. It was disarming. "I beg your pardon?" she asked, not sure she'd heard him correctly.

"The painting—it's a personal favorite?"

She looked up at it for a moment, then nodded, smiling. "In a way," she confessed. "One might say it's a reminder of happier times."

"I see." He studied the painting himself for a few moments. "I'm rather fond of it myself. It reminds me of some of the works by the great Impressionist painters—Monet, Cézanne."

"I take it you like Impressionist art," she concluded, smiling as she finished her wine.

"Impressionist, Renaissance—anything but abstract."

She raised an eyebrow. "You're not big on modern art?" she asked.

He shrugged. "When I look at a painting or a piece of sculpture, if I have to ask what it is, then to me it's not art," he responded with a grin.

Ashley laughed aloud. She couldn't remember the last time she'd really felt like laughing. The man—whoever he was—had sparked something in her that had been buried for a long time. "You sound like—" she stopped short, realizing she was about to tell him he sounded exactly like Brandon, and her smile vanished. "—like someone I once knew," she finished quietly.

He smiled. "I hope you mean that as a compliment."

Ashley nodded. "I do."

"I'm glad." He paused. "And now that I've met the artist, I'm glad I bought so many of her works. My only regret is that I didn't take them all."

"Bought most of my paintings?" Ashley turned, staring at him in disbelief. "Then you—"

He gave her a devastating smile as he extended his hand. "Allow me to introduce myself," he said graciously. "My name is Collin Deverell."

New York City, December 1986

Ashley sank into a tub filled with billowing clouds of fragrant bubbles and attempted to relax, but found it was not possible. Ever since the night of the opening, the night she first suspected someone had been in her apartment when she wasn't there, she'd been nervous and jumpy when she was alone here, especially at night. She was convinced that someone had indeed broken into her apartment, and that whoever had done it might return, possibly even when she was home.

She tried not to think about it. She turned her thoughts to the evening that lay ahead of her. It promised to be interesting at the very least. Dinner with Collin Deverell at a restaurant she had yet to try, Sign of the Dove. The last thing she'd expected when he introduced himself that night at the gallery was a dinner invitation. But he'd made it clear he was not about to take no for an answer, and she was grateful to him for almost single-handedly making the exhibit a resounding success. She didn't really feel like socializing, but she'd been wise enough to realize that cultivating his interest in her was definitely to her own advantage. After all, he was a wealthy collector, a wealthy, most generous patron of the arts whose enthusiasm for her work was giving her the means to fight for the one thing in the world that mattered most to her: her son. She needed the financial support he could provide if his enchantment with her landscapes continued to flourish. *All right*, she thought, *so his interest in me seems to be more personal than professional. So what?*

Ashley took a deep breath.

She stood up, reaching for a towel as she stepped out of the tub onto the tiled floor. She dried herself carefully, then applied a scented body lotion. As she watched the water

drain from the tub, she thought about the night she and
Collin Deverell had come face-to-face for the first time. He
had been, without a doubt, the most attractive man there.
He was charming and attentive and quite knowledgeable
about art, which hadn't surprised Ashley at all, given all
she'd been told about his private collection. And though she
was not looking for a relationship, when he invited her to
dinner, she'd accepted without hesitation.

She dropped the towel and slipped on her black silk robe
that resembled a traditional Japanese kimono. Tying the
wide red sash around her waist, she walked barefoot into
the bedroom and opened the double doors leading to the
walk-in closet. Looking through the long rack of clothes for
something appropriate, she finally selected a draped plum
jersey dress with sleeves tapering to the wrists, a slim skirt,
and slightly exaggerated shoulders. It was perfect, she decided. Elegant without being provocative. She chose a pair
of black pumps and a matching evening clutch bag, then
took everything back into the bedroom, laying it all out on
the bed. As she dressed, she thought about the position she
was placing herself in by encouraging Collin Deverell's interest in her. Though she knew virtually nothing about him,
she had the impression after talking to him that he was not
one to play games. If she encouraged this man, there could
be no turning back.

She stepped into her pumps and went over to her dressing
table, taking her red leather jewelry case from the drawer.
She selected a wide silver cuff bracelet, an amethyst pendant
and matching earrings. She pulled her heavy dark hair back
in a neat coil at the nape of her neck, then paused to study
the effect in the mirror. Dissatisfied, she removed the pins
holding it in place and brushed it out until it fell in loose
waves about her shoulders. It was by far her most flattering
look, she decided. She was not one of those women who
could pull her hair back severely. *A Bolshoi ballerina I'm not*,
she thought wryly.

The sound of the doorbell cut through her thoughts as
she was checking the contents of her bag. Switching off the

lamp on the night table, she went to open the door. He was every bit as handsome and elegant as he'd been that night at the gallery, she thought as she looked up into those velvety brown eyes. "Aren't you prompt," she said, keeping her voice light.

He nodded, smiling. "Timing is everything as far as I'm concerned," he answered.

It's like being on a desert island, Ashley thought as she looked around the crowded restaurant, taking in the wash of peach color, lace curtains, hanging plants, and strategically placed mirrors. Now, as she sat across from Collin Deverell, she found herself trying to figure out what it was he really wanted from her. It still was not entirely clear. In the car, he'd talked about art and the success of her exhibit and his personal favorites among her works. At the restaurant, he'd started off discussing his own extensive collection of valuable paintings, artworks reputed to be worth at least seventeen million, a figure he would neither confirm nor deny. Ashley remembered that there had been rumors several years ago that the collection had been stolen while he was traveling abroad, but that, she quickly learned, was another closed subject. If he wanted anything more than a strictly business relationship with her, he gave no indication of it.

"Is the smoked salmon all right?" Collin asked.

"What?" Ashley's thoughts returned to the present abruptly. "Oh, yes—it's fine."

"Then why aren't you eating? You've been rearranging it on your plate for the past ten minutes."

Ashley shook her head, feeling slightly embarrassed. "The salmon's perfect. It's just me," she insisted. "I've had a few things on my mind—"

"Your custody fight with your former in-laws," he guessed.

She looked up, surprised. She started to ask him how he knew about it, but then she felt silly. Of course it had been in all the newspapers. She nodded. "Yes," she admitted.

"You're fighting a losing battle, you know," he said easily as he leaned back in his chair, never taking his eyes off her.

Ashley looked at him, feeling the heat in her face as her cheeks flushed angrily. "You wouldn't happen to work for the Hollisters yourself, would you?" she asked, the anger building within her.

His jaw tightened visibly. "I wouldn't work for Bradley Hollister if I were starving and he was my last chance," he responded sharply. "I, my dear Ashley, work for no one—except myself, of course."

"Then why—" she began, confused.

Collin frowned. "When you do battle with a dragon, it's wise to know exactly what to expect," he told her as he reached for his glass. He took a long swallow. "You, unfortunately, have taken on the most formidable dragon of all. You should be prepared for the final confrontation."

She studied him intently. "And you intend to prepare me," she concluded.

"Perhaps." His face was expressionless.

"Why?" she asked uneasily.

"Let's just say—for now—that I happen to dislike Bradley Hollister as much as you do," Collin answered, signaling the waiter for another drink.

"I'd feel a hell of a lot better if you'd say a little more," Ashley admitted, puzzled by his statement.

"Some other time," he promised, making it quite clear that he had no intention of discussing it any further.

Ashley looked at the man across the table from her, and she wondered what his game was. Maybe she had been wrong in her first impression of him. Maybe he was playing games with her. Maybe there was more to the mysterious Collin Deverell than just an art collector who'd taken a fancy to her work. Maybe he'd bought all of those paintings for a reason, a reason he obviously wasn't yet ready to disclose. Why was he so interested in her legal war with the Hollisters? What was his own connection to them?

The waiter returned with Collin's drink. Collin took a

sip, pondered it for a moment, then smiled. "Not bad," he said, taking another sip. "Not bad at all."

Ashley started to stay something, then changed her mind. She had the feeling that no matter how many questions she asked, he wasn't going to tell her anything. Not yet. *Okay, I'll play along*, she thought. *I'll stick it out until I find out what you really want from me.*

All things considered, it turned out to be a most pleasant evening. Collin's refusal to discuss the subject of her custody battle and his own interest in its outcome had piqued Ashley's curiosity, but it also made her nervous. Sensing this, Collin had wisely elected to drop it, abruptly turning to more pleasant topics, such as art and current Broadway shows. They were both surprised to discover how many opinions they shared, but Ashley was even more surprised to find herself actually enjoying the evening. *I haven't enjoyed being with anyone since Brandon died*, she thought as the dark cloud of her husband's death descended over her once again. *But am I really enjoying being with Collin—or is it his implied hatred of the Hollisters that draws me to him?*

Over dessert, he asked to see her again. "I know this great little place off Lexington—the best lasagna this side of Rome," he told her, signaling for the check.

Ashley laughed aloud. "Lasagna! God, it's been years since I've had truly good lasagna," she confessed. "When I was growing up in California, my mother made it, but of course her recipe was handed down to her from her Italian ancestors—"

He looked genuinely surprised. "You're Italian?" he asked.

"Couldn't be more so if I'd been born on the banks of the Arno," she assured him. "My ancestors come from Tuscany, transplanted in the Napa Valley about three generations back."

"My mother was also Italian," he said as he took out one of his credit cards and gave it to the waiter. "She was born in Milan." He smiled in remembrance. "She was the most beautiful woman I've ever known."

Ashley smiled too. "And did she also make the best lasagna this side of Rome?" she asked.

Collin laughed aloud at the thought. "My mother never went near the kitchen, and if she had, my father would certainly have taken measures to make sure it never happened again," he said, amused at the idea of his mother actually cooking. "No, she didn't—cook or do laundry, or—God forbid—change a diaper, but she was a good mother. A wonderful mother."

Ashley studied him for a moment, having the feeling that she was seeing a side of him few outsiders were ever allowed to see. Though she knew virtually nothing about him, except of course what she'd been told by Melanie and Diana, she'd had the feeling almost from the moment they met that Collin Deverell was a loner at heart, a man who gave very little of himself away and had few close friends and no real confidants. Yet here she was, having dinner with him, glimpsing a side of him that was very human and vulnerable, a far cry from the polished, sophisticated man that was his public image. "I take it you were very close to your mother," Ashley said finally.

"I was," Collin responded quietly. "I loved both my parents, but I was always closer to my mother."

"What about your brother?" she asked. "Diana told me you're a twin. Aren't twins usually very close?"

"Usually," Collin said tightly, avoiding her eyes. The waiter returned then, and Collin scribbled his signature on the receipt stamped with his name and credit card number. "But in our case, the fact that we're twins hasn't made us any closer than if we'd been total strangers. All Justin and I have in common is the same parents and the same face." He paused. "You never did give me an answer, Ashley. What about tomorrow night?"

She nodded. "I'd be happy to share the best lasagna this side of Rome with you."

"She doesn't suspect a thing," Collin told Henry Harrison confidently as he got up off the couch in the library and went over to the bar. The gold phoenix medallion he always wore glistened in the light against his heavy green sweater. "She's a little curious. I think I probably should have waited to bring up the subject of her custody appeal."

"You're absolutely certain she's not suspicious?" Harrison asked, concerned.

Collin poured himself a drink. "You know me, Henry," he said with a grin. "I take chances, but I never take unnecessary chances."

"Everyone makes mistakes."

"My days of making critical mistakes are over," Collin assured him as he returned to the couch and settled down with his glass. "I only wish I could move a bit more slowly with her, but from what Bill tells me, there isn't time. Something has to be done *now*."

"Is it imperative that you, ah, recruit her now?" Harrison wanted to know.

Collin nodded. "I'm afraid so." He looked up at the older man and smiled wearily. "I can't do it alone, and you, my friend, are a bit too old for this sort of thing." He took a long swallow of his drink. "Ashley's my only option at this point."

"But can she be trusted?" Harrison asked, obviously concerned.

"If she can't be, then no one can," he insisted. "Ashley Gordon-Hollister has the strongest motive of all for wanting to see Hollister ruined. The bastard literally stole her son from her after her husband's death."

Harrison shook his head disapprovingly. "But will she comply with your somewhat unorthodox methods?"

Collin thought about it for a moment as he stared into the liquid swirling about in his glass. "I think," he began slowly, "that she would do anything short of—and possibly including—murder in order to get her little boy back."

"What do you know about Collin Deverell, Diana?" Ashley asked casually as the two women walked into Diana's office at the back of the gallery. Ashley's paintings were still on display on the stark white walls of the gallery and would be for another week.

Diana Gilling looked surprised. "Very little, actually," she admitted. "He comes in here quite often but doesn't usually attend any of the openings. He's not in the habit of talking about himself." She paused, curiosity written all over her normally cool, Nordic face. "Why do you ask?"

"I had dinner with him last night," Ashley replied. "He's a most interesting man—but a bit puzzling."

"Congratulations!" Diana responded enthusiastically.

Ashley gave her a quizzical look. "For what?"

"Having dinner with him." Diana seated herself behind the glass-topped desk in her small but immaculate office. "From what I hear, few women get that far with him— unless of course he happens to be sleeping with them."

"Well, I'm not!" Ashley protested hotly.

"I didn't think so," Diana said quickly. "The elusive Mr. Deverell is quite the loner, according to my sources. No family, except for his twin brother, and they haven't spoken for several years. No close friends, not even a regular woman in his life—just a series of one-night stands."

"Surely there's someone he's close to," Ashley pursued, her curiosity growing.

Diana shrugged. "If there is, they're being very tight-lipped about it," she said with a sigh. "Of course, it's a big city. I don't know everybody."

"Just everyone who matters, right?" Ashley asked, laughing.

"Everyone who might matter to someone like Collin Deverell," Diana corrected. "Including a few of the women who've had so-called intimate relationships with him. Even they don't really know anything about him—beyond what he looks like without his clothes and how good he is in bed."

"How good is he?" Ashley asked with a hint of sarcasm in her voice.

Diana smiled. "Are you really interested?"

Ashley drew in a deep breath. "I just want to know why he's so interested in me," she confessed.

* * *

"Why does it matter?" Melanie Masters pulled on her gray gloves as the taxi maneuvered through the heavy express-way traffic en route to Kennedy Airport. "The man paid over a quarter of a million dollars for your paintings, so obviously he's impressed with your talents as a painter. And if he's also interested in you as a woman, well, I think it's exactly what you need in your life right now."

"You know how I feel about that, Mel," Ashley said disdainfully. "Good God—Brandon hasn't even been dead a year."

"And neither have you," Melanie said promptly. "Ash-ley, I understand how you feel, how you felt about your husband, but he's gone and you can't bring him back. And if you're smart, you won't just lie down and die yourself. You've been like a zombie ever since that plane went down. It's as if you were on it with him!"

"In a way, I was," Ashley said sullenly.

"You've been alone too long," Melanie told her matter-of-factly. "I don't mean to sound cruel, but don't you think it's time to stop mourning? Brandon is not coming back, and what's more, I don't think he would have wanted you to spend the rest of your life living in the past."

Ashley stared out the window at the traffic around them. "I'm sure you're right," she said evenly. "Unfortunately, I can't help how I feel. I'm not ready to start socializing again. Not yet."

"Then how do you explain the smile on your face when-ever someone mentions Collin Deverell?" Melanie chal-lenged.

"He's a very interesting person, that's all," Ashley insisted. "I'm curious about him, about what he's really after."

Melanie smiled. "If you're not interested in him, why should it matter?"

"It bothers me," Ashley said. "I can't explain it, but it makes me intensely uncomfortable. I have the feeling that it's not me *or* my paintings he's after. Somehow, it's all tied in with the Hollisters and the custody hearing. That's why I agreed to see him again.''

''And that's the only reason?'' Melanie wasn't convinced.

''The only reason.''

As they approached the airport, a departing 747 flying low overhead interrupted their conversation with a deafening roar. ''You have been alone too long,'' Melanie insisted. ''You're suspicious of the man simply because he's shown an interest in you beyond your work. You're looking for an excuse to dismiss him.''

Ashley gave her a tired smile. ''Thank you, Dr. Masters. When I need your couch again, I'll let you know.''

''I'm right, aren't I?'' Melanie asked as the taxi slowed to a stop at the terminal entrance.

''I don't need an excuse, Mel,'' Ashley said tightly as she climbed out of the car. ''I told you—I'm just not ready for that. I may never be ready.''

Melanie stepped out of the cab and paid the driver. He took her luggage from the trunk and turned it over to a young porter. She didn't say another word until they were walking through the busy terminal toward the gate where she would board her flight to San Francisco. ''What if he really is interested in you?'' she asked finally.

Ashley was indifferent. ''What if he is?''

''You've got to put it all behind you sooner or later,'' Melanie pointed out. She paused to listen as her flight was called. ''For your own sake—you have to start living again.''

Ashley forced a smile. ''I will, Mel,'' she promised. ''Just as soon as I get Robert back.''

The forest-green Schiaparelli suit was perfect, Ashley decided, catching sight of herself in the mirror as she clipped a pair of antique silver earrings on her earlobes and hurried to answer the door. It was flattering, elegant, sophisticated, but definitely not provocative. She would not be sending out signals that might be misconstrued, not even by a man like Collin Deverell, who, according to Diana Gilling, had been overwhelmingly successful with women. *I only want to find out why he's so interested in my custody hearing*, she told herself. *That's all*, she thought as she opened the door.

"You're early, but—" She stopped short when she saw him. His trench coat was over his arm, and he was dressed in dark blue slacks, a white shirt, and a charcoal gray pullover sweater, a far cry from the expensive, hand-tailored suit he'd worn the night before, or the elegant tux he'd been wearing the night they met at the gallery. "Uh, come in," she said, finally finding her voice.

His expression was a mixture of mild embarrassment and amusement. "Obviously I forgot to tell you," he began in a low voice as he entered the apartment. "The place I told you about is a bit more casual. A relaxed atmosphere."

Ashley closed the door and drew in her breath as she looked down at the suit. "In that case, would you like a drink while I go change into something more—appropriate?" she asked.

He smiled. "Thank you, I would."

She went over to the bar. "What'll you have?" she asked, opening the ice bucket.

"Scotch and soda—neat."

Ashley put down the ice tongs almost as soon as she picked them up and reached for the scotch. "Where are we going?" she asked as she poured.

"Ever been to Pete's Tavern?" he asked, taking the glass she offered him.

She shook her head. "I'm new to New York," she told him. "I haven't seen much of anything outside the Mason-Gilling Gallery in the time I've been here."

Collin smiled. "I know how long you've been here," he said. "We met for the first time the day you arrived."

Ashley gave him a quizzical look. When she met him at the gallery, she'd had the vague feeling that she'd seen him somewhere before, but she'd assumed she must have seen a photograph of him in a newspaper or magazine.

He took a drink, his brown eyes twinkling with amusement. "At Kennedy Airport," he said, attempting to refresh her memory. "We were both heading for the same taxi . . ."

Her eyes widened in disbelief. "That was you?"

Collin grinned. "As I recall, it was definitely not one of your better days," he said lightly.

Ashley shook her head. "I don't have too many good days lately," she admitted.

"Nonsense!" he scoffed. Then he glanced at his watch. "Why don't you go change and we'll discuss this further on the way to the restaurant."

Ashley smiled. "Give me five minutes?"

"You've got three."

Ashley had never thought for a moment that Collin intended to walk to the restaurant, but now, as they walked down Fifth Avenue, not as chaotic at this time of the evening, she was glad he'd suggested it. It gave them a chance to talk, to get to know each other a little better. She had the feeling that this was as close as Collin let anyone get. *He's so charming, so outgoing, and yet it seems as though he's holding a great deal back*, she thought, looking up at him as they walked. *Maybe that's why I like him: we have that in common.* A part of Ashley was drawn to him, though she did not fully understand why. She wanted to trust him, just as she knew he wanted her to trust him. "You never did tell me," she began carefully. "Is this more appropriate for Pete's Tavern?"

He looked down at her for a moment. She wore slim black pants tucked into high, wine-colored boots, a loose-fitting garnet silk shirt, a wide black leather belt, and several heavy silver chains of varying lengths around her neck. Her fur-lined trench coat, which she hadn't bothered to button, resembled those worn by the troops during World War II. She looked uniquely beautiful, dashing for such a small woman. "It's acceptable," he commented nonchalantly.

"Thanks a lot!"

He grinned. "Relax," he told her. "You're just going to have to get used to the fact that you, my dear Ashley, are the kind of woman who's going to stand out in a crowd no matter where you are. A plain Jane you're not, and even if you were, you have a style that's entirely your own."

"I suppose I should consider that a compliment," she said, smiling.

"You should indeed," he said quickly.

As they crossed Fifth Avenue and headed east toward Lexington, it started to rain, not a downpour, but a soft, steady drizzle. Collin promptly opened the large black umbrella he carried and moved closer to Ashley, holding it up over their heads. They walked briskly along Twenty-third Street to Lexington Avenue, talking and laughing as they walked. Heading south on Lexington to Gramercy Park, they circled around the small private park to Irving Place. "This is it," Collin announced as he pulled open the door and ushered her inside.

Once inside, Ashley paused, her gaze taking in all the sights and sounds and delicious smells in the handsome but crowded bar. A group of young, casually dressed men and women sat at the bar itself, munching potato skins. Three men laughed over their beer in one corner. Collin guided Ashley through the bar to the dining room in the back. He spoke briefly to a waiter, who took them to a booth across the crowded, dimly lit room. As they seated themselves, Ashley looked up at a portrait hanging over their table. The man in the painting reminded her of some of the cowboys she'd seen in the old western movies on the late show, with his stern, craggy face and reddish-brown hair and mustache. The small gold tag at the bottom of the frame read MEL'S TABLE.

"Who is Mel and what are we doing at his table?" Ashley asked, amused.

Collin grinned. "I think he must have been one of the old regulars," he said, looking up at the portrait. "This was at one time O. Henry's old hangout, as you'll see on every menu and matchbook in the place. That's his table, over there.'' He gestured toward another booth. "This is the oldest remaining original tavern in New York City—dates back to 1864.''

"Do you come here often?'' she asked as the waiter returned with their drinks.

He shook his head. "I don't get to Manhattan all that often,'' he said. "I come in when I get a chance. I like it here because it's one of the few places I can relax and enjoy the nightlife—my kind of nightlife, that is. Not a lot of hustling going on here.''

She gave him a quizzical look. "Hustling?''

"Singles looking for a pickup,'' Collin explained. "That's not my style.''

"Oh. I see.'' She reached for her glass, but Collin stopped her before she could take a drink.

"I think we should make a toast.'' His face was serious.

Ashley smiled. "To what?''

Collin raised his glass. "To alliances, my dear Ashley,'' he said as their glasses clinked together lightly. "They have some definite advantages.''

Paris,
December 1986

Anton DeVries stood in front of 26 rue Armengaud, just outside the high green fence and stone wall surrounding the seven-story glass-and-steel office complex that was the world headquarters of Interpol, the International Police Organization. When he was finally permitted to pass through the front gate, which is kept locked at all times, he still was not admitted to the building until he'd been thoroughly checked out via a closed-circuit television camera. He was met at the entrance by Inspector René Dussault, a tall, slim, attractive Frenchman who appeared to be in his early to mid-thirties, with a thin, angular face, thick brown hair and a neatly trimmed mustache. "Good morning, Monsieur DeVries," he greeted amiably as he escorted DeVries inside and up the stairs to the second floor. "I realize this is a bit of an inconvenience, but it is all quite necessary," he said as he unlocked the white iron gate at the top of the stairs and motioned to DeVries to enter.

DeVries nodded; he understood only too well. He observed a group of Interpol's men, all formerly detectives with the Sûreté Nationale or the Paris Préfecture, as they went about the business of providing up-to-the-minute data on criminal activity around the world to 126 police forces in 78 countries via radio, phototelegraphy, and satellite. "We keep the world's most complete files on over two million known criminals," Dussault was saying.

"And the specific information we discussed over the phone?" DeVries asked impatiently.

"In my office," Dussault responded quickly. "This way."

DeVries followed the Frenchman down a long corridor to a small, sparsely furnished corner office. Dussault indicated a chair for DeVries as they entered, then closed the door. "I have been looking into the specific cases you inquired about," Dussault began, seating himself behind the cluttered desk. "I am not sure you will be pleased by what I have to tell you."

DeVries sat up ramrod-straight in his chair. "And that is?" he asked carefully.

The Frenchman pressed his fingertips together. "The robberies in question . . . there was nothing to indicate that any of them were even remotely connected."

"That can't be!" DeVries protested.

Dussault smiled patiently. "I thought you might feel that way," he said quietly. "I have something to show you, something I am certain will convince you." He rose from his chair and crossed the room to the door, switching off the overhead lights. Then he moved over to a slide projector atop a small file cabinet next to his desk. He turned it on, and the room was bathed in an eerie glow reflecting off the stark white screen. In another instant, an image appeared on the screen. "This is the man being sought in connection with the Ferrand-Bessèges robbery," Dussault explained as DeVries stared at the face on the screen, a heavyset, cherub-faced man with a wide nose, dark, curly hair and a bushy mustache. "The photograph was taken by one of their security cameras. The man posed as an electrician—a phony, of course. Unfortunately, this was discovered too late."

A series of photographs followed. A distinguished-looking older man with graying hair and horn-rimmed glasses: "He posed as an art dealer to gain entry to the château of the Baron de Martigny near St.-Raphael and made off with a Cézanne worth a king's ransom," Dussault recalled. Then there was a redheaded man with a full beard and a cane. "He pretended to walk with a marked limp," Dussault explained. "He took two million francs' worth of jewels from the dealer in Brussels—at least we *think* he is our man." The fourth was a young man who looked to be in his mid- to late thirties, quite attractive, with a dark, almost swarthy complexion, midnight-black hair and mustache, and a black patch over his right eye. "He is the main suspect in the theft of the two paintings in Rome," said Dussault. He showed DeVries a dozen other slides of men who were suspects in an equal number of thefts in Europe and North and South America, briefly explaining each suspect's involvement or suspected involvement and how Interpol came by the photograph or artist's concept. When he was finished, he switched off the projector and turned the lights on again. "At one point, we considered the possibility of an international ring of cat burglars," Dussault admitted. "There were some similarities, of course. Each robbery was brilliantly conceived, flawlessly executed, and very imaginative and daring. In many instances they were committed right under their victims' noses, literally. But there was never any concrete evidence to link either the thefts or the perpetrators."

"You're absolutely certain of that?" DeVries was unconvinced.

"Yes, monsieur, we are," Dussault said with finality.

"I'm not." DeVries got to his feet. "I'd like to see the files, if you don't mind."

"Not at all," the Frenchman said quickly. "I anticipated you might ask, so I took it upon myself to make copies you can take with you." He handed DeVries a large brown envelope.

"I'd also like copies of the photographs."

"Everything is there," Dussault assured him. "If you should need anything more—"

"You'll be the first to hear about it," DeVries told him. He tucked the envelope under one arm and walked out.

It is approximately a six-mile drive from Interpol headquarters in St. Cloud to Paris. Anton DeVries checked into the Hôtel Lancaster off the Champs-Elysées and went directly to his room. DeVries ordered a light dinner from room service and emptied the contents of the envelope Inspector Dussault had given him onto the bed. He put the photographs and drawings side by side on the bed and stared at them for a long time. The men in the pictures all looked strikingly different—different skin tones, different eye color, hair colors and styles varied. They had different builds and degrees of fleshiness, even in their faces, and yet there was something strangely familiar about each of them. Something he couldn't quite identify.

A young man from room service brought his dinner, and DeVries read the reports compiled by Interpol's staff as he ate. He was looking for something, anything that might prove his theory, and he found it when he compared the list of items taken in the robberies with the list of valuables taken from the Deverell estate. In each case, at least one item stolen matched an item on the Deverell list. Surely, he thought, excited, they could not consider that merely a coincidence.

He took another long look at the photos spread out on the bed, recalling what Dussault had said: "All flawlessly executed . . . very imaginative and daring." That was truly an understatement, DeVries thought as he stared into the faces of the men, looking for Collin Deverell in each of them. Deverell had vowed to regain what belonged to him, with or without the law, and he was nothing if not fiercely determined. *They have no idea what they're up against*, he thought, reaching for the phone.

He placed a call to Inspector Dussault at Interpol. "There is a link," he maintained. "But it's not a ring. It's one man—one brilliant, determined, very resourceful man."

"Impossible!" Dussault argued.

"Not impossible, not for this man," DeVries insisted. "We are not discussing your average cat burglar or con man. The man I'm talking about has brains and nerve in large quantities, and he's a world-class athlete to boot. The trouble is, he fancies himself a modern-day Robin Hood."

"It cannot be!" Dussault retorted hotly. "You have seen the photographs—"

"A series of very clever disguises," DeVries explained. "Damned near flawless, too. One man, Dussault—one man who has the intelligence and the nerve *and* the physical ability to get into just about anywhere. A chameleon who has a real talent for altering his appearance drastically and convincingly. It is possible, isn't it?"

"Possible, yes, but highly unlikely," Dussault concluded.

"I'm going to nail him—one way or another," DeVries vowed. "Then we'll see what's possible and what isn't." He slammed the receiver down on its cradle, annoyed with the Frenchman's unwillingness to accept his theory.

He walked back over to the bed and looked down at the photographs. *I underestimated you, Collin Deverell*, he thought, *but no more. I'm going to be watching you from now on because sooner or later you'll slip up—and I'll be there to make you pay for that slip. Then we'll see who has the last laugh.* He thought about the day he went to see Collin Deverell at his Long Island estate. Deverell had been a victim then. He'd been framed, probably by his own brother. *He was innocent—then*, DeVries thought. *Not anymore.*

* * *

It was snowing in Manhattan. Collin and Ashley were having dinner at The Cellar in the Sky on the 107th floor of One World Trade Center. From their table near the windows, they could watch the snow falling on the city as they ate. Collin was ravenous, devouring his canapés of smoked salmon and caviar as he carried on a curiously one-sided conversation with Ashley. Finally, he stopped talking, put down his fork, and stared at her for a moment, realizing that she'd done little more than move her lobster around on her plate. "What's wrong?" he wanted to know.

"It's nothing," she insisted, frowning.

"You're not eating."

"I'm sorry." She put down her fork. "I'm afraid I'm not very hungry after all."

Collin looked at her accusingly, pointing to the lobster. "Listen, woman," he growled with mock anger in his voice, "you're the one who ordered his execution. Now *eat* him so he won't have died in vain!"

Ashley gave a little laugh, shaking her head. "You're incorrigible," she declared with a sigh, "and I do appreciate your efforts to cheer me up."

Collin grinned. "It's the very least I can do—for the lobster, that is. Aside from providing for his survivors."

"I'm afraid I'm not going to be very good company for the next few weeks," she told him then, bowing her head slightly. "With Christmas only ten days away, I find myself thinking about Christmases past, when my husband was still alive and my son with us. The holiday season depresses me."

"An excellent reason not to spend Christmas alone," Collin said promptly. "I want you to spend the holidays with me—at Sea Cliff."

Ashley stared at him for a moment, not sure what he meant. "I don't know—" she began hesitantly.

Collin laughed, realizing what she was thinking. "You have nothing to worry about," he reassured her. "I'll be on my best behavior, and you'll have your own room. Scout's honor."

She laughed wearily. "I'll bet you were never really a Boy Scout!" she declared accusingly.

"Oh, but I *was*—and a Scout of distinction at that," he insisted. "I think I was probably the only eight-year-old in the state of New York to receive a dishonorable discharge from the Cub Scouts."

Ashley looked at him, smiling, suddenly glad she'd accepted his dinner invitation in spite of the black mood she'd been in when he called. Though she still had reservations where he was concerned, she honestly enjoyed his company. She was able to relax with him as she hadn't relaxed in a long time. He was easy to talk to and he made her laugh.

"Give me the bottom line, Ashley," he was saying. "What's it going to be?"

"I don't know," she said, shaking her head as she gazed into the darkness beyond the windows. "I need to think about it. I'm not sure you'd want me around in the mood I'll be in."

"Of course I do," he insisted. "I wouldn't ask if I didn't."

"Let me give you my answer in a day or two, all right?"

He looked at her for a moment. "I suppose that's fair enough," he said finally. "But I'll give you fair warning— I never take no for an answer."

The Christmas shoppers are out in full force today, Ashley thought as she walked alone up Fifth Avenue, glancing absently at the displays in the store windows. No matter how hard she tried, she simply could not summon up any holiday spirit. She'd been touched by Collin's concern and by his gentle insistence that she not spend the holidays alone, but she still wasn't sure she wanted to be with anyone for Christmas. She had her memories of holidays past, holidays spent with Brandon and Robert, and she was bound to those memories by a fierce determination to keep them alive with her undiminished love for both of them. *I'm the Ghost of Christmas Past*, she thought dismally.

She crossed Fifth Avenue at Fifty-eighth Street against

the light. A taxi driver heading south slammed on his brakes and honked his horn furiously. "Hey, lady—you color blind or somethin'?" Ashley didn't hear him. She just kept walking.

Ashley walked on, oblivious of the traffic, the pedestrians, the sights and sounds of midtown Manhattan, until she reached the entrance of FAO Schwarz, the world's largest toy store. She stood there entranced, admiring the brilliantly mechanized window display that looked like every child's fantasy. *Robert would love this*, she thought sadly. If only she could bring him to see it.

In her mind, she could see her son two years ago, when she'd taken him to see a department-store Santa in San Francisco, at the Embarcadero Center. She recalled how she'd felt when he told Santa Claus he wanted only one thing for Christmas: a baby brother or sister. Tears stung Ashley's eyes as she thought about Brandon's response. "Maybe we should start working on it," he'd laughed. "We might be able to deliver by *next* Christmas."

Impulsively, Ashley went inside the toy store. Whatever else Claudia Hollister was or had done to her in the past, surely she couldn't keep Ashley from buying Christmas presents for her son. Even that venomous old witch couldn't refuse to let Robert have them. Galvanized by her anger, Ashley made her way through the crowded lower level to the stairs. She wasn't quite sure what she was looking for, but she knew she would recognize it when she found it.

She thought about it as she climbed the stairs. Robert had always been creative; Brandon had said he inherited that from her. He'd been good with his hands, and she'd jokingly told him he inherited *that* from his father. She explored all the possibilities on the second floor and chose an erector set, some small building blocks from which he could create a veritable city, and modeling clay and paints. She made a dozen more purchases on the third floor. Then, as she piled her selections on the counter, she took one last look around, wondering if she'd forgotten anything. She dug into her oversize shoulder bag and took out her wallet, producing her credit card for the sales clerk. Would Claudia allow her to see Robert long enough to give him the gifts? she wondered. She had her doubts. She'd probably have to leave everything with Mason at the front door.

As she made her way down the stairs to the street level, she caught sight of a woman and a small boy admiring an electric train on display. The woman knelt down next to her son and hugged him tightly, and they were both smiling. Looking at them made the memories come flooding back again. Tears welled up in her eyes as she leaned against the railing, fighting back the rage that was building up within her. How long could she go on like this?

"I told you never to call me from your office, Bill," Collin said irritably as he picked up the phone and carried it over to the couch, cradling the receiver on his shoulder as he spoke. "It's too risky, dammit—someone might overhear you!"

"I'm not in my office," William McNichol said patiently. "I'm at home. I told my secretary I had an appointment outside the office today."

Collin was immediately concerned. "What's so important it couldn't wait until tonight?"

"I thought you should know immediately. There's talk of a possible takeover," McNichol responded tersely. "Hollister International wants to take us over—a friendly takeover, I believe the board calls it."

"Friendly, my ass!" Collin roared. "I knew my dear brother would eventually go too far. This *is* his idea, isn't it?"

"No, it wasn't his idea," McNichol said, somewhat hesitantly. "But he certainly doesn't seem opposed to the idea of a takeover."

Collin drew in his breath. "I wonder what they've offered him in exchange for his soul," he muttered under his breath.

"What?"

"Nothing, Bill, nothing. Just talking to myself," Collin said quickly.

"I thought you'd want to know."

"I do. I want to know everything that goes on from here on out—no matter how insignificant it might seem at the time," Collin instructed him. "I want to know as much about what goes on within Intercontinental Oil as Justin does—more if possible."

"I'll do what I can," McNichol promised.

Collin hung up slowly. So Justin had gotten in so deep with organized crime that he was now willing to allow Intercontinental Oil to be swallowed up by syndicate-controlled Hollister International. *He's gone too far*, Collin thought angrily. *He has to be stopped.* They *have to be stopped.*

He stood at the French doors, staring out into the garden as he thought about it, trying to come up with a way to prevent that takeover from coming about. *Justin's the key*, he decided. He needed to create a diversion, a way to make his brother's business associates distrust him enough to put their plans on hold, at least for a little while.

But how?

Ashley stood outside the high iron fence surrounding the Hollister town house on East Seventy-eighth Street, hoping to get a glimpse of her son, either coming or going. It had been three days since she'd had the gifts delivered by special messenger. Had Claudia given them to Robert? Had he even seen them? Did he know his mother was thinking of him, that she never stopped thinking about him? *I have to see him*, she thought desperately as she peered between the iron bars.

She pulled herself up straight as the front door opened and Robert appeared, alone, bundled in warm winter clothing. He walked to the top of the steps and paused, looking around as if he were looking for something before coming down the steps. He didn't see her.

"Robert!" she called out to him.

He looked around furiously, finally spotting her. "Mommy!" he cried out joyously, running headlong at the fence. "Mommy—I knew you'd come!"

Ashley reached through the fence, taking his small hands in hers, their fingers intertwined. Tears streamed down Ashley's cheeks as the dam within the depths of her soul finally burst and all the emotions she'd kept locked up inside herself for so long surged forth at the sight of her young son, the one person in the world she loved more than life itself. "I've missed you, baby," she gasped in a trembling voice. "God, how I've missed you!"

"I've missed you, too, Mommy," he said in a small voice. "Even when they told me you were gone forever, that I'd never see you again, I knew you wouldn't forget about me!"

"Not on your life!" Ashley swore, choking back her tears. "I told you we'd be together again soon, and we will be!"

"When, Mommy?" he wanted to know.

"Soon, baby. Real soon."

"Promise?"

Ashley bit her lower lip. "You bet." She paused. "How are they treating you? Are they good to you, Robert?"

He nodded, frowning. "I guess so. But I miss you."

"And I miss you, darling—but it won't be much longer now."

At that moment, Claudia Hollister appeared in the doorway. When she saw Robert with Ashley, she was furious. "Robert!" she called out angrily. "Come here this instant!"

"I'm talking to my mother, Claudia," Robert responded, not moving from his spot at the fence.

"I can see that, Robert," Claudia said coldly. "Now, do as I tell you!"

"But I want to talk to Mom—"

"Go inside, Robert," Claudia commanded sharply. "I'd like a few words with your mother myself."

Robert gave a reluctant sigh, then turned and pressed his face between the bars to kiss Ashley good-bye before running up the steps past Claudia and into the town house. Ashley got to her feet as Claudia approached. "You were told to stay away from here," Claudia said menacingly.

"He's my son." Ashley's voice was cold. "I have a right to see him!"

"You have no rights unless the courts give them to you!" Claudia snapped. "And that is highly unlikely."

"We'll see."

"Until that happens, you're to stay away from here," Claudia informed her acidly. "Understood?"

"Only too well," Ashley replied.

"Good." Claudia turned on her heel and walked away, disappearing inside the brownstone.

Ashley clung to the fence, crying uncontrollably until her sobs came in dry, choking gasps. Finally, she pulled herself fully upright and took a deep breath. She pulled a tissue from her coat pocket and dabbed at her eyes as she walked, dazed, down Fifth Avenue next to Central Park. The pain was as unbearable now as it had been the day he was taken from her in San Francisco. She couldn't take much more of this. She would do whatever was necessary to get him back, to have him back with her for good. If only she knew what to do or where to begin.

As soon as she reached her apartment, she telephoned Collin Deverell. "Does that invitation for Christmas still stand?"

As the Air France 747 began its descent to Kennedy Airport, Anton DeVries fastened his seat belt and returned the reports he'd been reviewing to his briefcase. Exhausted, he yawned and rubbed his eyes. Jet lag. He felt as though he hadn't had a good night's sleep since he left for Paris a week ago. He drew in his breath. It had been worth the trouble, he decided now. He'd found out everything he wanted to know—even if Interpol didn't share his theory.

It all made sense. Collin Deverell, suspected of doing away with his own property to collect the insurance, had been framed, wrongly accused of insurance fraud some seven years ago. By whom, DeVries had never been absolutely certain. *He*, however, had been sufficiently convinced to drop his investigation for the insurance company, but there had been nothing that could be done, legally, to recover Deverell's stolen property. So Collin Deverell had apparently taken the law into his own hands. He had gone from an innocent victim to a brilliantly successful thief and con man. Now it was a whole new ball game. Collin Deverell was as guilty as sin, and DeVries felt responsible somehow for letting him off the first time. He was obsessed with the idea of proving his theory and bringing Collin Deverell to justice. There was not the slightest doubt in DeVries's mind that Deverell had been the man who'd pulled off those robberies in Paris, Amsterdam, Brussels, London, Bogotá, Rio, and New York. Deverell thought himself a modern-day Robin Hood, striking out and taking back what he believed was rightfully his.

It was interesting. Deverell had gone to Morocco four years earlier to recover a valuable painting, a Renoir. He'd taken on William Harrington, a man with suspected underworld connections. According to DeVries's sources, Deverell had disappeared from the Harrington villa one day and was, for a time, believed to be dead. The odds had been against him then, but he'd somehow survived and come back stronger and more determined than ever. Over the past four years, he'd managed to recover all of his property.

DeVries recalled the day Deverell came to his offices in Manhattan. He'd been so angry, so fiercely determined. In his mind, DeVries saw the striking gold medallion Deverell had worn around his neck that day. The phoenix, that mythical bird that resurrected itself from its own ashes. Like the phoenix, Collin Deverell had risen from the ashes on the Sahara Desert, reborn of his rage and determination to avenge the wrongs dealt him. Like the phoenix, Deverell had endured.

Collin Deverell, DeVries thought, *was* the phoenix.

Sea Cliff,
December 1986

Ashley sat beside Collin in silence as he negotiated the sharp turns along Long Island Sound in his white Excalibur, bound for the Deverell estate near Sea Cliff. She still wasn't quite sure why she'd accepted his invitation. She knew only one thing: she could not bear to spend the holidays alone. She looked over at Collin. He seemed so strong, so self-assured. So in control of himself and his world. *If only I could be in control of mine*, Ashley thought grimly. "This is really beautiful," she observed aloud, attempting to make conversation with him. They had both been unusually silent during the thirty-five-mile drive from Manhattan, and she suspected that Collin had a great deal on his mind, as did she. "I think I'd like to paint here sometime."

He looked at her and smiled. "That's right—you've never been here before. I think you'll find it a pleasant change from that rat race in Manhattan," he said. "It's peaceful here, quiet—just the way I like it."

He brought the Excalibur to a stop and waited, tapping the steering wheel impatiently as a uniformed guard, who recognized him immediately, opened the huge iron gates leading into the Deverell estate. He waved to the guard as he put the Excalibur in gear and headed up the long, graceful, tree-lined driveway toward the main house.

"You've been terribly quiet today," he said finally.

Ashley didn't look at him. "I'm trying to figure out why you invited me out here."

"I brought you out here to seduce you, of course," he said with a grin.

She didn't smile. "I'm serious, Collin."

"So am I," he responded quickly. "I always mean business when it comes to that sort of thing."

"Why *did* you bring me out here?" she pressed on.

He took a deep breath. "I think you need a friend, Ashley," he said quietly. "I'd like to be that friend, but I get the feeling you don't quite trust me that far."

"And you think I'll trust you now?"

"I hope so."

She looked at him for a moment. He meant it. He wanted to get close to her. But he still hadn't told her why. "What's in it for you?" she asked hesitantly.

He glanced at her, and he wasn't smiling this time. "Does everyone always have to have an ulterior motive?"

"No," she answered carefully, "but people usually do."

"If you're so damned suspicious of me, why did you accept my invitation?" he asked then, turning his eyes back to the road.

She turned to face him again. "Curiosity," she said simply.

Collin grinned as he braked the car to a stop. "Curiosity, my dear Ashley, killed the cat," he reminded her. He slid out of the driver's seat and strode around to open the door for her.

She looked up at the magnificent brick English Tudor-style mansion as she emerged from the Excalibur. "It looks like a castle," she commented with an appreciative smile.

He shrugged. "I like it," he remarked offhandedly. "It's comfortable."

"Comfortable?" Ashley laughed aloud. "I'll bet when you and your brother were children, you got lost fairly often in this house."

He frowned. "I did, but Justin was never adventurous enough to get lost," he said tightly.

She studied him for a moment. She had the feeling that the mere mention of his twin brother was taboo. She followed him as he collected her bags and headed up the wide marble steps to the front door. They were met inside by two of the staff, who immediately took Ashley's luggage. "Take those things up to Mrs. Hollister's room," Collin instructed them.

"Yes, sir."

Ashley looked at him questioningly as the maids climbed the stairs, bags in hand. "I've had a room readied for you," he offered in explanation.

She smiled but made no comment.

"Excuse me, sir." The man approaching them looked to be in his sixties, reserved and distinguished-looking, and he spoke with a British accent. "There's a call for you—a gentleman in Nice. He claims to have the, uh, information you've been seeking," he said carefully.

"Yasmin?" Collin asked quickly.

"That's what he says, sir."

"I'd better talk to him, then." He turned to Ashley. "I won't be long. Henry will show you to your room and help you get settled." He turned and hurried down a long corridor off the reception hall.

Henry Harrison turned to Ashley. "This way, Mrs. Hollister," he said as he headed for the stairs.

Ashley followed in silence. The room that had been prepared for her was lovely. It was large and airy, decorated in cornflower blue and white, with a beautiful canopied bed and French doors opening onto a balcony that overlooked the lush, carefully tended gardens. "If you need anything at all, madam, just let one of the maids know," Harrison told her.

"Thank you, I will." She turned to face him. "Before you go, could you tell me something? . . ."

"Get back to me as soon as you have something definite," Collin said, cradling the telephone receiver on one shoulder as he leaned forward in his high-backed black suede executive chair. "That's right . . . Yes . . . I'll be in touch." He replaced the receiver on its cradle as Harrison came into the library. "You look as though the entire staff's threatened mutiny," he noted with mild amusement.

"Mrs. Hollister has been asking questions," Harrison responded with a worried look on his normally stern face. "She questioned me about what you really do, and—"

Collin laughed. "Is that all?"

Harrison looked confused. "Is that *all*?" he repeated incredulously. "How can you laugh about this, Collin? You've brought this woman here, knowing she's already suspicious of you—"

"She has to find out sooner or later," Collin interrupted.

The older man's mouth dropped open. "But now?"

Collin pursed his lips, then exhaled deeply. "Time's running out, Henry," he said finally. "I'd like to take things slow and easy, sure, but I can't. If I don't do something, and do it soon, Intercontinental Oil will face liquidation. I can't let that happen."

"But how can you possibly prevent it?"

Collin's smile was tired. "The same way I've done everything else over the past few years: by beating those bastards at their own game."

"Looks like we're going to have a white Christmas after all," Ashley observed, peering through the curtains in the music room, watching the snow fall on the garden. What she saw was a scene worthy of being immortalized on canvas. If only she'd been in the mood to paint.

Collin leaned back in his chair and smiled. "Christmas was always a special time here when I was a kid," he recalled. "My mother used to make a major production of it. She went all the way—a twelve-foot Scotch pine in the parlor decked out with ornaments from all over the world and imported hand-blown glass icicles. We had a crystal angel she found somewhere in Switzerland. There were always enough gifts for twelve kids. My mother could never make up her mind what we'd like best, so she just bought it all. My father used to say Bloomingdale's and Bergdorf Goodman were his silent partners, that they got more of Intercontinental Oil's profits than he did." He paused. "The thing I liked best about those family holidays was that it was the one time of the year we all spent together—we weren't all scattered to the four winds."

"I know what you mean," Ashley agreed with a bittersweet smile. "We didn't have a twelve-foot tree or imported ornaments or a lot of gifts, but we had each other and we were happy."

He studied her for a moment. "Where are you from originally, Ashley?"

"St. Helena. It's a town in the Napa Valley, north of San Francisco." She was still staring into the gray, gloomy sky, still watching the snow falling.

"Wine country," Collin concluded.

Ashley turned to look at him. "I grew up in the vineyards," she said. "The people there, for the most part, were like one big happy family. At Christmas, we had a nice meal and a few small gifts, never anything spectacular, but that was never very important. We just enjoyed being together, being with family and friends."

He looked at her for a long moment. "If you were happy there, what made you leave?"

Ashley shrugged, tugging at the bottom of her white beaded 1940s sweater, one of the many treasures she'd uncovered at her favorite vintage clothing store. "I don't know," she said wistfully. "I guess I was never satisfied. No matter where I was or what I was doing, I always wanted something more, something that was just outside my grasp. Does that sound foolish to you?"

"Not at all," he responded, shaking his head. "I've always been exactly the same way."

"I was looking for something I knew I'd never find in the valley," she admitted, putting her feelings into words for the first time that she could remember.

Collin hesitated momentarily. "And did you find it with Brandon Hollister?"

She looked surprised at his mention of Brandon's name. "Yes," she said quietly. "For five years Brandon and I were very happy. I felt I'd finally found everything I could ever want."

"I take it his parents weren't too pleased about your marriage," Collin said as he poured himself another mug of hot chocolate from the silver pot on the table beside him. "More cocoa, Ashley?"

She shook her head. "That's putting it mildly," she said. She ran her hands down the sides of her black silk pants. "They did everything they could to keep Brandon from marrying me. And after we were married, they never gave up trying to break us up. It reached a point where Brandon wouldn't even read their letters or return their calls. Of course, he'd divorced himself from them—emotionally, I mean—long before we met."

Collin sat up, interested by her comment. "Why?"

She turned to face him. Why was he asking so many personal questions? she wondered. She forced a smile. "Could we please talk about something else?" she asked. "The Hollisters are not my favorite topic for after-dinner conversation."

"Of course," he agreed, sensing her uneasiness. "Let's find something more pleasant to talk about." He brightened. "Art, for instance. I don't believe you've seen all of the Deverell collection . . ."

Christmas was pleasant in spite of the circumstances that had brought them together. Collin decided with a measure of satisfaction that it was the common bond they shared—a deep, burning hatred of Bradley Hollister that chewed at their souls like a rapidly growing malignancy—that drew them to each other. Hate, he reflected as he watched her across the dinner table, was an even stronger force than love. Hate had changed the course of history, had shaped men's destinies. Hate had brought him and Ashley together and would keep them together until their mission had been accomplished. *She needs me as much as I need her. Maybe more,* he thought. *She doesn't know it yet, but the outcome of her appeal has already been decided.*

He put down his fork. "When will your appeal be heard?" he asked, his tone deceptively casual.

Ashley took a bite. "Two weeks," she answered. "I think I'd be more comfortable with it if my lawyer were more

optimistic about my chances of winning.'' Collin saw fear
in her eyes. ''I have a feeling this may be my last chance.''

Collin reached for his glass. ''I think Morgan's probably
faced the Hollister power machine before,'' he told her. ''He
knows they don't fight fair.''

''Thanks for your vote of confidence,'' she said wryly.

He looked at her. ''Confidence has absolutely nothing to
do with it,'' he retorted. ''I think you should get your son
back. In fact I don't think he ever should have been taken
away from you to begin with. A kid's place is with his
mother. But Bradley Hollister is an unscrupulous man who
will do anything to get what he wants. It doesn't have to be
legal as long as it gets the job done.''

''That's what Morgan says,'' Ashley said, taking a sip
from her wineglass. ''He describes us as an unarmed David
going up against the all-powerful Goliath. The Hollisters
wield a lot of power in this state, and apparently they plan
to use some pretty heavy artillery against me.''

''People like Bradley Hollister operate above the law,''
Collin said simply, picking up his fork again and taking
another bite. ''Maybe you should consider doing the same.''

Ashley looked at him, surprised by his remark, but she
did not comment. Collin had turned his attentions once
again to his dinner, and she decided to do the same.

The subject did not come up again until much later that
evening, when they were having a nightcap in the library.
''I have a Christmas present for you, Ashley,'' Collin told
her as he handed her a glass of cognac.

She looked up at him, surprised. ''You shouldn't have,''
she began. ''I couldn't accept—''

He smiled patiently as his eyes met hers. ''You'll accept
this one,'' he said with certainty. ''The odds are against
you legally, my dear Ashley, but I'm not. I'm going to get
your son back for you—or, more precisely, we're going to
do it together.''

Ashley was still thinking about Collin's puzzling statement
when she returned to Manhattan on New Year's Day. What

did he mean? she wondered. What did he have in mind? And why was he so intent upon helping her? He'd admitted to sharing her hatred for her former father-in-law—but why? What had Hollister done to him? What was Collin after? What was his game? And what did he expect from her?

It was like a puzzle with half the pieces missing, she thought as she unpacked her bags. She put several garments aside to be taken to the cleaners. Picking up the beaded sweater, she looked at it for a moment. She always laundered it by hand. It was so old and fragile that she couldn't take chances with it. Take chances. What kind of chances was she taking by letting herself get involved with Collin Deverell? She smiled to herself. Was she involved with him? She'd stayed in his home for more than a week, and he had been a perfect gentleman the entire time she was there. He'd never made a move toward her, not even so much as a suggestive remark, except, of course, the joke he'd made about seducing her as they were driving up to the house. Yet he had asked so many personal questions—about her past, about her marriage, about her conflict with the Hollisters.

I wish I knew what's going on inside your head, Collin Deverell, she thought, puzzled.

At two o'clock in the morning in an office complex high above Wall Street, a uniformed security guard was making his routine nightly rounds. As usual, all was quiet and secure, but he methodically made his rounds every hour without fail. He double-checked each locked door, then went to the bank of switches on one wall and turned out all the lights in the offices at once. When he was satisfied that all was secure, he went on to the next floor.

Minutes later, the doors of one of the elevators opened and a slim, agile figure moved swiftly into the shadows. Clothed entirely in black, he moved with grace and assurance. He knew exactly where he was going and wasted no time in getting there. With a small, flat object resembling a nail file, he managed to pick the lock in a matter of seconds and entered the office as if he knew just what to look for and where to find it. He did not turn on the light. He moved about in almost total darkness with the confidence of a blind man who has mastered his environment. Crossing the room to a large painting next to a wall of built-in bookshelves, he moved the painting aside, exposing the front of a small wall safe. He took his time in cracking the safe, his trained ear pressed to the door as his fingers sought out the combination. He had it in no time at all and whipped the door open hastily. Grabbing all of the documents he found inside without taking the time to examine them, he stuffed them into the canvas sack he carried over one shoulder. Closing the safe, he replaced the painting and let himself out of the office, leaving everything appearing undisturbed. As he was leaving, he heard a noise in the corridor and ducked into the shadows. He had wanted to use the stairs leading to the rear exit, but he couldn't take the chance that someone else was on the floor. The elevator was closest—and quickest. Making sure he was not observed, he slipped into one of the empty cars and pressed the button to send it on its way.

As the car began its descent, Collin's mind was racing. He couldn't just leave the elevator and stroll nonchalantly across the main lobby to the exit as though he belonged there. No, there had to be a better way out. A way he could go back to his original plan and use the rear exit. As he searched his mind for an idea, he looked up and spotted the large, rectangular panels at the top of the elevator. Just beyond those panels, he knew from previous experience, was the trapdoor leading to the elevator shaft. If he could climb up the cable to the second floor when the car stopped. . . . Moving quickly, he reached up and forced one of the panels loose. With the agility of a trained gymnast, he vaulted himself through the opening and forced the trapdoor above it open. Reaching down, he replaced the ceiling panel before climbing through the trapdoor into the darkened shaft. He looked up into the blackness. Any minute now, the elevator would come to a stop at the lobby level. He pulled on his padded black leather gloves and hung onto one of the heavy cables and waited. When the car came to a full stop, he grasped the cable firmly, and with a swift, hand-over-hand movement, climbed up to the doors leading to the second floor. He swung out with the full weight of his body and grasped an iron bar alongside the doors. Gripping it with his left hand, he used all of the strength in his right to force the door open while standing on the dangerously narrow beam at the bottom of the door. His face dripped perspiration as he struggled with the heavy door, and every muscle in his body throbbed painfully. In that instant he saw his life flashing before his eyes like scenes from a movie. *This is it*, he thought. *Now or never.* When the door finally slid open, Collin fell onto the floor on the other side, breathing heavily and with profound relief. But he couldn't rest, not even for a moment. He scrambled to his feet and ran down the long, darkened corridor to the stairwell at the other end of the building. He slipped through the door, knowing it would lock automatically the minute it closed. Bounding down the three flights of stairs to the street level, he quickly picked the lock and slipped through the door, then headed down another corridor toward the service entrance.

Damn! he swore silently when he saw the heavy padlocks on the huge double doors. He hadn't anticipated this. He drew in a deep breath and dug into his pocket, pulling out a large key ring bearing a wide assortment of keys in varying sizes and shapes. Choosing one he thought was right, he put it into the lock. It refused to turn. "Son of a bitch!" he muttered under his breath. He tried another and another unsuccessfully.

This had better be it, he thought as he selected a fourth key. He slipped it into the lock and turned it carefully. It popped open immediately. Collin breathed a sigh of relief as he pushed the door open and ran swiftly into the cold night air. He hurried down a cluttered alley, dodging a wino who was sleeping it off, and turned on a side street that took him back to Wall Street, where his van was parked. As he climbed in and started the engine, he wasn't thinking about what had just happened—or almost happened—to him in that building. He was thinking about what William McNichol had told him, about what was in the computer printouts back at Sea Cliff. He was thinking about what Justin was doing to their birthright, to their father's memory. He was thinking about Ashley and what Bradley Hollister had done to her, to both of them.

Time was running out.

New York City, February 1987

Ashley was besieged by a mob of reporters as she emerged from a taxi in front of the New York County Courthouse on Pearl Street at Foley Square. Pushing past them, she climbed the concrete steps quickly and entered the hexagon-shaped classical-style building and made her way to the courtroom where she was to meet Elliott Morgan. The large, foreboding chamber was deserted when she entered. She paused in the doorway and looked around. Where the hell was Morgan? she wondered, glancing at her wristwatch. He'd said he would meet her there at 9:45. It was now 9:56.

Then she saw him, coming through a door on the other side of the room. As she walked toward him, the sound of her heels clicking on the floor echoed through the cavernous chamber. She began to feel the first waves of apprehension surging through her. Her stomach felt as though it were tied in knots; there was an unbearable pounding inside her head. Morgan took her arm and steered her over to one of the long tables at the front of the courtroom. "I'm not going to tell you any fairy tales, Ashley," he said as he sat down beside her. "I'm not going to try to soften the blow in any way. You've got to be prepared for this. It could, and probably will, get pretty ugly. Bradley Hollister's a powerful man, and his legal counsel believes in a no-holds-barred approach.''

''Tell me about it,'' Ashley said sullenly. Then she turned to face him. ''I want to win this case, Elliott. I want you to play by their rules. Do whatever you have to do to win.''

''That may be easier said than done,'' he said patiently. ''You know they're going to drag your name through the mud and back again—''

''I don't give a damn about my name,'' she replied. ''I only care about my son. I want him back with me—where he belongs.''

He looked at her for a moment as if wanting to tell her something, then abruptly changed his mind. He ran his fingers through his light brown hair. ''I had to make sure you knew what to expect.''

''I know,'' she said in a low voice. ''I've been there before. Now my name is going to be mud on both coasts. So what? Getting Robert back is all I care about.''

''It could be worse this time,'' he cautioned. ''This is Hollister's home turf.''

There was a gleam of determination in her dark eyes. ''So let's bury him in it,'' she said promptly.

The reporters and photographers began to swarm into the courtroom, ready to paw through the dirt the Hollisters' attorneys would be digging up in the course of their hearing. Ashley tried to ignore them, but their presence infuriated her. What right did they have to be there? she thought resentfully. She wished they had not been allowed into the courtroom at all, but there was nothing she could do about it.

Bradley and Claudia Hollister, with two of their attorneys, entered and seated themselves at the empty table across from Ashley and Morgan. Claudia looked over at Ashley once, only for a moment, and her eyes were as cold as ice. She frowned and adjusted the sable coat draped over her shoulders, then turned back to her husband, who did not bother to look at Ashley at all.

As the court was called to order and all present were

instructed to rise, Ashley caught a glimpse of a familiar face at the back of the courtroom—Collin! He did not look at her. In fact he deliberately avoided making eye contact. He slipped into a seat near the doors and tried not to be too obvious about it. *What is he doing here?* Ashley wondered.

She was not sure what bothered her most: the fact that he was there and apparently avoiding her, or her own nagging feelings about his presence. Had she been tricked? Were Collin's overtures, his attempts to get close to her, all a lie? Was Collin in fact in with the Hollisters, as almost everyone else here seemed to be? Was that why he'd asked so many questions about her marriage and her conflicts with her former in-laws? *How could I have been so stupid?* she asked herself. She felt angry and betrayed and hurt. She had actually begun to like Collin Deverell. He'd made her laugh as she had not laughed since Brandon's death. He'd drawn her outside herself, outside her grief. *Is he here to testify for them? God, there's no telling what he'll say happened between us that week at Sea Cliff!*

But even as that silent alarm went off inside her brain, Ashley realized that it didn't make sense. Collin was a rich man, influential in his own right. He didn't have to work for anyone. No, there had to be another reason for his presence. His words to her on Christmas night echoed through her mind: *I'm going to get your son back for you—or, more precisely, we're going to do it together.*

Please mean what you said, Collin, she prayed silently.

"You have to eat, regardless." Collin stood in the middle of Ashley's living room, arms folded, a look of determination on his handsome face as she attempted to evict him from the apartment.

"I told you—I'm not hungry," she protested irritably. "Don't you have better things to do than pester me?"

"Maybe, but none I'd rather be doing," he said with a wicked grin.

"Maybe some other time, okay?" she asked weakly. "I wouldn't be very good company tonight—"

"Listen—if you won't go with me, I'll just have to send out for something," he said stubbornly. "You have to eat something, and I have the feeling you also need someone to talk to."

She shook her head emphatically. She just wanted to go to bed and hide under the blankets. The first day of the hearing had been rougher than she'd expected, and she was drained, physically and emotionally.

"I'm a good listener. You know that," he added.

"I said I don't want to talk about it, all right?"

"Fine. We'll talk about something else."

"I don't feel like talking about *anything*!" she snapped. "I just need to be alone for a while! Now, will you please go?"

"Not on your life," he said firmly. "If you don't feel like talking, we'll just eat. And you're wrong. Being alone is just about the last thing you need right now."

"Thanks for the analysis, Doc," she said darkly, drawing her black silk robe around herself as if she were suddenly very cold.

Collin ignored her sarcasm. "You've got five minutes to get dressed," he said, looking at his watch. "If you're not dressed by then, you go with me as is."

She looked at him. "You wouldn't!"

He grinned evilly. "Try me," he challenged.

Realizing that he probably was not bluffing, she nodded, acknowledging defeat. "Ten minutes, okay?" she asked. "I'm no quick-change artist."

He nodded. "You have exactly ten minutes, woman."

"Apparently you were hungrier than you thought," Collin observed wryly over dinner at the Century Café.

"I always eat when I'm upset," she responded indifferently.

"So I see." Collin was amused. "But don't you think you might accomplish more by talking about it?"

She stopped eating and looked at him for a moment, tempted to ask him why he'd been in the courtroom that morning. Obviously he wasn't about to bring it up himself. She resisted that temptation. Though his unexpected appearance there had aroused her suspicions, Collin had become her only real friend in New York, the only person she'd confided in during the months she'd been in the city. She did not want to alienate him now, because she realized she did need someone she could talk to, someone to whom she could pour out her heart.

"Didn't your mother ever tell you it's not polite to stare?" Collin was smiling at her.

Ashley shook her head. "I'm sorry," she mumbled. "I was just thinking."

"About what?"

"About why you're so damned interested in me and my personal problems," she said honestly. "I'm curious."

Collin smiled patiently. "I was brought up to be a polite, helpful gentleman," he suggested. "Chivalry and all that."

Ashley shook her head. "Try again."

He grinned. "I'm dead serious," he insisted. "Chivalry isn't really dead, you know. It's just hard to find these days."

Ashley forced a smile she didn't really feel. "Very hard," she agreed.

Collin nodded. "My father used to say I was a throwback to another era," he recalled. "An era of dueling swash-bucklers."

"And highwaymen and pirates?" Ashley asked in a taunting tone, toying with her fork.

Collin flashed an easy grin. She didn't realize how close to the truth she'd been. "Touché," he said lightly. "I had that one coming."

She studied him for a few seconds. "Who *are* you, Collin?" she asked wistfully. "What do you really want?"

His eyes met hers. "I think," he said evenly, "we both want the same thing."

It's like watching the first hearing on instant replay, Ashley thought dismally as she sat in the courtroom the next day, listening as the Hollisters' attorneys painted a distorted mental picture of her for the judge. *I might as well have worn a scarlet letter tattooed on my forehead.* She glanced over her shoulder and saw Collin, once again seated at the back of the courtroom, near the doors. Would he slip out again at the end of the day without even letting her know he had been there? she wondered. Why was he there, if not to lend moral support?

It was much harder than she'd anticipated, even after having been through it before, to have to sit and listen to the Hollisters' attorneys ripping her apart in front of what seemed to be every reporter and photographer in Manhattan. She felt herself flinch inwardly each time the crowd reacted to a disclosure or accusation. *Don't let them get to you,* she told herself. *It doesn't matter what they think. Only the judge matters. He's the one who's going to decide your fate.*

She glanced cross the room at Bradley and Claudia, looking poised and confident as they listened to the testimony being given, and she thought about what Collin had told her. *They already know what the outcome's going to be. Why shouldn't they feel confident?* she thought resentfully. *They probably own seventy-five percent of the people in this room.*

"Yes, I was—involved—with her." The man on the stand was one of Ashley's former lovers, a man she'd dropped long before she'd met Brandon. "I was the one who ended the affair, but I always knew I could have her again if I wanted, and as a matter of fact I did—two years after her marriage."

Then Claudia took the stand. "My husband and I knew she was all wrong for our son when he first brought her home to meet us," she recalled. "We tried to talk him out of rushing into marriage, but he was so smitten that he refused to listen, even to us. Even after we told him what our investigators had told us about her . . ."

I'll give her credit for one thing, Ashley thought angrily. *She's an accomplished liar. She really does it incredibly well.*

As each of the Hollisters' "character witnesses" gave their testimony, Ashley watched the face of the judge, searching for a clue to what he was thinking, how he was responding to the things he was hearing. His face was expressionless. *It's like looking at the Sphinx*, she thought. It was maddening to think that her future, and Robert's, was in the hands of a man neither of them had ever even seen before. *It's not fair*, she thought with steadily mounting resentment.

"I don't think I can go through another day of this," she told Elliott Morgan when court was adjourned for the day. "I'm glad it's over. How soon do you think the judge will reach a decision?"

"It's hard to tell," the lawyer answered as he put his notes back into his briefcase. "The longer he takes to make up his mind, the better our chances of having the original decision overturned. It'll mean he's got doubts about the validity of their claims."

"Or it'll mean Bradley Hollister's told him to make it look good," Ashley said as she put on her coat.

Morgan looked at her. "Not everyone is on the Hollister payrolls," he said in a serious tone.

"You're absolutely right," she agreed gloomily. "You and I aren't." As she turned toward the exit, she saw Collin leaving the courtroom. *Why doesn't he talk to me, or even try to let me know he's here?* she wondered again.

"Most people prefer to sit down there, in the higher visibility area—the booths, or one of the tables," Collin explained. He and Ashley were having dinner on the balcony of the Grill Room at the Four Seasons. "But I happen to like it here in purgatory. It's more private."

Ashley looked at him, perplexed. "Purgatory?"

"That's what this section is usually called—purgatory or Siberia," he explained with a smile. "It's not the preferred seating area for those who like to see and be seen. Myself, I just come here for the food."

She fiddled with her fork. "I'm sorry I haven't been very good company tonight," she said finally, looking down at her plate. "The hearing's taken a lot out of me."

"Am I complaining?"

She looked up and forced a smile. "No . . . and I appreciate it. I really do."

"You should try to eat," he said as he finished his own meal. "You need to keep up your strength, even now. Especially now."

She looked down at the open, airy rectangle that was the Grill Room, an area defined by metallic-curtained windows on two sides and grained French walnut paneling on the other two. There was a row of five booths and thirty tables arranged throughout, all of them occupied. In one corner was a large, four-sided bar with well-spaced chairs. Ashley picked at the food on her plate absently. It was delicious, but she had no appetite. She rarely had an appetite these days. Since she'd been in New York she'd lost almost ten pounds. If it weren't for Collin's gentle pressuring, she probably would have lost a great deal more.

"Try the chocolate velvet cake for dessert," Collin suggested. "If it doesn't make your taste buds come to life, you'd better have the life support system turned off, 'cause they'll have to be dead."

"I couldn't," Ashley insisted.

"You've got to relax," he urged, signaling the waiter for another drink. "Regardless of what the judge decides, you *will* get your boy back. You have my word on it, and I never promise anything I can't deliver."

Ashley's smile was cynical. "Are you a mystic or a commando?"

"Neither." His face was serious. "But if you're willing to trust me, it'll all work out in the end."

She stared at him for a moment, tempted to ask why she should trust him when he would tell her so little about this mysterious plan of his, but she decided against it. She just shook her head. "I've been burned too many times recently to go on believing in miracles," she said solemnly.

His eyes met hers. "We make our own miracles," he said in a low voice. "It just depends on how far we're willing to go to make it happen."

She bit her lower lip, afraid to ask him how he intended

to precipitate this miracle he talked about, afraid she would not want to know once he'd told her. "Elliott Morgan thinks the longer the judge takes to make a decision, the better our chances of a favorable decision," she told him.

"Morgan is living in a fool's paradise, then," Collin said promptly. "Bradley Hollister is not a man who leaves anything to chance. Believe me, he already knows what the judge's decision will be."

Ashley took a deep breath. "But you can help me?"

He smiled. "Actually, my dear Ashley," he started, "we can help each other."

Ashley sat at the dressing table in her bedroom, attempting to apply her makeup with a trembling hand. An hour earlier, Elliott Morgan had phoned to say that the judge had reached a decision and that they were expected to be at the courthouse at eleven o'clock. He'd had no idea what that decision was going to be, and not knowing was making Ashley crazy. It had been only two days since the hearing concluded. Was it a bad omen? In two short hours, her destiny would be decided in a Manhattan courtroom. The judge's decision would also decide whether or not she would be returning to San Francisco, whether or not she and Robert would be reunited. If it was not the decision she'd prayed for, would she be able to give up, go back to California and attempt to pick up the pieces of what remained of her life? Or would she be able to summon up the courage to do whatever it was Collin had in mind?

She went to the closet and chose a tailored gray wool flannel suit with black velvet lapels and a matching velvet hat with a short veil. It was a vintage suit, late 1940s, from Dior's "New Look" collection, and it was in mint condition. She stared at it speculatively. It was the simplest, most conservative garment she owned, perhaps not exactly what a suburban mother might wear, but it would make her look solid and respectable to the judge. She took off her robe and sat on the edge of the bed to put on her pantyhose. Looking at the telephone on the night table, she considered calling

Collin to let him know the judge would be handing down his decision today. She decided against it. She had the odd feeling that Collin already knew. It was uncanny how he always seemed to know when something important was happening, how he always seemed to be in the right place at the right time.

Ashley would have bet any amount of money he would be at the courthouse today.

Ashley sat next to Elliott Morgan at the front of the courtroom as the reporters and other spectators filed in and seated themselves. Her eyes scanned the room, searching for Collin, but he was nowhere to be seen. Maybe he didn't know, after all. Maybe he didn't keep tabs on her as she'd once believed he did. Maybe he didn't have some deep, dark ulterior motive for wanting to help her get Robert back. *It doesn't matter now*, she thought nervously as she looked across the room at the Hollisters. They were both smiling, radiating confidence. *Bradley Hollister is not a man who leaves anything to chance*, Collin had said. *Believe me, he knows what the judge's decision will be.* And Brandon: *I don't like the way my father does business.* Ashley was so wrapped up in those recollections that she didn't see Collin enter and take his usual seat at the back of the courtroom.

Her thoughts snapped back to the present as court was called to order. Everyone stood up as the judge entered and made his way to the bench. As she sat down again, her heart was racing. *This is it*, she thought, her hands trembling. *This is really it.*

". . . I have reviewed the records of the previous custody hearing as well as the testimony given in this courtroom, and have given serious consideration to this matter," the judge said. "I have come to the conclusion that it is in the best interests of the minor child, Robert Brandon Hollister, to remain with the paternal grandparents, Mr. and Mrs. Bradley Hollister."

There was a loud murmur throughout the courtroom as Ashley jumped to her feet, trembling with rage. "No!" she cried out, the agonized howl of a wounded animal. *"NO!"* Elliott Morgan attempted to restrain her, but she pushed him away. The judge was pounding his gavel furiously, demanding order, but Ashley couldn't control herself. Unable to accept the reality that was assaulting her, she pushed past her own lawyer and ran from the courtroom amid popping flashbulbs and stunned whispers. As she pushed open the double doors and fled the room, Collin jumped to his feet and ran after her.

"Ashley, wait!" he called out. "Wait!"

She finally came to an abrupt halt at the bottom of the steps outside the courthouse, where Collin caught up with her. He paused for a moment to catch his breath, then took her in his arms. She was trembling violently. He stroked her hair and rocked her gently. "It's going to be all right, Ashley," he said softly. "It is going to be all right."

"It's over," she gasped, sobbing uncontrollably. "It's over. I've lost my baby—for good."

"No . . . you haven't," he said in a low, soothing voice. "It's not over yet, not by a long shot."

She pulled back and looked up at him, her cheeks streaked with tears. "You said that before," she said in a tremulous voice. "What do you mean?"

He shook his head. "Not here," he said firmly as he took his handkerchief from his pocket and wiped her face gently. "Let's go somewhere where we can talk, have a bite to eat—"

Ashley shook her head emphatically. "I'm not hungry."

"You'll eat," he said with gentle insistence in his voice. "You're going to need every ounce of strength you can muster in the weeks to come. And while we're eating, we'll talk. We'll figure out what our next move's going to be."

Before she could protest, he ushered her into his waiting car and took her to Barbetta's, an Italian restaurant on West Forty-sixth Street. Ashley had gone with him without argument because she'd suddenly felt as though she had nowhere else to go, but now, sitting with him in the marble dining room of the century-old brownstone, she was glad he had insisted. Though she wasn't really hungry, she had needed to get as far from the courthouse as she could. She'd needed to talk, and he was right, he really was a good listener. He had listened patiently as she poured her heart out to him, and she had the feeling that he really cared, that he was the one person in New York who gave a damn about how she felt, about what she was going through. When she'd finally stopped crying, Collin looked across the table at her and smiled wearily as he reached out and took her hand. "Now we figure out where we go from here," he said softly.

Ashley looked up at him, her eyes red and swollen from crying. "But I've exhausted every legal channel open to me—"

Collin put a finger to her lips and his voice dropped to a whisper. "I never said what I had in mind was *legal*, my dear Ashley."

Sea Cliff,
February 1987

As the taxi followed the winding road along Long Island Sound, Ashley thought about their strange conversation. She hadn't wanted to hear him out that afternoon at Barbetta's. He had definitely made it clear that he had something in mind, and no, it wasn't entirely legal. Still reeling from what had taken place in the courtroom, she had not been able to comprehend what he'd been trying to tell her. It was too much to have to digest at once. "Tell you what . . . you let me know when you're ready to hear what I have in mind," Collin had said patiently. "Just think about it, and let me know."

She *had* thought about it, in fact she'd thought of nothing else for the past two days. As she considered which would be worse—remaining in New York and perhaps seeing her son once in a while, when Claudia Hollister wasn't looking, or going back to San Francisco, where she knew she would never seen him again—Collin's words kept creeping back into her thoughts: *I'll get your boy back for you* . . . *trust me* . . . *I never said what I had in mind was legal.* . . . It didn't matter if it was legal or not, she had decided. It was her only hope now. She didn't care what she had to do or what he expected of her in return. She would do anything to get Robert back, legal or otherwise.

She had to see Collin, face-to-face. She'd downed two cups of coffee as she dressed, found a cabbie willing to make the long drive, and was on her way. Now, as the taxi slowed to a stop at the gates of the estate, a uniformed guard came forward to check it out. Ashley rolled down the window and waved to him. "My name is Ashley Gordon-Hollister and I'm a friend of Mr. Deverell's," she told him.

"Is he expecting you, ma'am?" the guard asked.

Ashley shook her head. "No, he's not. But if you'll just call the house and tell him I'm here, I'm sure it will be all right," she said quickly.

The guard nodded. "One moment, ma'am." He returned to his small booth at the gate and got on the phone. Moments later the big gates swung open, allowing the car to pass. As the taxi headed up the long driveway, Ashley leaned back in the seat and took a deep breath. *Please, Collin, don't let me down.*

The car slowed to a stop in front of the main house. Collin was standing in the doorway, waiting for her. "Why didn't you call?" he asked as she paid the driver. "I would have sent a car for you."

She shook her head. "Once I made up my mind, I decided we couldn't waste any more time," she confessed.

He looked at her, and she saw understanding in his eyes—and something else she didn't quite understand. "Come on inside," he said quietly. "We'll talk about it."

"You told me once that you hate Bradley Hollister as much as I do," Ashley said bluntly as they entered the library.

"Why?" She settled down on the couch and looked at him expectantly, waiting for his response.

Collin was standing at the French doors, his back to her, staring out into the garden as if he were looking for something specific. "He took your son from you," he began carefully, "but he also took something from me—or to be more precise, he's trying to take it from me. From my family." He turned to face her. "I intend to prevent that from happening. If you're with me, I believe we can help each other."

"What?" Ashley asked, confused. "What is it he's trying to take from you?"

Collin's jaw tightened visibly. "Intercontinental Oil."

"Your father's company?" She stared at him, trying to understand what he was saying. "But I thought—" she began.

"You thought I turned my back on the family business a long time ago," he finished for her. She gave a slight nod. "I did. I wanted no part of it after my parents died, and I never really thought I belonged in the executive suite anyway. But I also thought then that my dear brother Justin was capable of running the business. Turned out he was just running it into the ground." Collin looked at Ashley, suddenly realizing how little of himself he'd revealed to her since they met. *No wonder she's so reluctant to trust me*, he thought. He drew in a deep breath. "Ten years ago my father and mother were killed in an explosion on an offshore drilling rig in Venezuela. At the time it happened I could make no sense of it. There were so damned many unanswered questions. What were they doing in Venezuela to begin with? Why were they out there on that rig? And why did it explode? Not knowing drove me nuts for a while." He paused, staring into the distance as all the unpleasant memories came flooding back into his consciousness. "It had always been my father's master plan to one day have both of his sons running the company, side by side. Unfortunately, Justin and I didn't get along well enough to make it work, and when the time came, I just decided I didn't want any part of it. I sold out to my brother and dropped off the face of the earth for a couple of years." He went on to tell her how he'd returned to Sea Cliff to find his home had been violated and his paintings and other valuables taken, and, somewhat hesitantly, of the quest that took him to Morocco and altered the course of his life.

When he finished, Ashley was staring at him in disbelief. "You—you're a crook!" she concluded, astonished. "A thief!"

"Not at all," he said, shaking his head in disagreement. "I only take what's already rightfully mine."

"I see," she said carefully. "That makes your methods perfectly acceptable."

He looked at her. "Wouldn't you use whatever methods were available to you to get your boy back?" he challenged.

"Of course, but—" she started.

"Then reconsider your noble principles, Ashley," he suggested with an edge in his voice. "My way, good or bad, seems to be your only hope of getting Robert back."

Ashley backed off instantly; he'd struck a nerve. "All right . . . I'm in," she said, nodding in agreement. "I'm not at all sure it's going to work, but at this point I'm willing to try anything, legal or not."

He nodded too. "I had a feeling you would be."

"I still don't understand," she began carefully, her eyes meeting his. "What, exactly, does Bradley Hollister have to do with all of this—aside from the fact that his company is trying to take over your father's company? What's his connection to this syndicate?"

Collin faced her squarely. "He's the head of it," he answered grimly.

"I don't know why I'm finding it so hard to believe that my former father-in-law could be involved with the under-world," Ashley confided to Collin as they walked the grounds together that afternoon. "I know—probably better than anyone else—what an unscrupulous man he can be, how much power and influence he has. I also know that his own son—my husband—couldn't stomach his so-called business practices.''

Collin looked at her for a moment. "You really knew nothing of his connections with organized crime?" he asked.

Ashley's temper flared again. "Of course not!" she snapped. "Do you think I would have just sat back and let him take Robert from me if I'd had something like this on him? God, Collin, why didn't you tell me? I could have won the appeal—"

"Hold on," he said, placing his hands on her shoulders as their eyes met. "In the first place, you have to have proof before you can level an accusation like that, or you're just asking for trouble. Knowing wouldn't have done you a damn bit of good in that courtroom. That's why I didn't tell you before now."

"So what, exactly, do we do?" she demanded. "Fight fire with fire?"

"Something like that, yes—for now."

"For now?"

"I have a plan," he admitted. "I want to collect enough data to put Hollister and his people away for a very long time, and I have the means at my disposal to do it—if you're with me. I can't do it alone. What I have in mind will often require the skill of *two* able bodies. But together—together, Ashley, we can do it. We can get your boy back, save my father's company, and put Hollister behind bars where he damn well belongs."

"And how do you propose we do it?" Ashley wanted to know.

Collin frowned. "My father used to say a chain is only as strong as its weakest link," he recalled. "Hollister's chain of command has a hell of a lot of weak links. I figure if I—we—work on those weak links long enough, they'll crack." He bent down to pick up a twig, peeling the bark from it absently as they walked. "First of all, though, I have to train you."

"Train me? For what?" She looked at him cautiously. "Or should I even ask?"

He shrugged. "You've come this far, you might as well hear all of it," he said quietly. "You have a great deal to learn and not much time to do it."

"Like what?"

"The basics—lockpicking, safecracking, picking pockets—"

"Just the fundamental stuff every kid learns in high school, right?" Ashley asked dryly.

"Basically, yes." He broke the twig in half and discarded it.

"Used to be, breaking and entering wasn't so hard if you were smart and physically agile, but lately it's become a downright pain in the ass." He addressed the problem as casually as if he were discussing the weather. "The new alarm systems are complicated as hell. The more money an individual's got, the more sophisticated the security system. Many of them are heat-sensitive."

"Meaning what?" Ashley asked, not sure she understood.

"Meaning they're set off by a sudden change in temperature—such as that of a human body moving within their field." He paused. "Of course, if one body were to remain within that field until the job was done . . ."

"Oh, no," Ashley said, shaking her head. "This is insane. It'll never work—"

"It'll work, Ashley," he maintained confidently. "Of course, it will require some changes on your part—like giving up your apartment and moving in here . . ."

"Here?" She looked at him questioningly. "Why?"

"For a number of valid reasons, the most important being that we have to make the Hollisters—and everyone else—think you're ready to run back to San Francisco with your tail between your legs, so to speak."

"Thanks a lot!" She hugged herself tightly in an attempt to block out the cold.

"Listen—what does it matter what anyone thinks as long

as it gets results?'' he demanded angrily, losing patience with her. ''You want your son back or don't you?''

''Of course I do!'' she snapped irritably. ''But—''

''You're perfectly safe here, just as long as you don't forget to lock your bedroom door at night,'' he said with a mischievous grin, his mood changing abruptly. ''The only thing is, you should know that you can't be seen—at least not as Ashley Gordon-Hollister—in Manhattan.''

''What do you mean, I can't be seen as myself?'' she asked, not sure she understood what he was getting at.

''You'll be able to go into the city again once you've mastered the ability to don a convincing disguise,'' he promised. ''Until then, you'll have everything you need right here.''

''Isn't this an awful lot of trouble—'' she started.

''Perhaps, but it's necessary,'' he insisted. ''Trust me, Ashley. I've been playing this game for a long time now, and I've mastered it. I know what I'm doing.''

She studied him intently. The brilliant afternoon sunlight filtering down through the barren branches of the trees captured the individual strands of his thick hair, softly ruffled by the cool breeze, and transformed it into a million dazzling threads of varying hues of mahogany, chestnut, copper, and gold. What choice did she have? she asked herself. Collin was her last chance. Her only chance. ''When do I move in?'' she asked.

He smiled, relieved. ''Now. Today.''

She nodded. ''All right.'' She was silent as they walked along several more yards. ''Collin, exactly how do you plan to get Robert back?'' she asked finally.

And then he told her.

Ashley took one last look around her apartment as Collin carried her luggage from the bedroom into the living room. ''It's a strange feeling,'' she said quietly as she drew the drapes. ''I have a home in San Francisco, and one in St. Helena if you count my parents' home, and this apartment, yet I feel as though I don't really belong anywhere.''

Collin, standing in the doorway, said nothing. There were times he felt exactly the same way, even at Sea Cliff, in the home where he'd grown up.

She turned to look at him. "It's as if Brandon's death scattered my life—and Robert's—to the four winds," she went on. "Parts of me are here, parts in California."

"That'll all change, once this business is over," Collin promised. "Then we'll both be able to get on with our lives, maybe even find some sort of normalcy." He looked at his watch. "Come on, Ashley," he said, gently urging her. "We'd better get going. You can send most of this to storage."

Ashley nodded. She hesitated for only a moment in the doorway. Then, abruptly, she switched off the lamp and closed the door.

"I don't know why it bothers me to leave," she told Collin in the elevator. "In San Francisco, it was different—my whole life was in that house. Everything that was good and right with me was there . . . five years as Brandon's wife, four as Robert's mother, all the paintings I'd done in my studio. But here, there were no good memories, no real life to speak of."

Collin frowned, remembering the night he broke in, how cold and impersonal the place had seemed then. He was surprised leaving it bothered her at all. He looked down at the woman standing at his side. *A woman with her emotions shut off*, he thought. *We really are two of a kind, Ashley, you and I.* "It'll pass," he said aloud.

The uniformed doorman helped Collin carry Ashley's luggage out to his waiting car. Collin stopped to open the door on the passenger side for Ashley, then went to the back of the car to open the trunk. Ashley got in, looking around absently at the world she was about to leave behind. *For what?* she wondered. *What have I gotten myself into? What am I doing? Moving in with a man I know virtually nothing about—beyond the fact that he's a self-confessed thief—entering into a devil's bargain that could land me in prison for the next ten to twenty years. . . .*

"Ready?" Collin asked cheerfully as he slid behind the wheel and took out his car keys.

She forced a slight smile. "As ready as I'm ever going to be," she said tightly.

He grinned. "Relax," he urged. "You're not exactly a lamb bound for slaughter."

"Aren't I?" she asked dubiously.

"No, you're not," he assured her as he started the Excalibur's engine. "You'll see. It's—"

"Collin—look!" Ashley cried out suddenly. "Over there!"

Collin looked toward the park where she was pointing. A portly gray-haired woman was leading a small boy by the hand into the park. "That's my son!" Ashley gasped. "That's Robert!" She started to get out of the car, but Collin stopped her.

"Just what do you have in mind?" he demanded, his grip tightening around her wrist. "Are you going to mug the old lady and take the kid? You wouldn't make it out of Manhattan!"

She sank back into her seat. "I—I don't have anything in mind," she said, taking a deep breath. "I just wanted to see him—"

"And then what? What good would it do you?" he asked harshly. "It wouldn't make any difference, except maybe to make you even more miserable than you are already."

"Are you suggesting I stay away from him entirely?" Ashley cried. "I can't even think about—"

"Only for a little while," he replied calmly. "Then, when the time comes, you'll have him with you for good."

"Could I have that in writing, please?" she asked as he put the car in gear and headed toward Fifth Avenue.

"You still don't trust me, do you?" he chuckled, slowing the car to a stop at a red light before making a right turn.

"It's hard to trust a man who's admitted to being a thief and a con artist," she said finally.

"I'm doing what I have to do." Collin's tone was sharp. "And you're doing what you have to do."

She looked at him for a moment, stung by his words. "Where'd you learn to hit so hard?" she asked, sinking back in her seat.

"On a desert in Morocco," he said simply, concentrating on maneuvering the Excalibur through the heavy traffic.

She hesitated for a moment. "What does that mean?"

"It's a long story."

She sighed deeply. "Well, it looks like we're going to have plenty of time together, if you'd like to talk about it," she said. "Maybe ten to twenty, if we blow it."

He shook his head. "Maybe some other time."

Ashley was furious. She had the feeling he'd been on the brink of revealing something important about himself to her, but suddenly, as always, he closed the door on her again. "Dammit, Collin, you say you want me to trust you, yet whenever I try to establish that trust, you pull back," she complained. "How can I trust you when you won't trust me?"

He kept his eyes on the traffic, but she could tell she'd struck a nerve. "All right," he said slowly. "Maybe you're right. Maybe you do have the right to know."

And he told her about his journey to Marrakesh.

The mantle clock read three-fifteen. Ashley, wearing only a mauve silk nightgown, set on the edge of the canopied bed in her room, staring blankly at the blue walls. *I must be out of my mind*, she thought, anxiety building within her. *How can I even consider doing this?* But even as she wrestled with her doubts, she knew the answer to that question: she was doing it for Robert. There was nothing she would not do to get her son back. Nothing.

She rose to her feet slowly and walked barefoot to the French doors leading out to the balcony and pulled them wide open, allowing the cold winter air to rush into the bedroom. Ashley was oblivious of the bitter cold as she stepped out onto the balcony and gazed up into the clear, star-filled sky. She could visualize Brandon's face clearly; it was almost as if she could reach out and touch him. "You do understand, don't you?" she whispered.

"Well . . . it would seem we both have the same problem tonight."

Startled, Ashley looked down. Collin was standing in the shadows, bundled in a bulky sweater, the breeze tousling his hair. "What?" she asked when she finally found her voice.

"I take it you can't sleep either."

"No," she said, shaking her head. "I can't."

"I think it would be a good idea if you were to put on a robe," he said then, his voice tinged with amusement.

Ashley looked down, suddenly realizing that the breeze had plastered the sheer nightgown to her body. "You—" she gasped, horrified. She turned and ran back into the bedroom, slamming the doors behind her.

Collin shook his head, smiling to himself. He was sorry he'd called it to her attention. Ashley was a beautiful woman, and he would have liked nothing better than to— no, he couldn't allow his physical desires to get in the way of what he had to do. What *they* had to do. Not now. There was too much to do and too little time to do it.

New York City, March 1987

Anton DeVries was angry and frustrated, angry because no one accepted his theory that one man could have masterminded so many daring thefts across four continents, and frustrated because he was unable to get the evidence he needed to accuse Collin Deverell. There had to be something somewhere, something Interpol and the other law enforcement agencies had overlooked. Something *he* had overlooked. Something that would prove Deverell was in all the right places at the right times. Convinced that the more he could learn about the man himself, the more likely his chances of catching him, DeVries set out to learn even the most intimate details of Collin Deverell's life.

Now, in the Intercontinental Oil executive suite, high above Manhattan's financial district, DeVries found himself sitting across from Justin Deverell. Even knowing the brothers were identical twins had not prepared him for the startling physical resemblance. *It is virtually impossible to tell them apart*, DeVries thought as he looked across the desk at the chairman of the board of Intercontinental Oil. DeVries found it difficult to question the man about his brother: it was like interrogating Collin Deverell about himself!

"I'm afraid I can't be of much help to you, Mr. DeVries," Justin Deverell said. "My brother and I have never been close. In fact we haven't spoken to each other in several years. The only thing I can say about Collin with any great degree of certainty is that he's devoted most of his life to the pursuit of that great adventure, the ultimate thrill."

"I see." *Odd*, DeVries mused, *that identical twins could be so distant with each other.*

"I really don't understand," Justin said then. "The case was closed on Collin's stolen property some time ago. Has it been reopened for some reason?"

"No, not exactly," DeVries said quickly. "Some of the items have turned up—in Rome, in London . . ."

"And you have now changed your mind and think Collin may actually have committed fraud," Justin concluded.

DeVries shook his head, surprised at how quickly Deverell jumped to that conclusion. "No. Not at all."

Justin eyed him warily. "Then why all the questions about my brother's habits?"

"I believe, as I did then, that he was framed," DeVries maintained calmly. "By whom, I'm not sure, but—"

"Then why are you investigating it now?" Justin cut in sharply.

"I'm not at liberty to say, Mr. Deverell," DeVries said carefully. "I'm sorry."

"I see." Justin drew in a deep breath. "If you'll excuse me, Mr. DeVries . . ."

"Of course." DeVries got to his feet, extending his hand. "Thank you for seeing me, Mr. Deverell."

"I'm sorry I haven't been able to be of any real help to you," Justin said with a smile.

"Oh, but you *have*," DeVries insisted. "More than you realize."

He thought about it as he walked to the elevators. Justin Deverell's uneasiness had been obvious, but the reason behind it had not. Had his initial suspicions been correct? Had Justin Deverell been the one who framed his own brother? Or was it that he knew something about his brother's nocturnal activities?

It appeared Collin Deverell wasn't the only one who had something to hide.

"I'm never going to get the hang of this, Collin," Ashley muttered in frustration as she fiddled with the padlock on the garage door. She stopped abruptly and rubbed her hands together in an attempt to warm them. "It's cold out here and I'm no damn good at this."

"Nothing doing," Collin said firmly, shaking his head. "You're going to stay right here and keep at it until you can do it right—and do it fast."

"It'll never happen," Ashley lamented.

"Sure it will—unless you give up too quickly," he pointed out. "It took me a while to master it too."

She made a wry face as she brushed a strand of her hair away from her face. "I find that hard to believe."

"It's true," he maintained. "But Blackjack never gave up on me, and I'm not about to give up on you."

Ashley looked up at him for a moment. "You really think a lot of him, don't you," she said softly.

Collin gave her a tired smile. "It's damn hard not to like the guy who saved your neck."

She nodded. "Right."

"I owe him more than I've ever owed anybody." He

handed her another tool. "It's one debt I'll pay or die trying."

"Meaning his daughter," Ashley said casually, resuming her vicious attack on the lock.

"Yeah."

"And what if you don't find her?"

"I'll find her, all right," he said with certainty.

"Bingo!" Ashley cried triumphantly as the lock popped open in her hand. "Now can we call it a day?"

"Nope," Collin responded with a shake of his head. "Now you do it again and again, until you can do it fast and easy."

"I was once aiming for the Olympic fencing team," Collin explained as Ashley admired his ceremonial saber. "Made it as far as the '72 Pan-American Games, in fact."

"You must have been very good to have made it that far," Ashley commented, tracing the saber's elaborate grip with her fingertips.

"It was my whole life," he said, perching himself on the arm of the couch as he sipped his coffee. A fire had been lit in the fireplace, its flames filling the room with a soft glow.

Ashley turned to look at him, a puzzled expression on her beautiful face. "Why did you ever give it up?"

He shook his head. "I didn't really have much choice—at the time," he answered.

"I find it hard to believe that you would ever be in the position of not having a choice," she commented with a smile.

Collin got to his feet and walked over to the windows. "You'd believe it if you had known my father," he said then.

"Your father was the one who stopped you?" she asked incredulously.

He nodded but did not face her. "He felt it was a waste of time, that I had better, more important things to do with my life."

"Like preparing to take control of his company," Ashley concluded.

"Yeah." Though his face was in shadow, she could see the tension in his mouth, in the clench of his jaw. "The purpose for which Justin and I were born."

"You never told him how you felt?" she asked.

"I did. It just didn't matter." Collin turned abruptly and started for the door. "I'd suggest we call it an early night. We have a long day ahead of us tomorrow."

And he walked out, leaving her staring after him.

The days at Sea Cliff were invariably long and difficult. Ashley's nervousness and self-doubts about her ability to master the skills of the successful cat burglar made her a somewhat clumsy and awkward student, and Collin was an impatient and demanding tutor who made her repeat each step, each maneuver, until she could do it quickly and flawlessly. The same man she'd come to know in Manhattan as warm and relaxed and considerate was now tough, unyielding, and dispassionate, constantly demanding the impossible of her. Ashley tried to understand, telling herself that he had to be hard on her because there would be no margin for error when they were actually breaking into someone's home or place of business, but that knowledge hadn't made Collin any easier to get along with. *One mistake can be your last.* She repeated those words over and over again in her mind, like a mantra. *One mistake can be fatal.*

After dinner each evening they spent hours discussing what they had done that day and what they would be doing the next. He went through the steps with her and expected her to be able to repeat everything verbatim. They discussed types of locks and security systems and how to beat each of them. He prepared her to learn the high wire, as he called it, a cable generally used to gain entry to one building from the roof of another, and sensed her apprehension. "I don't use it unless I have to," he assured her, "but sometimes it's the only way."

Occasionally, after those sessions, they talked about the

people and events that had shaped their lives. Ashley told Collin about growing up in the Napa Valley and her dreams of becoming a painter, of making a better life for herself in San Francisco. "My father didn't approve," she recalled. "He thought I was setting myself up for a big disappointment." Her laugh was weak. "Little did any of us know then."

"There's nothing to be afraid of," Collin said confidently, leaning back against the trunk of the tree, his arms folded across his chest. "When I string a cable, it's so safe you could sail a baby on it."

"Could I have a guarantee, please—preferably signed in blood?" Ashley stood on a high platform several yards away, gripping a heavy metal ring rigged onto a thick cable running across the lawn to the tree where Collin stood.

"Better to learn it now than to have to do it for the first time when you're trapped in somebody's twentieth-floor apartment and there's no other way out," Collin said.

"That's like having to choose between the frying pan and the fire," Ashley moaned.

"Quit complaining and just do it," Collin ordered, stepping off to one side so he could watch her descent.

Ashley took a deep breath. "Here goes nothing," she said, shaking her hair away from her face. She swung forward, lifting her legs high as she jumped from the platform. She sailed along freely, coming to an abrupt halt the moment her feet touched the ground. Clearly pleased with herself, she turned to Collin, smiling, and made an expansive gesture with her hands. "Well?"

Collin nodded, his expression never changing. "Not bad," he conceded.

"Not bad?" Ashley looked properly hurt. "It was damn good for a first try!"

"You're absolutely right: it *was* damn good—for a first try," he agreed. "But good isn't enough when you're hanging four or five hundred feet up and sweaty palms or a slight miscalculation can prove lethal." He gestured toward the platform. ''Try it again, and this time, don't kick your feet. Let yourself glide.''

Ashley grimaced. ''You're a goddamned slave driver, Collin,'' she complained as she headed back to the platform.

He ignored her accusation. ''My life happens to mean a great deal to me,'' he told her as she climbed the ladder. ''There's no room for mistakes. Not in our business.''

''You call this a business?'' Ashley grumbled, wiping her hands on her black stirrup pants before grasping the ring he returned to her.

He was no more satisfied with her second attempt than he had been with her first. He made her repeat the exercise again and again until her form was flawless and her execution smooth. ''One more time,'' he told her as she climbed up to the platform again. ''This time, try for speed.''

''Shall I also try to break my neck?'' She gripped the ring again and launched herself forward, drawing her legs up as she came off the platform.

Seeing that she was coming down too fast, Collin called out to her, but it was too late. She was gaining momentum and would not be able to stop without hurting herself in the process. He leaped forward to catch her before she collided with the tree. She slammed into him as he caught her in his arms. He held her tight, staring into her large, frightened eyes. ''Are you all right?'' he asked in a low, husky voice.

''I—I think so,'' she gasped breathlessly.

''That was close,'' he said as he lowered her to the ground, hovering over her as she struggled to catch her breath. ''Too close.'' He could feel her heart beating wildly inside her chest, and his own pulse quickened as he suddenly became aware of how tightly their bodies were pressed together. Their eyes met and held. Suddenly, his mouth came down on hers, and he was claiming her with an intensity that took Ashley by surprise. With no time to think or control her own reactions, she began to respond to him, wrapping her arms around his neck, returning his kisses eagerly.

"I want to make love to you, Ashley," he whispered as he started kissing her neck. "Right here . . . right now . . ." His hand snaked up under her sweater, gently caressing her breasts.

The spell was broken by Ashley's realization that her nipples had hardened under his touch. "No!" she gasped, struggling against him, the weight of his body on top of hers pinning her to the ground. "No, Collin . . ."

"You don't mean that," he insisted, refusing to let her go. "Just now, when I kissed you—"

She shook her head frantically. "I can't . . . I'm not ready for this . . . not yet . . ."

He released her abruptly. "Don't worry, I won't rape you, if that's what you're afraid of," he said sharply as he sat up. "I've never had to take a woman by force in my life—and I sure as hell don't intend to start now!" He scrambled to his feet and turned away from her.

Ashley got up and brushed blades of grass from her clothes. Realizing how angry he was, she attempted to smooth things over. "I didn't mean to—" she began, reaching out to touch his shoulder.

He withdrew abruptly. "I think you'd better go on back to the house now," he said gruffly. "I'll be along later."

Ashley opened her mouth to protest, but changed her mind when she realized it would do no good. "All right," she said, walking away.

He watched her as she headed back to the main house. Damn, he wanted her! He couldn't recall a time in his life when he'd ever wanted a woman so much, but he'd blown it. Now she was not going to be quick to trust him—or to fall into his arms. Frustrated, he ran one hand through his hair as he turned to look up at the cable.

Taking a deep breath, he ripped it down violently.

Ashley sat on the edge of her bed, trying to sort out her confused emotions. She'd never been quite sure what she felt for Collin, and what had happened between them this afternoon had only served to further confuse her. She *had* responded to him. He hadn't been wrong about that. A part of her had wanted to make love almost as much as he did. Collin was the only man she could turn to now, the only one she could trust, and that made their relationship intimate. Making love, she told herself, had been the logical next step. But had her rejection of him alienated him?

He'd been unusually silent during dinner. He hadn't even looked at her as he ate. They had not had their usual discussion of the day's training session afterward. He'd gone off to the library alone and stayed there. Only Harrison, whom Ashley had quickly discovered was much more to Collin than a major domo, had been allowed to invade his privacy. Finally, Ashley had gone to her room. She'd heard his footsteps in the hallway when he went to his room, but he had not stopped to say good night as he usually did.

The year since Brandon's death had been unbearably lonely, especially after Robert had been taken from her. Somewhere deep within her soul, she'd wanted the kind of warm, intimate relationship she'd had with her husband, but it had always seemed to her that by surrendering to her longings, she would be cheating on Brandon. *That's a laugh*, she thought ruefully. *The scarlet woman's been living a nun's life all these months.* Then Collin had come into her life, Collin who had made her feel alive again, made her laugh. Collin, the man who'd given her hope where there had been none. They had been attracted to each other right from the start, that was undeniable. And though she didn't love him and knew he didn't love her, she also knew that sex between them would not be entirely without feeling. It could be the next best thing to love.

He's right, she thought as she shed her nightgown. *We only have each other now.*

She slipped on her black silk kimono and strode purposefully across the hall to his room. She tapped lightly on the door but did not wait for his response before opening it. When she entered, the room was in darkness except for a dim light coming through the windows. Collin, in his robe, stood near one window, staring into the night. "What do you want?" he asked in an irritated tone.

She crossed the room without a word and placed her hands on his shoulders, kissing him tenderly. He pulled back and stared at her for a moment, frowning. "Don't start anything you don't intend to finish," he warned.

"I fully intend to finish it," she whispered, stroking his chest as she kissed him again.

Suddenly his arms were around her, trapping her in an embrace as he kissed her hungrily. He reached down and untied the red sash to her robe, letting it fall open. He caressed her breasts, rubbing his thumb over one nipple, making it erect, as he kissed her neck. Taking her hand in his, he guided it inside his robe. "Touch me, Ashley," he said in a husky voice. "Feel how much I want you."

He backed up, perching on the edge of the bed as he drew her to him again. He reached up and pushed the robe off her shoulders, allowing it to fall to the floor. Cupping her breasts in his hands, he raised his head to kiss and nuzzle them, sucking gently at each of her nipples. Letting his hands roam over her nakedness in tender exploration, he then pulled her down on the bed beside him. "Do you know how beautiful you are?" he asked, still caressing her.

"You make me feel very beautiful," she responded, reaching for him again.

There can be no turning back now, she thought as their bodies came together.

Sea Cliff, March 1987

Ashley opened her eyes slowly and blinked. Sunlight streamed through the sheer curtains, filling the room with a brilliant glow. She turned her head slowly without raising it from the pillow. Collin was sleeping soundly beside her.

She lay there just looking at him for a long time, trying to come to terms with what was happening—*had* happened—between them. Trying to make some sense out of what she'd felt last night in his arms, what she was feeling now in the aftermath of their unleashed passions. She had enjoyed their lovemaking. Even now, she wanted Collin, wanted him to wake up and make love to her again. And even feeling as she did, she still felt an overwhelming sense of guilt. She felt as though her desire for Collin, the physical release she'd felt in their lovemaking, had been a betrayal of her love for Brandon. *It's not the same thing*, she told herself. *It's not the same thing at all.* With Brandon it was love, it was emotional commitment. With Collin it was—she wasn't quite sure what it was, beyond sex. Gratitude for what he'd done for her, for what he'd promised to do? Relief from the unbearable loneliness she'd felt since Brandon's death?

Collin began to stir. He turned over on his side, facing her, and opened his eyes. When he saw her, he smiled. "I thought you might have abandoned me and sneaked back to your own room," he said as he reached out and touched her cheek. "I thought I'd probably have to come looking for you."

"I'll bet you would have, too," she said lightly.

"Damned right I would have." He kissed her gently. "I want you right here with me, Ashley. Every night." He paused. "Any regrets?"

She shook her head. "No."

Collin smiled. "I was hoping you'd say that." He caressed her under the sheet. "God, I want you," he whispered, kissing her neck. "I think I've wanted you ever since that day I saw you at the airport."

"And I thought all you wanted was an accomplice," she giggled.

"Oh, I do," he assured her, tracing a line down the deep cleft between her breasts with the tip of his index finger. "I want you to be my accomplice—in every way possible."

He planted a row of tiny kisses from her jawline to the bottom of the soft swells of her breasts. Making small circles around each of her nipples with his tongue, he finally seized one in his mouth and began to suck at it intently. Ashley gave a shiver of pleasure as she ran her fingers through his hair, offering herself up to him. She felt his hand moving down over her hip, along her thigh, between her legs. His fingers probed the wetness he found there, welcoming him. He released her breast and sought her mouth again, kissing her urgently as he stroked her. Then he pressed himself into her, moving in a powerful rhythm until they were both gasping breathlessly as they came to a shuddering climax. Finally, Collin lay still on top of her, burying his face in her breasts. Ashley stroked his head as they both tried to catch their breath. Had it happened under any other circumstances, she would have been overjoyed to have found someone like Collin, who made her feel so alive, so completely satisfied.

But she also had the feeling that he would never belong to any woman totally.

As the blasting cold winds of March gave way to the promise of spring, Ashley became more and more adept at her newly acquired skills. Collin was now less impatient and not as demanding of her during those long hours of training, but he was increasingly possessive of her in bed. Ashley told herself it was normal, considering their unorthodox relationship: they were bound to each other not by love or even by an overwhelming physical passion, but by the nature of the secret life they shared. *We've only got each other*, she thought, lying awake in the darkness, trapped in his fierce embrace. *There's no one else either of us can turn to now.*

"Just remember why you're doing this," Collin told her whenever she was hesitant to try a new maneuver. "Tell yourself over and over again that you're doing it for Robert. It gets you through the first few times, and after a while it gets easier. Almost routine."

"Routine," Ashley repeated with doubt in her voice. "I don't think I'll ever consider this routine."

But the most difficult thing for Ashley to deal with was

not being able to venture beyond the safety of the walls at
Sea Cliff. Most of the time, she was either too busy or too
tired to think about it, but on those days when Collin made
trips into Manhattan, sometimes being away all day, she
would find herself wandering the grounds, lost in thought.

Now, as she sat on the wide marble steps outside the main
house, she could see Collin's silver Ferrari, one of the dozen
vehicles he owned, coming up the long drive. She got to her
feet and walked to the bottom of the steps to meet him as
the car came to a stop. "Am I glad to see you," she greeted
him as he got out of the car. "It's been one hell of a day
without you here."

"You may not be so happy to see me when you hear what
I've got to tell you." Collin wasn't smiling as he walked
toward her.

Ashley stopped in her tracks.

He looked at her. "It's not serious, but—" He stopped
short, shaking his head. "Robert's in the hospital."

"What?" She looked as though she might faint.

"Take it easy. It's not major," he said quickly, grabbing
her shoulders. "Just a tonsillectomy."

"How do you know?" she asked anxiously. "I mean,
how did you find out?"

He frowned. "I have my ways, Ashley." It was clear he
was not going to explain himself. Not yet.

"I've got to see him," Ashley said promptly, making it
clear that her mind was made up and the matter was not
open to discussion.

Collin shook his head. "Out of the question."

"The hell it is!" Ashley exploded. "This is my son we're
talking about, Collin! He's just a little boy—alone in the
hospital for the first time! I'm his mother! He *needs* me!"

"We can't risk it!" Collin argued. "We have to let everyone go on believing you've gone back to California—"

"I don't give a damn what they think!" Ashley snapped
angrily. "I have to see him!"

Collin paused for a moment, realizing he was not going
to talk her out of it. "All right," he said finally, acknowl-

edging defeat. Why had he ever told her to begin with? "Give me some time to think about it, okay? I should be able to come up with something."

Collin opened the door and looked around, making sure no one was looking. He ducked back into the stairwell, where Ashley stood clutching a large shopping bag. "The coast is clear," he said in a low voice. "Just remember our agreement, okay?"

She nodded. "Five minutes, no more."

"I hope Robert doesn't blow the whistle on us."

"He won't," Ashley assured him. "I'll make sure of it."

"See that you do." Collin opened the door again. "Let's go."

They moved down the corridor quickly, checking each of the rooms until they found the right one. "You go on in," Collin instructed Ashley. "I'll be right back."

She grabbed his arm as he started to walk away. "Where are you going?" she asked anxiously.

He grinned. "To secure an escape vehicle," he said, kissing her forehead. "Be right back."

Ashley went into the room and unzipped her jacket. The first bed was empty. In the second, near the window, Robert slept peacefully. Ashley crossed the room silently and stood beside the bed, looking down at him for a moment, overpowered by maternal love. "God, I miss you, sport," she said softly as she reached out to touch his hair.

His eyes blinked open, and he looked at her for a moment as if he thought he might be dreaming. "Mommy?" he rasped hoarsely.

She leaned over him and kissed his forehead. "Yes, baby," she said softly. "How do you feel?"

"I have a sore throat."

She took his small hand in hers. "It'll go away real soon," she reassured him. "You're my big, strong boy. You'll be out of here before you know it."

He looked up at her. "When can I go home, Mommy?" he asked. "With you, I mean?"

"It won't be long now," she promised, pushing his hair back off his forehead. "Not much longer, I swear."

Collin returned then, bringing a gurney with him. "Time's up, Ashley," he announced, pointing to his watch.

"Just one more minute, okay?" she pleaded.

"Who's that, Mommy?" Robert whispered.

"He's a friend of mine," Ashley explained. "He brought me here to see you."

"Ashley . . ." Collin's voice held a warning note.

She nodded. "Right." She bent down to kiss her son good-bye. "Listen, sport, there's something you've got to do for me, okay?"

He gazed up at her, eyes wide.

She glanced over at Collin, who was getting into an over-size green surgical scrub suit. "You can't tell anyone we've been here," she said slowly.

"Why not?"

"You just can't. It's got to be a secret, okay?"

He nodded. "Okay."

"Come on, Ashley," Collin hissed. He peered around the corner into the hallway. "Quick! Someone's coming!"

"Right." She kissed Robert again. "Remember what I said, sweetheart."

He nodded silently, holding back tears.

Ashley gave his hand a squeeze, then hopped upon the gurney and pulled her boots off. She blew Robert another kiss, then stretched out. Collin pulled the sheet up over her face, covering all but her bare feet. Giving Robert the thumbs-up sign, he pulled his surgical mask up over the lower half of his face and wheeled the gurney out into the corridor, passing Bradley and Claudia Hollister en route to the bank of elevators just beyond the nurses' station.

Once inside the elevator, Collin pulled back the sheet. "You can get up now," he told her. "We're quite alone."

She sat up and started pulling her boots on. "That was close," she said with a little laugh.

"You have no idea how close," Collin chuckled, pulling off the surgical mask. "We passed your in-laws in the hall."

"Former in-laws," Ashley corrected ruefully as she zipped her jacket.

"Now, are you satisfied he's all right?" Collin wanted to know as the elevator came to a halt on the ground floor.

She looked at him. "For now."

"You handled yourself very well up there," he told her as they crossed the busy hospital lobby together, "and it's made me realize something. You're ready to pull your first job."

Ashley held the flashlight and watched in silence as Collin reached into the rucksack and produced a small glass cutter. Moving quickly and expertly, it took him less than a minute to remove the glass from the skylight. "Damn!" he muttered irritably as he caught sight of the spiderweb of alarm wires now blocking their path.

"What's that?" Ashley wanted to know.

"It could have been one hell of a trap if I hadn't seen it in time," Collin replied as he reached into the sack again and came up with a long section of wire with an alligator clip on either end. Slowly, he traced the beginning of the alarm wire. Stripping it, he swiftly connected the alligator clip to the end of the alarm, then pulled out a pair of pliers and cut the wire carefully. Ashley tensed, expecting the alarm to go off, but it didn't. Her body sagged with relief when she realized Collin had succeeded.

"Is that all there is to it?" she asked as he unrolled the scaling ladder.

Collin shook his head. "If breaking and entering were that easy, more people would be doing it. Unfortunately, this is just the beginning."

They climbed down through the skylight. Collin took two pairs of specially designed infrared goggles from the rucksack and gave her a pair. "Put these on," he instructed.

"What for?" she asked. This was something he hadn't showed her before.

"They'll enable us to see the invisible beams," he explained as he put his on and adjusted them.

"Invisible beams?" she asked with a growing sense of alarm.

"Heat sensors," he told her, picking up the rucksack. "They're set off by a sudden change in temperature. When you step into the beam, nothing happens. It's when you step *out* and the temperature drops suddenly that all hell breaks loose."

She put the goggles on and looked around. There were beams of light everywhere. "How do we avoid them?" she wanted to know.

"That's the tricky part," Collin answered. "Some of them are high enough to duck. Others are low enough to step over. But some are placed in a way that you almost have to be an Olympic gymnast to avoid them."

"Swell," Ashley grumbled.

"Follow me and you'll be okay," he assured her.

"Is that a promise?"

They moved carefully through the house, ducking, crawling, and jumping in order to avoid the beams of light that were crisscrossed throughout each of the rooms. "There's nothing I enjoy as much as a real challenge," Collin remarked, attempting to relieve Ashley's tension.

"You should be having the time of your life, then," she responded grimly.

"The safe's in the library," he told her as they made their way down the hall to the room he'd indicated. The minute she stepped inside, Ashley thought she was going to faint. In front of the alcove where the safe was hidden were at least twelve beams blocking their path. "What a disappointment to have come this far and have to give it all up now," she lamented, ready to turn around and leave.

"I'm not going anywhere without getting what I came for," Collin said stubbornly.

Her eyes widened in disbelief. "Listen, I don't know what's in that damned safe, but I do know it can't be worth going to prison for!" she protested.

His face was serious. "Oh, but it is, and I'm not leaving without it," he insisted. "And neither are you."

"Damn you!" she snapped, annoyed with him for placing their lives on the line like this over some jewelry and a few incriminating papers put there by a syndicate bigwig. "It's impossible. You can't possibly pull it off—"

"You're right," he cut in quickly. "I couldn't pull it off alone, but you and I together can do it."

"How?" she implored.

"Come here and I'll show you." He led her as close to the beams as she could get without setting off the alarm, then he got down on the floor and crawled on his stomach underneath the lowest one. She watched with a mixture of amazement and fear as he opened the safe and pulled out some jewelry. "Might as well take this for good measure," he said, passing the items to her between the beams. "Careful now—don't let them touch."

Ashley nodded. "Not on your life," she said as she put them in the canvas bag she carried over one shoulder.

Collin went back to the safe and took out a bundle of papers bound together with a rubber band. "Here's what we're *really* after," he said as he passed them to her. "Enough of this and we can send Hollister to prison for a very long time."

He closed the safe while Ashley stuffed the papers into her bag. "Now what?" she asked as he slipped the rucksack over his shoulder.

"Now comes the fun part," he said. "When I give the word, I want you to run as hard as you can go, back where we came in."

"Run?" she gasped. "Why?"

"Because in about ten seconds, all hell is going to break loose," he told her. He took a deep breath. "Ready, set . . . GO!" He stepped through the beams and set off an alarm so loud that the entire house seemed to reverberate from it. Ashley thought her eardrums were going to burst as she and Collin sprinted up the staircase toward the attic. They climbed up the scaling ladder hastily, then pulled it up through the skylight. Collin rolled it up and turned to

Ashley, who was paralyzed by her fear. "Come on!" he urged. "We've got to get the hell out of here!"

He scurried along the rooftop with the agility of a cat, Ashley trailing close behind. He raced along the top of the high stone wall with the balance and assurance of the trained athlete he was. Ashley was sure she was going to fall at any moment. *If I'm lucky, I'll break my neck and die instantly*, she thought dismally. *Anything would be better than going to prison. Anything*.

Collin grabbed the rope they'd used to climb the wall when they came in and gave it a hard yank to make sure the hook was still securely in place. He bounced down the wall easily and beckoned Ashley to follow. She grabbed the rope and started down haltingly.

"Hurry!" Collin called. "Let yourself fall! I'll catch you!"

I wish I could believe that, Ashley thought. She took a deep breath, closed her eyes, and let go of the rope. She felt herself falling for only a moment. Collin caught her easily and lowered her to the ground. He pulled the rope free and they raced across the road and down into the wooded area where they'd left the Excalibur. He hurriedly removed his gloves and unzipped his black overalls, revealing the tux he wore underneath. Stuffing everything into a laundry sack, he slipped on the white dinner jacket he'd left in the car and watched as Ashley shed her overalls like a snake shedding its skin. Underneath, her white chiffon evening dress unfurled like a flower dropping easily to her ankles. "I felt like I had an inner tube around my waist for a while there," she lamented as she unzipped her boots and kicked them off.

While she put on her high-heeled sandals and shrugged into her mink coat, Collin took her overalls and boots and put them into the laundry bag, which he stuffed into the trunk along with the rucksack containing his tools and everything they'd taken from the safe. As he slid behind the wheel of the Excalibur, he heard police sirens in the distance. "Not a minute too soon," he breathed as he started the engine and drove up onto the main road. "At least we'll be going in the opposite direction."

Less than a mile down the road, they heard more sirens, this time headed in their direction. "Damn!" Collin muttered, slamming his fist against the steering wheel angrily.

"I think they're coming from up there," Ashley said, pointing ahead. "There's no way you can outrun them now."

"I wouldn't even try." Collin pulled off on the shoulder of the road and shut down the engine.

Ashley looked stunned. "What in God's name do you think you're doing?" she implored.

"No time to explain," he said as the police car approached, its headlights blinding them. "Just follow my lead."

"What choice do I have?" she asked weakly.

The police car came to a stop in front of them. Collin got out of the Excalibur and went to meet the officer. "What's the problem?" the policeman asked, getting out of his car. "Oh—Mr. Deverell. I didn't recognize you at first."

"Quite all right," Collin said with an easy grin. "I seem to be having a bit of engine trouble, and I'm afraid I'm not very mechanical."

"I'll take a look at it if you like," the policeman offered helpfully. "I don't know much about these fancy foreign jobs myself, but I am pretty good with cars."

Collin smiled. "I'd appreciate it. I have tools in the trunk, if you need anything."

Ashley's face went white. *Is he nuts?* she wondered. *He's practically giving him an engraved invitation to look in the trunk!*

"Let's take a look under the hood first," the policeman suggested. He glanced over at Ashley. So she was the one. Everyone knew Collin Deverell had a woman living with him now, but no one had ever gotten a good look at her. That place of his was like a fortress: no one got in unless Deverell wanted him in. The woman looked nervous. "You're a long way from home, aren't you?" he asked casually as Collin raised the Excalibur's hood.

"We've been at a party in Manhattan all evening," Collin said. "But those fund-raisers can be so dreary sometimes, so we decided to leave early and take advantage of the magnificent evenings one can only find out here." He dropped his voice to a conspiratorial whisper. "Actually, there's nothing wrong with the car."

The officer looked at him. "Oh?"

"Well," Collin began slowly, nodding toward Ashley, who watched them anxiously but was unable to hear what was being said, "you know how it is . . ."

The policeman smiled knowingly. "Oh—yeah." So that was why the woman was nervous. He'd obviously interrupted something. He turned back to Collin. "Sorry about the inconvenience," he said apologetically. "There was a robbery this evening at the Van Hydes, and—"

"Oh, yes—we heard the sirens," Collin said, nodding. "The Van Hydes aren't home?"

The policeman shook his head. "On vacation. Whoever their burglar is, he's one slick operator. The cars already on the scene say he managed to sabotage their high-tech security system and still get into the wall safe."

"Really?"

"Yeah. I'd hardly call him our average second-story man." He paused. "I've got to get going. Have a good evening." He winked.

"I thought for a minute there you were going to take a bow," Ashley said as he got back into the car.

Collin grinned. "One does like to hear good things about one's work," he pointed out. "I'm no exception." He started the engine and pulled away at the same time the police car departed.

"Is that what you call it? Your work?" she asked.

"What would you call it?" he wanted to know. "A hobby? A sport?"

"I'd call it a perversion," she said. "I'm just glad you were convincing enough to throw him off."

He grinned. "When you don't wish to arouse suspicion,

you do whatever you're doing in plain sight," he said simply. "Right under their noses."

"Your philosophy?" she asked.

"One of them."

"What did you tell him?" she wanted to know.

"Simple. That you and I were parking," he answered with a lewd grin.

"Oh, great!"

"You did well tonight, Ashley," he said then. "I think it calls for a bit of a celebration. Get that bag under your seat."

She pulled out a large brown paper bag. Inside was a bottle of Dom Perignon. She gave a low whistle. "I'm impressed!"

"Don't forget the glasses," he told her.

She reached into the bag again and pulled out a package of paper cups. She roared with laughter. "Now this is the ultimate in style," she declared. "Dom Perignon and paper cups!"

He grinned. "It was the best I could do on short notice."

"How appropriate!" she laughed as she uncorked the champagne and filled two of the cups, passing one to Collin. "Know what? Until I met you, I never realized how dull my life really was!"

Collin laughed too. "At the risk of sounding cliché, my dear, you ain't seen nothin' yet!"

New York City, June 1987

Anton DeVries slammed the newspaper down on the desk in rage, once again frustrated by his inability to accumulate enough evidence on Collin Deverell to have him arrested—or even to convince Interpol of the validity of his theory. *I should have let him go to prison for fraud*, he told himself again and again. He recalled his last conversation with René Dussault in Paris. The inspector had not been able to accept what DeVries considered to be all too obvious. It was merely coincidence, the Frenchman maintained, that the items taken in those robberies were those taken from the Deverell estate in 1979. After all, Collin Deverell was a man of means, an heir to one of the world's great fortunes. A man known publicly for his philanthropy, his good works. Hardly the kind of man one could consider a likely thief.

Even DeVries's own supervisor had remained unconvinced. "You yourself said the man was innocent when everybody else—myself included—was ready to slap him with a fraud charge."

"He *was* innocent—then. He was set up by God only knows who," DeVries insisted. "He's not innocent anymore. He's the one who pulled all these jobs."

DeVries recalled his conversation with Justin Deverell: *My brother has devoted most of his life to the pursuit of the great adventure—the ultimate thrill.*

The fact that no one believed his theory had only fueled DeVries's determination to bring Collin Deverell to justice. It had become an obsession with him. Often, he would lie awake at night thinking about it, trying to come up with a way to trap the man, but Deverell was too damned unpredictable.

Don't look down, Ashley thought as she inched her way along the top of the stone wall. Collin, several steps ahead of her, made his way to the balcony off the master bedroom and made the five-foot leap from the wall to the balcony as naturally as if he'd been climbing stairs. Ashley approached more cautiously. "I don't think I can do it, Collin," she confessed.

"Sure you can. You've made a jump like this dozens of times," he reminded her.

"I'm shaking."

"This is a hell of a time to get cold feet." Collin pulled the wide straps of the rucksack down off his shoulders and dropped it near the French doors. He turned to Ashley again, extending his arms. "Grab my hands," he instructed.

She stared at him for a moment, then did as he told her. Grasping both of his hands firmly, she tried not to look down as she jumped across to the balcony. As she paused to catch her breath, Collin dug into the rucksack and took out a slim black leather case resembling a manicure kit. He took from it an odd-looking narrow metal instrument and went to work on the lock, opening it within seconds.

"What kind of lock does it take to keep you out?" Ashley kidded him.

Collin grinned as he pushed the doors open. "One that hasn't been invented yet."

She followed him into the darkness. He took her hand and led her through the master suite and down the staircase. Once in the library, they put on their infrared goggles, expecting to encounter the heat sensor alarms they'd faced so frequently in the past two months. They had *not* anticipated what they encountered now.

"Damn!" Collin muttered under his breath, running a hand through his hair nervously. "Who'd have thought it?"

"They're not heat sensors?" Ashley asked, puzzled. The look on his face alarmed her. Collin was not the type to scare easily.

"I wish." Collin drew in his breath. "Lasers."

She looked at him. "What?"

"They're goddamned lasers," he said, turning to face her. "Walk into those and you won't set off the alarm— you'll be fried!"

Ashley swallowed hard. "So we're calling it off?" she ventured in a small voice.

"Not a chance," he said, shaking his head. "We need what's in that safe, and we're not leaving until we get it."

Ashley gave him a frightened look. "But you just said . . ."

Collin's eyes scanned the room quickly. "There has to be something here . . ." he muttered. Then he caught sight of a woman's compact lying on a small table near the door. "The mirror—of course!"

Ashley stared at him. "I think your brain's already been fried," she lamented. "Collin, I always knew you were a basket case. You've just confirmed it."

Collin snatched up the compact and opened it to make sure the mirror was still intact. "It just might work," he said optimistically.

"Just what crazy idea do you have in mind?"

He gave her a sly smile. "Ever see a scorpion sting itself?"

Realizing what he was planning to do, Ashley's heart almost stopped. Her pulse was racing as Collin dropped to his knees and positioned himself near the crisscrossing rays of dazzling white light. With a steady hand a surgeon would have envied, he slowly inched the mirror into position, catching the deadly beam and deflecting it carefully. Ashley looked on, feeling as though she would faint at any moment, as he redirected the laser slowly downward, toward its own source. As the light was deflected back into itself, there was a flash of blinding light and a loud roar. Ashley stumbled backward as smoke filled the room. Collin rocked on his heels and pulled off his goggles, smiling with satisfaction as he wiped perspiration from his brow.

"Not bad—even if I do say so myself," he commented, obviously quite pleased with himself. He scrambled to his feet and closed the compact, placing it back on the table, then wiped his hands lightly against the legs of his black overalls. He gestured to Ashley. "Shall we?"

"Whatever's in there must be pretty damned important for Dunwald to go to this much trouble," Ashley remarked as they approached the safe.

"It is," Collin responded. "You might say some people would be willing to kill for it."

Ashley's eyes opened wide. "Kill for it?"

"Dunwald's the keeper of the flame, so to speak. He knows almost as much about the mob's operations as Hollister does, and he has enough evidence to put them all away for a long time. That information is Dunwald's life insurance policy: as long as he has it, nobody will touch him.''

"That must be comforting."

"I guess you could say that." He handed her the rucksack after taking out an instrument resembling a doctor's stethoscope. She looked on in silence as he used it to detect the faint sound of the tumblers clicking while he turned the dial carefully. Within seconds, the safe was open and he was examining its contents.

"Anything we can use?" Ashley wanted to know.

Collin nodded as he looked over one of the documents. "Plenty, but I was hoping the really important stuff would be here," he admitted. "Apparently old Dunwald wasn't altogether sure of his own high-tech security system."

Ashley smiled wearily. "Maybe your reputation's preceded you."

"The bastards," Collin mumbled, still reading. Abruptly, he swept the entire contents of the safe into the rucksack and slipped the wide straps up over his shoulders, securing it to his back. He turned to Ashley again. "Let's go."

They ran from the library, up the stairs to the master suite. Out on the balcony, Collin leaped across to the wall, with Ashley following closely behind. They scurried along the wall until they reached their waiting van, then jumped down onto it. As Ashley climbed down the ladder on the side of the van, Collin leaped to the ground and slid behind the wheel, starting the engine. In the distance, he could hear police sirens. Someone, he decided, must have heard the explosion when he blew up the laser and called them. *It's going to be close*, he thought.

"What the hell am I paying these people for?" Collin demanded angrily, slamming the telephone receiver down with such force that the bell sounded.

"There's a problem?" Harrison appeared unruffled as he collected the silver and plates. Collin had taken yet another meal in his study while he placed his usual half-dozen late-night transatlantic calls.

"Damned right there's a problem! It's called incompetence," Collin growled, leaning back in his chair. His hair was mussed and the faint lines around his eyes and mouth seemed to have suddenly deepened. "I've been paying those goddamned investigators a helluva lot more than they're worth."

"I'm sure," Harrison said calmly, placing the used tableware on the tray. He was accustomed to these angry outbursts and knew Collin would tell him whatever he wanted him to know.

"How many years have they been on my payroll now, Henry?" Collin asked, knowing that Harrison knew full well that he already had the answer.

"At least five years," Harrison estimated.

"Five years." Collin thought about it for a moment. "Five years to locate Yasmin, and all they've given me is a few dead-end leads and a lot of feeble excuses!"

"Europe is a big place, Collin. Millions of people," Harrison reminded him. "What you expect of them is much the same as looking for the proverbial needle in a haystack."

Collin's jaw tightened visibly. "I was there, remember?" he asked, annoyed. "It took me a while, I'll admit that, but I *did* locate all of my property—and recovered every piece, I might add. Why can't a platoon of PIs locate one young woman?"

"I'm sure I don't know."

Collin looked at him for a moment. "Doesn't anything ever get to you, Henry?" he asked, suddenly curious.

"Yes," Harrison responded with a slight nod. "You do." He picked up the tray and started for the door.

"Where's Ashley?" Collin called after him.

"I believe she's gone upstairs."

After Harrison was gone, Collin took a few moments to review the notes he'd made on a yellow legal pad. He was angry and frustrated by the lack of results. He'd made a promise to Blackjack, and he intended to keep it, one way or another.

Somehow, he would find Yasmin.

* * *

"The longer we're together, the more aware I am of how little I really know about you," Ashley said, breaking the silence as she lay awake in the darkness, a willing captive in Collin's arms. "Even when we make love . . . I get the feeling you're holding a part of yourself back."

"You know everything you need to know about me," Collin said quietly, staring up at the ceiling.

"I know practically nothing."

"There's not much to tell."

"I know why you do what you do," Ashley pressed on. "I'm even beginning to understand it. But I don't really know *you*—who you are, what you want out of life after this is over, what you like or dislike—"

"As to what I want when this is all over, I can't give you an answer because I don't really know myself—yet," he said, turning over on his side to face her. "I haven't taken the time to seriously think about it. And as for what I like, I think you have a pretty good idea."

"I'm not talking about—" she began.

"And as to the other, I could say the same thing about you," he went on. "I don't really know anything about you, other than the obvious things—that you're a very talented and successful painter, that you were once very much in love with your husband and probably still are, in spite of who his parents happen to be, and that you'll fight to the death for your son. Aside from that, you appear to have an invisible wall around yourself, designed to keep the rest of the world out." They really were two of a kind, he decided. How many years had he spent deliberately avoiding emotional entanglements in his pursuit of a carefree, uncomplicated lifestyle? And how many more had he continued that way because of the pain of losing his parents and the hatred with which people like Hollister and Harrington and even his own brother had branded him? Collin thought of the night he broke into Ashley's apartment, of the cold, impersonal surroundings he'd found there. How void of sentimentality it had been! He understood Ashley's unwillingness to care after the death of her husband and the loss of her son: he'd been there himself. Yet now, with her, there was something deep within him that *wanted* to care.

Ashley hesitated for a moment. "I never really thought about it," she began slowly, "but I suppose after Brandon died, after Robert was taken away, I just shut it all off. I didn't want to get hurt again."

"You wanted to be safe."

"I guess you could say that." She paused. "What's your excuse?"

"In my—*our* line of work, one can never afford to let anyone get too close," he said evasively.

"Not even your own partner?" she asked.

He pulled himself up on one elbow. "I'd say we're about as close as a man and woman can possibly get," he said, lightly tracing her jawline with one finger as his mouth sought hers. His hand moved slowly, searchingly, down over her breasts, caressing her as their bodies came together. Finally, he pulled back and looked down at her in the darkness. "You are beautiful," he said huskily. "I'm going to hate like hell to lose you."

She reached out, touching his lips with the tip of her finger. She wished she knew what was really going on inside his head, what he was thinking, what he was feeling. She wished she knew what *she* was feeling. There were times she was overcome with guilt after they made love, thinking about her husband and how much she had loved him, how much she missed him. Other times, she wanted only to stay within the protective circle of Collin's arms, wanted to think that when all of this was over, it would not mean she was never going to see him again.

"Make love to me, Collin," she whispered. "Just make love to me."

"My pleasure," he said, bending his head to kiss her breasts. He sucked at her nipples, first one, then the other, as his hand moved down over her belly, between her legs. She slid one hand between their bodies and started to stroke him as they continued to kiss. Then, in one swift movement he was on top of her, inside her, leaving her breathless. She clung to him, moving with him, until the room began to spin wildly. He took her with several quick, sharp thrusts, then fell off her in exhaustion. They lay there for a long moment, neither of them moving, neither of them speaking. Finally, Collin broke the silence.

"Tomorrow, Ashley," he told her. "Tomorrow, you start learning the fine art of disguise."

He taught her to use wigs and makeup and tinted contact lenses. He coached her in affecting mannerisms and speech patterns. He showed her how to alter the shape of her body with specially padded clothing and lifts in her shoes. He helped her master various accents and dialects. One afternoon when he felt she was ready, he directed her in the application of her makeup, helped her choose the right dress and a long auburn wig, and gave her some last-minute coaching on her French accent. Then they tested her new "identity" on the unsuspecting servants, who were completely fooled.

"What do you think, Henry?" Collin asked when the three of them were alone in the library.

"It's remarkable," the older man commented. "If I were to see her on the street, I honestly would not recognize her."

Ashley laughed. "Think Danielle could fool 'em in Paris, Henry?" she asked.

But it was Collin who responded. "The question is, can Danielle fool 'em in Manhattan?"

"Relax, you look wonderful—and I'd be willing to bet that no one here will ever connect Danielle Langon with Ashley Gordon-Hollister," Collin reassured her as they entered the crowded Rainbow Room, high above midtown Manhattan in Rockefeller Center.

She leaned close to him. "I feel like my slip's showing and everybody knows it except me," she said under her breath.

"Your slip is definitely not showing," he said with a devilish grin. "Nor are you—anywhere."

She looked at him. "You are a wicked man, Collin," she told him.

"You should know, luv."

They were shown to their table and were seated. Collin introduced Ashley to those he knew who ventured over to the table in the course of the evening. Ashley handled herself with a quiet kind of dignity that did not betray the nervousness she felt inside. Once, when they were alone, she confided that she felt as though everyone were staring at her.

Collin smiled. "Of course they are," he agreed. "They're staring because you're so beautiful."

"Sure."

"You are, you know." The band started to play, and Collin jumped to his feet and grabbed Ashley's hand. "C'mon—let's dance."

"But—"

"I really want to dance."

She shook her head. "Oh, all right."

Out on the dance floor, he took her in his arms and guided her around slowly, his eyes continuously scanning the crowd. When he found the man he'd been looking for, he made an abrupt turn and leaned close and whispered, "Look over my shoulder—the man sitting alone at the corner table."

Ashley did as instructed. The man looked to be in his late fifties, with strong, regular features and slate-gray hair. "Our pigeon?" she asked.

Collin nodded. "Hanover Jarrett, in the flesh," he said in a low voice. "You don't recognize him?"

"No," she said, shaking her head. "Should I?"

"He's a senior vice-president of Hollister International," Collin explained. "He's Bradley Hollister's right-hand man, and he's had his eye on you since we arrived."

Ashley rolled her eyes upward. "Great."

"Actually, it *is* great," Collin told her. "Better than great, in fact."

"So he's interested," Ashley said. "What do we do next?"

"Not we, my dear—you," he said with a sly smile. "Encourage him."

"And just how am I supposed to do that?"

"Use your feminine wiles."

"I think I lost my feminine wiles a long time ago," she sighed.

Collin grinned. "Take my word for it: you haven't lost anything in that department," he assured her. "Smile at him, let him know you've noticed him. If my hunch is right, he'll do the rest."

"Wonderful."

Collin guided her across the crowded dance floor in the direction of Jarrett's table. Whenever their eyes met, Ashley lowered her head slightly and smiled. Jarrett gazed appreciatively at the sight of a beautiful woman, but made no move. "This is ridiculous," Ashley whispered to Collin.

"Not at all," Collin disagreed. "Just think of it as fishing."

"Okay. He's not biting."

"He will be. Before the evening's over, he'll ask you to dance."

"Terrific. I'll be the only one on the dance floor with my own shark," she said darkly.

"Listen, you just get him hooked," Collin told her. "I'll reel him in."

"I'm counting on it."

The music stopped. Collin and Ashley returned to their table. "He's still watching you," Collin observed, looking in Jarrett's direction. "Look back—and smile, for God's sake."

Ashley shifted in her chair to look across the room. Spotting Hanover Jarrett watching her, she smiled again. "If I have to do this much longer, my face is going to crack," she muttered.

"Sssh—here he comes," Collin said under his breath as Jarrett got to his feet and crossed the room to their table. "May I have this dance?" he asked as the band started up again.

Ashley glanced at Collin out of the corner of her eye. He nodded slightly. She rose to her feet gracefully. "I'd like that," she responded.

Collin watched with interest as Jarrett led Ashley onto the dance floor. As the man took her in his arms, Collin was taken by surprise by the intensity of his own reaction to the sight of her with someone else. It aroused feelings of jealousy that he did not completely understand. *This is crazy,* he told himself. *She doesn't belong to you. A few months from now, she's going to walk out of your life and you'll probably never see her again.*

Finally, he got to his feet and made his way through the crowd, incensed by the way the man was holding on to her and annoyed by the way his own feelings were getting in the way of the job he'd come here to do. He approached Jarrett from behind and patted the man's shoulder. "Mind if I cut in?" he asked pleasantly.

Jarrett was clearly displeased but forced a smile. "Of course," he said agreeably as he released Ashley.

"Thanks, pal." Collin took Ashley in his arms and held her close as he whisked her across the dance floor. "We can go as soon as the music stops," he whispered, watching as Jarrett returned to his own table.

She gave him a puzzled look. "But I thought—"

He grinned. "I just lifted the old boy's wallet."

Ashley was confused. "I still don't understand why you picked his pocket," she said as she followed Collin into the library. "What good is his wallet going to do us?"

"You'll see." Collin went to the wall of bookshelves and released the lever to open the panel leading to the computer room. As they entered, he opened the wallet and examined its contents. "Driver's license . . . credit cards . . . bank automatic teller card." He looked up at Ashley and grinned.

"I'll bet this one couldn't even tell you what U.S. currency looks like. He's got a string of plastic here as long as my arm. Both arms."

"So what are we going to do?" she asked. "Go out and run up a bunch of bills for him?"

"Nope. He's going to do it himself. He doesn't know it yet, but he is," Collin said. "Kill the lights, Ashley."

She nodded and switched off the overhead lights as he took a seat in front of one of the terminals. She took a chair next to him. The entire room was bathed in an eerie green glow from the displays on the screens. "What have you got in mind, Collin?" she asked.

"That depends," he said slowly, still scrutinizing the cards in Jarrett's wallet. "Let's see what we've got here." He punched in an entry code. The screen immediately came to life. He studied it for a moment, then tackled the keyboard again. One by one he accessed all the computers: the Department of Motor Vehicles . . . Social Security . . . Veterans Administration . . . records of all the stores and oil companies having issued credit cards in the name of Hanover Jarrett. The printer ticked away steadily as Collin stared at the screen, analyzing every entry. "I don't get it," he said finally, baffled. "I would have been willing to bet this would turn up something, but so far he's clean."

"Maybe he is exactly what he presents himself to be," Ashley suggested.

"Not if he's one of Hollister's henchmen," Collin growled. "There's got to be something. All we have to do is find it."

"Even if it takes all night?"

"Even if it takes all night," he said firmly. Then he entered yet another access code.

"Whose computers are you breaking into this time?" Ashley asked.

"ManhattanBank's," he answered, his gaze fixed on the screen.

Ashley let out a groan. "I had to ask."

A sign flashed on the screen: YOUR AUTHORIZATION CODE, PLEASE?

"So much for that idea," Ashley commented. "This is going to be impossible."

"There's no such thing as impossible, something I think you'd know by now," Collin reminded her. He thought about it for a moment. "Roland Leder, the bank's senior veep, set this system up himself. All I have to do is put myself inside his head—think as he would."

"This ought to be interesting," Ashley muttered.

"Leder's a creature of habit. My guess is that he'd want to keep it simple enough for the personnel who access it daily, yet change it often enough to prevent break-ins." He thought it through carefully, then turned back to the keyboard and tapped out a possible code.

THAT IS AN IMPROPER AUTHORIZATION CODE. The screen went blank.

"Damn!" Collin took a deep breath and tried again. Again, it was wrong.

He refused to give up. He tried again. And again. And finally an idea hit him. He took a chance and gave it one more try. There was a long pause before the response flashed on the screen: SYSTEM ACCESS COMPLETE. PLEASE PROCEED.

"All right!" he shouted, elated. "We're back in business!" He went into the bank's record-keeping system, summoning up a complete history of Jarrett's banking transactions. Collin studied the screen, checking every entry as the printer clicked away, preparing a printed record of all the information obtained. "I knew it!" Collin declared triumphantly.

"Knew what?" Ashley asked, eager to be let in on his discovery.

"Look at this," he said, pointing to the data on the screen. "The amount and frequency of the transfers—"

"What does it all mean?" she asked, baffled.

"It means, my love, that our friend Hanover Jarrett is a crook."

She looked at him. "Now *there's* the pot calling the kettle black."

"I'm serious." Collin stared intently at the flashing images on the screen. "Income from God knows how many sources . . . large amounts transferred to half a dozen numbered Swiss accounts. Jesus, this man's done more laundering than a Chinese cleaners!"

"How does that help us?" Ashley wanted to know.

"Simple," Collin maintained. "It's all tied in with your beloved ex-father-in-law. When we bring him down, we bring the whole underworld empire with him. This printout," he said, gesturing toward the printer, "goes to the federal prosecutor along with everything else that has Bradley Hollister's fingerprints on it."

Ashley started to say something, when she was interrupted by the appearance of Harrison, who brought Collin a yellow envelope. "This just arrived," he announced.

Collin ripped open the envelope and pulled out the cable, reading it hastily. "It's about time!" he declared, a broad grin crossing his face.

"You must have won the Irish Sweepstakes," Ashley said.

"Better than that, luv," he said, laughing. "You and I are going to France. The Riviera, to be precise."

Nice,
August 1987

"I had no idea how far you'd really go to prove a point," Ashley teased Collin as they crossed the huge circular *salon royal* of the glamorous belle époque Negresco. She glanced up absently at the gleaming Baccarat crystal chandelier as a bellboy, in traditional red breeches and white gloves, walked briskly ahead of them with their luggage. The floor was covered in 720 square yards of Aubusson carpet and the walls adorned with the artworks of Picasso, Léger, and Cocteau.

"Who's proving a point?" Collin asked with a wicked grin. "Even in our line of work, the pros do take vacations."

She looked at him for a moment. They were both making jokes, but they knew how important this trip was—for more than one reason. The cable he'd received two days earlier had informed him of the whereabouts of Blackjack's daughter, Yasmin, and Collin was determined to keep the promise he'd made to his good friend the day he left Morocco. Nothing on earth could have prevented Collin from making this journey. As they had been preparing to leave, he'd discovered that Tommy Petrano, one of the syndicate's most powerful men, was also headed for the Côte d'Azur. "We'll kill two birds with one stone," he'd told Ashley.

Their suite was magnificent, Empire in style and overlooking the Promenade des Anglais and the blue Mediterranean. As soon as the bellboy left them alone, Ashley took off her dark glasses and removed the blond wig she wore. "Thank God," she breathed, relieved. "The damned thing was driving me crazy." She ran her fingers through her own hair, letting it fall down past her shoulders. She walked over to the windows and stared out at the sea. "So how do we find this Tommy Petrano?" she asked finally.

Collin turned to face her. "I've already located him," he said calmly as he removed his tie.

Ashley looked surprised. "But how—" she stopped short when she saw the amused look on his face. "The bellboy?"

"Close. There was a message at the desk when I picked up the key." He held up a small brown envelope. "It seems Mr. Petrano is being most cooperative: he's staying with a friend at a villa near St.-Jean-Cap-Ferrat."

Ashley took off the white linen jacket she wore over her royal blue summer dress. "Why is that convenient?" she wanted to know.

"Because it just happens to be the same villa where Yasmin is now residing," Collin said simply.

"So where do we go from here?"

Collin grinned. "How do you feel about a little gate-crashing?" he asked.

"You're kidding!"

"Not at all. There's a gala tomorrow night at the home of Baron de Villeurbanne I'm just dying to attend," he said with a devilish gleam in his eyes.

The expansive, Italian-style villa overlooking the Mediterranean was even more splendid than anything Ashley had seen en route to St.-Jean-Cap-Ferrat from Nice. Built of Italian marble and fruitwood, with wide steps leading up to the main entrance and a large lily pond in front, it looked like something out of a movie. As they got out of their rental car, Ashley noticed that the whole place was lit up. "I take it this is *not* going to be an intimate gathering of a few close friends," she quipped.

"Sure it is," Collins aid, grinning. "Just a simple little affair for three hundred of the baron's closest chums."

"Right."

"Trouble is, the baron's a real bastard and doesn't have three close friends, let alone three hundred. My guess is that everybody here tonight is like us—they all want something. The difference is, we're not going to be as obvious about it."

They had gone over the plan at least a dozen times on the way to the villa, and Ashley had memorized every step. Collin was convinced that Petrano had brought along the papers to transfer the large block of stock he held in Intercontinental Oil in exchange for some property he wished to purchase from the baron, and Collin intended to prevent that transaction from ever taking place. Now, as they prepared to enter the villa, he turned to Ashley, using the phrase he always used to make sure she knew her moves by heart: "You know your lines, luv?"

"Chapter and verse," she assured him.

"You'd better, because this is going to be your toughest part yet."

"I'll just be happy if my crash course in French doesn't fail me," she said as they climbed the steps together. "Do you think anyone's going to believe I'm an actress about to make my first French film?"

"*Everyone* will believe it," he said confidently.

They were admitted to the villa by a young white-coated houseboy, who did not bother to ask their names before escorting them to a large ballroom enclosed almost entirely in glass, overlooking the water. Ashley scanned the group of elegantly dressed men and women briefly. "Your estimate of three hundred guests didn't miss by much," she whispered to Collin.

"I never miss by too much," he chuckled softly, leading her into the crowd.

As they mingled with the guests, both together and independently, Ashley found herself relaxing in spite of the reason for their presence here. *I'm getting better at this*, she thought as she chatted with some of the guests. *God help me, it could lead to a whole new career.*

She glanced across the room at Collin, who was engaged in conversation with a man she recognized as a prominent French art critic. When he looked her way, he gave the signal—a single tug of his earlobe—to let her know it was time to make her move. Excusing herself from the women she'd been talking with, she hurried upstairs, making sure she was unobserved. Taking her lockpicking tool from the small evening bag she carried, she went to the door Collin had indicated at the end of the long hallway. She tested the knob to make sure it was indeed locked, then went to work on it. Within seconds, the door came open. "Yasmin?" she said in a low voice as she entered.

A young woman who appeared to be in her mid-twenties emerged from the dressing room, wearing a long, heavily embroidered purple silk caftan. She was exquisite, small but shapely, with a piquant face, high cheekbones, a small chin, and large, dark eyes. Her hair was dark and luxuriant and hung to the middle of her back. Her heritage was apparent in her exotic looks and her manner. "I am Yasmin," she responded in French, in a voice that was soft and melodic. "Who are you?"

"I'm here with a very good friend of your father's," Ashley explained, also in French, though not with as much fluency or confidence.

"That is not possible," the young woman said coolly. "My father has been dead for many years. He died in prison, convicted of a crime he did not commit. It was his last wish that I come here and live with the baron as his mistress. The baron is my protector."

Ashley frowned. "I hate to be the one to tell you this, but the baron's done one hell of a snow job on you," she responded. "Your father is very much alive—and your being here, being used by the baron, is the *last* thing he wants. We've come to get you, to send you home to him—where you belong."

"No. I could not possibly go with you," Yasmin said with finality.

I've got my work cut out for me, Ashley thought dismally.

In another part of the house, Collin was putting the second phase of their plan into action. He crept down a hallway in another part of the villa's second floor, headed for the suite now occupied by Tommy Petrano. Methodically avoiding the closed-circuit television cameras installed throughout the villa, he finally found the suite he'd been looking for, but the position of the camera outside the door made it impossible to get inside and still avoid being seen by the security people in the control room. But Collin had anticipated such a situation. He took a piece of stiff wire from the sleeve of his jacket and bent it into an L shape, then pulled a small hand mirror from one pocket. Attaching the wire to the mirror, he carefully attached the other end to the base of the camera, then positioned the mirror directly in front of the lens. Knowing it would appear as interference on the screen in the security control room, he knew it would be only a matter of minutes before someone came up to check it out.

He let himself into the suite and located the wall safe. As he worked feverishly at the dial, he wondered how Ashley was doing with Yasmin. Would she have any trouble convincing the girl to go with her? Would Yasmin even believe Ashley was really trying to help her? It wouldn't surprise him at all if the girl wasn't capable of trusting anyone now.

Touching the phony passport in his pocket, the one he'd had made for her before leaving New York, he looked at his watch. Had they already left the villa? Were they waiting for him outside as planned? Had Ashley encountered any problems with Yasmin? Ashley knew they didn't have much time. He pulled the door of the safe open and hastily searched its contents. "Damn!" he growled as he realized the papers he'd been looking for were not there. What the hell could Petrano have done with them? Surely the stock had not already been transferred. He didn't have time to search the villa. He would have to wait for another chance, another time.

As he started to close the safe, he spotted a small chamois bag. Snatching it up, he emptied part of the contents into the palm of his hand. Diamonds! He smiled to himself as he slipped them back into the bag, thinking that the evening was not a total loss. He hurried over to the window and hastily disconnected the gutter. Then he deposited the bag into the pipe and let it fall down to the ground below. He'd collect it later, after— The sound of footsteps outside the door cut through his thoughts. "Son of a bitch!" he muttered to himself. Now there was only one way out—through the window.

"I am sorry I did not believe you at first," Yasmin told Ashley at the Nice Airport, where she was preparing to board a flight to Casablanca. Then she turned to Collin, holding up the thick brown envelope he had given her in the car. "I will be most happy to deliver your message to my father."

"You do that," he said with a tired smile. "Now, go—

they're calling your flight. I think your father's waited long enough to have his daughter home again.''

Yasmin nodded. Impulsively, she embraced each of them. ''I cannot thank you enough,'' she said with tears of joy in her eyes. Then she turned abruptly and hurried through the gate, pausing just long enough to wave at them one last time.

''You really are a man of your word, aren't you,'' Ashley said as she and Collin walked through the busy terminal together.

Collin shrugged. ''I never promise what I can't deliver.''

''Come on—this is me you're talking to,'' she chided him gently. ''I've come to know what a soft touch you really are.''

Collin grinned. ''Don't let it get around, okay?'' he asked in a conspiratorial tone. ''It'll ruin my reputation.''

She laughed. ''Your secret's safe with me.''

''The papers weren't in the safe,'' he said then.

Ashley looked at him, surprised. ''Why didn't you tell me before now?''

''There wasn't any point,'' he said grimly. ''Yasmin had to be our first priority, besides, I had to come up with another plan.''

''So it's back to the villa, right?''

''Wouldn't do any good,'' he said with a shake of his head. ''Petrano's leaving France tonight.''

''Where does that leave us?'' she asked, frowning. ''We need to think—''

''I already have a plan,'' he assured her.

She gave him a puzzled look. ''But how—'' she started.

Collin grinned wickedly. ''Ever hear of a man called D. B. Cooper?''

As the mechanics and other airport personnel scurried about on the airstrip where the small private jet was being refueled, Collin moved among them unobtrusively. Loading suitcases into the plane's cargo hold, he began to perspire, not because he was nervous, but because he was too hot in the paratrooper's jumpsuit he wore underneath his bulky mechanic's coveralls. *It won't be much longer now*, he told himself. His normally thick, wavy hair was combed straight back and the fake beard and mustache artfully applied. I just hope, he thought as the long black limousine approached, that Tommy Petrano doesn't see me.

Collin watched in silence as Petrano emerged from the car and made his way to the aircraft. *It's got to be there*, Collin thought, eyeing Petrano's attaché case. *If it's not, I'm sticking my neck out for nothing.* He looked on silently as Petrano climbed the steps and disappeared into the cabin. *This is it*, he told himself as he climbed, unobserved, into the cargo hold and pulled the door shut behind him. He hoped the plane departed on schedule. Ashley would be waiting for him at the designated spot, and if he had to float around in that raft too long, he might end up at sea. As carefully as he'd planned everything, Collin knew only too well that there were a multitude of things that could go wrong. The plane could be off-course. Fierce winds could carry him out to sea—or too far inland. But he was most concerned about the one element over which he had absolutely no control: Petrano's reaction, should he be caught. Was he armed? Collin wondered. Instinctively, he touched the revolver he carried inside his overalls. Would he have to use it?

Collin knew he would only be able to estimate the plane's location by the length of time they'd been in the air. It was a gamble, but it was the only option available to him unless he wished to reveal himself to Petrano, which he definitely did not want to do. Feeling the vibration of the aircraft as it taxied down the runway and lifted off, he started peeling off the overalls. Removing the fake mustache, he checked the parachute before strapping it on. So far, everything was working, he thought as he double-checked the deflated rubber boat he'd brought along for a possible landing at sea. He opened the door connecting the cabin to the cargo hold and looked around. Petrano was alone, as he'd expected him to be, reading a newspaper. Moving quickly and silently, Collin crawled out of the hold, just far enough to

enable him to reach the attaché case sitting on the floor at
Petrano's side. Snatching it quickly, he pulled it back into
the hold and slipped it into the heavy canvas bag he'd
strapped to his chest. *No time to check the contents now*, he
thought as he looked at his watch. It was almost time to
make his next move.

Counting down the minutes made him think of that
dreadful night he'd spent in that vault in Paris. It had been
a dangerous situation then, and it was even more dangerous
now; but Collin had come to thrive on the challenge of not
only outwitting his adversaries, but cheating death itself. He
fully intended to cheat it again, tonight. He forced open the
door. The wind was ferocious, but not strong enough to
make him lose control. The plane was flying below ten thousand feet. He could drop approximately a thousand feet before opening his chute; that way he would not be spotted by
other aircraft in the vicinity. He would be nothing more
than a small speck in the gray, gloomy sky. He leaned forward and let go of the door, falling into the night at approximately sixty-five miles per hour. When he was sure
he'd gone as far as he could go safely without it, he deployed
the chute. The wind caught it immediately and carried him
toward the Mediterranean. As he fell nearer to the earth,
he could see the lights of Nice to the northeast. He tried to
orient himself toward them. *Be there, Ashley*, he prayed. Then
he pulled the cord that would inflate the rubber boat. It
opened immediately. He held it to his chest, mentally preparing himself for impact. Just before he hit the water he
saw the signal—headlights flashing three times—that let him
know Ashley was there.

Regaining his equilibrium, he pulled himself upright in
the boat and waved to her as he paddled inland with his
hands. "It worked, dammit!" he called out to her. It was
a long shot at best, but it had worked!

"You're incredible!" she said, laughing, as he climbed
out of the rubber boat onto the beach. "I've said it before
and I'll say it again: you're certifiably crazy!"

Collin grinned. "You have to be a little bit crazy in this

business,'' he reasoned as he pulled the attaché case out of the canvas bag and proceeded to pry it open. He removed the documents and gave them to her. ''There they are—my ticket to regaining control of Intercontinental Oil, and the beginning of the end for Hollister and the syndicate.'' Then he pulled a large bundle of currency from the case and started throwing it into the water.

''Wait a minute!'' Ashley shrieked. ''Are you nuts? There must be almost half a million dollars there!''

Collin laughed. ''Relax, Ashley—it's no good to us. It's funny money.''

She stared at him. ''Counterfeit?''

''Every bit of it.'' He threw the sack into the water. ''Come on, my gorgeous accomplice,'' he said, putting his arm around her, ''let's go home.''

Sea Cliff, September 1987

Wearing only her black silk robe, Ashley stood on the balcony outside the master bedroom suite, staring thoughtfully at a photograph of her son. It had been months since she'd seen Robert, and a great deal had happened to her in that time, but one thing had not changed: not a day passed that she did not think about him, anxiously awaiting the day when they would be together again. When Collin had explained to her that it would be necessary for her to leave the country for a while with her son—just until he'd nailed Bradley Hollister and the all-powerful syndicate, until Hollister was safely behind bars where he couldn't hurt anyone again—she'd even resigned herself to that.

How many times over the past six months had she justified the things she'd done by telling herself it was all for Robert? How many times had Collin tried to curb her impatience by telling her that his plan could not be rushed, that if it were to work it would take time? She turned and looked back into the bedroom, where Collin was sleeping soundly. A part of her did not want to leave him. Collin had made her laugh, made her feel alive again. *Am I falling in love with him?* she asked herself. Or was it the dangerous nature of the secret life they shared, putting their freedom—possibly even their lives—on the line every time they pulled a job? Were her growing feelings for him tied up with the realization that he was her last hope of getting Robert back? She wasn't sure.

Collin began to stir. He rolled over on his side and opened his eyes. "Ash?" he called out to her. "Where are you?"

"Right here," she said, walking back into the bedroom. "I couldn't sleep, and I didn't want to wake you."

He extended one hand to her. "Come here, woman," he said with a wicked grin. "Now that I am awake—"

Ashley laughed. "Jesus—don't you ever get enough?"

"That's like asking a flasher if he's tired of his favorite raincoat, but you didn't let me finish," he scolded as she sat down on the bed beside him. "I was going to say that now that I'm awake, we should talk."

"I'll bet."

"I was."

"About what?" she asked.

"About whatever it is that's bothering you," he said, fingering the front of her robe. "You've been in a strange mood ever since we came back from France."

"It's the same thing that's been bothering me all along," she admitted. "Seeing Yasmin and sending her home to her father just made me think about how long it's been since I've seen Robert."

Collin looked at her for a moment. "It won't be much longer now," he promised. Then, in a half-joking tone, he asked, "Anxious to get away from me?"

"No, I'm not, now that you mention it—" She stopped short, horrified.

He laughed. "That's what I like—an honest woman,"

he chuckled, tugging at the sash on her robe. "And just for the record, I'd hate like hell to lose you, too."

"Would you, now?" Ashley said, smiling. "Why?"

"Lots of reasons," he murmured as he slipped his hand inside her robe and stroked her breasts. "Like this . . ."

Anton DeVries studied the data spread out on the desk in front of him. *So,* he thought, intrigued, *my man is becoming a creature of habit.* After reviewing all of the available information on burglaries committed in the New York area over the past six months—burglaries he believed had been masterminded by Collin Deverell—he had discovered a pattern. The thief chose his victims carefully. He planned meticulously. His timing was damned near flawless. And it seemed his most recent targets were all individuals with suspected ties to organized crime. *Now, there's a switch,* DeVries thought with mild amusement. *One crook ripping off another.*

But it did limit the possibilities of where he might strike next.

"The safe's in the library," Collin told Ashley as he brought the van to a stop outside the high wall surrounding a large Georgian mansion in East Hampton. "We can go in through the music room."

"And the alarms?" she asked, remembering the floor plan they'd studied together the night before.

"A piece of cake. If it had looked too difficult, I'd have elected to use the tunnels."

She looked at him. "Tunnels?" she asked. "There were no tunnels on the layout . . ."

Collin grinned. "There wouldn't have been, since not too many people know about them," he said. "This place was originally built during the Prohibition era by a notorious bootlegger who hid his stuff from the feds in tunnels he had dug under the house."

"How did you know—" Ashley stopped short. She didn't even have to ask. Of course he knew. Even if no one else knew, Collin would know. Somehow.

"Let's get to it," Collin said as he climbed out of the van. "We don't have all night, you know."

She nodded. "How well I do know."

They climbed the stone wall surrounding the property and scurried across the lawn to the patio at the back of the house. Moving quickly, Collin disconnected the alarms and picked the lock on the glass doors leading to the music room. Once inside, he checked the rooms with his infrared goggles. When he was satisfied that the place was free of heat sensor alarms, he turned to Ashley. "All clear."

She nodded and followed him silently as he made his way to the library. As she started to pass him and enter the room, he grabbed her arm and pulled her back. "You almost blew it by not looking down!" he snapped.

"What the hell are you talking about?" she demanded angrily. Then, looking down, she spotted the dim beam of light coming from two small built-in devices on either side of the lower doorframe. "Step over," he instructed.

Once inside the library, they located the wall safe with no problem and opened it speedily. Collin passed all the papers and jewels he found inside to Ashley, who stuffed everything into her canvas shoulder bag. "That's it," Collin announced as he closed the safe. "Now we can—" He stopped short, catching sight of a car's headlights as it came up the drive. "Someone's coming." He ran across the room to the wall of built-in bookshelves and began pulling books from the shelves, searching frantically for the lever that would open the entrance to the tunnels. "Ah-hah!" he shouted triumphantly as the panel slid aside. "Come on!" He grabbed Ashley's hand and pulled her into the tunnel just as the panel started to close again.

"How do we get out of here?" Ashley asked as they ran through the darkened tunnel, barely able to see an inch in front of their noses.

"This way," Collin responded, urging her on. "This one should come out close to the wall."

"Should?" Ashley asked breathlessly.

"Okay, it will—I think." They climbed the stairs to the

doors at the tunnel's end, and Collin forced them open. As they emerged, only thirty feet from the wall, they could hear the sound of dogs barking.

"Guard dogs?" Ashley asked, pausing to catch her breath.

"Probably. We'd better run for it." They both broke into a dead run, not stopping, not looking back, scaling the wall with lightning speed. It was not until they were running for the van that Ashley stopped long enough to look up and see the silhouetted figure of the man perched up on the wall, the barrel of his gun aimed at her.

"Stop!" he called out.

Startled, she dropped her canvas bag. As she bent to pick it up, Collin spotted their assailant—and the gun, glistening in the moonlight. "Ash, look out!" he shouted, lunging forward instinctively. Just as he knocked her out of the way, a single shot was fired and Collin fell to the ground. Ashley scrambled to her feet, realizing he'd been hit.

"Collin!" she screamed.

"Go, Ashley! Get to the van!" he rasped, gripping his right shoulder.

"I'm not going anywhere without you!" She struggled to help him to his feet. "Come on, Collin—you can make it!"

"You've got to get out of here!" he said, grimacing with pain.

"*We* have to get out of here." She was trying to drag him the ten yards to their van.

"I'll only slow you down . . ."

"Stop or I'll shoot!" the man called out in a threatening voice.

Ashley ignored him, pulling open the back doors of the van with one hand and helping Collin inside as the man leaped down from the wall and came after them. She closed the doors quickly and climbed into the driver's seat, speeding away as several warning shots were fired.

"I've got to get you to a hospital," she told Collin as she headed for the highway.

"You know better . . . than that. There's no . . . way

we can . . . go anywhere near a . . . hospital,'' Collin argued with what little remained of his strength. ''Doctors have to report gunshot wounds . . . the police would be called . . .''

''Just what the hell am I supposed to do?'' she demanded angrily. ''Just sit here and wait for you to bleed to death? You need a doctor!''

''Get back . . . to Sea Cliff . . .''

''What good will that do?'' she asked, more worried now than angry.

''Henry . . . he was a medic . . . during the war,'' Collin groaned. ''He'll know . . . what to . . . do.''

''I hope so.'' She turned the van and headed for home.

Ashley stood in the doorway, looking on as Harrison bandaged Collin's shoulder. *Thank God he's going to be all right,* she thought, still trembling with fear. It had all been a terrible nightmare. She could still see the faceless guard up on the wall, the barrel of his gun gleaming in the pale moonlight as he took aim. She could still hear that shot being fired, see Collin falling to the ground. She barely remembered getting him into the van, driving away, begging him to let her take him to a hospital. She had been so afraid that by the time she got help for him, it would be too late.

Henry Harrison's words cut through her thoughts. ''I'm relieved your father isn't alive to see this, Collin,'' he was saying. ''He would never forgive me for my part in this madness.''

Collin grinned. ''Sorry to get you out of bed for this, old man,'' he said, sounding almost like himself again. ''Hope it hasn't been too much of an inconvenience.''

''Inconvenience?'' Harrison looked disdainful. ''After so many years, Collin, I'm quite accustomed to your rather bizarre nocturnal habits.''

Ashley stepped forward then. ''Is he going to be all right, Henry? Will it heal properly?''

Harrison gave her a weary smile. ''He's far too mean to die, if that is your concern,'' he assured her. ''He's going to be as good as new, though I'm not at all sure we can consider that a blessing.''

"Henry's been putting up with me since I was a kid," Collin pointed out, "and I haven't done away with him yet.''

Harrison turned to look at him disapprovingly. "And you were a bit of a problem then, too," he recalled. "Like that time when you were ten years old and broke your leg falling from a tree while spying on one of the maids. I won't embarrass you by going into the details of what you were trying to see.'' He turned back to Ashley. "He has never been sick a day in his life. Not even a cold. He has had his share of broken bones, however, and he was stabbed once and shot twice—this makes the third time—but he's never been sick. His parents always worried that he'd come to a bad end. Sometimes I think they may still be right.''

"My father was never wrong," Collin added. "As he would have been the first to tell you. The only crucial mistake *he* ever made was having the poor judgment to get himself killed—and taking my mother with him in the process.''

Ashley followed Harrison into the hallway. "Is he really going to be all right?'' she asked in a hushed tone.

"Certainly," Harrison answered without hesitation. "If we can keep him down long enough for that wound to heal. The bullet didn't go too deeply, but we do have to watch for signs of infection.''

She was openly relieved. "Thanks. That's what I needed to hear.''

When she went back into the bedroom, Collin was sitting up. She sat down in a chair near the bed. "Are you in very much pain?'' she asked.

He shook his head. "Henry gave me something. I don't feel much of anything right now.''

"Something's bothering you," she ventured.

He nodded. "That guard—did you get a good look at his face?''

She shook her head. "It was too dark. I couldn't see

much of anything except the gun," she admitted. "And that's something I'll never forget as long as I live."

"I think it was DeVries," he said then.

"DeVries?" Ashley looked at him, stunned. "The insurance investigator?"

"The one and only," he said with a grin.

"You don't seem terribly worried about it," she told him.

"Don't let my surface demeanor fool you," he said with a tired smile. "I *am* worried. If I'm right, if DeVries is the one who shot me, I have a great deal to be worried about. It means I'm becoming predictable to him, that he knows where I'll turn up next. The one thing I'll never do is underestimate Anton DeVries. He's brilliant and he's dangerous. He's dangerous because he's vindictive. It seems yours truly is the only blemish on an otherwise flawless record, so for DeVries, it's no longer a question of a man doing his job. He's not going to stop until one of us is defeated—or worse."

"How do you know so much about him?" Ashley asked, curious.

Collin gave her a half smile. "When you've been at this as long as I have, and you take as many chances as I do, you make it your business to know as much as possible about your enemies."

"What is it with him, Collin? Is this some sort of vendetta? What does he really want from you?"

Collin grinned. "What he wants, luv, is my head," he answered. "On a silver platter, if possible."

New York City, October 1987

Ashley walked alone up Madison Avenue, the collar of her mink coat turned up to conceal the lower half of her face. She wore dark glasses and a large fur hat, deliberately avoiding eye contact with the people she passed. As she crossed the street, headed for the Mason-Gilling Gallery, she saw something in the window that caught her eye. As she drew closer, she recognized the painting on display. It was one of her landscapes of the Napa Valley, a painting she'd given Diana Gilling before her exhibit last year. As she paused to look at it for a moment, she was surprised by the strength of the emotion that overcame her. *It's as if someone else painted it*, she thought, staring at it intently. *But then, maybe that's the truth. I was someone else then. I was a woman who had everything—a good marriage, a beautiful son, a successful career. Respectability. And what am I now? I'm a criminal, no matter what my reasons for stealing. A thief, living with a man who's made me do things I would never have believed I would ever do, a man I've fallen in love with but can't ever have a future with.*

"It's beautiful, isn't it?"

Turning toward the sound of the woman's voice, Ashley's heart almost stopped. Diana Gilling stood next to her, bundled in a full-length blue fox coat and matching hat. "Oh—yes," Ashley responded in a faltering voice. "Yes, it is."

"The artist grew up in the wine region in California," Diana explained. "I think all of her paintings came straight from the heart."

Ashley looked at the painting again. "I'm sure they did."

Diana smiled. "It *does* show, doesn't it?" she asked in a cheerful voice. "I only wish I had more of her works to display. Now that she's not painting anymore, her landscapes have skyrocketed in value."

"You own this gallery?" Ashley asked, altering her voice so Diana would not become suspicious.

Diana nodded. "Just coming in from lunch . . . and I'm afraid I'm in a bit of a rush. Good talking to you, Ms.—"

"Ellis," Ashley said quickly. "Penelope Ellis."

"Ms. Ellis." Diana smiled as she opened the door to go into the gallery. "Do come by again."

"I will," Ashley promised. "I most certainly will."

My paintings have increased in value, Ashley thought as she headed west to Fifth Avenue, remembering Collin telling her once that he considered it a good investment to buy an artist's works early in his or her career because there was every chance that later on in the game, their worth would double or even triple. Most collectors felt the same way—obviously to her advantage.

She paused outside Cartier at Fifth and Fiftieth, peering through the window at a magnificent diamond and sapphire ring. It was the most beautiful thing she had ever seen. *How long has it been since I've taken the time to really admire a painting or a piece of jewelry?* she asked herself. She couldn't remember. She couldn't recall how long it had been since she'd stopped caring about such things.

"You've got excellent taste," said a familiar masculine voice from behind her. Startled, she jerked around. Collin stood behind her, smiling. "That's a gorgeous ring. Want me to see what I can do?"

"No!" she said quickly, keeping her voice low. "Absolutely not!"

"You like it, don't you?" he asked, the brisk wind blowing through his hair.

"I love it," she admitted, turning to look at it again. "If I ever marry again, that's the kind of ring I want."

Collin frowned. "Before you can marry again, Ashley, you're going to have to exorcise the ghost of your first husband from your soul." He shoved his hands down in his coat pockets and walked away.

What's eating him? Ashley wondered.

"I think I've got something here," Ashley announced as she barged into the library. She was carrying a large cardboard box, which she set down on one corner of Collin's desk. "It was right here under our noses all along."

Collin looked up from the notes he'd been making on a yellow legal pad. "What has been under our noses all along?" he asked curiously.

"This." She reached into the box and took out a fat manila envelope. "Unless I'm misinterpreting its contents, what we have here is some very incriminating evidence against Bradley Hollister and the syndicate.''

He took the envelope and pulled out the papers it contained, reading them carefully. Then he looked up at Ashley. ''Where did you get this?''

''They were in our safe back in San Francisco, among Brandon's personal papers,'' she explained. ''When I decided to come here last year, I closed up the house. I didn't want to leave anything important behind, so I boxed up everything that was in the safe and brought it along.''

''You've had it all right here, all this time?''

She nodded.

''Why didn't you ever mention it before?'' he asked.

She shrugged. ''I never gave it much thought until I started asking myself if Brandon's estrangement from his parents could have had anything to do with his father's syndicate ties,'' she admitted. ''This morning, I decided it was worth checking out—and my intuition paid off.''

His face was serious. ''Ashley, you've got enough here to nail Hollister all by yourself! Names, dates, places— Jesus, it's worse than I ever dreamed!'' He looked up at her again. ''The man's a murderer. A goddamned cold-blooded murderer!''

She shivered. ''I know. I still can't believe it, even knowing him as I do.''

''It says here that he ordered hits on a U.S. senator, a union leader, and a leading presidential contender,'' Collin said, reading it again. ''Do you know what this means?''

She nodded, frowning. ''It means Brandon was an accessory. He knew and kept it quiet.''

He looked up at her. ''It's not easy for a son to go against his own father, no matter what the man's guilty of,'' he said quietly, trying to ease her pain. ''Believe me, I know.''

''If your father had done all those things, would you have kept quiet?'' she challenged.

Collin's eyes met hers. ''I don't really know the answer to that,'' he said honestly. ''My father was no saint, believe me. He was tough and domineering and unyielding and his ambition took precedence over just about everything else in his life. To a lot of people he was a first-class prick. He took my dreams away from me and tried to turn me into something I wasn't, and in a way I always resented him for it. But he was my father, no matter what else he was, and I'd give anything right now if he and my mother hadn't gone to Venezuela.''

"So you believe Brandon was right in not telling what he knew?" Ashley asked.

He shook his head. "I didn't say that," he said slowly. "What I'm trying to tell you is that he had his reasons. Apparently he couldn't live with his father, knowing who and what he was, but he just couldn't bring himself to send him to prison."

"He was a lawyer!" Ashley cried. "It was his duty!"

"He was a son first and a lawyer second," Collin said gently. She started to cry, and he took her in his arms and held her close. "It's okay, baby," he whispered, stroking her hair. "It's all right."

"Does this mean Operation Swampland is off?" Ashley asked Collin that night in bed.

Operation Swampland was the code name Collin had given the final phase of his plan. Now that he'd recovered his personal property and accumulated enough evidence on Hollister and other key members of the syndicate to put them all away, he'd discovered it wasn't enough. It wouldn't get back all the Intercontinental Oil stock Justin had handed over to Hollister. Collin knew that in a matter of years Hollister would be out of prison and back in business, if indeed he was ever put out of business. He knew only too well that Hollister would be able to continue to run his operation from prison, much the way Al Capone did years ago. Collin wasn't about to let that happen if he could find a way to prevent it. He wanted to strip Hollister of his power and ruin him financially, so he'd come up with a plan. Up until now, it had involved the sale of a large amount of phony stock. But even that hadn't been enough. Collin decided he had to go for all or nothing, so he'd purchased a large section of totally worthless land that was, ironically, practically in the backyard of the oil-rich fields in Venezuela that had made his father a very wealthy man many years ago. By the law of averages, that land should have been just as rich in oil, should have been worth a fortune, but, as it turned out, it wasn't even suitable for cattle. Of course, Hollister didn't know that, *couldn't* know that. Using all the right connections and some very convincing documents—including phony geological reports—Collin was sure he could get Hollister to take the bait. He was counting on the man's greed to make him part with his Intercontinental stock.

Collin shook his head. "Afraid not," he said, almost apologetically. He knew she was nervous about coming face-to-face with the Hollisters, but he could think of no other way to accomplish his goal. "I still need that Intercontinental stock Hollister's been sitting on for the past six months if I'm to gain control and prevent that takeover."

"Are you sure this is going to work?" she asked dubiously.

"I'd bank on it," he said confidently. "Blackjack used to say you couldn't cheat an honest man: men are swindled by their own greed. A deal that's too good to be true is usually just that, but men like Hollister don't see that until it's too late."

He had bought the land in South America in the name of the MACS Corporation, a dummy corporation he had set up for just that purpose. Ashley had found it amusing that MACS was really *scam* spelled backward. They had deliberately let it leak that Muhammed Hassan, a wealthy Middle Eastern oil magnate, would be staying in New York City with his wife, Leila, while negotiating the purchase of the land in question from the MACS Corporation. Collin had seen to it that every businessman worth his stock in town knew about the mysterious Hassan and his purpose in coming to the States, knowing that it would only be a matter of time before Hollister picked up on the promising South American land deal and moved to beat Hassan to the draw.

He'd taken a suite at the Plaza in the name of Muhammed and Leila Hassan and picked up his messages at the desk every day without fail. As for the offices of the MACS Corporation, he'd rented a post office box and had a special telephone line installed in the library that transferred calls from a vacant office he'd leased in Manhattan. When Ashley accused him of going to great lengths—and expense—to pull this one off, his response had been: "Believe me, it will be worth it. Only the end result matters." His hunch had paid off: Bradley Hollister had left a message for Hassan at the Plaza, inviting him and his wife to dinner.

"I'm not sure I can pull this one off, Collin." Ashley's words cut through his thoughts. "They *know* me—I was married to their son! They've seen me in court more often than most people see their in-laws at family reunions! No matter how I disguise myself—"

"They won't recognize you," Collin insisted.

"Can we risk it?"

"We have no choice," he maintained. "This, my dear, is how we ultimately create a diversion so we can get in there and take your son."

She looked at him in the darkness. "Then it won't be much longer?"

"Not much," he answered.

Ashley was silent for a moment. "It's hard to believe it's finally going to happen," she said at last.

"I never promise what I can't deliver," he said simply.

You're a goddamned fool, he thought. *Why can't you just tell her you're in love with her?*

Ashley sighed as she climbed the stairs and went into their bedroom. Their room, she thought sadly. For how much longer? She told herself she should be happy. She had every reason to be happy. Everything she had done in the past six months—including getting involved with Collin in the first place—had been for Robert. God, she'd been counting the days until she could have him with her permanently, but now that it was really happening, her joy was mixed with an overwhelming sadness. Why?

The answer was simple: Collin. She was in love with him. She had not wanted to fall in love with him; in fact she'd made a concerted effort not to. But still it had happened, and now she had to face the fact that she was going to have to walk away from it. This was her only chance of getting Robert and keeping him, at least until Hollister was convicted and sent to prison. Collin had said it himself.

She thought about it as she lay on the bed, staring blankly at the wall. Collin had never said he loved her. He'd never even expressed any real regret at the prospect of her leaving, aside from that offhand comment about hating to lose her. She suspected that he was too obsessed with his need for revenge to feel love or anything else. She wasn't sure *what* he felt for her beyond physical desire. Even in their most intimate moments, when he was capable of a fierce tenderness, he never said he loved her, never told her how he felt.

"I've come up with a solution," Collin announced over dinner that night.

Ashley looked up from her filet mignon and smiled placidly. "Great," she responded. "What's the problem?"

He reached for his wineglass. "You've already forgotten?" he asked in a teasing voice. "Your persona for our evening with the Hollisters, of course. I've come up with a way to further conceal your identity from your former in-laws."

"Plastic surgery?"

"Nope. You're going to be blind," he replied cheerfully.

"I'm *what*?" She almost dropped her fork.

"Blind," he repeated. "You know—dark glasses, white cane, guide dog—"

"I know what being blind is," she cut in sharply. "What I want to know is how you intend to pull it off."

"The same way we've done everything else," he said, attacking his steak. "By training you for it."

* * *

"Is this really necessary?" Ashley asked as Collin taped her eyes shut. "Couldn't I just close my eyes and feel my way around?"

"Wouldn't work," Collin insisted. "If you were to fall or bump into something, the first thing you'd do would be to open your eyes so you could make a course correction. It's a normal reflex action. But someone who's really blind can't do that. You, my dear Ashley, have to learn to maneuver just as if you had actually lost your sight."

"Will my eyes be taped when we're at the Hollisters?" she asked worriedly.

"Not if you learn your part well now," he said, helping her to her feet. "You're a quick study. It shouldn't take you long to get the hang of it."

They started with what Collin referred to as "the basics." He gave her a slim white cane and led her to the center of the room. "Now, feel your way around," he told her. "Use the cane the way an insect uses its antennae." In ten minutes, she managed to knock over a lamp—which Collin rescued before it hit the floor—break two vases, and fall over the same stool three times. Collin made her do it over and over until she was able to maneuver easily without the use of her eyes. "Now comes the next step," he told her.

Then he took her to the kitchen. "Let's see you whip up that dreadful protein drink of yours," he challenged.

"You've got to be kidding!" The tape over her eyelids was driving her crazy.

"Not at all. It's all part of the game."

He leaned against the counter, arms folded across his chest, watching her with amusement and trying not to laugh at her mistakes. She ended up breaking two glasses and a saucer and spilling the contents of two canisters before finally getting the mixture into the blender. When she tried to pour it into a glass, more went onto the counter than went in her glass.

She tasted the fruits of her difficult labor and made a face. "This stuff tastes horrible!" she gasped, spitting it into the sink—and on the counter.

Collin took the glass from her, laughing. "Next time, luv, don't use baking soda instead of protein powder," he told her good-naturedly.

"Baking soda! Why the hell didn't you tell me?" she demanded angrily.

"That wouldn't have been fair."

"Fair! You louse! You wouldn't know fair if it walked up and slapped you in the face!" She pounded his chest furiously, but he only laughed, pulling her into his arms and holding her close.

"Now comes the fun part," he said.

The next day, he taped her eyes shut again. This time, he took her out on the grounds and turned her loose. She spent one very long afternoon bumping into trees, tripping over garden hoses, stumbling, and falling down. Collin was unmerciful. He insisted they repeat the exercises every day for the next week.

"You're ready," he told her at the end of that week. "You have to be. We're having dinner with the Hollisters tomorrow night."

Ashley studied her reflection in the mirror. Her makeup was perfect—too dramatic for Ashley Gordon-Hollister, but definitely right for the beautiful and exotic Leila Hassan. She looked older, more sophisticated. Almost regal. *Now comes the hard part*, she thought as she turned her attention to the black wig, still on its block.

Collin came into the room as she was struggling with the wig, attempting to conceal her own dark brown hair beneath it. "Here—let me help you with that," he offered as he came to her rescue. He put the wig on the dressing table and picked up a handful of oversize pins. Carefully wrapping her own hair tightly around her head, he pinned it in place, then slipped the wig over it and anchored it. "How's that?"

She turned to face him. "You tell me. How do I look?"

"Like the wife of a very rich and very successful Middle Eastern oil tycoon," he pronounced.

"I have a feeling this thing's going to give me a dreadful headache."

"Take a couple of aspirin before we leave," he suggested. "If you didn't have so damned much hair—"

She laughed. "I never thought it would be a curse."

Collin stepped in front of the mirror and went to work on his own disguise. Ashley witnessed a startling metamorphosis take place. She looked on, intrigued, as he applied a dark stain to his face, neck, and hands. Then he used a special adhesive to apply the black mustache and beard, making sure it was precisely in place. He covered his own brown hair with a dark wig that curled over his ears and the nape of his neck. After that came the tinted contact lenses, which turned his brown eyes almost black. He slipped into his white silk shirt and diamond cuff links, and Ashley came to his assistance when he continued to fumble with his tie.

"I think all men are helpless when it comes to tying their own bow ties," she teased.

"It's probably some genetic defect," Collin agreed as he reached for his padded jacket. When he put it on, he immediately looked twenty-five pounds heavier. "Now for the finishing touch." He sat down on the edge of the bed, took his left shoe off, and slipped a bottle cap inside before putting it back on. Then he stood up and crossed the room, walking with a pronounced limp. "What do you think?" he wanted to know.

"I think I'd better call the police," she joked. "There's a strange man in my bedroom!"

"Is the limp noticeable enough?" he asked.

"Absolutely," she replied. "What happened to you?"

"A compound fracture from a collision during a polo match."

"Why the bottle cap? Couldn't you just fake a limp?"

"I could," he answered, "but I might forget. The bottle cap reminds me to limp." He walked over to the dressing table and handed her the dark glasses. "Shall we go, Madame Hassan?" he asked, gallantly offering her his arm.

She looked up at him. "Do you really think this is going to work, Collin?"

"I'd stake my life on it." His eyes met hers. "In fact that's exactly what I'm doing."

"What brings you to New York, Mr. Hassan?" Bradley Hollister asked cordially. The four of them were having a drink before dinner in the Hollisters' drawing room.

"I am sure a man as thorough as yourself already knows the answer to that question, Mr. Hollister," Collin replied, speaking with a heavy Middle Eastern accent. He reached out and took Ashley's hand in an affectionate gesture. "That is, I presume, why you have invited my wife and myself to dinner this evening."

"Well, yes," Hollister admitted, caught off-guard by Collin's directness. "I've heard about the South American land deal you're working on, and to be perfectly honest, if it's a potentially profitable endeavor, I might be interested in a piece of the action myself."

"I doubt that," Collin said with a patient smile. "You see, Mr. Hollister, it is not at all what you might think. The newspapers have been very misleading. I am not looking for another oil field. Quite the contrary."

Hollister looked surprised. "But—"

Ashley spoke up then. "You see, Mr. Hollister, my husband and I are both horse fanciers. We are looking at that land as a possible location for our breeding farm."

"My wife is absolutely correct," Collin agreed. "The land is no good for anything but grazing."

"You're joking!" Hollister laughed.

"Not at all," Collin replied. "This has long been a dream of ours."

"But why not raise horses in your own country?" Hollister asked carefully.

"That would not be very practical," Collin answered. "You see, no horse feed is grown in our homeland. It would have to be flown in on a regular basis. It would be most expensive in the long run."

"I see." Hollister sipped his drink thoughtfully. Claudia sat there like a cold, perfectly polished statue, smiling but contributing nothing to the conversation. Ashley suppressed a smile. Hollister really had no idea he was being taken. Not only did he not recognize her, he didn't see through Collin's disguise either, and Collin was certainly a well-known figure in Manhattan. Nor did he suspect that the MACS Corporation was just a front, that the land in question was worthless. Ashley could almost smell his greed, and she was enjoying herself tremendously.

"Mrs. Hollister, could I impose upon you to direct me to your powder room?" she asked then.

"Of course," Claudia said pleasantly. "I'll show you—"

"No, that will not be necessary. If you could just direct me . . ." Ashley insisted.

"Leila is very independent," Collin explained. "She does quite well for herself. She refuses, under any circumstances, to be what you Americans call handicapped. Leila is as capable as any sighted person."

"I-I didn't mean to offend—" Claudia stammered.

"It's quite all right, Mrs. Hollister." Ashley would have liked to scratch the woman's eyes out, but resisted the temptation.

"Through the door and to the left. Right at the top of the stairs. It's the second door on the left," Claudia told her.

"Thank you," Ashley said graciously.

She made her way up the stairs carefully, using her white cane as an antenna, the way Collin had trained her to do. She found the bathroom with no difficulty. The real problem arose when she was heading back to the stairs.

She found herself hesitating at the closed door to Robert's bedroom, wanting to go inside but knowing she shouldn't. Finally, logic was defeated by her fierce maternal instinct. She turned the knob slowly and opened the door. The room was in darkness. She entered and walked over to the bed, prepared to make her excuses by saying she took a wrong turn if she were to be discovered. Looking around to make sure she had not been observed, she removed her dark glasses and gazed down at the sleeping child. She realized now that she had needed to see him, needed to reassure herself.

It's all for you, my baby.

"You really think Hollister's going to take the bait?" Ashley asked Collin as they drove back to Sea Cliff that night.

"Oh, he'll take it, all right," Collin said confidently. "In fact, luv, he already has."

Ashley couldn't hide her surprise. "He has? But—"

"He's already asked for geologicals on the land. He called in one of the top firms in Venezuela," Collin explained. "I couldn't let him see the real report, of course, so I had a phony one drawn up. The report that's waiting for him at his office will convince him beyond the shadow of a doubt that there's oil—and a lot of it—on that land."

Ashley was intrigued. "How'd you manage the switch?"

"Simple. Hollister's been asking for information on Intercontinental's assets, so I persuaded Bill McNichol to make the switch. He's been spending so much time at Hollister's offices that no one's suspicious when they see him there."

"How did you know when it would arrive?"

"Easy. I called the geologist and pretended to be one of Hollister's people. I asked when the report would be sent out," Collin said, obviously quite pleased with himself.

"You think of everything, don't you?"

"I try to make sure all the bases are covered."

Ashley smiled as a thought came to mind. "You know, there's a much easier way to get Bradley Hollister's attention," she said.

"Yeah? How?"

"Just slide a piece of cheese under his door."

Sea Cliff,
November 1987

The bedroom was in darkness except for the pale light of the full moon streaming through the French doors. Collin lay awake next to Ashley, watching her sleep and cursing himself for having let his emotions get out of control. *You idiot, you knew it would be a mistake to let yourself get too involved with her,* he told himself.

He sat up and reached for his robe. Putting it on, he stood up and tied the sash, then walked over to the windows. Moonlight illuminated the lily pond at the front of the house, making it look like a gigantic mirror. He stood there for a long time, staring into the night, trying to make some sense of what he was feeling. He'd pursued this woman, used her for his own purposes, and now it had blown up in his face and he was in love with her. And in a matter of days he would be putting her and her child on a plane for Rome. That was the way she wanted it, wasn't it? A fresh start, a new life? After that, it was not likely that their paths would ever cross again. He looked over at Ashley. She was sound asleep. Lying on her back, her dark hair fanned out on the pillow, the sensuous curves of her body were defined by the thin sheet covering her. He couldn't tell her that he loved her. God knew he tried, but the words just wouldn't come. He'd tried to show her in his lovemaking, but he was never quite sure she'd understood the message he was trying to convey. *Why can't I just lay all my cards on the table?* he wondered.

He left the bedroom and went down to the library. As he seated himself at the desk, he opened the drawer and took out a large brown envelope. In it was everything Ashley was going to need to begin her new life in Italy: passports, birth certificates, driver's license, even a marriage license and death certificate to prove she was a widow, that she'd been married to an Italian citizen. He opened her passport and stared at it for a long time. *I've blown it*, he thought. *What should be my moment of triumph is actually going to be the darkest day of my life.*

All his life he'd been a risk taker, a gambler in every sense of the word. As Justin had so aptly—and so often—put it, he'd spent his life in search of the great adventure. It was true. He'd believed that without risks, life just wasn't worth living. Yet there was one risk he'd never been willing to take. He'd never been willing to gamble on love, on commitment. The funny part was, to this day he wasn't exactly sure why.

Early in life, he'd decided he didn't want to further complicate his life with emotional commitments. To the women in his life, he regretfully confessed that he simply didn't want the responsibility for another person's happiness. He enjoyed women, enjoyed sex, but he had to be free to come and go as he wished. They had all accepted that without protest. They'd all understood that no matter how passionate he was in bed, there was no future with him and never would be.

He had also rejected the prospect of making a commitment to his father, to the company. He didn't want to be tied down, he told himself. Trouble was, he didn't know exactly what he did want. At the time of his parents' death, he was still uncertain. He'd turned his back on it because he'd seen what it did to them, how it controlled their lives. His father lived only for Intercontinental Oil. With the passing of years, there was less and less joy in his father's life, and the company became more and more important to him, until nothing else mattered. And Justin . . . his brother, his mirror image, had become as obsessed as their father with the power the company gave them, until he ended up a bitter, angry man whose greed in the end had stripped him of the very power he sought. Even their mother, their beautiful, passionate mother who embodied the romance and the soul of her Italian ancestors, had been a victim of the company. In the last years of her life she'd spent most of her time alone. She'd been nothing more than an unlisted asset of Intercontinental Oil, a beautiful hostess at the parties her husband gave for business associates, an intelligent traveling companion, a lovely centerpiece at business-connected social gatherings. Not that she ever complained. It was her duty, just as it was Collin's duty, to accept the future for which he'd been born. His mother's sense of duty had been her undoing, and now it threatened to be Collin's as well.

In his own way, Collin was as obsessed as either his father or Justin. He was bent on revenge, and that was the worst kind of obsession. It had consumed him with hatred and bitterness, leaving him incapable of any kind of positive emotion. Where he had once shunned emotional involvements because he was afraid to care, he avoided them now because he was unable to care. Somewhere along the line, his need for revenge had stripped him of the passion of his youth, of his zest for life, for meeting each new challenge that confronted him head-on. The adventurer in him had been replaced by a man who was cold and calculating, who operated like a machine—without passion, without emotion of any kind. It had been necessary, he told himself, in order to survive in this world he'd entered. He'd never missed that other Collin . . . until Ashley came into his life. Ashley aroused feelings in him he'd thought dead and buried long ago. She made him feel things he didn't want to feel. And somewhere along the way, she'd made him love her. But Ashley wasn't like the other women in his life. With Ashley, it would have to be a total commitment. All or nothing.

And Collin wasn't sure he'd ever be able to give her that.

Anton DeVries was in the computer room at his company's Manhattan headquarters, staring at the display on the computer screen. After weeks of collecting and analyzing the data available to him, after weeks of cursing himself for having let Collin Deverell get away, he knew, with a gut-wrenching certainty, where the man was going to strike next. He pursed his lips thoughtfully. This entire case bothered him. He had looked at both sides of the coin, and still he did not know which way to go. He knew what Deverell was doing and why. Morally, the man was in the right, but by definition of law, the man was certainly a thief. Still. . . .

"Still chasing after that mysterious thief of yours?" Duncan Cresswell, DeVries's new supervisor, had come into the room.

"Uh-huh." DeVries never took his eyes off the screen.

"Tell me, Anton, does this mystery man of yours have a name?" Cresswell asked as he poured himself a cup of coffee and took a seat at the next terminal.

DeVries nodded. "I'll tell you what it is just as soon as I know," he responded curtly. He'd endured enough humiliation in his previous attempts to convince others in his organization of Collin Deverell's guilt.

He would say nothing more until he had an airtight case against him.

"We got the son of a bitch!" Collin shouted jubilantly as he put the telephone receiver back on its cradle. "Goddamnit, we got him!"

"What's happened?" Ashley asked as she rose from her place on the couch across the room.

"The trap, my love, has been sprung," he announced, taking obvious pleasure in the news he'd just received. "Hollister just signed the papers to purchase our swampland from the MACS Corporation—and signed over every last share of Intercontinental stock he owns! Hollister International now owns all that worthless land—and I have control of the company!" Then his expression changed. "In just a matter of days, Ashley, you will be reunited with your son—once and for all."

"How do you figure?"

"Simple. Friday night, Hollister and his wife are attending a costume party at the Rainbow Room. You and I will also be there."

Ashley gave him a quizzical look. "What for?"

He grinned. "The confrontation, of course."

Her mouth dropped open. "You must be crazy!"

"Not at all, my dear," he assured her. "You wouldn't want to have gone through all of this and not have the pleasure of letting your former in-laws know who's orchestrated their downfall, would you?"

"I'll be satisfied just getting Robert back," she answered honestly.

"And you will," he said. "But to accomplish that, you'll have to face them."

She looked at him suspiciously. "Exactly what do you have in mind?"

"We confront them. We tell them what we know and what we have on them," he explained as casually as if he were explaining the rules of a parlor game. "You're going to offer them a trade: your silence in exchange for full and legal custody of your son."

"And if they refuse?"

"They won't," he said confidently. "Believe me, they won't."

She hesitated for a moment. "You'd be willing to let them off the hook that easily?"

He shook his head. "I didn't say that."

"Then what, exactly, are you saying?"

"You're the one who's promising silence. They'll return your son to you. Once you're safely on your way to Italy, I'll deliver the evidence to the proper authorities."

"Deliver it? Do you think that's such a good idea?"

He shrugged. "I'm willing to take my chances," he told her. Then he reached over and stroked her cheek with his fingertips. "Don't worry, Ashley. It's going to work like a charm."

"And if it doesn't?"

"It will," he said.

"But if something should go wrong?"

"Just leave everything to me. I still have a few tricks up my sleeve."

Ashley looked at him for a moment. "Collin, do you ever

think about having a family of your own—a wife, children?''

He hesitated, tempted to tell her exactly what he *had* been thinking about. ''Nope,'' he lied.

''Why not?''

He frowned, deliberately avoiding her eyes. ''I'm not cut out to be a family man—any more than I was meant to be an executive,'' he said tightly, busying himself with papers spread out on his desk.

''I see.'' She turned away from him. ''So what will you do once this is all over, when I'm gone and you have full control of the company?''

He looked up. ''The truth? I have no idea.''

''You've gotten very good at this,'' she said coldly. ''You could always make a lifetime career of it.''

His jaw tightened visibly. ''I guess I deserved that.'' He paused. ''You know, I thought you'd be in a better mood now that you're going to get your boy back.''

''So did I.'' She walked out, slamming the door.

He wanted to go after her but didn't. *You're one stubborn bastard*, he told himself. *You should tell her.*

Before it's too late.

Ashley set up her easel in the music room, where the morning light was best, and placed a huge sketch pad on it. She folded back the cover, then paused. It had been a long time, she realized now, as she took one of the black felt-tipped pens from a canister on a nearby table and pondered the blank page before her. Finally, she started to draw, the pen making bold strokes across the stark white page, something deep within her soul taking over with just as much power and passion as it had in the past.

''Once an artist, always an artist.''

Startled, Ashley swung around. She'd been so involved in what she was doing that she'd lost track of time. She had no idea how long she'd been drawing when Collin entered the room, so silently that she hadn't been aware of his presence until he spoke.

She looked at him accusingly. "Do you always have to sneak around like that?" she asked, recapping her pen.

He shrugged. "Force of habit, I guess," he said as he came forward. "Anyway, you wouldn't have known I was here if I'd come in blowing a trumpet." He gestured toward the easel. "Going back to being an artist when this is all over?"

"Probably." Her smile was forced. "I don't know how to do anything else."

He gave a low chuckle. "You make it sound like a last resort."

She turned back to the easel. "Maybe it is."

He shook his head in disbelief. "Come on, Ashley—we both know better than that," he scolded her. "Artists—real artists—have it in their blood. When they're away from it for any length of time, they can't wait to get back to it."

Her eyebrows shot up questioningly. "You seem to know an awful lot about it."

"My mother was a frustrated artist," he offered in explanation. "She was actually quite good. I suspect she could have been a success had she decided to pursue it seriously." He glanced at the easel, then turned to Ashley again. "You're a great deal like her."

Ashley smiled, knowing that it was, coming from Collin, the highest possible form of a compliment. "I can't remember ever wanting to do anything else," she confessed. "When I was very young, I was fascinated with images and color and how I could create them on paper. Later on, when I first started to do landscapes, I felt a little like God—as if I were creating new worlds to be enjoyed." She paused, a question hanging on her lips. *Dare I ask it?* "What about you, Collin?" she said finally, deciding to risk it. "Have you decided yet what you're going to do after we—after this is done?"

He shrugged. "A part of me—a big part—wants to go back to fencing," he admitted. "Ever since I left the professional ranks I've felt as though there were something missing inside of me. I still think I've got it, but I'm a little old for Olympic competition now."

"But?" Ashley asked, waiting for the other shoe to drop.

"But," he began, "I seem to have taken responsibility for the future of the company. Once I've regained control, I'm going to have to run it."

"Why?" she asked.

"There is no one else, Ashley," he pointed out. "I certainly can't let Justin stay on as CEO, not after all that's happened."

"Can't you do both?" Ashley asked, putting down the pen. "I mean, look at all the top-level executives who take up tough, time-consuming sports—like polo."

Collin shook his head as if he'd already dismissed the idea. "I've never felt anything could be accomplished by spreading myself too thin. By trying to accomplish too much I could end up not being worth a damn at anything."

Ashley smiled crookedly. "Somehow, I doubt that will ever happen to you," she said.

He smiled too, but his eyes reflected a hint of sadness. "You've only seen me when I'm focused on one thing," he reminded her.

"I think you could do anything you put your mind to," she maintained.

"I don't think so."

She paused. "You have so much to offer, Collin. You've really never thought about settling down?"

"There's more to having a family than financial security, sweetheart," he pointed out, his expression suddenly grim.

Her eyes met his. "I wasn't talking about money," she told him.

He stared at her for a moment. He opened his mouth as if he were going to say something, then changed his mind abruptly. "No woman in her right mind would want me for a husband," he said. There was something in his eyes that looked like regret, but it was gone before she could capture it. He turned away, looking at the drawing on the easel. "What is this, anyway?"

Ashley drew in a deep breath, frustrated. "Our costumes for the party," she said irritably.

"I was thinking we could just rent something."

"Nonsense," she argued. "If there's one thing I've learned from you, it's that if you're going to do something, you might as well do it in a big way."

He grinned. "Touché," he conceded. "A highwayman and a she-devil . . . typecasting if ever there were such a thing."

She laughed. "If it were typecasting, we'd both just wear black—and ski masks."

"That would be just a little too obvious."

"True."

He continued to study the sketches she'd made. "Think you can get these little numbers whipped up by Friday?"

"No problem," she said confidently. "Diana once told me about a place on Eighth Avenue that can do just about anything on twenty-four hours' notice."

If only everything were so easy, she thought.

"What do you think?"

Collin scrutinized the two costumes on the dressmaker's dummies that stood in the middle of the music room. "I have to admit you were right, Ashley. We'll make one hell of an entrance in these."

"The sword is real," she explained as he checked out his costume. "An old saber I found in an antique shop in Manhattan. I thought it was you the minute I saw it." She paused. "Something for you to remember me by."

Collin didn't respond to this last statement. He walked past her to the other mannequin. Her costume included a long black wig from which two cone-shaped seashells, painted silver, protruded. "Horns?" he asked.

She nodded. "This one has its own special effects," she explained, showing him one of the elbow-length red leather gloves that went with the ensemble. "There are pouches in each glove just below the wrist, filled with flash powder. A flick of the wrist, and smoke appears.''

"Clever," he commended her.

The costume itself was spectacular, bright red silk with a daringly plunged neckline and uneven hemline, the fabric layered all over for an unusual effect. For a belt, Ashley had chosen a heavy chain and padlock, and a dog's spiked collar would serve as a necklace. "There's only one thing . . ." Ashley was saying, studying the dress as though something were still missing.

"What?" he asked, not sure he understood.

"Got a cigarette lighter?"

"A lighter?" He gave her a quizzical look as she spied one on the table at her left and snatched it up. Before he could stop her, she dropped to her knees, flicked the lighter open, and turned up the flame, putting it to the fabric.

He was stunned by her actions. "Are you nuts?" he yelled. He moved to stop her, but she pushed him away. He watched, puzzled, as she methodically burned the edges of the fabric, putting out the flame as she went along, before it could get out of hand. "What the hell—"

She looked up at him and smiled. "A devil would have walked through the flames of hell," she explained. "Entirely appropriate, don't you think?"

"You know your lines?" Collin asked as they neared their destination.

"Chapter and verse." She was trying to study the documents he'd given her in the darkness of the car, with only the light from the headlights of other cars as they passed to read by. Everything was there: plane tickets, birth certificates, passports, driver's license, even Italian currency. "How long will we have to stay in Italy?" she wanted to know.

"Six months, maybe longer." He kept his eyes on the road. "Long enough for the federal prosecutors to nail Hollister and his goons."

"Have you delivered the evidence yet?"

"It's on its way. Express."

"Then what?"

"Then we wait. They'll do the rest."

There was an uncomfortable silence between them. Finally, Ashley spoke. "I love you, Collin."

He hesitated for a moment. "You'll be a hell of a lot better off if you don't," he said tightly.

"Oh, stop being so goddamned noble!" she snapped. "It doesn't become you."

"I'm being practical," he insisted. "I don't know how to be noble."

"I think that's the most revealing thing you've ever said to me," she said irritably, furious with him for shutting her out this way.

He raised a hand to silence her. "This isn't the time or the place—"

"Time. Time is something we don't seem to have a lot of—in case you haven't noticed—"

He cut her off sharply. "This is all pointless," he said angrily. "I do love you, okay? I admit it. But that's not enough for someone like you. I know it and you know it. What you're looking for is what you had with Brandon. You want security—marriage, kids, the whole nine yards. I'd make a lousy husband. I never think beyond tomorrow. I'm not into long-range plans."

Her eyes met his in the darkness. "Who are you trying to convince—me, or yourself?" she demanded.

He didn't answer, because at this moment he didn't know the answer.

The Rainbow Room provided an elegant Art Deco backdrop for an array of costumed guests, most of whom had already shed their masks and were eating, drinking, and dancing, all in the name of charity. "It's like a human Fort Knox," Collin remarked, unimpressed. "There's enough gold and ice in this room to cover the national debt."

Ashley's glance swept over the crowded dance floor. She felt more like an observer than a participant in this high-society circus as she anxiously scanned the guests in search of the Hollisters. "Are they here yet?"

He shook his head. "I don't think so. I haven't seen them." On the surface he was calm because he knew it was necessary, but inside he still felt the emotional turmoil of their earlier conversation, of the confession he hadn't planned to make. *She forced my hand, damn her.*

"Maybe they're not going to show," Ashley whispered.

"They'll show," he assured her.

"But if they don't?"

"They will."

Ashley wished she could concentrate on the task at hand. Tonight, of all nights, she needed a clear head. Tonight her fate was to be decided. Hers, and her son's. Yet all she could think about was the confession Collin had made just an hour earlier. *Damn him*, she thought, frustrated.

"There they are," Collin was saying.

That got her attention. "Where?"

"Over by the door. They just came in." He nodded toward the entrance.

Ashley forced a smile. "Leave it to Claudia to be fashionably late," she commented dryly. "Are you sure it's them?"

Collin nodded. "Hollister took off his mask," he said, never diverting his eyes from his prey. "No mistaking that bastard."

Ashley nodded but said nothing.

"Let's go," Collin said.

She looked surprised. "Now?"

He nodded. "No time like the present."

Ashley got to her feet slowly, trembling inside. This was it. Suddenly she wasn't sure she could pull it off. What if it all backfired? What if it blew up in their faces? Collin was half-dragging her across the dance floor, not giving her a chance to reconsider. "Don't take your mask off until it's time for the unveiling," he instructed.

As if I want to take it off at all, she thought.

They followed the Hollisters to a table near the windows.

Bradley and Claudia had just seated themselves when Collin, with Ashley in tow, approached them. "Mr. Hollister?" he addressed the older man by name.

Hollister looked up. "Yes?"

"You don't know me, but we have important business to discuss," Collin said without making an introduction. "Mind if we sit down?" He pulled up a chair without waiting for Hollister to answer.

Ashley seated herself next to him. Looking across the table at Claudia, she decided it was entirely appropriate that her former mother-in-law had come dressed as Marie Antionette. *If only I had a guillotine handy*, Ashley thought.

"I don't believe I caught your name," Hollister was saying, eyeing Collin cautiously.

"I didn't throw it," Collin said easily. "I'll get right to the point, Hollister. You bought some land in Venezuela that actually belonged to me. In exchange, you handed over to my representative a very large block of Intercontinental Oil stock."

"Hassan," Hollister recalled.

"Precisely," Collin acknowledged with a nod.

"What about it?"

"You came up on the short end of the stick, Hollister," Collin told him, taking great pleasure in the revelation. "That land is worthless."

Hollister shook his head, amused. "The geologicals—"

"Fake," Collin maintained. "I should know. I planted them in your office myself."

Hollister's smile quickly vanished as the realization hit him. "A con game . . ."

Now it was Collin's turn to smile. "You catch on fast, Mr. Hollister."

"You're a fool to admit this." Hollister's tone held a warning note.

"I don't think so," Collin said easily. "You see, my partner and I have managed to accumulate a great deal of evidence to prove your—shall we say—unethical business practices." He went on to describe in detail the contents of some of the documents they'd obtained. One look at Hollister's face told him he had the other man exactly where he wanted him. "We have all the evidence the federal prosecutors will need to put you away for a long time."

Hollister's face went white. "What do you want from me?" he managed in a suddenly strained voice.

Collin removed his mask. "I don't think that's going to be too hard to figure out," he said, turning to Ashley. "What do you think, partner?"

Ashley removed her mask, slowly, savoring the look of shock on their faces when they saw her. "I think you're right, partner," she said, turning to the Hollisters again.

"You—" Claudia gasped.

Ashley smiled triumphantly. "I told you I'd see you in hell."

Ashley still couldn't believe it had really happened. Even now, en route to the airport, with Robert sitting between her and Collin in the back seat of the limo, she found it hard to believe that Bradley and Claudia Hollister had actually given up without a fight. That she had custody of her son again—legally. Collin had been right all along.

Collin. Ashley looked at him, shrouded in silence, staring through the window of the moving car at something only he could see. He hadn't said ten words since they left Sea Cliff. She wondered what he was thinking right now, what he was feeling. He'd said he loved her. She believed he'd been telling the truth that night. Yet in the past three days, he'd shut her out as if she'd ceased to exist for him emotionally. It was business as usual when they went to the Hollisters' to get Robert this morning, but it seemed as if a part of Collin had died in the process of regaining his possessions. She wondered if he felt even a fraction of the pain she was feeling at this moment. Could he really say good-bye, knowing they might never see each other again?

She realized time had run out for them as the limo passed through the entrance of Kennedy Airport. This was it. This was really good-bye. She blinked back tears. *It's not fair*, she thought bitterly. *I never thought there could be anyone after Brandon—and now that there is, I'm losing him.*

Their driver parked near the entrance to the busy TWA international flights terminal, then got out and opened the doors for them. As he went on to take Ashley's luggage from the trunk, with the aid of a porter, Colin helped Robert and Ashley out of the car. "Take care," he said in a low voice, squeezing her hand as she stepped up onto the curb.

She nodded. "I guess this is it," she said in a faltering voice.

He nodded. "Got everything?"

"Everything that's mine," she answered. "I love you, Collin."

He hesitated momentarily. "I love you, too. For what it's worth."

"It's worth everything to me," she said softly.

He kissed her tenderly. "You know, you're the only woman I've ever known—aside from my mother—who's accepted me just as I am."

"I wouldn't want you any other way," she said as a tear escaped from the corner of her eye and rolled down her cheek. "I'll never forget you."

"Nor I you."

She bit her lower lip to keep it from trembling. "Does it really have to be good-bye?"

"I think it would be easier for both of us," he said quietly.

Her eyes met his. "Since when did you start looking for the easy way out?" she asked, her voice suddenly cold.

"I'm thinking of you."

His attempt to pass it off on her was more than Ashley could take. It was the last straw as far as she was concerned. "Like hell you are!" she snapped. "My well-being's just an excuse and you know it!"

"Ashley—" He attempted to calm her down, but it only served to further infuriate her.

"You're a goddamned coward, Deverell!" she exploded, not caring how many people heard what she was saying.

"You can dangle on a wire a thousand feet above the earth or outrun armed guards or take on the entire underworld, but you're afraid of love! You won't take a chance on yourself, on us!"

"Ashley—"

People were staring, but she no longer cared. After all she'd been through in the past months, she wasn't giving up now without one hell of a fight. If he walked out on her now, he'd damn well know what she thought of him for doing it. "What are you going to do, Collin—spend the rest of your life hiding from yourself?"

His jaw clenched tightly. "There's no point in making a scene, Ashley," he said in a voice that was low but firm.

She drew in a deep breath and let it out in frustration. "You're absolutely right," she said with a sigh of resignation. "It is pointless. If love isn't enough for you, then it's all pointless." She turned away, leading her son toward the entrance, then turned back abruptly to face him again. "I was in love before. You know that. When I lost Brandon, it almost killed me, but I'm not afraid to take a chance on love again just because I might lose that person. If I learned anything from what Brandon and I had together, it's that love is worth fighting for. It's the one thing in life that's really worth a gamble—even if it's a long shot at best. It's just too damn bad that you, for all your high-stakes gambling, can't see that!"

Collin didn't respond. There was nothing he could say or do that would change anything now. He was still convinced that he was doing the right thing for both of them. The only possible thing. He watched in silence as she disappeared through the glass doors, as she walked out of his life in almost precisely the same spot she'd walked into it less than a year ago. Then he got into his car and nodded to Harrison.

"Let's go," he said tightly as he slammed the door.

Harrison looked at him dubiously. "Are you sure?"

"I'm sure, dammit!" Collin snapped. "Now—go!"

* * *

Ashley was fighting back tears as she stood in the long line at the Alitalia ticket counter, waiting to check their bags and pick up their boarding passes. Even knowing how Collin felt, had always felt, about making commitments, a part of her had believed their love was strong enough to change his mind, strong enough to make him come around, even if it didn't happen until the last minute. She realized now she'd been wrong, and that realization was a painful one. It hadn't been enough, not for Collin.

All these months, she'd survived on hope. When Robert was taken from her, it was the hope that, in the end, justice would be served and she would regain custody that kept her going. When that failed, and she met Collin, it was the hope that he was genuinely trying to help her, and that his plan would work, that kept her sane. And in the end, it was hope, hope that their love would be enough to break through the emotional barrier Collin had erected around himself, that it would be enough for him once there was no longer a common cause, a common enemy to bind them to each other. Now her hope was gone. She'd done what she'd set out to do, but in the end she found herself feeling as if she were the loser.

As the man ahead of her moved aside, Ashley stepped up to the counter and presented their tickets. Watching the clerk punch up her reservations on his computer terminal, she found herself thinking of all the times she'd watched Collin work his own brand of magic at the computer keyboard, transferring funds from one bank to another, setting up reservations, ordering tickets—and in the end, framing syndicate members, turning them against each other. Collin had enjoyed living on the cutting edge of danger. He'd thrived on it. What would become of him now? How would he handle being an executive, being tied to a desk day after day? He thought he didn't have a choice, that it was his responsibility. All those years, he hadn't been able to see beyond his obsession with revenge, and now he was left with nothing to show for it but the burden of having to run a company he'd never wanted in the first place. He knew what he *had* to do, but he still didn't know what he *wanted* to do. She felt sorry for him. He was trapped in a life of duty and there was little happiness on the horizon for him. If only he could have seen . . .

She forced a smile as she took the tickets and boarding passes the clerk had placed on the counter in front of her. "Enjoy your flight, signora," he said pleasantly in Italian.

"*Grazie.*"

She looked down at her son, who clung to her timidly, openly wary of the crowd of strangers around them. After all he'd been through, he wasn't going to overcome his fears overnight. It would take time, if indeed he ever did get over it. God help him if he ended up like Collin, never able to trust or to love.

The traffic on the highway going to Sea Cliff was bumper-to-bumper. Collin sat alone in the back seat of the limo, oblivious of the river of automobiles or the endlessly honking horns, lost in his own thoughts. He was thinking of Ashley, remembering the first time he saw her, right there in that same airport. She'd looked so damned beautiful that day, all in black, her face framed in black fur, her dark eyes flashing. Ashley was a beautiful woman under any circumstances, but when she was angry, she was magnificent! Even then, even knowing he'd only intended to use her for his own selfish purposes, she'd stirred something deep within him.

He recalled how she'd looked that day at the courthouse, when she lost the appeal, how he'd wanted to protect her . . . the day he taught her to use the high wire, how incredibly sexy she'd looked, how much he'd wanted her then . . . the first time they made love, how she'd looked standing naked in the shadows in his bedroom as she came to him . . . the afternoon he taught her to fake blindness, how furious she'd been with him when she discovered she'd put baking soda in the blender . . . and today, at the airport. Never, even if he lived to be a hundred, would he forget the anger and the hurt in her eyes. He had done that to her. After all they'd been through together, all they'd come to mean to each other, he had hurt her badly. He had also hurt himself.

He loved her. He loved her more than he'd ever believed he could love any woman. But what did he have to offer her? Sure, he could give her that big house at Sea Cliff and all the art treasures. He could give her a different car for every day of the week and the most magnificent jewels in the world. He could make love to her. But it would never be enough, not for a woman like Ashley. She needed stability. Good God, she probably even wanted more children! And he wasn't sure he even *liked* kids. But more than that, she would want a total commitment. She would want all or nothing. No, he knew he'd never be able to give her what she'd have to have from him.

What are you going to do, Collin, spend the rest of your life hiding from yourself?

Was that what he was doing? Hiding from himself? Had the years left him so bitter, so cynical, that it was no longer a question of not *wanting* to care, but not being *able* to care?

You're a goddamned coward, Deverell! You can dangle on a wire a thousand feet above the earth or outrun armed guards or take on the entire underworld, but you're afraid of love!

Collin closed his eyes. She was right. He was a coward. He was hiding from himself. He loved her but he was afraid to take a chance on it, afraid he might fail. Afraid he couldn't live up to her expectations—or his own. Love was the one thing he'd never been willing to chance.

He thought about it. His destiny had been decided the moment he took on Hollister and the syndicate. He'd committed himself to regaining control of Intercontinental Oil—and to running it himself, once he was in control. He had no choice. There was no one else now. It had to be him. It wasn't the life he'd wanted for himself, but it was his responsibility now.

The future suddenly looked pretty damned bleak. But then, any future without Ashley would be bleak as far as he was concerned. With her, at least he felt alive. At least there would still be a reason to get up in the morning. And maybe, just maybe . . .

"Henry—turn around at the next exit!" he shouted. "I've got to get back to the airport before it's too late!"

"Has Flight 803 for Rome departed yet?" Collin demanded, struggling to catch his breath. He'd run all the way from the car through the terminal to the Alitalia ticket counter.

The clerk shook his head. "That flight is boarding now."

"Which gate?"

The clerk gave him the gate number.

Collin broke into a dead run, pushing his way through the crowd, not stopping until he reached the boarding gate. He looked around wildly. At first he didn't see her. Could she have already boarded? His heart was racing. Then he spotted her, kneeling in the line, talking to her son. He ran up to her and grabbed her by the arm. "I've got to talk to you," he rasped as he dragged her out of the line.

She looked at him, startled by his behavior. "Collin! What in God's name—"

"I love you!" he told her. One look at his face told her he meant it. "I want to marry you—if you'll have me!"

She looked at him, her mouth open.

"If I'll have you?" She started laughing and crying at the same time. "You idiot! You crazy, wonderful idiot!" She rushed into his arms as the other passengers began to whisper among themselves. "You really are nuts, do you know that?"

"Is that a yes?"

She nodded emphatically, mascara streaming down her cheeks. "Yes!" she cried happily.

"Think you can stand the dull life of an executive's wife?" he asked as he pulled his handkerchief from his pocket and wiped her cheeks.

Ashley threw back her head and laughed heartily. "I have a feeling that life with you will *never* be dull—no matter what you're doing."

San Remo, Italy, July 1988

"I hate to leave here," Ashley told Collin as they walked hand in hand along the promenade of colorful tiles. "The past few months have been so peaceful—"

"Uh-huh," Collin agreed with a satisfied smile. "You do mean in comparison to this time last year, right?"

"Definitely in comparison to this time last year," she said, resting her head on his shoulder as she watched Robert running along the promenade several yards ahead of them. They had finally managed to put the nightmares behind them, and she was reluctant to let anything interfere with the peace they'd found on the Italian Riviera.

"With Bradley Hollister behind bars, there's nothing to keep us here," he reminded her. "No court in the country will ever take Robert from you—from us—again, and I do have responsibilities back home. Bill McNichol has been doing a first-rate job, but I can't expect him to keep doing it all forever."

"What about Justin?" she asked. "He has been running the company for the better part of ten years."

"I wouldn't trust my dear brother any further than I can see him," Collin said with what seemed to be a note of regret in his voice as he looked out at the yachts in the harbor. "I am glad he wasn't convicted. After all, he was nothing more than a scapegoat for Hollister's people, but as for letting him run Intercontinental Oil, well, he's going to have to prove he can be trusted before he gets back into the executive suite." He paused. "And you, my love, have a career of your own to resume. Or have you given up painting?"

"Not a chance!" she responded, pausing to admire her diamond and sapphire wedding ring. "But I've been thinking about something else I'd like to do—soon, if you approve.''

He raised an eyebrow questioningly. "And just what would that be?''

"I think it would be a great idea to give Robert a brother or sister,'' she told him. "You do want children of your own—don't you?''

He looked down at her, surprised. "Are you, in your own subtle way, trying to tell me the rabbit's dead?''

Ashley laughed. "No—not yet, anyway,'' she assured him. "But it is something to think about, isn't it?''

"It might be, at that,'' he agreed. "I never thought about it before, but I do rather like the idea of having a family—a large family.''

She looked stunned. "Now, wait a minute—''

He gave her a wicked grin. "Twins do run in my family, you know,'' he said teasingly. "Maybe two boys this time, then two girls—''

"If you want a second set, you're going to have to have them yourself!'' she said with a laugh, pulling away from him and breaking into a run. "I think you'd better sleep on the couch from now on!''

"No way!'' he shouted as he ran after her, catching her in a bear hug. Then he kissed her playfully. "Woman, I plan to keep you *very* busy for the next few years . . .''

In his office in Manhattan, Anton DeVries stood at the windows, staring absently at the magnificent New York skyline. On his desk was a newspaper detailing the trial and ultimate conviction of Bradley Hollister and several key syndicate kingpins. Among those acquitted was Justin Deverell, former chairman of the board of Intercontinental Oil. Control of the company had been assumed by Deverell's brother Collin, who had yet to put in an appearance at any of the company's board meetings, but it was expected that now that the convictions had been handed down and Justin Deverell had been officially ousted from the company founded by their late father, Quentin Deverell, Collin Deverell would return from wherever he'd spent the past six months to assume his position as board chairman. The eyes of Wall Street would be on Intercontinental Oil over the next year, especially in light of the events of the past six months, the newspaper reported.

To this day, DeVries did not completely understand what it was that made him let Collin Deverell slip through his fingers when he'd been so close to nailing him. He knew only that something deep inside him told him that the man was no criminal, in spite of what he'd once believed. He drew in his breath and reached for the mug on his desk, taking a long swallow of the cold, bitter coffee it contained. Then he went to the drawer and took out a cable he'd received several weeks ago, reading it for the hundredth time:

HAVE DECIDED TO RETIRE STOP TIME HAS COME FOR ME
TO BECOME RESPECTABLE BUSINESS AND FAMILY MAN STOP
WANTED YOU TO BE FIRST TO KNOW STOP
DEVERELL